LOCKHEED ELITE

LOCKHEED ELITE

a novel

T Y L E R
W A N D S C H N E I D E R

LOCKHEED ELITE

Sign up to Get Updates on upcoming things at:

www.tylerwandschneider.com

Did you enjoy the story?

Reviews of this book are welcome and encouraged on your personal blog as
well as sites like Amazon (all countries), Goodreads, iTunes, Google Play,
BookBub and many others.

Should you like to reach Tyler for any reason, you can do so at the website shown above. He is always up for interviews, guest blog posts, and
giveaways.

© 2017 Tyler Wandschneider
All rights reserved.

Paperback ISBN: 9780692909591
ISBN: 0692909591
eBook ISBN: 978-0-692-91898-2
Kindle ASIN: B073VHM3QG (ISBN: 978-0-692-90960-7)
Library of Congress Control Number: 2017910019
Stars in Hand, Seattle, WA

For my lovely wife, Maryna,
who loves and guides this dreamer into reality,
And for my darling daughter,
who sings to my heart, even from her mama's belly,
And for my sisters, brothers, nieces and nephews,
who bring me joy though the distance is long,
And for my friends,
the steel from which I am sharpened,
And for my parents,
the very fabric of my being,
This story is for you.

Your Husband, Father, Brother, Uncle, Friend, and Son

ACKNOWLEDGMENTS

I longed for the day I could say this book was no longer mine. Realizing that truth came in a sudden wave of emotional relief. Perhaps a relief not unlike the one you feel at the end of a very long day. Putting a book out into this little world of ours is no simple task. Sure, we have the tools to simply scramble some words together, and in minutes we can publish. What I'm talking about here is doing it right, and in all honesty, we did *Lockheed Elite* exactly right.

I wrote precisely one book before starting this one and I took everything I learned about writing over those five years and put it into *Lockheed Elite*. At that point in my writing career, I knew some stuff, but when you're that green, you don't really know what you don't know yet, so you feel like you know a lot. Oh, how wisdom conquers folly with a stiff swat to the back of the head. Thankfully, I realized I knew nothing compared to the greats, but I was discovering that I had potential and that's why I labored on. I realized this when I started publishing the rough draft of *Lockheed Elite* chapter by chapter on Channillo. com. There I encountered an audience who liked both my writing style and the content I had to offer. And therein lies my first nod of appreciation. To the authors and readers of Channillo.

com, know that your encouragement and praise for *Lockheed Elite* ushered me from one chapter to the next.

So I wrote on until I hit the end.

At that point I was done, wasn't I? Not in the least, dear reader. In a way, it was just the beginning. This was the point where I enlisted a couple alpha readers. These friends filled the exact requirements I needed for this task. They read a ton, and they possess a unique ability to tell me, with bold honesty, what they think. If they would have told me so, I would have gone back to the beginning and started over. In retrospect, I should have enlisted them earlier because their task was on large scale issues, but that's a confession for another time. Many thanks to Micky and Matt; I envy your candor every day.

Some say that it takes a team to write a book. True, as you've seen above. But there's more to it, perhaps. A team gives a sense of tangible work done on a project, an idea that there are those who put some sweat into the operation. But there are those who have helped in indirect ways too. So let's not forget my wife, Maryna, who woke to an empty bed many mornings because I was up working on this thing before the world had shed the sleep from its eyes. Or the near full Saturdays I spent locked in a room typing and dreaming away while she was working on our first home. I remember one day very distinctly; I looked up from my laptop and gazed out the window and saw her tirelessly cutting blackberry bushes out from where they were choking out a bush by the road. There's a profound sacrifice there that I fear I may have overlooked at the time. Honestly, I can't remember if I closed the laptop and went outside to help her. I'd like to think that I did, but truthfully, I may not have, and I know that I should have.

So, to my wife, Maryna. I see your sacrifice, in its entirety, in these writing projects, and I appreciate what you do for us and for this little dream of mine. Thank you, from the bottom of my heart.

Thank you, all.
Tyler

CHAPTER 1

Anders Lockheed held a folded wad of cash to the side of his empty beer bottle. To an unsuspecting bystander, this was nothing more than a payment for his crew's next round. To an appreciative third-shift bartender at Slips, this was a payment of a different kind.

Passing by several thirsty patrons, Nira offered a knowing nod to Anders who held up four fingers and a steeled glance. Without breaking her stride, she bent over, plucked his order from the fridge, and with fluid motions and a hooked metal flat bar, popped the cap off each bottle.

She strode the few steps over to Anders and rested the beers on the bar. Her hands dropped to the towel at her waist, and he slid his empty bottle over. A moment later, she cupped her hand over his—and the bills—and gave him a wink. A wry smile curled at the corners of Anders mouth, and he smoothly slipped his hand away.

He'd bought four beers this way, usually a few times a night, tipping double or even triple the standard and, most important, securing the staff's silence if anyone came around with questions. It was an understanding Anders didn't mind having.

He then shot her an appreciative grin, fingered two beers in each hand, and began weaving his way back through the crowd, settling murmurs as he passed by. He found his table and sat down beside two of his crew, Jones and Wick. On the opposite side of the table, their next interviewee, Severn, fidgeted in her chair. As instructed, his crew refused to say a word to her since she arrived, letting the hopeful recruit's mind race in anticipation.

Severn was one of several recruits handpicked by Anders for the chance to join their ranks. If their research was correct, she'd be more than capable of handling herself in the roughneck lifestyle among this crew. And like the others, she'd paid handsomely for the interview; however, this guaranteed nothing but the sit-down.

Although he'd prefer anonymity, Anders' team ranked among the best salvage crews in the known galaxy, which afforded certain benefits—like hand picking the best recruits. On the books, they were a tight-knit crew, each job done perfectly and within the confines of the law. They paid their taxes to the Galactic Alliance as soon as they took payment, and except for one recent job, they'd never been late on any promised delivery.

Off the books, however, they held a different creed. Sometimes a job required a few unorthodox methods to get it done right. No way around it. As such, Anders felt there was no need to tell the GC all the "minor" details of their operations, like their occasional noncompliance with the law. He always said, "Life's just easier for everyone if the all-seeing Galactic Command doesn't see it *all*."

After letting Severn stew in nervous silence for a several moments, Anders handed her a beer and said, "Okay, so you're here." As if she wasn't invited. "Now what?"

Jones and Wick grabbed the other beers Anders had left sweating on the table.

"What do you mean, now what?" Severn snapped back.

His curved eyebrow checked her attitude, and he let her rest in her poor choice of words. Anders knew she'd act tough right off. All the hopefuls do, but he sought other traits in a new recruit too. Among a rugged toughness, everyone knew he required loyalty and intelligence; but more than that, he looked for those who carried a moral compass that didn't *always* point north. A bonus that gave Anders the ability to bend the rules out in the cold and black when the job required it.

Most crews operated in much the same way; it wasn't hard to find. But what he looked for were the ones who didn't hide it. During an interview, if a recruit *pretended* to be perfect and law abiding, then they were willing to lie to the captain's face. A huge telltale sign of an unworthy candidate.

In Severn's case, he already knew she was smart based on the history Wick researched, and loyalty was always earned. That part was easy for him, but it left two traits that he needed to test. Sure, it was simple to act tough in the interview—anybody could do that—so Anders had a plan to test her toughness and her ethical boundaries.

Collecting herself, she tried to recover with, "What else would you like to know? I already told you I was a first-class ranger, washed out of the Galactic Command Ranger Elect."

"The GC," Anders said pointedly, noticing her attempt to relax herself. "What are your ties with them now?"

"Oh, please," she replied, glancing away from the table. "Everyone knows what happens when you get kicked out of GC training."

"I do," he said, "but I wanna hear you say it."

"They abandon you," she said. "No more money. No more training. Nothing. Too many wash out than what GC can provide for, so they refuse to be responsible for anyone who fails to make their ranks."

"So whatcha gonna do now? Cuz we ain't hirin' a scrawny little punk like you," said Jones in his deep, commanding voice. He let his dark eyes stare down into hers.

"Well," she said, throwing her hands up from elbows propped on the table, "nothing, I guess, seein' as how I spent the last of my dough on this broke-ass interview. What the hell is this?" she said, looking back at Anders. "You take my money for an interview, but you're not even hiring?"

"Oh, we are," squawked Wick, donning a wry smile. "Just not you."

Severn nearly bit, and Anders saw her catch herself. It pleased him to notice a sense of understanding wash over her face. A calmness flooded her body as she relaxed into her chair again.

She simply replied, "Too bad for you then."

"Why's that?" asked Anders, satisfied to enter a new stage in the interview.

"I hear your team is the best," she complimented.

Jones leaned in, his dark skin lightening under the dim light hung over the table. "We are."

"I can make it better," she said with an air of confidence.

"Wick," Anders turned to him and asked, "is this true? She washed out?"

"Yup, I checked. They want nothing to do with her—she's done. Discharged for disobedience." Wick relaxed in his chair and sipped his beer, proud of his contribution to the interview. He wasn't a soldier like the rest of them, but he was definitely one of Anders' best assets, able to infiltrate almost any networked system. Not to mention his ability to whip up any type of gadget that might prove useful in a tight spot. He was, for lack of a better term, a super-space-genius. Truth be told, Anders could probably sell Wick's *innovations* and support the crew comfortably without having to do these jobs, but he found no joy in that.

"All right," said Anders. "If you're so disobedient, then why should we pick you? We've got dozens of ship rats like you wantin' to join our team."

Severn smiled. "In my five years at GC, I finished more than half my training. I've completed hundreds of missions for GC—I know their ways and how they think. I've gone up against some of the biggest outlaws and won, and I can fight better than any man here in the bar, not to mention any other ship rats interviewing this shift, wherever they are. I'm the best candidate you have, and we both know it. Besides it's too late for me to transfer to law, and my discharge would be a problem there anyway. I need work, I need it now, and I need it for life."

Silence.

Anders didn't hear a single word explaining her disobedience, so he waited for her to finish her answer. He was more concerned with that than her sudden change from keeping order working for the military to working for a scav crew. In Anders' case, he wasn't worried about that. His work didn't involve illegal activity—not on a regular basis anyway. A crew that listened to orders was paramount.

To Anders' satisfaction, she realized what he was waiting for and simply added, "Just don't order me to kill or go to bed with you and disobedience won't be a problem."

Anders glanced at Wick, who nodded, confirming his research matched her explanation. Then he looked at Jones, who returned his questioning look with a dead stare. Having worked alongside the pair for many years, he knew that their responses meant they were willing to take the next step with Severn. As long as Anders was up for it. Regardless of her background, Anders saw something in her and went with his gut.

"Prove it," he said, initiating a final test.

"Prove it?" Severn repeated.

Anders stared at her. "Prove to me you're out of GC. Prove to me you need this job. And prove to me you can beat out the other candidates."

"How?" she asked. Anders noticed a faint reluctance.

He leaned close to the table, placing his label-less brown bottle on the same sweat ring it had left before. Eying Severn for a moment, he flicked his gaze toward the bar, prompting Severn's sharp eyes to follow his line of sight. "You see those two meatheads sitting together?" He pointed at two enormous, identical men wearing tank tops, cargo pants, and big black boots. Twins who also chose to dress alike.

"Yeah, I see 'em," Severn replied.

Anders shot her a challenging look. "They interviewed earlier and are waiting for my decision. I want you to pick a fight with them. Tell them they lost the job to you."

Severn threw up her best poker face. With her lean, muscular build, Anders trusted she could beat down almost any man, but winning a fistfight against two brutes twice her size? He wondered if she'd ever had the "opportunity" to try her hand at a fight so unbalanced. But her thinning eyes said she wanted this job, needed this job.

"No problem."

As she rose from her chair, she downed her beer in three gulps, never breaking eye contact with Anders. The look she gave him almost broke his serious composure, but he steeled himself regardless. Then she slammed the empty bottle on the table and turned toward the twins, projecting as much confidence as she could manage. But before she had a chance to leave the table, Anders grabbed her wrist, tugging her attention back to him.

"One more thing." He grinned. "If you want a spot on the team, you have to win." He let go and pointed to the hulking men at the bar for emphasis.

"I wouldn't have it otherwise," she said. She glanced at Wick and gave him a wink before turning away. "Take notes, boys," she said over her shoulder.

Severn shuffled her way through the maze of tightly packed tables where loud, obnoxious patrons enjoyed their many drinks. As she closed in on the bar, where the twins sat beers in hand, Anders asked Wick and Jones, "So, what do you think? Is she for real?"

"I believe so," said Wick. "It's not hard for GC and the law to fake her extrication inside their networks, but her story checks out everywhere else too. All the info I have in my network confirms she's been totally abandoned by GC and has no connection to the law. I'm in."

Their attention was briefly diverted as one of the twins yelped when Severn yanked him backward off his stool by his shirt. They watched as she stepped over his downed body and swung a hard right cross, leaving him unconscious on the floor. The crowd in the area groaned with surprise.

"Yep. Me, too," said Jones. "I'm in." He nodded at the fight. "They're gonna be pissed. Did you even tell them you were sending the recruit over to pick a fight?"

"No," Anders said dryly. "They need punishment for dropping the ball on the last job. We always deliver on time—they need to remember that. It's how we keep our repeat business."

"Kanor's gonna kill her. I don't see how she's gonna punish them," Wick said, adjusting his seat for a better look but was distracted by a familiar bleeping on Anders' comm.

"Another attack?" Jones asked.

Anders looked up from the comm. "No, but they'd better figure out where those mechs are coming from." He looked up at the partially completed construction in the ceiling. "You see all the defense prep Cambria's doing in the hangar? They're even doing it in here too." Wick leaned over to glance at the comm, so Anders tilted his hand to give him an eyeshot.

Jones replied with, "Yep, and I don't wanna be here if this place gets hit."

"My autolink to GC," Wick said, losing his focus on the fight for a moment, though slapping thuds could still be heard while Severn and Kanor were locked in a torrent of thrown and blocked punches.

"Yeah, it is," said Anders, answering Wick and looking back at his comm. "Looks like they've decommissioned something."

"Nice. Always a good take on those," Wick said, refocusing on the fight as Kanor lifted Severn in the air. "You should stop the fight before something bad happens."

"No. She either needs to toughen up or they need a lesson," Anders said, scrolling through the information on his comm. "She'll get a few punches in, and that'll be good."

"Ah, Cap?" Jones said.

"Looks like it's some kind of starship," Anders said, ignoring how Wick and Jones had adjusted themselves in their seats.

"Captain!" Wick said, scooting his chair quickly away from the table while grabbing both of their beers.

Anders looked up just in time to see Wick slide to safety. Then he saw Jones stand up and take one step back, shoving his chair backward with his huge calf. Before Anders looked up in the direction of the fight, Severn landed on the table. Anders' eyebrows curled in a mix of disappointment and confusion as they peered at each other while she slowly toppled over with the table. As the table edge slammed to the floor, she awkwardly rolled over her shoulder and then stood up, brushed herself off, replaced the table, and said, "Excuse me, I'll be right back." Without missing a beat, she re-entered the fight at the bar with the twins.

Anders watched her run and jump knees-first into Kanor's chest. Severn on top, they tumbled to the ground, and Anders' attention was drawn back to his comm, which made another bleep as it downloaded more information about the decommissioned starship.

"Ooo!" said Wick as Severn landed a healthy strike to Kanor's jaw. "If my source linked to that comm is right, we have about two hours before GC sends that info out on the open networks for all to see. What kind of ship is it?"

"It says it's a destroyer-grade class M1A MKIII starship," Anders replied. "And it's close, too." He glanced at the fight again, as Severn ducked a weak counterpunch from Kanor, and added, "She's pretty good."

"She is, but she won't be able to last long, Cap," Jones said, growing sympathetic to the unbalanced fight.

"She'll be fine. From what I've read, she can handle herself," Anders said as he watched Ciris, the first twin Severn had knocked out, come to and stand up behind her. It was clear she didn't know he was there when he wrapped his beastly arms around her in a sweaty bear hug. Anders went back to his comm, reading more about the possible job. His interest in it was growing, and when he finally found the location of it, he was convinced he'd found their next job.

While reading his comm, Anders saw Wick quickly look away from the fight.

Anders gave Jones a look and then glanced at Severn. He eyed her form and how she stood well balanced with one leg back for power strikes. She was lean and strong and most certainly ready for his crew. He turned back to Jones. "We need this job, and it's gonna be a long game. I'll have to call in Jug."

Jones paused, knowing what Anders' suggestion meant, and then simply nodded.

Wick shook his head and looked away again. "I can't watch this." He grabbed his beer and drank the rest of it down.

Anders grinned at him but then stood up to see the crowd, now formed as a semicircle, enclosing the fight with the bar. The crowd shouted with a unified "oh." Ciris was still holding Severn in a bear hug, while Kanor stepped in, ramming his forehead into the bridge of her nose. The cartilage shattered with an audible crack, and Severn's head snapped back at the force of the impact, nearly smashing into Ciris' face.

Broken nose.

Ciris released Severn and stepped around her wobbling form to stand next to his twin.

Kanor frowned at his brother. "How did you piss this one off?"

Anders smiled, noticing Kanor's puffy eye and busted lip.

"I didn't—I thought you did," replied Ciris with a swollen eye blackening with passing moments.

"Hey, what's your deal, chicky?" asked Kanor.

"What, can't a girl get a decent fight around here?" Severn produced a crimson-colored smile, refusing to acknowledge the pain radiating through her nose.

Anders was satisfied with his new recruit. Though she had a broken nose, it was clear she had landed plenty of solid shots herself. He had effectively punished the twins for their mishaps on the last job and put her through an appropriate test. She was tough as rivets and willing to follow difficult orders.

"Really?" Ciris said. "Fine with us."

Anders rose from his chair and made his way toward the fight. The twins approached a still unbalanced Severn, ready for another round. She kicked at Kanor to force him back, but Ciris grabbed her leg with a quick hand and dragged her forward until she was too close to escape. Each of the twins then settled a massive hand on one of Severn's shoulders and reeled their free hands back, forming solid fists. The sheer force of their grips nearly paralyzed Severn, and she choked out a scream of pain.

The twins prepared to punch her simultaneously, a hit that would end the fight for good.

"Oh, damn," she whispered and closed her eyes.

"Wait!" Anders yelled, stopping the twins. He raised his hand with his comm. "We got something. Bring her with, she's in."

Anders knew they understood what had happened by the way they nodded acknowledgment for the command. They released their grips on Severn. She nearly fell to the floor, but Ciris nudged her upright with a bump of his hand before he walked away. Kanor quietly paid their bill. He, too, left a large tip, as Anders had, but his money was an apology for the absolute mess they left.

Heading out of the bar, Anders grabbed his old brown leather jacket from the back of his chair. He flipped the jacket on, wafting the smell of the worn leather into his face, and then gave Severn one last look before turning toward the exit. Even bloodied and wobbly, he saw something in her. She somehow had the kind of moxie he didn't know he was looking for.

CHAPTER 2

Severn followed her new crew as Anders led them out the front door of Slips. Of the drink holes on Cambria, Slips remains the largest of the three, and Severn had frequented the place many times to watch Anders' crew. It became an integral part of her preparation for the interview, though it proved tough to get any staff, or patrons for that matter, to speak about them.

With the interview over and a real shot at joining the crew ahead of her, she, though in much pain, was eager to start her mission and excited to see the inside of their ship. She'd studied it a few times as well but only the exterior while it was docked in the hangar, which was two flights up in the elevator and a long walk down the corridor.

As they approached, sounds from the hangar billowed out into the corridor. Tools clattered and clanged, air guns whirred, and the noises of other machines echoed inside the steel walls that formed the enormous hangar. When Severn entered, a familiar metallic aroma filled the air and her senses seemed to heighten. The sight of oil spots on the floor became a quick reminder to watch her step while the sound of machines buzzing tickled frequent looks over her shoulder. And the smell of secondary lift engines whirring alive to carry dozens of ships through the airbreak out to the black were a constant warning of the fierce competition sailing the void.

Anders' crew was the best, and it showed as people watched them parade through the hangar as if they owned it. Severn felt an immediate pride as she walked among the crew everyone wanted a piece of, whether to be a part of them or to take them apart. She hadn't realized how empowering it would feel, how tall she'd walk while in their company. It was as if her body knew who she was with. Her back straightened, her shoulders widened, and her neck held her head higher. All she'd heard about them while on the other side was just talk. But now, getting a real taste of it, it exhilarated her.

Maybe it was the adrenaline from the success of the interview, but the hangar seemed more awesome than before. The ships lined up in their two rows seemed cleaner and sharper. Their noses pointing at each other over the large middle aisle appeared to honor one another in a ship-like salute. At the stern of the ships, in the large space between them and the wall, a people conveyor stretched the entire hanger leaving room enough for any of the several manned lifts that buzzed around.

Anders led the crew to the left-side people conveyor where Severn welcomed the chance to stand stationary. There she stopped her nosebleed and cleaned up most of her bloodied face by spitting on her sleeve and wiping it down. Jones stood next to her, so she tapped him on the shoulder. When he glanced down at her, she asked, "Is it straight?"

He glanced intently around her nose for a moment as she scrunched her face and moved her mouth around in an attempt to force it back into its naturally centered position. He shook his head with the nonchalance of an honorable first mate. "It's skewed a bit to your left."

"Damn." She huffed and knelt down to view her reflection in the conveyor's glass. Using the reflection as a guide, she cupped her hands over her nose and began to adjust it. Blood trickled out of her nostrils again as her cartilage cracked and crunched with each push and tug. Anders, even though he stood ahead of the rest of the crew and thought to be out of earshot, turned to observe.

Severn finished and stood up, blinking the unshed tears from her eyes attempting to prove to her onlookers that a little pain couldn't shake her. But Ciris, now wearing a bright red rope burn around his neck from Severn's sneak attack, smirked at her as if he thought he'd put her in her place. Kanor, standing beside his brother, grinned as well. The meaning in their looks was clear.

Severn wanted to shut that attitude down and, with it, any future comments they might make about busting her up. She needed to make a statement that said, "You may have bested me this time, but I can hurt you whenever I want." And she needed to say it without another scuffle. So she did the only thing she knew might work.

In her most intriguing tone, she whispered, "Hey."

She'd hoped only the twins and maybe Jones would look, but unfortunately, everyone turned their attention on her, including Anders. However, she had already committed to her play, so she went for it.

She jerked her arm back as far as it would go and threw a punch, aimed in the general direction of the twins. Both Ciris and Kanor recoiled when they saw her fist coming, even as she stopped her blow into empty air short of their faces.

Jones bellowed out a single, mighty laugh, and Wicked snickered. Even Anders managed to chuckle. Jones then winked at her, approving her actions. Severn could handle herself well, but she knew it'd always be good to have a beast like Jones on her side.

A rush of pride surged through her body urging her to stand tall again. She'd put Ciris and Kanor in their place, right where she wanted them. And as a bonus, the small victory felt like a painkiller, soothing her bruised face.

Their time on the conveyor ended, forcing them to step off in front of the open cargo hold of *Elite One*, Anders' ship. He had a permanent dock in the first slip in the hangar. Slip 101A, which meant it was on the port side, closest to the airbreak to space. Cambria was one of the oldest docking stations in the galaxy. Some crews rented rooms here for months at a time while they worked on and upgraded their ships. Mostly though, it was used as an in-and-out resupply station. Slip 101A was a long sought-after spot on Cambria, and Anders had procured it indefinitely. The only slip owned by anyone, a story Severn couldn't get her hands on, further proving how tough it would be to infiltrate his crew.

"I want us flying in five minutes," Anders ordered as they stepped toward the steel ramp that led into an oversized cargo hold.

"Where do you want her?" asked Kanor, gesturing to Severn.

"Wick, put her in sick bay," Anders replied. "Get her fixed up."

"Check," answered Wicked. "Follow me," he said to her.

The entire team, with the exception of Anders, entered the ship, eagerly posting their positions. Severn hung back, letting Wicked walk ahead while she stayed hidden in the shadows at the cargo door and watched Anders.

This crew had a solid reputation, but she still needed to know what she was getting into. It was important to watch everyone. So she grabbed ahold of the cargo door opening and swung her body outside to see what Anders was doing. The ship's port-side engine mount cast a shadow on her from the airbreak, so she hid herself in the darkness.

Anders began what seemed to be a preflight ritual of giving the hull a thorough once-over. Then he pulled out a handheld scanner that looked like someone had slapped it together in some machine shop and examined the openings for the landing gears. He ran his palm along the belly of the ship and seemed to caress the hull appreciatively. He even smelled it, as if he were enjoying the aroma of space itself, something Severn had never thought possible. When he seemed satisfied, he walked the few meters over to the airbreak and gazed out into the operational space next to the station and beyond.

Outside the station were dozens of local ships transporting supplies from the storage pods in close orbit. Beyond the working area, planet Esandrea; behind her, two moons enslaved to her pull.

Anders approached the airbreak, his skin reflecting a rich combination of blue and purple. The brown leather jacket he wore turned black as space in the fluorescent light. Being this close to the airbreak, she heard the buzzing of the thing, and it drained out all the other sounds of the hangar.

He raised his hand and placed it on the glowing force field. He looked tiny up close to the hangar's twenty-meter-tall by twice-that-wide opening into space. He paused and inhaled, filling his lungs with the hangar air. Severn reflexively did the same. Then he slowly exhaled, throttling it down with zeal as he pushed his hand through the field and into the vacuum outside. He held it there, experiencing the cold, the pain, the nothing mere centimeters away that stretched his arm into the beyond. When his exhale finished, he pulled his hand back inside and rubbed it until the blood flow stabilized. Severn had never seen anyone do something like this and was amazed, yet partially convinced of a modicum of insanity within Anders.

He turned toward her, and Severn, totally exposed standing on the ramp, suddenly realized he was about to catch her watching him. What would he think of her? But she was surprised to see an unchecked reaction from him instead. He hadn't realized someone had invaded what clearly was a private moment, so she reprieved them both by offering a question. "Does it hurt?"

His annoyed response caused her to jump. "Get in sick bay now!"

Angry at being scolded as if she were a child, she eased herself inside and hustled on her way. She'd been on many ships, and usually the sick bay was found somewhere behind the open machine shop at the end of the cargo hold. On *Elite One* two main corridors opened forward of the back of each side of the machine shop, and she chose the port-side one, assuming it would loop around near the cockpit and she would find the sick bay somewhere before it. The corridor was dimly lit but curved to the right, enclosing the sick bay directly behind the machine shop. She entered it, relieved to find her large pack nestled into the corner. She hadn't realized she'd left it at the table when the fight was over. She suddenly remembered seeing Wicked carrying it on the way to the hangar. She was grateful and thanked him for his thoughtfulness.

"No problem," he said. "You seemed a bit preoccupied."

"I was," she agreed while looking around the room.

A small relief settled over her when she noticed how clean they kept the sick bay. Come to think of it, what she'd seen of the ship so far was pretty well kept. A great many things hung on the corridor walls, but they were organized, and the walkway was clear. The cargo hold too. And the sick bay might even pass a military inspection.

Wicked pulled her from her own inspection of the area as he patted the blue-sheeted surgeon's bed, inviting her to sit down. Knowing what this was, she sat without protest because, for some reason, Wicked was easy to trust. Within minutes, he had her arm swabbed with alcohol, set up with an IV catheter, and injected with all the vaccinations required for space travel. The Galactic Command had already set her up with these vaccines, but Wicked wouldn't allow her to skip them. It was better to make sure than risk ending up dead.

Wicked approached her again, this time with what looked like a modified helmet and another syringe.

"What the hell is that?" she asked, eyeing the helmet.

He handed it to her. "It's pressurized. I'll put it on you while you sleep. It'll keep your eyes from bruising on the account of your broken nose."

"Oh," she said. "While I sleep?"

"Yup," Wicked said, raising the syringe. "There's a side effect with this one. It'll knock you out for—"

"What? No!" she interrupted him, swatting at the needle. Unconscious with a new crew was a horrible thought, regardless of how comfortable she felt with Wicked or what she'd heard about this crew in particular.

"Hey!" he replied, raising his voice and a thumb over his shoulder. "It's this or the door. Captain's orders!"

Under the threat of losing her opportunity and with much apprehension, she acquiesced, ultimately betting on the crew's reputation. So she calmed herself and let Wicked pump the fluid into her arm. A moment later, she fell into blackness.

CHAPTER 3

Wick endured the smallest pang of guilt for what he had to give Severn, but it was standard procedure for a new recruit—not that they had them regularly. It was Anders' wish, and Wick trusted his decisions, so he did it. The truth was, and Wick understood this, the top crew around couldn't trust what new recruits were up to when they came aboard. What Wick really gave Severn was a vaccination, but what she didn't know was that it also contained the chemical nerohypnothol. A drug designed to put her to sleep until she was *intentionally* awakened, which gave him the opportunity to implant a tiny bug in her jaw.

As soon as she fell unconscious, Wick injected the bug into the soft tissue in her lower mandible with a syringe, the pain of which would be concealed by the punches she had taken during her interview. The twins may not have known what Anders was up to, but Wick and Jones understood how well thought-out their captain's plans were. When Wick finished, he secured her to the surgeon's bed to keep her from flopping onto the floor during takeoff and flight and then headed down to his station for takeoff.

In the engine room, Wick fell into his normal rhythm. The first thing he did was tap the top of his old helmet for good luck. Then he fired up his central system, which monitored the actions of every other station on board. He designated the bottom right screen of his grid of nine to watch over Severn in the sick bay—someone had to keep an eye on her. Next he checked in with the twins on the port- and starboard-side gunners, and then Jones who was, as always, copiloting next to Anders. Wick monitored them and all of the ship's systems from his small command center while eagerly waiting for the intercom speakers to crackle with Anders' orders.

The excitement billowed in his chest as his mind raced and his hands danced around the system. A small tweak rerouted energy from the trash dump and cargo bay door to the engines and inertial dampeners for the next ten minutes. Another adjustment pumped a little more O_2 into the cockpit, gunner seats, and engine room for added alertness. Wick took care of a thousand things the crew never even thought were done. His enjoyment of his role on this crew drifted far beyond what he could describe. It was his life, and he loved being the engine master for this crew. He also loved his command center, his pride and joy with every part of the ship linked into his central location. Monitoring, adjusting, optimizing everything.

Anders finally broke radio silence and called out the ship's takeoff while Wick watched over the ship on the monitors. *"Ready to move in three"*—the crew casually took hold of nearby grab bars for stability—*"two, one."* Wick never grew tired of how smoothly this crew operated. They had done this a thousand times, and they understood takeoff was exactly three minutes after Wick flipped his Good-To-Go switch, igniting a green light at their posts.

Wick felt the ship lift off her perch as she drifted sideways through the airbreak and out the hangar door. He envisioned her fall over the edge toward Esandrea, and once she was far enough away, Anders would ease the thrust forward, pitching the ship upward and away from the planet. The command center livened up with every decision Anders made, and Wick witnessed everything as it happened as if he were in the cockpit.

Anders set a course to the destroyer's coordinates in the Darigon system, and Wick alerted him the FTL drive was charged. Anders responded that he was ready to jump, so Wick flipped another switch turning on a yellow light next to the green one at everyone's post.

"Jump in two minutes. On my ready," Anders said over the comm.

From the engine room, Wick confirmed that the entire crew made their final preparations. The twins on the gunners booted up their scanners, ready for any raiders that might make an appearance. The ship was most vulnerable the few moments before a jump, when nearly all power was routed to the engine. Wick monitored the warp drive, and in the cockpit, Jones staffed the scanning probe to make sure they wouldn't jump through or into anything nasty. Finding no problems, each crew member comm'd up to Anders, giving the systems-all-clear check, and, satisfied, the captain sounded off his count. *"Ready for jump in three, two, one."*

Wick smoothly engaged the warp drive, feeling the small inertial tug on his body for several moments. After a short while monitoring the systems, Wick became convinced the ship was stable in her sailing speeds far exceeding light. So he flipped off the yellow beacon, signaling to the crew that the flight was stable. Not a moment later, Anders came on the intercom and ordered the entire crew to the sick bay for mission planning.

CHAPTER 4

Anders arrived with Jones and saw that Severn was still lying unconscious on the surgeon's bed. The twins showed up next, and lastly, Wick, who, Anders assumed, had been making some last-minute adjustments to the warp drive.

"We have a couple of hours before we arrive," Anders started.

"What are we after?" asked Ciris.

Anders gave a devilish grin. "GC is about to put out on the wire first-come rights to scav a destroyer-grade class M1A starship."

Ciris and Kanor whistled, knowing how large a score something like that was. "All right," said Kanor. "A simple claim stake. I like it."

"It's not as *simple* as you think." Anders' voice dropped to a serious tone, and everyone in the room gave him their full attention. "This ship is probably three times our size, and no doubt some of the toughest crews will be after it. I'm not the only one with a genius on board who can hijack GC's network to receive advanced screenings of goods."

Wick smiled.

"Contrary to what Kanor just said, this is not an in-and-out claim stake." He paused, assuring himself the fullest attention. "I want the whole ship this time. We scrap all of it and we're set for a couple of years at least. Then we can do away with these piddly-dink jobs and plan some real stuff for a change." The crew nodded in agreement. Anders could tell they were eager for a big win.

Anders eyed Severn on the bed and caught himself staring at her face for a moment. Then he addressed Wick. "Is she hooked up?"

"Yeah, the bug's in her jaw. She'll think the soreness is from the twins' nice little love tap," Wick replied. "It's always recording, and we can listen in anytime."

"Yeah, next time let us know if you're planning to include us in your little audition," said Kanor.

"Next time deliver the goods before the deadline, or I'll leave you out in the void," Anders said sharply. "The lot of ya! Last chance, understood?"

"Aye, sir," the twins replied in unison.

"All right, wake her up, Wick," Anders said.

Wick walked over to a cabinet and removed a vial and syringe, then brought them over to Severn. He drew out some of the fluid from the vial, plunged it into her arm, and then removed the IV catheter before plunking a tiny adhesive bandage on her arm. He stepped back, waiting. After a couple of breaths, Severn's eyes popped open, as if she had been startled awake from a long nap. She blinked a few times to focus and then began to panic as a result of the amount of synthetic adrenaline contained in the fluid. Her level of alertness confused her; the rush of energy forced her breathing to quicken and made her body sit upright, then lurch forward.

Wick placed a hand on her back. "Relax and breathe. It'll pass."

She took a deep breath, worked her sore jaw, and looked around. She recognized Anders, Jones, and Wick, but when she directed her gaze at Ciris and Kanor, she jumped off the bed, grabbing at them.

Anders hooked his arm around her midsection to slow her down. "Relax, you already dealt with them," he said. "Sit down."

She sat back on the bed, taking deep breaths. She took a few moments and calmed herself.

"You good?" he asked, looking into her eyes. When she nodded, he continued. "Good. The three of you. What's done is done. That's an order." He glanced at Ciris and Kanor and then at Severn. "I don't want any animosity between you on this mission. Got it?"

Reluctantly, they all nodded.

"If it was a test," Severn said, "then why start a beef between potential team members?"

"Oh, you'll fight plenty as full-fledged team members," Anders answered. "You'll get over this one quick. Besides, I had to know if you had it in ya."

"Well, do I?" Severn asked.

Wick grinned at the opportunity. "In a manner of speaking."

"We'll know more after our shifts," Anders said.

"What's happening during our shifts?" Severn asked.

"As of right now, I'm merging our personal shift into our work shift, and we'll stake a claim on an abandoned GC starship," said Anders. "Tell me, did GC put you through a field medic rotation as part of your military training?"

"Yeah, for two years," Severn replied.

"Good. For now, that's your duty when needed. Soldier, otherwise, and if you prove useful on this job, I just might have a use for you."

"You'll be calling me partner by the time you take your next rest shift," she said.

"No, I won't be," Anders replied. "Get up and get to work. Wicked?"

"Yes, sir?" he asked as he fell into step beside Anders.

"How's Bertha coming along?" Anders asked.

With a grimace, he answered, "It'll be a little while yet."

Anders gave Wick an intense look, and Wick knew right then what the man was planning to do. "You have two hours to get her ready," Anders said.

"But it'll—"

"Move!" Anders said, cutting him off. "Use Severn if you have to, and make sure they'll be out for more than a single shift this time!"

He turned to the twins. "Ciris, Kanor."

"Sir," they answered.

"Get the suits ready, and fit Severn for one in case we need to send her in too."

"Yes, sir," they replied, leading Severn out the sick bay door.

"Jones," he said finally.

"Sir."

"Get me all the Whistling Slingers we've got. Then you and I will prep for a double belly buster." He groaned. "I want a tight connection this time. This'll be our biggest tow yet!"

"You're not seriously considering..." Jones began.

"Yes, I am, and no more questions!" Anders shouted. "Move it!"

CHAPTER 5

The hours passed while Anders monitored his crew working around the ship. Wick relentlessly worked on Bertha and Anders silently hoped he'd get her operational. Without her, the plan would inevitably fail, and Anders would be left to defend the ship the old-fashioned way: brute force. His crew could handle any ship easily enough one-on-one, but with a claim this size, Anders expected several non-friendlies to make an attempt on the starship. Anders needed a good plan, and Bertha was it.

Ciris and Kanor spent the time checking the suits and fitting Severn for hers before heading up to maintain munitions. Meanwhile, Jones and Anders collected eight Whistling Slingers, discovering that only six were in good working condition. When Anders asked Wick to fix them, Wick calmly replied, "Which would you rather have, Bertha or the two Slingers, cuz I can only do one. I am a genius, but you ask the impossible."

Anders wisely chose Bertha over the Slingers and silently hoped there would be fewer than seven other crews. It was possible but unlikely.

As they neared their destination, only Wick's work on Bertha remained unfinished. Anders was there to help, doing whatever Wick asked, when Jones came over the intercom.

"We'll be arriving in sixty seconds. Brace for FTL drop," he said.

Anders nonchalantly grabbed a nearby support, and Wick, crouching, pinned his lower leg between the floor and the bottom of Bertha, locking himself in position. She was a large, round, tubular machine, illegal in the state in which she was designed, but Wick, in his never-ending genius, had built her in a way that camouflaged her true purpose. In her illegal form, she was an enormous electromagnetic pulse generator. Large enough to paralyze all ships within her range. Her victims would be forced to replace much of the wiring directly connected to main power sources. Her immense power surge would fry them to the point of total severance. Any ship that flew would be able to make such repairs, of course, but it would take an average of ten hours to complete, and Anders would need every minute of that for his getaway.

When they dropped from FTL, Anders left Wick to join Jones in the cockpit so he could get a good look at the starship they'd be salvaging. He arrived to find that Ciris and Kanor, along with Severn, had beaten him there in their curiosity.

There she was. A destroyer-grade class M1A MKIII starship, the only one he knew to have ever been decommissioned.

"She's rolling mostly on one axis," Jones reported. "We can do this easy."

"Don't count this as easy just yet," Anders commanded. "How fast?"

"Scanners say one radian per second by maybe less than an eighth."

Anders stared at the ship.

"One by an eighth?" asked Severn.

"She's rolling over along her long axis once every six seconds or so," Jones said, "and with every rotation, she flips head over ass less than an eighth of a radian."

"That might make sense if I knew what a radian was," Ciris chirped.

"Quiet!" Anders ordered. "Check the long-range scanners. Anyone coming?"

Jones immediately flipped the switch on the long-range scanners, sending out a pulse. Within seconds, two blips hit back. "Two incoming," he replied. He paused as more blips hit. "Three. Four." And another. "Five ships. All less than twelve AUs away." He looked at Anders.

"Good. That—"

Blip, blip.

"Two more ships, sir. That's seven total," Jones added.

"All headed this way?" Anders asked.

"It would appear so, sir."

Anders glared at the starship thoughtfully.

"Is that bad?" Severn said.

"We only have six working Slingers," Jones answered.

"Five, actually," said Wick, entering the cockpit. "I needed another platinum pack. Had to take it from one of the Slingers. We're out of spares but Bertha's up!"

"That's good, Wick, thanks," Anders said. "But that leaves two ships unimpeded."

"C'mon, we can take 'em out," encouraged Kanor.

"Maybe, but that's a last resort," Anders replied. He may have been a roughneck, but rendering a ship flightless could very well kill the crew. Anders always avoided that play, almost to no end.

"Typical male beefiness," Severn said. "Fight first, think later, eh, Kanor?"

"Got a problem with that, Chicky?" Kanor replied.

Her face flushed red, and she grimaced.

"Wanna finish this?" he taunted.

"Anytime, beefy tits," she said, gladly accepting however Kanor wanted to finish the fight.

"Cage Challenge," he said calmly.

The whole crew gasped, except for Severn and Anders. Anders' face raged with anger knowing this would jeopardize the mission. By the look on Severn's face, Anders might have guessed she didn't know what a Cage Challenge was—but everyone else knew what they were. He always thought locking fighters in the animal transfer cage in the belly of the ship was a bit primitive, but it sure settled scores. In some cases, it even heightened crew morale, but he didn't have the time for this now.

Anders knew he couldn't prevent it, but he still tried. "No challenge. We're on the job!" He had to make an attempt. The mission was on a tight schedule.

"No one can cancel a challenge, Cap. No disrespect, sir, but you can't," Jones respectfully rebuked.

Anders knew that fact, no matter how much he wanted to ignore it. If a challenge could be canceled, then the point of it would be lost.

With much hooting and howling, Kanor shuffled his way out the cockpit as Ciris gave Severn a shoulder bump on his exit.

"Sir?" Severn asked.

Though she said only the one word, Anders read the entirety of her question on her face. She wasn't scared, that was clear. She just wanted to know what to expect.

"You two are about to finish the fight you started in Slips."

"Oh," she nodded, a bit bemused. "Why?"

Maybe she didn't know what it was. Anders threw a hand on her shoulder. "We're locked in a tin can most of the time. People tend to get a bit wound up."

"So," she said, "you challenge a fight to settle a score?"

"Exactly," Anders said, letting go of her shoulder. "It's simple. Two people have an argument that you can't resolve. Someone calls for a challenge."

"No one can cancel it," Jones added. "Even the captain."

Anders grimaced. "A rule I'm regretting at the moment. But when it's done, the argument is over, and things are considered settled."

Severn pondered for all of one second before saying, "All right then, better get this done quick." And she was out of the cockpit almost before she finished.

Anders and Jones eyed each other, unsure if they should be impressed or concerned. Then Anders fell back into captain mode and pointed at the controls.

"Position us above the starship, just clear of the rotation, so we have a three-hundred-sixty visual on the incoming ships."

"Yes, sir."

"How much time do we have?" Anders asked.

"Maybe forty minutes before the first of them shows up."

"Get the shields up and stay on the scanners," Anders ordered angrily as he turned to give instructions to Wick.

"Sir?" Jones asked.

"What?" he snapped, knowing what Jones was going to say. He was a loyal first mate, but loyalty to the captain meant loyalty to all of the crew, so...

"I have to support the challenge. I'll get us set up, but I need to be down there." He spoke with respectable candor, even as Anders growled in frustration. Jones then added, "And so do you, sir."

Anders looked out at the ship and then down the hallway. "If we lose this claim, we're—"

"I know, sir. But we'll get the claim."

"You, too?" Anders said to Wick.

Wick loved Anders, and he knew it. Anders had saved Wick from an unsavory person who had enslaved him to design equipment that would help their crews pull off some of the most notorious interplanetary crimes. Anders had thought Wick's skills could be better used on his crew, so he helped stage Wick's death. Anders had nicknamed him Wicked for how he'd designed his own death. After the event, Wick had devoted his life to Anders' crew, which had only consisted of Anders and Jones at the time.

Wick hated to go against Anders on this, but he had to, for the sanity of the crew. A Cage Challenge was nearly sacred.

As usual, Anders had to act quickly to get his crew in line so they could focus on the mission. It wasn't the fight that concerned him. That would take only a few minutes, ten at the most. It was the injuries that concerned him. He couldn't afford to have anyone seriously injured or stuck in sick bay on this.

When Anders arrived at the cage in the belly of the ship, the lights already illuminated the fight area. Wick, Jones, and Ciris were perched up at the cage, watching, fingers gripping the chain-link fence. Kanor was inside, shirt off and sweaty. Severn was clearly disgusted by the thought of having to rub up against such a beast. He wasn't fat in an obese way but large and muscular; still, he had decent insulation wrapped around him that rippled over his core with every step he took.

Kanor and Severn were finishing their stretches inside the cage as Anders walked in. Jones quickly showed Anders his portable handheld scanner, confirming he had an eye on at least the immediate area outside the ship.

"You ready?" Kanor grunted as he took his stance facing Severn.

"Are you?" she replied, and that's when Kanor rushed her. It surprised her, and she almost froze, but then she threw an instinctive right hook that connected with the top of Kanor's head. It wasn't enough though. Kanor drove his shoulder into her stomach, and they both tumbled to the ground.

Stunned, Severn was on her back, trying to catch her breath, as Kanor unmercifully brought a fist down in a hammer strike toward her nose. The pain she must have already been feeling in her broken nose made her impulsively bow her head forward, causing the strike to land on the hardest part of her skull.

There was a snap, a scream, and a loud thud that all near the cage heard. The thud was Severn's head whipping back and banging against the poorly matted steel floor. The scream was Kanor, and the snap was the sound of multiple bones in his hand breaking. Kanor recoiled, cradling his wrist as he shrieked in pain, and Severn rolled over, nearly knocked out but quickly regaining her wits. As she stood up, she faced away from the fallen Kanor. With a deep breath, she turned to finish the job but was met with Ciris entering the cage.

"Oh, did you forget?" he said with a smirk. "The challenge is to settle the fight you started back at the bar. You started that with both of us, so we both get to finish it."

His statement pleased Anders, as it made him realize something.

Ciris charged at her like Kanor had, but instead of tackling her, he brought up his foot and kicked her in her abdomen, sending her flying backward into the chain-link cage wall and tumbling to the floor. Ciris turned with his arms raised in victory to find praise from the onlookers but was met with a solid right cross from Anders, who had walked into the cage behind him. Ciris was unconscious before he hit the ground.

Anders stood over his motionless body. "I guess you forgot. I'm the one who started the fight in the bar." Though he was relieved that the fight had ended quickly, Anders was pissed that a hand was injured, now limiting one of his crew.

"Fight's over!" Anders yelled at everyone. "Get these two meatheads to sick bay and get back to your stations."

Stunned at how quickly everything had gone down, no one moved. The entire fight had lasted less than one minute.

"Now!" bellowed Anders, as if he had aid from a series of speakers behind him.

Jones and Wick stepped in to help up Kanor and Ciris, and Anders walked over to Severn, who was curled up on the floor, cradling her stomach.

"You all right?" he asked.

"I'll manage," she answered. "You better do hazard pay."

"If you make the team, you won't have to worry about money. Now get up!" he said before turning to walk away, fighting the urge to help her up. Then he turned back, succumbing to the desire to help her, and reached out his hand. Though she was quite tough, he noticed the softness in her hand and the elegance with which she stood up. Refocusing himself on the job, he immediately turned and made his way back to the cockpit.

On his way, Anders stopped at the sick bay to reset Kanor's bones and place a splint that wouldn't allow him to wear a space suit. He decided then that he and Severn would do the space walking on this mission.

Within fifteen minutes, Kanor and Ciris were stationed on the turrets on the port and starboard sides, with Jones, as usual, in the cockpit. Wick was suited up to help Anders and Severn set the Slingers, and they gathered in the cargo hold.

CHAPTER 6

Severn observed Anders as he smoothly commanded his crew. His attentiveness to the crew members in his immediate area kept them alert and on task. He used the comms to stay in close contact with members around the ship. Those crew members knew Anders was addressing them even without having their name called. They all understood when it was their job and answered accordingly.

"How many?" Anders said into the comm as Wicked stepped in line next to him at the port-side wall of the cargo bay.

Severn was already suited up and locked in. Anders clamped Wicked and then himself to the safety rail, securing them all to the ship's wall. They each had an additional line to the ceiling of the cargo bay directly over the two-square-meter door in the floor. Around that would-be-opening were the five working Whistling Slingers.

"Fourth one just arrived," Jones answered.

Their ship, *Elite One*, was positioned above the dead, rolling starship, and some distance away, surrounding them, were four other salvaging crews waiting to make their move.

"Who are they?" Anders asked.

Jones replied immediately, "Night Hawk, Raider, Smooth Sailing, *and* Great Haul."

"All right, *Great Haul*. There's a little luck we needed," Anders said, facing Severn. "We won't be sending them a Slinger."

"Friends?"

"Not exactly," Wicked answered.

"More like a mutual, unspoken agreement not to use force," Anders replied. "They're more about smarts and respect. If they're beat, they go home."

"So, really, we have just one more crew to worry about then," said Wicked.

"Yep, let's hope for another friendly," Anders said. "All right, we all ready?"

Over the comms, every crew member sounded off ready, with the exception of Kanor.

"Kanor?" Anders said. No response. *"Kanor? Report."* Still no answer. "Damn him."

"The others have arrived," Jones announced. *"If we're gonna do this, we need to go now."*

Severn imagined Kanor sulking in his gunner seat, refusing to work with her. Could be a dead comm too. She wasn't going to worry about it now though. She needed to focus on her part.

"You'd better get your head in the game, Kanor," Anders ordered, *"We're a go. Depressurizing the cargo hold now."* He turned a knob on the control panel in front of him, locking all doors leading into the ship from the cargo hold, and a green light illuminated on the panel. He pushed it, initiating the decompression of the air inside the cargo hold, and they waited.

After a few minutes, an orange light signaled the cargo hold matched the vacuum in space, and Anders instructed Severn to pull the lever on her left. As she did, the cargo door in the floor slid open. From there, they pulled their tethers from the wall and shuffled over to the opening.

"Stay on the gravity plates," Anders instructed her, holding his arm out, as if to provide a sort of railing for her.

Severn neared the opening and leaned over the edge, careful not to lean over too far. There was no force to pull her into the opening, she knew that, but still she approached with caution. The ship itself was a dark gray with wide swaths of smooth jet-black strokes perfectly camouflaging the ship against the star-filled backdrop. Not a single light shone from the ship, and by all accounts, it indeed appeared abandoned.

"There she is," said Anders. His voice somehow put Severn at ease. Not at ease in the sense that she was nervous and needed to settle down; more like her need to impress had been lifted. His awe in the ship below and his cool focus on the job instilled in her a desire to do nothing more than work with this team to stake this claim.

"Nice," Wicked said, drawing the word out long and smooth.

Anders then reassured his first mate of their find. "*She's a beaut, Jones.*"

The starship was nearly three times as long as *Elite One* and twice its breadth. Anders had mentioned this would be their biggest haul yet.

"Probably should have asked you this already," Anders said, turning to Severn, "but have you ever spacewalked before?"

"Yes," she lied, eager to get out there. Besides, she couldn't let him in on any experience she lacked. Her mission depended on him hiring her.

"Good enough," he said. "Just do what I do."

Wicked made his way around the opening to position himself opposite them and near the Slingers. Anders gracefully stepped over the edge as if he were heading down a flight of stairs and sunk through the opening while floating across the hole. He reached the other side perfectly, with his entire body below the ship, except for his hands, which landed on the grab bar at Wicked's feet. He turned to face Severn.

"Your turn, c'mon," he said, waving her on.

She was relieved that Anders became calm and helpful at this point. She pinned him as crass, but it seemed in moments of serious, deadly work, he became the leader everyone needed. Helpful and direct.

Severn stepped down over the edge. Her approach to the other side was a little less graceful than Anders' and a bit lower than needed. She quickly realized she was going to miss the grab bar and panicked, before remembering she was still tethered to the cargo hold ceiling. With the aid of an extended hand from Anders, she was guided to the grab bar and turned to position herself as Anders had.

"Have you selected the targets?" Anders asked.

"Uploading now," Jones voice replied in her helmet speakers.

Just then, Severn's visor lit up with information. On the left were personal health stats for each crew member: how much air, suit pressures, heart rates, and BP measurements. On the right were active comms, in network and out. No outside networks were linked, but all six crew members were active and green lit.

"Face the ships," Anders instructed Severn, turning her body with his grip on her upper arm.

"I see them."

Off in the far distance, the ships lined up horizontally as if suspended in attack readiness, pointed at the derelict starship; they belonged to the seven other salvage crews hoping to make the claim. Five of them were outlined with a fluorescent red light on the visor. Two of them were not.

"Who's the other friendly?" she asked.

"That would be Davie's crew," Jones answered.

"He's a close friend?" asked Severn.

"Not exactly, and he's a she," Anders responded. "She's an old friend and pilot I used to fly with."

"You did more than fly, sir," said Ciris.

"Oh, I see," said Severn. "Maybe she *should* be a target then. You never know, she might have a bigger grudge than you think."

"No, Jones was right," Anders said. "She hates me, but she won't attack. Unfortunately, this will piss her off a lot more though."

Wicked began handing Whistling Slingers down, one after another, as Anders and Severn floated them into position.

"Don't turn any on yet," Wicked explained. "The ships will pick up the signals and think we're planning to attack. We need to look focused on the claim."

"Check," Anders acknowledged.

After Wicked handed Anders the last Slinger, he made his way over to Bertha to wait for Anders' go.

Severn and Anders hovered beneath the ship with the five Slingers. Keeping them close by proved a difficult task. Anders managed three of them, and Severn focused on the other two. Just when she had one where she wanted it, the other would drift, and she'd have to make an adjustment on that one. Back and forth she went, with one hand holding the ship and one hand gently nudging a Slinger.

"We're set. Wicked, charge Bertha. Jones, be at the ready on the emergency shutdown. Ciris, Kanor, weapons offline."

The crew responded with their acknowledgments just as Severn finally had the Slingers where she wanted them, though they still drifted some. Anders seemed like an expert at the task, and it annoyed her.

"Ready," Jones said.

"Jones, on Wicked's mark, full shutdown," Anders instructed. *"Wicked, call it when you're fully charged. I want full knockout."*

"Nearly there, I think," Wicked replied from inside the cargo hold. *"We're in a vacuum. I can't hear how revved up she is."*

"Gimme a best guess," Anders instructed.

"Eighty-five percent," Wicked called out. *"Ninety."*

"What's going to happen?" Severn asked, immediately regretting that she may have sounded panicked.

Anders looked at her as if to say, "If you can't handle this, then you might as well just shove off now and get out of the way."

Before Severn's embarrassment could set in, Wicked announced, *"I've got full power, we're a go."*

In that instant, Jones' voice said, *"Check, shutting down."*

The entire ship went dark. Generators shut down, the lights followed, and then their suit systems went out as well. The comms were on a separate remote controlled by Wicked. The last thing to shut down was the main engine, and with that, something Severn hadn't expected happened—but not before Anders realized his mistake.

"Let go!" he yelled to Severn as he released his grip on the ship and unclipped his tether at his belt line.

"What? No!" she called out, but before she could finish her protest, he had unclipped her tether.

"Let go! Don't push. Just straighten your arm, *then* release," he said.

"Why?" she asked, too frightened to let go of her only lifeline. Without it, she was at risk of floating in space forever. Letting go was the last thing she could do.

"Do it now, or the ship will throw you off into space. You won't be able to hold on while she spins," he said calmly. His intentional coolness motivated her hands to let go.

Just then the edge of the opening began to drift away, and Severn realized what was happening. With the shutdown, it was impossible for the counterthrusters to disengage at the exact moment the torque of the engines stopped, which forced the ship to roll over. Thus, *Elite One* lifted up and away from Anders and Severn and began to roll on her long axis.

"Grab those two," Anders said, pointing at the Slingers nearest Severn. Anders grabbed one close to him, maneuvering it like a saddle between his legs; it was nearly as big as a small horse's back. He then grabbed the handles of the other two Slingers and watched as his ship nearly made one full rotation.

"Wicked, no time better than now," Anders called.

CHAPTER 7

As the ship rolled on her axis, Wick held onto Bertha inside the cargo hold to resist the inertial push on his body. The machine vibrated violently as if she were warning him of her awesome, and quite illicit, power. Wick, fearing her, almost heeded that warning, but he had an important job to do. There was certainly no turning back now, so he shut down not only the comms between the crew members but also the space suits that some of them wore. These were the last of the live circuits manned by this crew, and Wick held the power of them in his hand.

Everything went silent—except for Wick's pounding heartbeat and his now labored breath inside his helmet. The moment he had with himself, alone in the cargo bay, suit and comms off, with everyone's life in his hands, became a quite sobering one.

But it fueled his motivation. His crew depended on him, so he slammed his palm down on the big red button trigger, and Bertha immediately cried out with a muffled pop. Her shell casing bent and contorted with a nasty invisible force, and then everything was silent again.

He waited one more moment for good measure and then turned on the remote casing strapped to his forearm. Once rebooted, which ate up only twenty seconds, he turned back on the suits worn by himself, Anders, and Severn. Then he lit up the comms again and ordered, *"Comms up, check in."*

Then he examined Bertha. Though she was a one-shot deal, he could fix her for another run. Still, he shook his head in awe of the thing. Though he understood her complexity completely, he still admired the awesomeness of her power.

While he gawked at Bertha, the speakers in his helmet cracked when Anders checked in first, followed by Jones and then the rest of the crew.

CHAPTER 8

Severn checked in last after the others acknowledged their comms were back online. Then she noticed Anders eagerly watching the far-off ships. The interior cabin lights and bright exterior searchlights remained on. Once off, Anders would know the targets had been impaired by the electromagnetic pulse, and he'd have his cue to send in the Slingers.

"*Nothing's happening,*" he reported.

"*Geez. Give it a second,*" Wicked retorted. Then he tacked on, "*Sir.*"

Just then, the lights went out on one, two, three ships. They also began to roll as *Elite One* had. Then the rest went dead.

"*Ah, there they go,*" said Anders, relieved. "*They're out. Jones, start her up.*" By now, *Elite One* had rolled over several times.

Anders turned on and targeted the Slinger he held in his right hand. Severn waited and watched, and when she felt comfortable mimicking how he had done his, she prepped hers as well. After he had fired his—which was as simple as flipping a switch, aiming, and letting go of the thing—he used the air jets on his suit to meet up with her.

Within moments, Anders had fired the last two Slingers, and they both watched as the final one thrust forward, increasing in speed as it sailed effortlessly toward the targeted ship.

When the first one he'd fired was within a ship's length of its intended victim, it fired three cables with grapples at the ends, plus an additional high-powered magnet for good measure. The cables latched onto the hull of the ship, and the Whistling Slinger changed direction, dipping down below the ship.

"Thank you for making me let go," Severn said to Anders. "I figured out what you were trying to do *after* the damage would have been done, so thanks."

Anders appeared to shrug his shoulders in his suit. "I should have warned you sooner. It slipped my mind."

"Ahh," she said, playfully. "So you aren't perfect."

She laughed, but he didn't as they watched the Slingers begin to slowly gain speed towing five of the seven ships away.

"Where are they headed?" she asked.

"Away from here," Wicked said. *"They'll be dark for several hours."*

"Emergency systems will keep the air flowing," Jones added, *"but they'll be a long way off, and we'll have our ship and tow gone by then."*

"We still have work to do," Anders said, *"but we need a ride."*

Within minutes, Jones had righted the ship and positioned it next to Anders and Severn, who, through the many motions of launching the Slingers, had themselves flipped over. Their feet now pointed toward the ship's cargo opening. Anders put his hands over his head, squeezed a small button on his palm, and then arched his palms back, exposing his wrists. Air rushed out from his suit, projecting him slowly toward the opening. Severn mimicked this technique and was inside with him in no time. At the control panel, Wicked slid a net across the opening behind them.

"All crew on board," Anders announced, and immediately the ship began to make its way toward the sleeping giant of a starship.

From the cargo bay, they watched through the opening as the rotating starship quickly filled the view. Though it was spinning, the surface features became clearer as Jones approached.

"Where we going in?" Anders asked.

"My scans show the forward chassis bulkhead is the best shot," Jones said. *"You'll see a series of hatches spanning across her beam. We can gain access there."*

"Good," Anders replied as he spotted the hatches. *"I have a visual on the target. Wick, get on the starboard grappling."*

In a hustle, Wicked posted up in front of the cargo hold's starboard-side podium, while Anders stood at the port-side controls. He held a joystick located on the panel that housed the corresponding screen, which showed a view of the starship, still rotating, with a simple crosshairs displayed in the center. Anders moved the joystick, and a camera followed the order. He flipped a switch on the console, and the screen split in two, triggering an additional grapple.

"Better use two," Anders said, toggling between the two screens, making the aiming adjustments on the separate grappling systems.

Flipping the same switch on his console, Wicked replied, "I figured."

Amazed at their control under the pressure, Severn couldn't help but be in awe of how well they worked. She also couldn't help but wonder how they were going to stop that monster of a ship with such a small one of their own with just a few grapples.

"Are you sure we can stop that thing?" she asked, worry fighting its way into her voice.

Wick laughed. Anders responded with, "We're not stopping it, rookie."

Wick turned to her. "We're landing on it."

"Then we'll take 'er somewhere else," Anders added.

"*Hold on to something*," Jones announced. "*Gonna match her rotation*." Then added, "*On* two *axes*," as if to tell the crew they owed him a favor.

Severn, caught standing between Anders and the opening on the floor, stuttered at what to do with herself. She made a motion toward Anders but then quickly cut back toward the opening. It felt closer, and for some reason she assumed the grab bar in the opening would be a good place to hold on. In hindsight, this wasn't the best grab bar with which to support herself, although it gave her a beautiful view of the starship below.

"*Here we go*," said Jones. "*In three, two…*" He paused for the beat of one instead of announcing it.

Immediately, Severn felt inertia push her starboard as the ship went laterally to port side. Then she noticed the rotational speed of the starship below slow down as Jones matched the speed. That distracted her from the ship's new movement, which pushed against her arms, which held on to the grab bar. She stiffened her body against the force. But it was too late, and her knees were planted too close to the edge for balance. She was like a one-sided door hinge, her hands at the cargo door, and with the ship's motion, she was rotating up and over the opening. Before she knew it, the force of the ship's movements felled her over the edge.

"*Ahheek!*" she screamed.

She closed her eyes, figuring she'd be shot out into space forever.

The net, however, provided her with a reminder that this crew knew what they were doing. When she calmed down and opened her eyes again, she noticed Anders had turned to see what had caused her to scream.

"What the hell was that?" asked Ciris.

Kanor chimed in next. *"Sounded like a little girl got scared."*

"You gonna be okay, kiddo?" Anders asked her, clearly annoyed.

"Yes," she replied sheepishly.

"Heads up," Jones said, pulling their attention back to the target. *"I've matched the rotation the best I can, we gotta do this quick."*

Severn flipped her body over on the safety net so she could crawl off it. Mere meters away was the starship, so close she could see its surface clear as day. All kinds of protrusions, panelings, and labels littered the hull. Military sequences of letters and numbers delineating access hatches, compartments, and even turret pockets.

Recognizing this familiarity motivated her, and when she spotted the row of hatches where they'd be entering, she popped up from the net ready to get on with the job. She had been caught up in the romance of being part of an elite scav crew, and now she needed to get her head back in the game.

CHAPTER 9

Now that Severn's bout with weightlessness was over, Anders refocused his attention at his task at hand—setting the grapples on the starship.

"Wick, you ready?" he asked, eyeing the starship. On the small screen by his joystick, Anders aimed the crosshairs on a surface long enough longitudinally for two angled connection points, one forward and one aft just left of the hatches.

"Yeah," Wicked replied. "I got the right side, call it."

"Check. Go on three, two, one."

When Anders finished his count, they fired together, and four grapples shot out from the hull of their ship toward the derelict starship below. The arrow-like heads of the grapples pierced the hull with tremendous force, and with no time wasted, the heads exploded, releasing several smaller grapples inside the ship that stuck into nearby steel supports, beams, and chassis.

Another beautiful invention by Wicked.

The heads were equipped with a special device that welded them to the supports using an electric charge, creating a connection stronger than the lines and even the supporting elements on the ship.

"*We have contact,*" Anders said. "*Give us some tension, and we'll reel us in.*"

"Check," Jones replied. *"Easing thrusters off now."*

Elite One inched away from the starship as the pair of ships, now connected, rotated together, which allowed inertial forces to tighten the lines. Wicked's port-side lines were a bit longer, so the starboard-side lines went taught first. The entire crew, Anders was sure, felt the lessened pull of the artificial gravity as the grappling lines exuded a centripetal force on *Elite One*, which resulted in a small but noticeable "push" on them "upward."

Wick began reeling in his grappling line first, and once their ship was level with the starship, Anders started reeling in his lines as well. While they brought the ship "down" to the starship, Jones deployed the landing gears, and shortly *Elite One* was pulled in tightly and was securely moored to the starship three times her size.

"We're locked on, Jones. Get us out of here."

"Aye, Captain," Jones replied. He went to work, slowly reducing the rotation of the two ships, and Anders felt the artificial gravity return to normal.

Anders, Wicked, and Severn remained at the connection point to monitor the stresses of the connection. At first, they felt vibrations as the connections creaked and groaned from below, but nearly an hour went by without any issues arising. Finally, Anders concluded things were holding well, so he called it—besides, the air was getting low in their suits, so then was as good a time as any.

Anders gave the last of the orders that closed the hatch, repressurized the cargo hold, and released the crew to get some food and rest. Then he said, *"We'll board our new claim when we're ready and see what kind of treasure we really have."*

Over the comms, Anders heard the crew's hooting and hollering as they celebrated the largest claim they'd ever staked.

Anders knew it wasn't over yet but still felt it was a small victory worth letting the crew acknowledge. Hiding and salvaging a ship this size was never an easier task than merely staking the claim on it. They would have to keep it hidden for months on end, slowly picking it apart and selling off pieces, never letting anyone know where they were keeping it. Anders had his spot, though, and he was confident in its secrecy.

CHAPTER 10

Stepping into the engine room in search of Wicked had become a hide-and-seek of sorts for Anders, never sure what he'd find him doing. Through years of adjustments and use, Wick had transformed the area into his own command center, complete with state-of-the-art machining and all manner of tools. He might be found up front at his computer station working on the ship's network; or center-room waist deep in the engine making some kind of tweak; or somewhere on the workbenches diving into something entirely new. Anders welcomed the renovations, even encouraged them, since this was also where Wick designed all his clever things.

Anders found him behind the engine but working in a particularly well-lit area of the workbenches. "Are they ready?" he asked.

"Just about," Wick answered, looking up from under his lighted headgear, his one eyepiece magnifying his left eye. On the wall in front of him were many tools that appeared to be handy for working on small objects; to the right of that hung a clock Wick had built from spare parts, the creepiness of which drew Anders' attention every time he neared the damn thing. It wasn't the makeshift tail, wagging with the beat of each second; it was the eerie cat eyes that seemed to watch him. Wick was the only one who thought it was cute. Above the clock was Wick's old helmet, the only remnant of his past that he kept. He never spoke about it, and anytime Anders asked about it, Wick swiftly navigated the conversation to something else. He hadn't asked about it in quite some time.

"When can we launch them?" Anders asked as he fingered a few bemusing gadgets on the worktable.

"I'll be ready in about fifteen minutes. We should launch 'em through the trash dump," Wicked said as he returned his focus to his hands, soldering the remaining wires to a small green motherboard.

"The trash dump?" Anders asked, having never considered the trash dump to launch *useful* things into space.

"Yep. I figure it's the quickest way to get them into the black."

"True," Anders replied, stepping closer to inspect the five completed spheres. "What are you calling these?"

"I'm thinking something like Cloakspheres, or Cleres for short."

"Ah, decently clever," Anders said. "I'm sure it'll work, but do you know for how long?"

"That's the thing," Wick replied. "It's hard to say how long they'll last because we can't accurately predict how many signals they'll be filtering."

"Gimme a for-instance," Anders said.

Wick curled his mouth in thought. "I'd say they'd be depleted of power if someone were actively pinging this exact sector for about twenty minutes straight."

"Twenty minutes," Anders repeated. He sat on a stool next to the worktable. The leather on top was cracked, exposing the yellowed cushion inside. One of the bolts fastening the legs was loose and squeaked as he shifted to get comfortable.

"In reality," Wick said, "no one would do that. When searching for ships, your navcom pings a sector, and when the signal doesn't come back, it moves on to the next sector."

"There's no reason to ping any one sector more than once."

"Exactly," Wick replied. "So we don't need a lot of power."

"What about the power to keep them in flight alongside us?"

"Oh, please," Wick said, clearly insulted that Anders assumed he hadn't already solved that problem. "Hold this." He handed Anders a small piece of metal.

"A magnet?" he asked, glancing at the worktable littered with gadgets.

"Sort of." Wick winked. "It's a combination of nickel and cobalt where I've altered the polarity so its magnetic pull is specific to the signal I run through this machine here." He placed his hand proudly on a larger piece of the same metal wired to the engine and a small laptop. On the screen was a wireframe rendition of *Elite One* now connected to the derelict starship.

"What did you do?" Anders asked, eager for another of Wick's inventions.

"Watch," Wick said while he keyed commands into the laptop.

Before long, Anders felt a tug on the magnet in his hand. "What the—?" The movement startled him into letting go of the magnet. It didn't fall as he expected. Instead, it remained floating in the air, exactly how a feather might, then slowly drifted to the floor.

"The force I've managed to get from this is drained from the pull of gravity, but, as you can see, much less."

"I don't follow," Anders confessed with a questioning look.

"I've been working on this for a long time, and I've discovered a way to manipulate the pull of magnets from a one-directional pulling force to a multidirectional push or pull force."

"Seriously?" Anders asked, relieved he understood this part but had no idea how it worked.

"Yes. It's very weak but strong enough in zero-g to sustain these spheres in flight at six points around the ship. I control them from here, where you'll see six dots floating around us on the laptop display. One above and below, one in front and in back, and one on each side." He used the wireframe graphic on the computer screen as a prop.

"So, when we launch them, they'll follow us—"

"And at the same time cloak us from any signals searching for a big-ass starship," Wick said with a proud grin.

"Don't ever leave this crew," Anders said. "You're an absolute genius." Compliments from Anders were a rarity, but he knew Wick deserved one. "You should know that the only reason we've managed to stay alive and well fed out here is because of you and what you bring to the game."

"Thank you, sir." Wicked's shy eyes shot to anywhere but Anders'. "I don't plan on going anywhere, sir."

"Good," Anders said. "I'll gather the crew and meet you at the garbage dump in fifteen."

"Aye, sir." Wick nodded, then had a thought. "Sir, can we meet in the cockpit? I'm just dumping the spheres through the garbage dump. No one really needs to see that. The exciting part is locating them around the ship and testing the operation. We can do that from the cockpit."

"That'll be fine," Anders agreed. "I'll see you there."

CHAPTER 11

Wicked clenched his laptop under his arm as he passed the captain's bunk, nearing the cockpit. As he drew nearer, the soft clank of his hustled boots on the steel grating faded into the distinct sounds of conversations held by the crew already inside.

Even though the cockpit was crowded with the entire crew, his first glance shot straight out the viewport into space. There weren't any portholes on the ship, other than the one at the cargo door, so looking out the viewport in the cockpit was his default instinct when entering the cockpit.

His mind instantly calculated whether his system for signal cloaking would work. The destroyer connected below the ship stretched out in front of the viewport for what seemed like kilometers but in reality was only a couple of *Elite One* ship-lengths at best. Nevertheless, almost as if it were a reflex, he thought through his design one last time.

Satisfied, he acknowledged the crew—although not all of them were eager to see yet another display of his intellect. Ciris and Kanor wore their typical smug looks, just as they did whenever they had to watch Wick introduce another of his inventions. He brushed it off though; somehow he understood they didn't really hate him, they only struggled with not really understanding anything he talked about, which fueled their misplaced grumbling.

They weren't alone though. Wick felt a bit too much on display in these moments, but Anders always told him that when the crew saw how valuable Wick was to the sustainability of their ship life, they would appreciate him all the more. Still, it felt odd.

"Whatchu got this time, Wick?" Jones asked, inviting him into the cockpit with a wave of his huge hand.

Wicked stepped inside the tightly packed cockpit. "What I got this time is something that will hopefully give us some peace and quiet," Wicked said as he slid into the copilot's chair. "People will be looking for us, for this destroyer, and the cap asked me if there was anything I could do to make us invisible."

"Let me guess," Ciris piped up. "You're going to make us invisible." He and Kanor chuckled and finished with a misfired fist-bump. Twins in their thirties should've had something like that down by now. But it was the least of their usual mishaps.

"Ah, no," Wicked replied. "Besides, that would be like killing a bug with a shotgun—a waste of energy, resources, and just plain unnecessary." The twins grimaced.

"So what is it then?" Severn asked as Wick finished booting up his laptop.

"Well, I have a little machine down in the engine room that will be hosting invisible leashes for—" He raised the pitch of his voice and his hands to introduce the six spheres now floating into view in front of the ship. They lined up perfectly, waiting for positioning instructions. "I call them Cloakspheres, or Cleres for short."

The twins scoffed, and Kanor mumbled something that sounded like mocking. Their derision was collectively overlooked, as usual.

"So they're a cloaking mechanism," Jones said.

"Not exactly," Wicked replied. "They only cloak us from signal searches. Usually when ships don't want to be seen, they use scrambling devices. They work pretty well, but they still send a tiny bit of a distorted signal back to the source, so it ends up looking like some kind of interference. Nothing as clear as a ship, but it's something."

"Right, so we know *something* is there, and if someone's looking for anything, they might still check out the area where the distortion occurred," Jones said, following along swiftly. He was usually the best at understanding Wicked's explanations, and he appreciated the participation.

"Exactly!" Wick said. "What I've done here is create a system that causes the signal to pass over us. When it reaches us, instead of immediately bouncing back, it gets absorbed and passed from one Clere to another, around the ship and then beyond. So the signal never returns to the pinging vessel. It appears as if there's nothing but empty space where our ship is."

"And we're in the clear," Severn added, catching on to his pithy naming. "I like it. You're pretty smart, Wick." By the look on her face, she was unsure if it was too soon to use his nickname, but then he gave her a little wink, thanking her for acknowledging his clever naming of the Cleres.

"I'm guessing you need to station these around the ship?" Jones asked.

"Yes. I have their locations preloaded, and since you'll be monitoring their positions as you sail this boat, you should hit this command." Wick held three separate keys down for a moment. "That will run the routine to send them to the designated positions. If they ever get off course for any reason, hit it again, and they should reposition."

"Should?" Jones teased, as if he thought Wicked's invention wouldn't work.

"Will," Wick replied.

"Tell me more about how this all works," Jones said.

"All right, while they're getting that set up," Anders announced, "the rest of us are going to prep for boarding the starship."

"Yes!" Ciris exclaimed. "That's what I like to hear!" With childlike enthusiasm, he scrambled off toward the cargo hold ahead of everyone else.

"Wick," said Anders, "meet us in the cargo hold when you're done here. Kanor, man the turret for any surprise visitors."

As the crew replied with their ayes, all took to their respective commands. A short time after Wick finished up with Jones, he made his way through the starboard-side corridor to the cargo hold where Anders was working with Severn and Ciris. They had their suits on and seemed ready to explore the starship. Wick quickly donned his suit, which Anders had laid out for him, and joined them at the port-side controls of the cargo bay.

"First things first, check for suit pressurization," Anders said. "Wick?"

"Check."

"Ciris?"

"Check."

"Severn?"

There was a pause before she found the bar on her arm displaying her suit stats.

"Ah, there it is. Check!" she said, excitedly.

"*Jones and Kanor, check in,*" Anders ordered.

"*Check,*" replied Jones from the cockpit.

After his higher-ranked crew mate, Kanor responded, "*Check.*"

"*Exiting team is a go. Ready to reclaim the cargo hold pressure.*"

"*Reclaiming in three, two, one.*"

After Jones finished his count, the cargo hold whirled for a moment as the air left the chamber. When the torrent of decompression finished, Anders released his grip on the grab bars and turned the key on the controls to open the hatch at the floor. As it retracted, it revealed the same net that had saved Severn from losing herself in the black. Beyond it, the derelict starship lay in wait, a meter or so below.

"Wick, you're up," Anders ordered.

With the gravity still generated in the cargo hold, Wicked stepped toward the opening while carefully handling his steel-headed harpoon. At the hatch, he took aim through an opening where he'd pulled back the net and fired his shot. The arrow launched through the hatch, tugging a cable behind it, and embedded itself just forward of the middle hatch on the destroyer. Wicked repeated this process with a second shot, placing another harpoon and cable just aft of the same hatch.

With both cables secured to a spring-loaded tensioner, Anders clipped himself to a climber and ordered Ciris to join him with his thermal lance. As they eased through the opening in tow behind the climbers, Wick closed the net the best he could around the cables, and Severn joined him at the opening to watch as the captain and Ciris descended onto the hull of the starship.

Before they reached the surface of the hull, Wick spoke. *"Cap. Ciris. See those green buttons on your suit at your knees?"* he said.

Anders and Ciris glanced at their knees.

"What'd ya do this time, Wick?" Ciris asked. Wick was convinced Ciris liked it when he surprised them with little helpful gadgets while on the job, though Ciris would never admit it.

"I installed them last night. For all of us. Press it now," he replied.

Anders pressed the designated buttons, and his feet gently drew toward the steel hull and then snapped into place.

"Grav boots, y'all!" Wicked said. *"Took a while to get the configuration right. It'll be a little weird walking, but it'll save you a lot of time trying to move around, and now you won't have to waste a hand holding on to something. I mean, still connect your magnetic leash, but you can trust them to hold you to the surface."*

"I think you just earned a little bonus, Wick," Anders said as he positioned himself on the surface.

"Yeah, all right. Pretty cool, kid," Ciris said, forcing a compliment.

When Anders and Ciris finished torching the hatch open, Severn and Wicked latched two black crates to separate climbers and sent them down the cables to the landing crew before heading down themselves. Anders and Ciris floated the crates through the hatch, and once the crates passed through the access tunnel, Wick remotely engaged the magnetic system on them to make them stick to the steel floor inside the small corridor.

Before long, the four of them maneuvered their way inside, opened the crates, and collected their appropriate equipment for exploration: standard bio scanners, atmosphere testers, internal mapping scouts, comm device amplifiers to penetrate the steel walls, and, of course, handguns equipped with oxidized ammunition.

Exploring and scaving a new ship they'd claimed was by far Wick's favorite part of being on this crew. To him, his life was perfect.

CHAPTER 12

With every passing hour, Severn became more impressed with how smoothly Anders' crew worked and how swiftly they executed his orders. No one complained, and the work got done. She saw that kind of well-oiled teamwork only in the military. "Impressed" was a hard-earned compliment from her.

So far, very few orders had come to her from Anders, but she readied herself close to the action and observed their work. She hadn't yet formulated what her exact duties were on this crew, but she was quickly learning how she might fit in.

They entered the ship into a short, narrow corridor wide enough for two people to walk side-by-side. The hallway opened up to a much larger corridor to the left. To the right, the smaller hallway hooked left, heading forward. Ciris and Wicked were on the floor in that corner, and from what Severn could see, they were getting something ready. This smaller hallway they were in seemed to be some kind of access for behind-the-scenes maintenance.

"First things first," Anders said while standing near the open doorway to the greater corridor. "Wick, you and Cy get going on the mapping. Set the scanners to seek atmo and pressure. I wanna know right away if any of these compartments are gonna blow if we open them."

Wicked dug through his equipment, plucked something out, and tossed a small black disk over his shoulder into the space in front of Severn. She went to grab it, thinking he was tossing it to her.

"Leave it," Anders said, anticipating her motions.

She jerked her arm back as if she'd break something if she touched it and let the thing float with increasing speed up to the steel gray ceiling of the corridor. The disk snapped to the ceiling with an invisible force, and a moment later, a large white beacon appeared in the bottom right corner of her visor, with the text EXIT next to it.

Severn then witnessed Wicked release sphere after sphere; later, she would learn he called these Hounds. They were small self-traveling scanning probes, and they traveled through the ship, mapping all accessible spaces. Two floated off beyond Ciris and Wicked, and four more zipped past Severn and Anders into the main body of the ship.

Immediately, Severn and the others began receiving real-time updates rendering the space of each room and corridor as the Hounds made their way from EXIT. As the three-dimensional map grew, four locater beacons appeared, grouped together, signaling each one of the crew with their names and a designated color. Severn smirked at the magenta color she was assigned.

Watching this team work excited Severn, but Anders had mentioned something she couldn't ignore. "Sir, you said earlier that somethin' could blow?"

"Nah," Wicked answered for him. "Sometimes these abandoned ships have stray sectors that were never decompressed. If you don't know and open one—"

"BOOM!" shouted Ciris. The volume of his voice crackled the comms, and everyone except him and Anders jumped at the shout.

"What the—?" Severn said as she stepped back, bumping into the wall behind her.

"Cool it, Ciris," Anders said. "I don't want that crap on the job, and you know it. I'm dockin' you a tenth."

"Damn, Cap, I was just goofin' around. You don't gotta cut my pay," Ciris pleaded, but Anders said no more. Severn offered Wicked her attention again, hoping he'd finish his explanation now that Ciris' little outburst had been dealt with.

"As I was saying," Wicked continued, "you don't want a surprise like that. If you manage to pop a handle to a door behind a pressurized room, even just a little pressure," he pinched his gloved thumb and forefinger together, "it could send you barreling into a wall. Best case, you get knocked out."

"And worst case?" she asked.

Wicked looked at Anders. He nodded.

"We lost someone that way. That's why we have the Hounds now."

"Bayne," Anders said.

"Bayne," Wicked repeated softly. "The door was barely latched shut, but it still held pressure. Bayne gave the handle a good tug, the door flew open, and before we even realized what was happening, Bayne was flying through the air. He hit the wall so hard he…broke his neck."

Anders spoke with a heavy heart. "He died instantly. There was nothing we could do."

It was a short, somber moment as the men remembered their fallen shipmate.

"*To Bayne*," Jones said over the comms. The rest repeated the salute, except Severn, who hadn't known him. It felt disrespectful to her new crew to salute their dead compatriot.

"Focus," Anders commanded, reeling his team back to the job. "Remember our boy, but we still got work to do. We got a good map to start with, so let's move."

"Put me to work, Cap," Severn said, unable to curb her eagerness to get on with her mission.

"You're with me. We're looking for the bridge. Looks like it's this way." He pointed to the main hallway behind them. "Wicked, Ciris, get as much of the easy-to-grab sellable scrap as you can."

"On it, boss," Ciris acknowledged, taking credit for Wicked, who was already unpacking his spooling machine and router, ready to head the other direction.

Anders and Severn took the first right, heading fore in the main corridor. The ship was dark except for the headlamps beaming from their helmets. Random debris floated about, and dust wafted through the light beams. Or was it frost? A thin layer of frost coated most surfaces, so it could be.

Otherwise, the ship was clean and felt, for the most part, new. The interior was crisp, clean, and empty. Severn wondered if Anders would ask himself why the military command would decommission a ship in such seemingly good shape.

They reached their first intersection, which led into an even larger hallway. This one clearly served as a main thoroughfare. Before they turned into it, Severn noticed a small blue arrow glowing in the darkness on the wall. When she turned her head, focusing her headlamp on it, the arrow glinted a slick black against the lighter wall behind it.

Anders caught her staring at it and said, "It's Wick."

"What's Wick?" she asked.

"It's another one of Wicked's things," Anders said.

Severn looked at the arrow again, realizing what he meant. "Oh. I see. The Hounds paint arrows pointing back to the hatch."

"*You likey?*" Wicked asked, excitedly interjecting himself.

"*Don't feed his ego, Severn,*" Jones' voice thundered over the comms.

"*It's kind of hard not to. Is there nothing you haven't thought of?*" she asked.

"*Nope. I'm omniscient,*" Wicked replied.

"*Oh, brother,*" she said. "*Sorry I asked.*"

The comms echoed soft amusement, and then the chatter slowly died down into silence as the crew's attention drifted into their work.

CHAPTER 13

Ciris and Wicked spooled roll after roll of wiring from the ceiling conduits that spanned the immediate corridors. Though dealing with the debris floating around from tearing up the ceiling was a nuisance, this was the most accessible and the easiest thing to collect and sell. Besides, Wicked had devised an easy way to spool the wiring on large cylinders. The harder pieces would be salvaged later as the ship was skinned a bit more each time they visited.

As he and Ciris moved through the ship, they collected thousands of kilograms of copper and nickel wire. Then they came across the mainframe computer line where they hit the mother lode. There alone they removed three entire rolls, doubling their take in a single location.

Sending them up to the cargo hold was a cinch. Jones turned off the grav plates in the cargo hold, and Ciris floated each finished roll up the access tunnel and into *Elite One's* hold. They easily loaded a couple dozen rolls as large as Jones' massive upper body before Anders checked in from the bridge.

"Wick, we're at the bridge door. How's the pressure?"

"Lemme check," he answered as he made his way over to the computer setup inside his case near the exit. The small laptop logged anything pressurized and any biomaterial found by the

Hounds as they scanned the ship. *"It looks clear, Cap. You should be able to open it."*

"Check. Opening," Anders answered.

After relaying the information to Anders, Wick checked the scan logs and found something he'd never encountered on a scav job. *"Ah, Captain?"* he called over the comms.

"Check," Anders answered, pausing at the bridge door.

"Hold on, Wick," Jones interrupted from the cockpit. *"Captain, we have a problem."*

"What is it, Jones?" Anders asked.

"I have two ships inbound," Jones reported. *"Looks like scav crews by their sig."*

"How far out?"

"Cap," Wick tried to interrupt.

Jones continued with his report. *"We got maybe thirty-five minutes."*

Wicked understood that Anders needed more information from Jones. *"Armed?"* Anders asked. But Wick was growing more concerned with what he was seeing.

"Nothing unusual, so I'd assume yes." Jones' tone indicated that he didn't have much more to contribute. *"You know as much as I do."*

"Kanor," Anders said, enlisting his gunner.

"Check."

"I want a warning shot across their bows if they break the barrier."

"Check."

"Cap!" Wicked said louder, forcing himself to be heard.

"You're going to shoot right off the bat?" Severn asked. *"Shouldn't we get back to the ship first and figure this out?"*

"It's just a warning, kid," Jones said. *"It lets them know we're working at high risk and to not come near."*

"It's standard," Anders said. *"We do it out of respect."*

"Plus, it lets them know I'll send one up their ass if they get too close," added Kanor.

"Such a tough guy," Severn said.

"Captain Anders!" Wicked yelled through the comms.

"What is it, Wick?" Anders replied, almost annoyed.

"We've got something else on the scanners," Wicked said.

"Pressure?" Anders asked.

"No, worse. I've got a bioactive reading."

"That's a new one," said Jones.

"Wicked, what is it?" Severn asked. *"That sounds living."*

Wick answered, *"It is."*

"Where is it, Wick?" Anders asked. *"Is it moving?"*

"No. Stationary. Cold but alive. Quarter-ship, halfway between you two and us."

"Mark it on our visors. Ciris, meet me there. Severn, head to the exit and help get Wick and the equipment back up."

"I ain't checking that out, no way, uh-uh," Ciris replied.

"You get your ass there, boy," Kanor announced, breaking his radio silence. *"It's your job."*

After a beat, Ciris acquiesced and started a hurried trek toward Anders, leaving Wick by himself. In the tiny, silent corridor, Wick glanced around as if to double-check the corridor really contained just him. After a few breaths, he forced himself to return his focus to the scanner logs to look for any other anomalies.

CHAPTER 14

Anders' curiosity manifested as both a raised heartbeat and a cautioned pace as they neared the location of the bioactive reading. Part of him entertained a concern that whatever the "bioactive thing" was could hear the thump of his grav boots and might run off. Silly thought, really, but still, this experience was a first for him.

They passed doorways every so often until they crossed a corridor and found themselves outside of a door to a room that, by the rendered map, appeared to be sectioned off on all sides by hallways.

Anders nodded to a wide-eyed Severn as she continued on her way, leaving him behind. He couldn't tell if she was frightened in general or worried for him. Either way, there was no room for frightened crew members on his team. But still, he fought the urge to keep her next to him.

Ciris turned a corner, passing Severn, and joined Anders. The captain waited until Severn's beacon reached the exit before he approached the door, which took only a few moments but felt like an hour.

"You packed up, Wick?" he asked, breaking radio silence.

"Check," Wicked answered. *"I'm sending Severn up on the climber now."*

"Check. Let me know when you're on ship."

"Check," Wick replied.

"What room do you think this is, Cap?" Ciris asked, attempting to conceal his anxiety.

"I'm not sure, but judging by the proximity to the bridge and the size of the uncharted area behind it, I'm guessing it's the captain's quarters. Not to mention the sign on the door that says 'Captain's Quarters.'" He gave Ciris a look that told him, very briskly, to smarten up.

"All right, Cap, we're on ship," Wick announced from the cargo bay. *"I'm leaving the door open, and there are two climbers ready for you."*

"Wait, if you come back in a hurry," Severn said, *"just turn off your grav boots and jump up through the access tunnel."*

"Good thinkin'." Anders gave Ciris an impressed look. *"All right. Wick, double-check the pressure behind this door."*

"Already did."

Just then, two of Wicked's Hounds went screaming past Anders and Ciris, heading toward the exit.

"Wick, your Hounds are going crazy," Ciris reported.

"I recalled 'em. It's an emergency mode," he replied.

"Wick, send one back here. I want to send it in to map whatever's behind this door."

"Aye, Cap."

Moments later, one Hound soared back over to Anders and positioned itself at eye level at the captain's quarters door. After a nod of acknowledgment between Anders and Ciris, who was now standing at the wall opposite the door with his gun drawn, Anders pulled the handle up, releasing the door from a closed position. Anders pushed and stepped back while the Hound drifted in, beams of light scanning the interior.

Anders watched as a map of the interior space was created on his visor. The first room formed, showing a large space with equally sized blacked-out unmapped areas on either side enclosed by already mapped corridors. There was also one other access door opposite the one they were posted at.

"Wick, show me the bio-reading," Anders said.

A moment later, a blue blip appeared inside one of the unmapped areas of the room.

"See it? Still hasn't moved," Wicked replied.

"Check," Anders acknowledged and turned to Ciris. "Let's go."

Anders stepped inside the room. His headlamp revealed a living area, complete with a couple of couches, a large table for meetings or dinners, and a personal workstation. Ciris joined Anders inside, and they walked around, checking the room's layout. Then they moved toward the door leading to the next room, the one signaling a positive bio-reading.

As they approached the door, Wicked said, *"Pressure is clear, sir. Complete vacuum inside."*

"Check," Anders said as he motioned for Ciris to stay back and cover him. Anders too pulled out his weapon, unsure if it would do any good. No one had ever encountered live bio-readings in the vacuum of space. Anything surviving the elements of space would surely be no match for a simple gun.

"At the door. Ready to open," Anders announced to the crew.

"Good luck, Cap," Wicked said. *"Stay alive."*

"Yeah, Cap," Jones said. *"Don't get dead. And don't be afraid to run."*

"You don't even have to run that fast either," Severn said, *"just faster than Ciris."*

Anders chuckled while looking at Ciris.

"It's true, I guess." Ciris smirked, but Anders could tell he was trying to hide his fear of the unknown.

Anders and Ciris exchanged nods, worried but ready to reveal whatever was hiding behind the door. Before he could lose his nerve, Anders popped the door open in a swift movement. As the door swung around, he stepped back, and both men watched in silence as the room came into view. The comms were silent too. In fact, no one said anything for what felt like an eternity while the Hound drifted in and scanned the room.

"*Cap?*" Jones finally said.

"*Nothing,*" he replied. "*No movement.*"

Anders watched as the Hound finished its scan and came out of the room. The mapping showed a bedroom. Inside was a tall cabinet protruding from the wall and a bed with nightstands on either side. On the bed was the blue blip.

"*I'm going in,*" Anders said, deftly gathering his wits.

He stepped into the bedroom, and his headlamp illuminated only a quarter of the room until he passed the foyer. Then the light spread out in all directions, revealing everything the scans had—except the surprise Anders saw lying on the bed.

A woman.

Lying there as if she'd been positioned for eternal rest: not covered by bed linens, but clothed in a lower ranked military uniform, and strapped to the bed with restraints at her legs, waist, and chest.

Anders slowly approached her, his grav boots thudding on the carpeted steel floor. There she lay, motionless, seemingly not alive. Until Anders noticed something that made him stop short.

She was breathing.

Her chest rose and fell with a slow, rhythmic motion, exactly how Anders' chest wasn't. His breath came and went in a panicked rush as he stared at the inexplicable sight before him. A woman, without a spacesuit, living and breathing in the vacuum of space.

"Ciris, get in here," he tried to say. But his first attempt failed; it emerged as a breathless, choked noise. He wet his throat and tried again, and this time Ciris came hustling in, gun raised.

"Cap, what is it?" Jones thundered over the comms.

Anders didn't say anything as he watched the beautiful woman breathe. She couldn't be more than maybe in her mid-twenties, with fair skin and shiny black hair. Her lean body lay straight and motionless. Except for the breathing.

"It's a woman," Ciris said, surprising not only himself but the rest of the crew. *"Not in a suit. Just…lying on the bed."* There was a sort of detachment in his voice.

"And she's breathing," added Anders.

"Cap, did you just say there's a breathing woman down there?" Jones asked. *"Without a spacesuit?"*

"He did," Ciris said. "Cap, we should go. We should leave this and never come back. This is not right."

"Cap," Jones said in a tone that could only mean he was reporting bad news. *"Those ships have arrived, and they're advancing at a steady rate."*

As he processed that news, Anders snapped out of his stupor. He knew something was wrong with this, but for some reason, he felt this strange woman was no threat. She seemed so peaceful. She slept soundly, and yet he felt he couldn't leave her there.

"Wick, keep the grav plates off in the cargo hold," Anders said in the voice he used before he rattled off commands to each crew member. *"Kanor, fire a warning shot now. I don't want to wait for*

barrier. Jones, position us facing directly at the ships. Severn, head to sick bay and prep the surgeon's bed. Ciris, grab the bed linen at her feet. We're taking her with us."

"No! Cap, we should leave her. I don't know what she's doing here or why or how or anything. All I know is something this weird is better left behind."

"Do it now," Anders said with a finger in the air. "Or that's it. You and your brother can find another crew."

"Do it, Cy," Kanor added. *"If you don't help him, he'll just carry her on his own and you know it. And then we'll be out of a job."*

With much reluctance, Ciris acquiesced to Anders' command.

Anders went to the head of the bed, releasing the restraints on his way. He couldn't hear it, but he felt the vibrations of the Velcro tearing free. He gathered the bed linen, pulled it up over the woman's face, and tucked the covering into itself, wrapping her tightly. Ciris began helping, and together they wrapped her entire body in the blanket. Anders noticed it wasn't hard to bend her body, as if the temperature were not absolute zero. As they nudged her up from the bed, her body rose and maneuvered at their slight direction.

As if maneuvering a long balloon, they pushed her body back to the exit hatch. Looking up the access tunnel, Anders saw Wicked eagerly peering over the edge of the opening, hoping to get a glimpse of this woman.

"Grab her as she comes up," Anders said.

"Check," replied Wicked.

Anders and Ciris positioned her body as if it were an arrow heading through the access tunnel and pushed her up. She floated a little off course, so Wicked flipped over the opening and stuck his arm down, guiding her head through before it collided with a grab bar. Wicked eased her body towards himself and positioned her flat as he floated her over to an open area.

By the time Wicked gently placed her on the floor and held her there to keep her from drifting in zero-g, Ciris and Anders were through the opening. Anders made his way over to the control panel and closed the opening in the floor as soon as Ciris clipped the climbing cables free. Anders then eased on the grav plates, letting the dozens of spools of wires and other things come to rest on the floor.

"Jones, we're clear. Pressurize the cargo hold. Do it slowly," Anders ordered.

"Check."

Jones began to pressurize the area while Anders, Wicked, and Ciris watched the woman's chest rise and fall. Severn was peering at them through the airlock leading toward the sick bay.

Anders' suit depressurized as the cargo hold gained pressure. When it balanced, he unclipped his helmet, and the others did the same. Severn hurried through the airlock, now working as a regular door, and joined the others, eager to see this woman.

"Let's get her to sick bay," Anders said as he slid his arms underneath the woman's back and head. Ciris, Wicked, and Severn also grabbed hold of her, supporting her as they walked.

"She's so cold," Severn said.

"But she's soft," Wicked added. "Not stiff at all. Anything in the black that long would be stiff as steel by now." He looked at her. "Much colder too."

Anders had never seen Wicked with such a confused look before. He was the resident genius. He shouldn't have been stunned like this.

"You're saying she should be colder?" Anders asked.

"Yes," Wicked replied. "We shouldn't be able to hold her without protection. She's cold, yes, but nowhere near absolute zero—well, cosmic background temperature, which is just a few degrees warmer, but—"

"No one cares," Ciris interrupted, anticipating a physics lesson.

"I do. So what does this mean?" Anders asked as they squeezed through the opening to the sick bay and placed her on the bed.

"I'm not really sure. Somehow, she's able to keep most of her body heat. And..." He paused, making sure he wanted to admit it. "She can breathe out there." He pointed at her chest rising. "In a vacuum. Where there are absolutely no gases to breathe at all."

"Captain!" Jones thundered over the intercom. "They aren't responding to Kanor's warning shots. You need to get up here."

"Damn," Anders said. "Severn, check her out. I want your best medical report when I get back." Anders turned to leave, but he faltered when everyone gasped and recoiled from the woman. Severn stifled a shriek.

Anders turned back, only to see that the woman had opened her eyes and was staring at the ceiling.

"Back! Everyone back," he warned his crew and drew his gun.

At the sound of Anders' voice, the woman's eyes drifted in his direction.

CHAPTER 15

"Everyone out, now!" Anders ordered. "Ciris, get up to your tur-ret," he added, working both situations methodically. Ciris took off in a hustle.

Anders positioned himself between the woman and his hus-tling crew. They fled into the corridor outside of the sick bay while Anders stood guard at the door, close enough for escape at the first sign of hostility. He remained still, tense, ready to fight or flee, and observed the woman, who hadn't moved since wak-ing. She lay there, staring at him with curious eyes, and he saw no threats in her behavior.

But this woman had been breathing, living, in the vacuum of space.

Anders couldn't classify her as anything but dangerous.

In Anders' mind, anyone—or anything—with the ability to do the impossible was equally capable of doing harm. So he had to deal with this woman. Somehow. Right now. Because to make this situation infinitely worse, ships were currently press-ing through the unspoken no-fly zone all scav crews adhered to. Anders knew that meant one thing: piracy.

And since they'd outright ignored Kanor's warning shots, Anders would have to defend his claim any minute.

He didn't have time to deal with this woman properly.

So he stepped back toward the door and pointed his gun at her chest.

"I mean you no harm," he said to her calmly. "But I don't know if you mean me harm, and I don't have time right now to find out. So I'm gonna lock this door. And you're going to stay in here for the time being."

She didn't reply. She simply gazed at him silently from the surgeon's bed.

Anders added, "I'm locking you in here, but you are not a prisoner." He paused. She kept staring. "Understand?"

He gave her a few beats to acknowledge him—she said and did nothing—and he was about to repeat his question when Jones interrupted him again over the intercom. "Captain, I think they're moving into attack positions. We gotta get in this or get out. Now!" The speakers crackled, then silence.

Anders bolted out of the sick bay door, closed it, and set the lock.

The woman inside didn't budge.

"Wick, get to the engine room and monitor the systems. When this is over, I want to know how they found us!" Wicked opened his mouth, as if to offer an explanation, but then he thought better of it and took off toward the engine room.

Anders began his hustle toward the cockpit, and Severn, anticipating orders coming her way, fell in step with him.

"Severn," he said, handing her a helmet from a nearby supply cubby, "put this on. You're the only one who won't be strapped in for this. Turn it on and test the comm link." He darted around a corner, heading to the cockpit, and she trailed behind him, listening closely. "I want you running gopher. Check in with Kanor. Make sure he has all he needs. He may have you reload his ammunition. Your first priority is to keep him and Ciris loaded. Keep announcing your position on the comm so we all know where you are. When you're asked to do something, repeat the order and do it. Got it?"

"Check."

"Good. Now go!"

She hesitated, frowning.

"What?!" he said, hustling along.

"Where is Kanor, exactly?" she asked.

"Up!" He pointed for emphasis. Then he sprinted into the cockpit, leaving her alone in the corridor.

He dropped into his seat next to Jones, assessing the situation as quickly as possible. The small steel room echoed with proximity warnings, and beacons flashed from every direction. The heated air was thick and warm, and Jones was already sweating, a sheen on his feverish skin as the pressure of the situation closed in on him.

Anders slipped on his headgear. *"Crew, check in."*

The crew outside the cockpit checked in one at a time with their location and status, ending appropriately with Severn as the runner.

Jones filled Anders in. "We got three bogies." He pointed at the oncoming vessels, one on either side of their ship and another heading straight toward them. Jones flipped a switch that activated the scanners. A glass interface stood before the viewport and illuminated targeting information for each enemy vessel with reality-augmented diagrams of the situation. A few seconds later, a monitor on the main console spat out an information stream of each approaching ship.

"Standard approach?" Anders asked. Jones confirmed. "Do we know them?"

"Dunno, too far out yet," Jones said. "They're coming in steady. Sixteen-hundred-fifty knots."

Anders typed in commands on his keyboard, and then the ships were labeled from left to right as Alpha, Bravo, and Charlie.

"Hail Bravo," Anders commanded.

"Check. Hailing Bravo," answered Jones.

"This is Captain Anders Lockheed. Can I get a callback?" He glanced at Jones, and Jones returned the look, both of them tense.

"I know who you are, Anders," Bravo replied.

Anders growled off-comms, "Alan Thomas. That son of a b—"

"Got a big load there, don'tcha?" Alan kept talking, his voice cracking through the speakers.

"We've staked this claim fair, Alan. Don't do anything stupid."

"Yeah, you did," Alan replied smugly. *"But there's just one problem."*

"Raider," Anders said off-comms to Jones. Jones sighed.

"Look, Alan," Anders said, *"your brother was fixin' to jump us with his lackeys. It was an honest defense."*

"Yeah, maybe," Alan retorted, *"but you're making me go help him, and I hate doing that. You're costing me money and time, and I think you owe me a big piece of that there starship. She's a beaut."*

"Sounds fair enough," Anders said. *"We can bring you in. Go ahead and take your friends and go help your brother. I'll be sure to send you a cut."* Anders shrugged at Jones, knowing full well Alan wouldn't go for that. He was ruthless and took what he wanted. This was going to end in a fight.

"Nah, I think I'm gonna take it and make a call to the GC about your little EMP. They're gonna take all you got for that and lock you away."

"Go ahead." Anders laughed. *"They've already looked. They don't know what the hell they're looking for. As far as they'll be able to see, this was a clean claim."*

On internal comms, Anders said, *"Wick, prep a smoke screen. Three hundred meters, port and starboard side and forward."*

"Check," Wicked replied. *"Three minutes."*

Off-comms, Jones muttered, "Anders, we need this one."

"Heading to Ciris," Severn interrupted.

"I know we do," Anders replied. "We don't have the fire-power to take them on and keep the tow at the same time. This is too big right now."

Most of the crew, including Jones if he were thinking clearly, would agree that being latched to a huge starship with three crews pressing in with the intent on taking them out was a bad situation. It'd be next to impossible to defend themselves and keep the starship. Anders knew he was cornered. For now.

"Maybe you're right," Jones admitted. "But if we lose this payday, we're in it big time with Boozer, and you know it."

"Heading back to Kanor," Severn announced, out of breath.

Anders didn't need Jones to tell him the trouble they'd see if they didn't make this claim. They needed this claim—lest one of their crew would pay the ultimate price. But if they stayed here, they'd all pay.

Anders hit the internal comms. *"Kanor, Ciris, warning shots."*

"Check."

"Check."

Hailing Bravo, Anders said, *"Alan, you've got a warning shot coming your way. Next one's in your face. Fair warning."*

"You're outnumbered and outgunned, Anders," Alan said as three shots crossed his own bow.

Anders flicked off the comms and said to Jones, "Prep the warp drive."

Jones hesitated.

"This is unwinnable. Do it!" Anders shouted. Then he addressed Wicked. *"Wick, drop a Lucy. Long range."*

"Check," Wicked answered. *"Smoke screen in thirty seconds."*

"Check," Anders acknowledged.

"Heading back to Ciris," Severn announced tiredly.

"Cap, we can take 'em," Kanor shouted through the comms, eager for a fight.

"Alan, last warning," Anders said.

"I don't think so, Mr. Elite One," Alan mocked.

"Wicked, do it." Anders said on internal comms.

"Sending smoke screen now," Wicked replied. *"Confirmed. All three en route."*

From the cockpit, Anders and Jones watched the only missile they'd be able to see soar toward Alan's ship, *Enraged*. As it closed in on the enemy vessel, Anders said to Jones, "Release the starship."

Jones, with much reluctance, reached for the toggle to release the cables.

Over the internal comms, Anders announced, *"Brace for FTL jump in thirty seconds."*

With a grumble, Jones popped the toggles, releasing the four heavy-load cables connecting their ship to the starship. Anders steadied *Elite One*, keeping up the illusion they were still connected, until the missiles exploded a quarter of the way between them and the three other vessels. It was a fiery spectacle that ballooned out in all directions, followed by a huge screen of white dust painting the space between them.

Concealed from the enemy ships seeing their escape, Anders eased the controls back, lifting up the nose and pulling away from the starship. Then he flipped the ship over and took off. In a few seconds, they were clear of the starship, and Anders addressed the crew again, *"FTL in three, two, one."*

Anders never liked running from a challenge, but he was sure he'd made the right call. With their ship tethered to the starship, they were stuck in too vulnerable of a position. If it had been anyone but Alan, he'd have considered staying for the fight. But Alan...he wouldn't have left *Elite One* in working order. Anders had taken the only option he had to keep his crew and ship safe: to leave now and come back later for an ambush.

CHAPTER 16

With the ensuing battle canceled by Anders' decision to flee, Severn was left feeling overworked and, ironically, a bit unused. She'd run back and forth between Ciris and Kanor, but they'd never asked her for anything. It had taken until her third trip before she realized they were messing with her, making her "check on the other" for no reason. But though the prank annoyed her, she refused to let it sink in. She decided now was the time to make good on Anders' request for a medical report on the new guest. Doing right by him was her way in.

Before checking on the woman in the sick bay, she made a quick stop at her bunk and grabbed the only clean change of clothes she had. She'd noticed the woman was of similar height and build and thought giving her some real clothes might help calm her down, if she needed calming. Besides, a skintight jumpsuit was not the best outfit for a new and strikingly beautiful woman on a ship full of men. Severn knew that from experience.

Confirming her suspicions, she arrived at the sick bay to find Ciris and Kanor peering through the small glass window of the locked door, fumbling over each other as they stared at the guest. They were also passing a bag of potato crispies between themselves, alternating stuffing their mouths and gawking. Crumbs rained down through the grated floor. Wicked, a few feet away, watched the brothers in amusement.

Severn huffed as she approached and then cleared her throat to put an end to their peeping. "You don't have a chance, boys," she said. The twins pretended they didn't hear her. Rolling her eyes, she gestured to her armful of clothes. "Move, please. I need to get in there."

When they stepped aside, she glanced through the window. The woman was still awake and lying flat on the bed the same way as when they'd left her earlier, as if she were lying still for a body scan. And despite the fact she was strapped down, she didn't look the least bit uncomfortable.

"She hasn't tried to get out?" Severn asked the others. They all shook their heads, with the exception of Wicked, who said, "Nope."

"Hm. Would you come in and watch over me?" Severn asked Wicked.

"Me? I'm not sure—"

"It'll be fine, Wick," she said. "You can protect me."

He sputtered for a second, then nodded. "Okay. Sure."

Before she went in, Severn noticed Ciris and Kanor were almost salivating over the idea of watching the woman change. Severn's eyes rolled in disgust. She wasn't about to let that happen. "Hey!" she called to them. "Leave, the both of you. In fact, go find the captain and tell him I'll have the med report soon."

They shot her a couple of disappointed looks, but they turned around without a fight and walked away, grumbling something accompanied by laughter.

Once they were out of sight, Wicked unlocked the door, and the two of them entered the room. Severn walked up to one side of the bed, while Wicked loitered on the other. Severn immediately noticed the woman's eyes following her as she moved. She shuffled over to the counter where she placed the clothes, then opened the cabinets to rummage for any recognizable exam instruments. She found one device and plucked it off the shelf.

With her back to the room, Severn heard the distinct crunching sound of someone moving while seated on surgeon's bed exam paper. Then Wicked nervously murmured, "Severn?" She spun around to find their mystery guest had unstrapped herself and sat up. The woman now straddled the bed, one leg dangling on each side, and was observing Wicked with her calm, curious eyes. Wicked was slowly backing toward the wall, unwilling to get close to the strange woman.

Severn found it amusing that all the men on the ship were so scared of this woman. Sure, she was weird—breathing in the vacuum of space and all—but she hadn't yet made any attempts to hurt anyone. "Relax, Wick," Severn said. But Wick didn't even look her way. Instead, her voice caught the woman's attention.

The woman turned her head and now gazed at Severn, nothing written on her face except pure curiosity. Like she was using her eyes for the first time ever, watching strictly for the purpose of observation. It was as if she'd never seen people—or anything—before. The look reminded Severn of one of her friends from boot camp—Aura Ishii.

Aura suffered a massive concussion during a training exercise and was diagnosed with severe amnesia. When Severn was finally allowed to see her friend, the doctors warned her that Aura had lost all memory. Of everything. She couldn't remember how to talk or how to eat, much less the faces and names of her friends and family.

Aura had been reduced to a blank slate.

That's why Aura was the first thing Severn thought of when looking at this woman now. Like her memory had been wiped clean, and she was becoming aware of the world for the first time. All she did was observe. She didn't even know how to react to what she was experiencing. There was no fear, no joy, no anything; like she hadn't learned yet what types of experiences drew out those feelings. There was only curiosity behind her eyes.

Severn slowly approached the woman and spoke in a soft, nonthreatening voice. "We're not going to hurt you. I just want to check you out." She sat the VitalScanner on the counter, deciding it would be better to make first contact with the woman *without* cold, sterile instruments. Instead, she reached out for the woman's arm and added, "Do you mind if I check your pulse?"

The woman's only response was a tilt of her head as Severn held her wrist and pressed two fingers to her skin. The woman watched Severn's hands work.

After checking her pulse, Severn pulled her fingers away and said to Wicked, "She's warm. Normal temperature, as far as I can tell."

"How is that possible?" Wicked whispered, then regained a normal voice. "She was as cold as the black. Even had some frost on her. And that was, what, half an hour ago?"

"Well, she's normal now. So is her pulse." Severn gently placed the back of her hand on the woman's forehead. The woman didn't react. Severn then leaned in to look at her eyes, but she didn't notice anything out of the ordinary. The eyes were a soft gray-blue with normal round black pupils. Though they did cross a bit when Severn leaned in, almost touching noses with her.

Severn felt the woman was calm enough to let her use the VitalScanner, so she picked it up. "I'm going to use something to record your vitals now. It's normal. We all do it, and it doesn't hurt." As she was prepping the scanner, she remembered that during her brief medical training she'd been taught to ask a lot of questions. So she said, "Do you have a name?"

Her tone seemed to spark something in the woman, like she knew she was supposed to contribute to the conversation but couldn't quite figure out how.

Severn gave her a chance to answer, but she didn't.

"We all have names," Severn continued while placing the round, smooth, flat silver end of the handheld scanner to the woman's bare forearm. It wasn't the right place for it, but she didn't want to startle the woman by suddenly touching her neck with it. "My name is Severn," she continued as she gestured with her free hand at her own chest. Then repeated, "Severn."

"Do you have a name?" she asked again, slowly shifting the scanner to the woman's neck. The second the scanner reached the correct place, the woman spoke.

"Severn," she said with a soft voice.

Severn jumped but managed to stop herself from recoiling. She took a breath, placed a hand to her own chest, and said, "Yes. My name is Severn." She gestured to the woman and repeated, "And you are?"

The woman answered again, "Severn."

"She thinks you're giving her a name," Wicked said softly, mustering the courage to peel himself from the cold steel wall.

Severn considered that for a moment, then stepped back, using the same introductory gestures as before and saying her own name. Then she gently squeezed the woman's shoulder and said, "Aura."

The woman made eye contact with her for a second, then with Wicked, and then came back to Severn with a look a shade closer to understanding. She repeated, "Aura."

Severn smiled and replied, "Yes. Aura." She looked at Wicked and gave him a small shrug, unsure of how to continue.

"Just do your medical checks, and let's inform the captain," Wicked said. "She seems normal, so let's finish."

"Probably right," Severn replied. "Aura, I'm going to check a few more things, okay?"

Aura still wore a blank look, but Severn got the feeling she was all right with what she was doing to her. Severn verified a normal temperature, heartbeat, and blood pressure from scanning her neck. As far as she could tell, the woman's heart and lungs were healthy with no irregular rhythms. With some quick poking, prodding, and general movements like having her squat and stand up with her arms outstretched, Severn concluded that Aura wasn't injured anywhere either. Aura appeared to be perfectly healthy.

"I think she's good," Severn said to Wicked, then turned back to Aura. "I don't see anything wrong with you. Except for you not being able to talk to us." Severn smiled, and Aura mirrored the gesture. It seemed genuine.

"I'm gonna get her changed now," Severn said, sending a knowing look to Wicked. He didn't move until, "Wanna step out?"

Busting with a sudden realization, he offered, "Oh, yes. Of course." He stuttered his step though. He went for the door but then stopped and turned to Severn as if to stay. But then, quick as he could, he nervously jammed out the door. Severn figured he was concerned for her safety, not that he was hoping to watch. She knew he wasn't the type.

CHAPTER 17

"Captain, wait," Jones said, catching Anders before he stood up to leave the cockpit.

"What is it?"

"I think we have to tell Wick what's going on." A calm undertone resided in Jones' deep voice which somehow always made Anders consider his thoughts a bit further. Anders knew Jones was right on this point, but he hated the thought of telling Wick something so dangerous.

He knew he was a bit overprotective of him, but felt it was with good reason. He could tell Wick was finally beginning to feel safe as part of his crew. New name, new crew. It had helped Wick move on from his past.

"I was hoping to wait until after a few more jobs, when we could settle with Boozer. This starship claim was going to provide the scrap sales to do that for us. It was a huge payday," Anders said. But even as he spoke, he acknowledged the truth of the matter: It was better and safer for Wick to know that the secret of his faked death had gotten out.

"Wick dropped a Lucy on the hull, right?" Jones asked.

Anders nodded with pointed eyes, "I'm not losing that ship."

"All right. We take a step back and put a plan together for returning to it then. We can still take the claim," Jones said as he keyed in ambiguous flight adjustments on the console. "How did Boozer find out? And who else knows?"

"I'm not sure." Anders sighed. "He's asking a pretty big sum to keep quiet." He leaned back in his chair and rested his weathered boots on the steel bench at the back of the cockpit. "If *he* knows, anyone else could know." He paused in his thoughts. "And that means Maddix knows."

"Then there's no use in paying Boozer off then, is there?" Jones said.

"No, I guess not." Anders stared at the controls on the ceiling, simultaneously appreciating his first mate's critical thinking and wondering how he could find out more about who might know their secret about Wick. If Maddix knew, no amount of money could buy Wick's freedom. His genius was far too priceless to Maddix to simply take a payoff. Wick had invented a lot of wonderful devices that made Maddix's illicit dealings more lucrative.

"Cap, you know what we need to do," Jones said.

"I guess I do. I—"

Ciris popped his head in, interrupting them. "Yo, Cap. Chicky needs to see you. She's gonna have the med report soon."

Anders nodded. "Thanks. Can you send Wick up here?"

"Sure, why not?" He turned to leave, muttering under his breath, "Like I have nothing better to do than to play messenger boy."

"You *don't* have anything better to do than to play messenger, boy," Jones retorted as Ciris skulked out. He and Anders shared a quiet laugh. "Why do you still put up with those two, Cap?" A muffled beep from the dashboard pulled his attention. "Water supply's down to half."

Anders waved a hand nonchalantly, "We'll fill it up when we go see Boozer."

Jones spun back around. "Might as well stock up on everything else while we're there. And sell the wire Wick got from the starship."

"Yup. Probably break even on that one," Anders said, disappointed.

"Yeah well, it is what it is, Cap. So, you gonna try and talk to Boozer to find out who all knows?"

"I figure it's a start. Tell Wick what's up so he doesn't go showing his face when we dock."

"He's not gonna like being ship-bound for it," Jones said.

Anders agreed. There was nothing worse than heading into a port and not leaving the ship. Might as well be staring a burger only to find out it's made from Farlinian dog.

"We'll figure it out soon enough," Anders said.

"What about the woman?" Jones asked. "We gonna keep her around? The twins might get a bit too frisky."

"Jones," Anders said with a deep sigh, "I have no idea what the hell to do about that. And you're right about the twins. Plus, she's obviously military."

"Then she's a military problem." He smiled jokingly. "I mean property."

They shared a chuckle, but there was a truth there where Anders found a shade of relief. At Port of DeMarus, he could take her to a Galactic Command post and leave her with them. She was, after all, found on their decommissioned ship, wearing military-issued clothing. But then…

"Hey, Jones, why would GC leave that woman on the ship?"

Jones shrugged and, like a good first mate, offered another question to keep his captain thinking: "Who said she was on the ship when they decommissioned it?"

Anders went back to staring at the steel bulkhead at the rear of the cockpit with his fingers interlocked and resting on his belt buckle. He sat there for several moments, trying to work through all of his problems, before the sound of footsteps reigned in his attention. "Must be Wick," he muttered.

"Hey, Cap." Wick strolled in with his patented boyish smile. "Cy said you wanted to see me."

"Yeah, have a seat," Anders said, motioning to where his boots had been resting seconds before. "Got something to go over with you."

"Sure thing." He took a seat, allowing his smile to morph into something more thoughtful. "What's up?"

"Well," Anders started, "it seems that word is out about you not being dead."

Wick's thoughtful look collapsed into one of horrible dread. He said nothing.

"Don't worry about it, kid," Jones said. "We got you."

Wick tried to look relieved, but it was a struggle. "How?" he finally managed. "Who?"

"We're not sure how," Jones replied, "but we got a message from Boozer saying he'll stay quiet if we pay him off."

"Oh, man," Wick moaned. He, like everyone else, knew Boozer was a fool, but the man still meant business. "How much?"

"Don't worry about that," Anders said.

"Screw that!" Wick yelled, surprising both Anders and Jones. "How can I not? I'm a part of this crew, just as much as the next guy. Or person, now, I guess. Whatever we pay on my behalf affects us all. I wanna know how much."

Anders opened his mouth to reply, but he couldn't figure out how to phrase it.

"It's why he took the starship gig," Jones answered for him, easing Wick back into his seat.

Wick's eyes darted in every direction, as if he were looking at the thoughts inside his own head. Then he grimaced. "Oh, man. I knew this job was way too big for us. I kept wondering why we'd try for something…" He let out a breath and sat back, digesting the magnitude of the price. "Geez. Boozer's crazy."

"Yup," Jones confirmed.

"And he's serious?" Wick asked.

Both Anders and Jones wore deadpan looks.

Wick went pale and then green in the boney parts of his face. "I have to go back to Maddix, don't I?"

"No!" answered both Anders and Jones.

"So what do I do then?" Wick asked.

"Nothing. We're going in to port to see Boozer, sell the wire, and stock up," Anders said. "You'll stay on board, hidden, and we'll go find out what we can."

"It's a good plan," Jones reassured him.

Wick thought for a moment. "Aye, sir. It's a good plan," he said, deflated. "Got plenty of work to do ship-bound anyway."

"See, Cap? We gotta trade up on those two knuckleheads and get us someone new with as much heart as my boy Wick here," Jones said, clapping Wick's shoulder.

"Truth, brother. That's the truth," Anders said with a chuckle, slipping back into captain mode. "All right, Jones. Get us on a heading for Port of DeMarus. Slow. Give us two days to get our cargo straight, take inventory, and figure out what's up with our new passenger."

"Aye, Cap," Jones said. Anders stood up and put a hand on Wick's back, leading him out of the cramped cockpit.

"Just do what you do, Wick. Get *Elite One* shipshape and ready for the next gig. My guess is Boozer will give us some job to make good on what we owe, so we might as well get a jump on being ready."

"Aye, sir," Wick said and looked him in the eye. "Thank you, Anders. Sir."

Anders said nothing but let a faint smile tug at the corners of his mouth.

CHAPTER 18

Anders was eager for Severn's medical report on the woman but more so for a moment alone in his quarters. He didn't sit at his desk to log the events of the day like he normally would have. Nor did he remove his gun, knife, and small utility flashlight from his belt. This time, he walked straight to his bed, let himself collapse with a single bounce, and lazily shut his eyes.

But a captain's nap can only last about as long as a captain can go without thinking about his ship, his crew, or the work ahead. And there was too much begging for his attention right now. So after a few short moments passed in which he lay there restlessly, Anders groaned and then slithered out of bed, intent on his next task: tending to his newest guest.

He figured that Severn had most likely gone back to her bunk by now, and, indeed, that was where he found her. He walked through the door unannounced, startling her. She was seated at the desk posted at the side of her bunk, writing in a small notebook. Anders figured it was some kind of journal, as she immediately covered it with another piece of paper. He'd never understood journaling; a waste of time it was. Now that he thought about it, so were his captain's logs.

He then noticed the woman. She was perched on Severn's bed, peering at Anders. When he smiled, she returned the smile, efficiently shimmied off the bed as if she were almost weightless, and approached him with an outstretched hand.

"Aura," she said softly.

Anders, a little taken aback, held his gentle smile and took her hand in his. Her handshake was firm and matched the strength of her lean body. She was smaller than Severn, much thinner, but only a bit shorter. Her pitch-black hair reached her shoulders in straight, unsnarled strings.

"Anders. Pleased," he replied and looked to Severn for an explanation.

"It's all she's been doing with everyone. She just introduces herself."

He released his grip, but Aura continued to look at him expectantly. "All she's been doing?"

"Yes, I guess I should fill you in." Severn stood from the desk, shifting papers one more time. It was obvious she didn't want him seeing what she was writing. She joined the two of them in the center of the room.

"What can you tell me so far?" Anders asked, motioning toward Aura.

Severn brushed Aura's arm and gave a gentle squeeze at her shoulder. "She's perfectly healthy, as far as I can tell. Blood pressure is normal, heart rate is normal, I didn't hear anything abnormal with her breathing, and her body temperature rose to normal sometime during our run-in with the other ships."

Anders' eyes seemed to paint Aura's entire body from limb to limb, waist to torso to head. Not in an invasive manner; more to appease his curiosity about her extraordinary survival. "She's human, right?" he said, feeling funny asking the question.

"Yes, she's human, Captain," Severn replied lightheartedly.

"I had to ask. It's a bit unbelievable, considering."

"That is true. I would've wondered myself, but as far as I can tell, she's real flesh and blood," Severn said.

"What else can you tell me about"—he paused questioningly— "Aura?" He'd noticed Aura was observing the conversation. She was following who was speaking and watching their lips move. He got the distinct feeling she was studying them, and when Severn told him the rest, he understood why.

"It's not really her name," Severn said. Anders returned a wanting look and at the same time noticed something in Severn's face. She was hiding something. She continued before he could read into it. "When I was in boot camp, there was a girl, Aura Ishii. She suffered a blow to the head, resulting in a severe case of amnesia. She lost all of her memory." Anders watched Aura study Severn as she spoke. Severn continued, making a list with the use of her fingers. "She lost the memory of language, family, friends, education…everything." She shrugged. "In the passing days, Aura looked at us exactly the same way this woman is. Like she's observing, trying to figure out…her existence."

"A little out there, but understandable, I guess," Anders said. "So you think she's suffered some kind of amnesia?"

"However she was able to survive in space, her mind and body did reach absolute zero. Just think about what that could have done to her brain."

"Think about it," Aura said with a smile. Anders and Severn both looked at her, curious. But Anders figured she was just repeating what she had heard.

"So her brain and body reached absolute zero and survived, but the cost was memory loss?" Anders said.

"It's the only thing I can come up with to explain it," she said. "And remember, I'm not a doctor."

"What does Wick think?" Anders asked.

"He agrees. He's a little freaked out by her, but he thinks she's suffering from something like that."

"It looks like she's picking up language pretty quickly, and she doesn't seem scared of us. Has she eaten anything?"

"Yes, she has," Severn said.

"All right. What do we do now?" Anders asked.

"I think we just wait it out. Give her a bunk, food, let her follow us around, and see what comes of her memory."

Anders thought it over. His first concern was the safety of the crew, but it seemed like the woman was no threat to them right now. Food and water rations weren't a concern; they'd be in port in two days' time and the last count put them at forty-four more sailing days without the need for new provisions. They had the room and, with Severn, help to care for their mystery guest. He was good with keeping Aura around for the time being.

"All right," Anders said. "You're in charge of her. Make sure she doesn't break anything, keep her fed, and keep me posted on her progress."

"I think I can handle that. Anything else?" she asked.

"We'll be in port in two days. We can reevaluate then."

"Aye, sir. Which port, may I ask?"

"Port of DeMarus," he said before turning to leave.

CHAPTER 19

Severn breathed a small sigh of relief when Anders left, then noticed Aura's own sigh when she returned to her seated position on the bed. Her eyes grazed over the room as if to rummage for something to occupy herself.

Severn then realized that regardless of her amnesia, Aura needed things to do. "We should go see Wicked," Severn said to her, receiving no particular reaction from Aura other than a faint smile. "All right then, give me one minute." She let a finger fly in the air. Then she placed her focus back on her note and added:

PORT OF DEMARUS - TWO DAYS' TIME
HE'LL HIRE MARKO

She pulled a canister roughly the size of a large finger from her bag. With a twist, the thing popped open, and Severn ripped her note from the notebook, rolled it up and stuck it inside. She then reconnected the two pieces with a twist in the opposite direction. There was a snapping click, indicating it was tightly locked, and a faint green beacon began flashing. She slipped the canister in her pocket and stood up to address Aura.

"You ready to go see Wicked?" she asked.

Surprisingly, Aura looked as if she understood they were going to do something; she slid off the bed again and followed Severn. After leaving the bunk, Severn led the way to the engine room, anyone's best guess if looking for Wicked.

Just before reaching the open doorway to Wicked's engine room, the sharp sound of a heavy piece of metal slamming to the steel floor grating shot out of the room. An expletive followed.

Severn stopped short of the doorway and noticed a confused, almost worried, look on Aura's face. It was when Aura shrugged, as if to ask if she was supposed to do something, that Severn laughed quietly. Aura watched her laugh to herself, and Severn realized she hadn't regained emotions of the sort. Not yet anyway.

When Severn entered the engine room with Aura, she found Wicked snarling and huffing at his current project. She noticed a wrench on the floor near the doorway and picked it up.

On Wicked's work bench was a steel gray box, maybe the length of her forearm on each side, but the box didn't interest her. Attached to the top of it was a glass globe, partially sunken into the metal, with a steel rim that appeared to secure it in place.

"Hey, Wick," Severn said, pulling his attention. "What is that?"

"Oh, nothing. Just something I've been working on nearly my whole life," he said, throttling a long breath out through tight lips. He tossed a pair of pliers on the bench before standing to greet them.

Severn noticed his irritation. "Uh oh, not working?"

"No. Never has," he said. "But I'll get there. What's up? You need something?"

"Um, no, we were just bored and thought we'd come down here to bug you." Severn stepped aside to let Wicked see that Aura was with her. Aura had already found her attention drawn to Wicked's work benches and their contents. She picked up objects and looked at them. They watched her for the better part of a minute. Aura eventually picked up a particular piece of equipment, stared at it for a moment, and then appeared to understand exactly what she was looking at. She began to strip the exterior parts off with quick, nimble fingers.

"What is that? Is she—?" Severn started.

"No, it's all right. Let her do that. It's a busted booster rocket for a Slinger. I've been meaning—" An astonished look came over Wicked's face as Aura fiddled around with the interior of the booster for a few moments, replaced a couple of pieces, then reconstructed the exterior with the parts she'd removed. All in the span of several breaths.

"Did she…?" Severn asked.

"Um," Wicked stammered. "Yeah, she fixed it." He stepped over to the bench, reaching his hands out, addressing Aura. "May I?" he asked. Aura nodded, and he took the booster from her, looking it over. He poked his fingers in and turned it around, checking the components she'd added, and then handed it to Severn. "She fixed it. Exactly how I would have."

"Really?" Severn asked, holding the so-called booster and not knowing what she was supposed to be looking at.

"I mean, it's not all that difficult, but she did exactly what I was planning to do. Considering what's happened to her, that's quite amazing." Wicked turned back to Aura and asked, "Are you some kind of mechanic?"

Aura seemed like she wasn't going to say anything, as usual, but then she answered him.

"Aura," she said in her soft voice and gave a light smile. She also reached out her hand.

Reflexively, Wicked shook it. "Wick."

Aura grimaced like she didn't like the name. But then her face lit up with a bright smile, as if she couldn't hold back a burst of joy. "Hi!"

The two stared at each other, their hands ever so slowly shaking, neither one of them letting go. Severn watched, unable, or unwilling, to break up the moment. But then Aura's attention drifted back to the work bench, and Wicked released his grip on her hand. Severn noticed that he didn't really want to.

"You should let her do more, Wick," Severn said. "See if it helps her memory."

He scanned the projects on the work bench, the many things awaiting their fixing. "Oh, I know," he said as he picked up a small piece. "I've been meaning to get to this." He handed Aura a thin, rectangular object, and when she rolled it over, Severn noticed the slits in the cover over the circular opening of the intercom box. "This is from Ciris' bunk. Somehow he spilled a drink on it and fried the motherboard. If she can fix it, it'll take her a while."

"This could be good. Can I leave her here with you for a while?" Severn asked.

Attempting to hide his enthusiasm, Wick replied, "Yeah, I don't mind. It'll be nice to have someone else in here for a bit. Gets a little lonely sometimes."

"Ooh." Severn made a pouty face. "Poor baby."

"Shut up," he replied, defensively.

Severn was glad she'd found a friend on this crew. She liked his innocence. "Thanks, Wick," she said, motioning to Aura. She didn't mind hanging out with Aura but was glad she'd have some time alone. She glanced behind Wicked and noticed his wall of monitors.

"Wow." She gave an arching whistle. "You sure do keep an eye on us." Tucked in the corner were a series of nine monitors hung in a grid pattern that formed a sort of curved display. The work bench there held several servers and a few keyboards. Each monitor showed a different sector of the ship, and each one flipped to a new sector seemingly at random.

"Yeah, we do, but not for what you may be thinking. If you'll notice"—he pointed to no particular monitor—"there are no cameras in any of the bunks."

"Well, that's a start," she said, not yet convinced.

Aura passed behind them as she walked over to another work bench. She seemed to be on a rushed hunt for something in particular.

"We set it up this way," Wicked said, "so we could do away with having to call the entire ship just to find one person." Aura banged on something three times with a hammer. After a quick glance, Wicked continued his explanation. "We used to hit the comms and call out to the entire ship and have whoever we were looking for ping us back or have them come find us. Now, since I'm in here all the time anyway, you can ping me and ask, 'Hey, where's Cap?', and if I know or can see him, I'll tell you. If not, you're on your own. The constant intercom calls got pretty annoying, so Anders wanted something else."

"And this is the best you could come up with? No personal comms or something?" she asked with a smile.

He grimaced. "It's annoying to wear a comm all the time."

Severn nodded in understanding as she watched Aura drag a stool over to her work bench. The legs produced a horrible sound as they scraped across the jagged steel grating. Severn and

Wicked both winced at the ear-piercing sound, but Aura didn't seem to mind it.

When Aura sat at her leisure, Severn pointed to one monitor in particular. She knew it was the trash dump but asked Wicked about it anyway.

"That's the trash shoot," Wicked replied. "Don't send anything through there unless you're me or the Cap or it's your turn on garbage duty. We have a strict schedule about when we use that."

"Sounds serious. I'm not scheduled for today, am I? I have a lot of nothing to do," she said, hoping to gain some information.

"No, no." Wick shook his head. "Ciris is due to collect the trash for a while. Besides, newbies don't get that duty until they've been on for more than six months. We had a new guy once who was dumping supplies to his actual crew that was following us. We didn't catch on for a month, but when we did, Cap nearly sent the guy out the trash dump himself!"

"Ouch," she snapped, then had a thought. "Trash dumps are pretty shady business. I'm surprised Anders allows them."

"Oh, he doesn't. The shoot incinerates the trash first, so it's only ash that leaves." He leaned into her with a whisper. "The guy stealing stuff didn't use the incinerator. That's how I caught him."

"Ah. Good to know," she said with a wink. "All right, I'd better let you get back at it."

"Okeydokey, but what should I do with her?" he asked, stealing a glance at Aura.

She was face deep in the intercom box, her eyebrows scrunched with concentration, and a faint humming began to fill the air around her.

"Looks like she's pretty good doing that," Severn replied. "Try to talk to her here and there. Maybe her memory will start to come back."

"Maybe she has it, but just doesn't speak our language," he said with a wry smile.

Severn cocked her head as if to consider it but then said as she left, "Maybe she's pretending and is plotting a trap for us all." She couldn't see Wicked as she left but his total silence made her imagine a spooked look on his face and smiled to herself.

CHAPTER 20

When Severn left Aura alone with Wick, he didn't expect the experience to be so much like no one else was there. He usually endured a modicum of anxiety when around anyone. Even Anders. Even in his shop. He had been taken advantage of so much that a natural tension formed when in the presence of others. Not so with Aura. Immediately, he felt she belonged in his shop with him.

For quite some time, the two of them focused on their work and nothing else. Quiet thuds and clanks sounded intermittently as they switched from one tool to another. A soft expletive would escape from Wick's mouth, plus a huff here and there from Aura—though she displayed no real emotions. She appeared content in her work. She hummed a lot, though, while she worked. It was a sweet, soft sound and seemed to increase her focus.

When Aura began soldering wires to the small black motherboard of the intercom box, Wick slid some eye protection onto her head. She didn't appear to notice.

"You really should protect those beauties," he said, embarrassment immediately rushing over him. But the only reaction from her was the tiniest curl of a smile. It would have gone completely unnoticed if he weren't watching her. Relief flushed the red from Wick's face when he realized his compliment probably didn't even register as anything to her.

"Okay, I'll talk to you later," he said awkwardly before he stepped back toward his work bench. As he did, his eyes were drawn towards the motion on the monitors. He saw Severn in the mess hall talking to Ciris. It didn't seem like a heated conversation, as he would have expected from those two. It looked normal, which was strange, and that made him watch a while longer. They chatted for a few more minutes, and then Severn pointed to a nearby trash can. Wick found her behavior odd, first talking with him about the trash dump and then to the guy scheduled to perform it.

"She sure is a curious one," he whispered to himself. He was about to let it go, but then Severn pulled a small black cylinder from her back pocket and tossed it in the trash while Ciris' back was turned.

Wick pulled his stool closer to the monitor and sat there, watching them finish their conversation. It wasn't long before Severn walked away, and then a few beats later, Ciris left as well. That's when Wick decided to leave the engine room. Before he passed through the doorway, however, he thought it polite to at least let his silent friend know that he'd be stepping out for a moment. She gave him a quick glance and smile before he shot out the door.

He hurriedly walked through the narrow corridors to the cargo hold, the metal grating beneath his feet ringing out with each step. Grazing his fingertips along the walls seemed to help him stabilize as he hustled through the tight space. He then hopped onto the stairs that led to the mezzanine, which was a short walk from the mess hall. From there, he would have arrived at his destination quickly, but Anders called to him from across the cargo hold, on the starboard-side mezzanine.

"Wick! Glad you're here. I need a hand for a moment."

"Ah, I have som—" He paused. "Right now?" he shouted across the two-story cargo bay. The not-so-perfect pressure that was nearly impossible to maintain made everyone speak louder. The echo in the hold didn't help.

"Yeah. Can't wait. Should be quick. C'mon." Anders was already almost at the bottom of the mezzanine stairs across the hold, so Wick started his climb down to the first landing. By the time Wick landed on the hold floor, Anders had made it to the paneling by the large rear cargo door. Wick knew Anders aimed to make some room inside the hidden compartment.

When Wick joined *Elite One*, Anders' first task for him had been to create a hidden cargo space behind a square panel as tall as Jones. One that inspectors would never be able to discover or open. He'd wanted to make sure no scanners would be able to detect a space back there. So Wick had built a device to place on the back side of the panel that disrupted scanning equipment. To any scanner, there appeared to be nothing behind the panel except the outside of the ship.

In addition to that device, Wick had built a locking mechanism that could only be unlocked by someone standing on the opposite side of the cargo hold. Which is where Anders pointed for Wick to go, which is why Wick knew what Anders was planning.

Wick knelt to the floor, pulled up a small steel grate, and turned what looked like a flow control valve for a series of pipes. There was nothing in the pipes but a cable that ran over to the secret compartment, unlatching it.

Anders popped off the panel and set it aside.

"What's up, Cap?" Wick asked, hoping his assumption was wrong. "What are we doing?"

"We need to get this hold ready."

"Why? We got something going on?"

"Not yet. I just want to be ready. I'm sure Boozer's going to have something for us to do."

"I don't understand." Wick only wanted to be relieved of having to help. He needed to get to that trash can to see what Severn had tossed. Clearing out the hold wasn't in the crew's best interest.

Anders worked harder and became more vexed with each question. As his anger grew, Wick found it increasingly difficult to tell Anders about the thing Severn had tossed. He decided to tell him, but Anders continued before Wick could open his mouth.

"Boozer usually has a need to smuggle something when people owe him a favor. I don't enjoy that kind of work, so I'd like to be ready to do it quickly and secretly."

"Okay. So what am *I* doing down here?" Wick immediately regretted saying that because it only enraged Anders more.

"You're helping me," Anders said sternly as he tossed a folded heavy canvas at Wick. It slammed into his chest, and dust puffed up into his face. Wick caught it, coughed, and was nearly knocked over.

"Fine," he huffed. "Where are we putting this junk? I warned you to leave this empty in case we needed it in a hurry. I was planning on—"

Anders cut him off. "You also assured me that your Cleres would hide us while we were on the destroyer, but that didn't go over the way you planned, did it? Some things don't go as planned. One more word and I'll have you load this junk into your bunk. Just put it over there," Anders said as he ducked back into the compartment. He pointed his finger and waved behind him to nowhere in particular.

Crestfallen, Wick silenced himself, knowing there was nothing more he should say. Except, "One of them must have called in help before we deployed the Slingers. It's the only thing I can think of. It was a big haul, so it makes sense that other crews would team up." He knew Anders needed the information, but he also understood that he should be quiet, so he said it with a reserved softness.

Anders paused as if to consider the new information and give a response, but he quickly went back to work. He probably would have already thought about that anyway, so Wick may not have given him any new information. The item in the trash can was new information, but at this point if he were wrong, he'd be on the cap's bad side even more. So he let it go.

For the next several minutes, they hustled back and forth silently, emptying the hidden compartment of tarps, boxes, old engine parts, and many other things that Wick, quite frankly, thought could be trashed. That thought again piqued his interest in what Severn had tossed. He wanted to get his hands on it, to see if she was hiding something, or...

At the height of his rekindled interest, Wick heard a sound that crushed his thoughts.

The sound of the trash dump alarm.

It rang out similar to the fire alarm, but it only lasted one beat to let everyone on the ship know that someone had used the dump. Since everyone probably knew this was a scheduled dump, no one would be startled by the alarm, except Wick.

It was another five minutes of moving junk from inside the hidden compartment before they finished and Anders released him from his "quick" chore. Normally, Wick would have shared with Anders what he wanted to do, but he was angered by the impromptu chore, the quasi accusation about the Cleres, and the attitude the captain had, so he kept it to himself out of spite.

"Next time I ask for some help, could you be a little less grumpy about it?" Anders asked. It was more of an order than a request, and it made Wick want to storm back to his engine room in a huff. He still wanted to check the mess hall trash can first, though, on the off chance that Ciris had missed it.

"Yes, sir," Wick said.

"All right, now get outta here," Anders said, pointing in the direction from which Wick had come.

Anders stormed up to the mezzanine on the starboard side, and Wick, much in the same way, went up the port side.

CHAPTER 21

"Damn kid!" Anders huffed as he dropped into his chair, letting out a harsh sigh.

"Uh oh," Jones said with a grin. "What happened?"

"These guys need to start getting their crap together." A few toggles on Anders' console took some rather aggressive switching. "We make a lot, we pay aplenty, and still they grumble when they have to do a little work around here," he said.

"Ciris?" Jones asked. "I heard the trash dump."

"No." Anders waved him off while sorting through a list on the monitor in front of him. "Wick. I asked for his help in clearing out the stash, and I was met with a bowl of crappy attitude."

"I'm sure it wasn't that bad. He's usually good with helping out."

"He is, but this time he got under my skin," Anders said, then took a deep breath. "But maybe I was a bit hard on him."

"No worries. It'll help toughen him up. Let it go," Jones said. "What's next?"

"That's about it. The stash is clear, I called into port for a hookup and supplies, I got Kanor cleaning the artillery and packing ammo, Ciris did the dump, Wick's doing his thing, and Severn's watching Aura."

"Sounds like you could take a breather then," Jones said.

"Nah, I'm all right. I need to catch up on the Wire 'n' see what's been going on."

"Not much good," Jones said. "You can expect some heavier screening when we get there. Should probably leave Aura here, just in case. I mean, I know you're thinking of turning her over, but you might want to check things out first. I've been staying on top of the Wire, and a bit of a funk is in the air these days."

"What's been going on?" Anders asked while flipping through the Wire news on his screen.

"You can read about it, but the short of it is this," Jones said, as if to prepare the captain for some tough news. "Cambria got hit pretty bad not long after we left."

"What?" he asked, eyebrows raised. "What happened? By what?"

"They think it was the same thing that's been wreaking havoc over in the Darigon System."

"Same kind of attacks?"

"Exact same."

"So it's spreading to other systems now, and GC still doesn't know who's behind it?"

"Looks that way."

"Damn. I figured it'd hit closer to home soon, but Cambria?" Anders said. "That's one hell of a jump from Darigon."

"Yeah. A bit surreal, huh? We can still go back and do our thing, but it's crawling with GC, and she's beat up pretty bad."

"Do they have pictures of the mechs that did it?" Anders asked.

"Yeah, one sec," Jones replied while typing on his console. A few moments later, Anders began scrolling through the pictures on his screen.

"Wow. They're looking pretty good."

"It's freaky how they're improving with every attack."

"No kidding," Anders said. "They're looking more and more like people, but it's still obvious they're machines. Has GC figured out how to tell them apart from labor mechs?"

"Not yet. That's why it's so difficult to stop these attacks," Jones said. "And they're not even truly attacks."

"No?" Anders asked. "Looks like it to me."

Jones tilted his head and raised his eyebrow as if to tease forward Anders' ability to believe what he was about to say. "I've been reading up on them, and it seems that whenever they do their thing, they just, all of a sudden, start shooting up a place, not really at anything or anyone in particular. Then they stop and watch how everyone reacts. They watch the people run for cover, watch the police or GC arrive, and watch as they close in on them. When we begin to engage them, it's like their will to fight back diminishes. They seem to resist just enough to test how authorities manage the situation. They pick a fight and then lose the fight. Intentionally."

"Interesting," Anders said. "They're studying how the authorities respond to different attacks."

His statement seemed to give Jones an idea.

"Check this out," Jones said as he keyed into his console. "The attacks all happened at financial institutions, authority stations, police and Galactic Command, large public areas, government locations, and large aircraft hubs. All on and off a planet."

"Someone's planning a big job," Anders realized.

"You don't think it's Boozer, do you?" Jones said.

"No way. He's way too small for something this size," Anders said and then paused for thought. "Now Maddix, on the other hand..." He put his finger in the air.

"If it is Maddix, then we need to keep Wick far away from this. If Maddix finds us, then Wick's a slave again and we're as good as dead."

"Check," Anders said, realizing that he'd have to do whatever Boozer wanted to keep him quiet.

No matter the cost.

There wasn't a lot of conversation after they came to this conclusion. They sat silently in their chairs, scrolling through the news on the Wire, Anders plotting and planning in the back of his mind. Worry was also brewing in his chest for what lay ahead at Port of DeMarus and for him and his crew. Staying too long at port could prove more dangerous than he would like, so he would need to get in, meet with Boozer to, unfortunately, take whatever deal he'd be offering, and get out.

After a long time sitting together, both Anders and Jones decided to turn in for sleep. They also decided to try to enjoy the next day, the last day before getting to Port of DeMarus, where they would find out how deep they'd have to go to keep Wick from Maddix.

CHAPTER 22

Anders understood exactly how large Port of DeMarus was. Big enough to pass through genpop unnoticed if you knew how to pass through inspections, but the port was also large enough to attract a certain kind of nuisance that had been popping up as of late.

Port of DeMarus received more than 150,000 interstellar travelers every thirty days. That wasn't counting the two million for local interplanetary travel. Port of DeMarus was sized to meet this demand, and so at a half hour out, not only the breadth but also the depth of its massiveness filled the limits of *Elite One's* oversized cockpit viewport.

Jones maneuvered the ship into the approachway lit with massive red beacons in four enormous lines, demarcating a square, tube-like runway for incoming vessels. All around the approachway, local vessels buzzed through their normal operations, servicing the port and standoff stations with deliveries, repairs, and the like.

Anders stepped into the cockpit to join Jones on the final approach. It was always helpful having the copilot keep an extra set of eyes out the viewport. Traffic at ports this size was never slow and easy.

"Have you called for a docking?" Anders asked as he threw on his leather jacket before easing into his chair.

"Not yet. Prolly should, though, since we're closing in," Jones replied.

"All right. I'll do it. What's the channel here again?"

"One," Jones said with a smirk. He popped the all-comms switch for the crew on his console. *Prepare for docking in ten.*

"One. Why can't I remember that?" Anders asked, shaking his head and reaching for the controls on his console.

"Cuz you like to overcomplicate shit."

"Maybe, but I wager that'll save our asses one day," Anders replied, bringing a handheld comm to his mouth. *"Port of DeMarus, docking master, Captain Lockheed here. Over."*

The comm speakers crackled, and a moment later, a voice responded, *"Dock Master Scotty here. I read you, Captain Lockheed. State your business."* The man spoke with weathered and raspy voice, but he did so quickly.

"Looking to resupply. We need to purchase two months' rations, sell some gear at the Port Bazaar, and get a drink at one of your famous watering holes. One overnight, class-three cargo ship. Got room?"

"Yeah, we got room. Not sure for the likes o' you." He laughed. *"I heard o' you. Been havin' trouble 'round here lately with some wild folk 'n' their machines. You ain't gonna cause no ruckus, are ya?"*

Anders eyed Jones curiously. *"No, sir. Just some quick business. We'll be outta your hair within a couple shifts."*

There was a pause.

"All right, Captain Lockheed. Proceed to Docking Bay Seventeen G. That's as close to the bazaar as I can getcha."

"Thank you, sir, that'll be fine."

"Dock master out."

"Classy old-timer there," Jones said with a chuckle.

"Wild folk and their machines?" Anders asked. "They have some trouble here too?"

"Not sure, Cap. I suppose Boozer'll know something."

"I don't wanna owe him anything more than I already do. We'll ask someone else."

"Aye."

Jones navigated the airspace around the station with ease and finally glided through the airbreak and into the hangar bay. There he found his designated docking ground crew swinging their bright orange batons. From their guidance, Jones rested the ship on a temporary perch in Bay Seventeen G. Anders and Jones then began shutting down the ship's systems, and after the engines quieted, they both left the cockpit and headed to the cargo hold to meet with rest of the crew.

Kanor and Ciris could barely contain their excitement for trading the confinement of the ship for the warm and toxic environment found deep in the belly of Port of DeMarus.

"Listen up!" Anders shouted as everyone, including Aura, lined up in front of him. He stood between them and the cargo bay door to freedom. "I don't want to be here longer than necessary, so I booked us for a day's stay." He eyed Ciris and Kanor. "Don't go too far or get too stupid. You're all on call in case we gotta jam outta here quick."

There wasn't as much muffled disregard for Anders' on-call requirement as there usually was. Jones and Wicked had known the order would be coming. Severn was too new to think it unfair. And Aura didn't know enough to get upset. So the only scoffing came from the twins.

"Kanor," Anders continued, "you and your brother sell the wire we scaved from the starship." Kanor nodded, accepting his task. "Get as much as you can for it. We're gonna need it. Drop the money and receipt off in the lockbox before you head out, and be back in less than thirty hours." Anders knew that it was a fifty-fifty shot they'd make it on time, and half of him wasn't sure if he'd care if they ever came back. "Jones. Severn. You're with me. We're going to see Boozer and set things straight, and with any luck, we'll be outta here a couple bucks richer and on to the next gig."

Anders paused, reluctant to give the next order. Finally, he said, "Wicked, shipbound until further notice."

"Damn, kid. What'd you do?" Ciris said, amused by Wicked's predicament.

Kanor, on the other hand, wasn't so appreciative. He knew the shipbound order meant something big, so he elbowed Ciris in the arm to shut him up.

"Any questions?" Anders asked.

Surprisingly, Aura raised her hand.

"What is it, Aura?" Anders asked, unsure if she understood what had been happening for the last few minutes.

"Mm," she started. "M-may I stay? W-work?" She pointed at Wicked.

The crew, in unison, turned to Wicked for some kind of explanation.

"Yeah," he said, "she's been kind of saying random things all day. Not much has made sense until now."

"Looks like she's starting to remember then. Good," Anders said and then addressed her. "Yes. You stay here with Wicked." He nodded to Wicked. "You okay with watching her?"

"Yeah, she's harmless," Wicked answered with a shrug.

Anders nodded. "Okay. Keep her on board."

"Check," he said, nudging her shoulder and waving for her to follow him.

Wick and Aura disappeared down the small corridor leading to the engine room, while Kanor and Ciris began collecting the material they'd be selling at the bazaar. Anders led Jones and Severn down the cargo ramp, bent on meeting up with Boozer.

CHAPTER 23

Anders had Severn lead the way through the port's thick crowd. She formed a sort of wedge for him and he in turn for Jones, who brought up the rear, bumping into everyone who came close to him. At first, Jones whispered an apology to each person but soon grew tired of it. They should see him coming.

The three of them held this formation as they snaked their way through the terminal. Old and well established, Port of DeMarus served more travelers than any other station. But the presence of the public eye wouldn't matter, Anders knew, when he was behind Boozer's closed doors. He needed to negotiate his way back to his ship, somehow keeping Wick's faked death a secret and everyone else on his crew alive. His only hope depended on Boozer's willingness to renegotiate the terms they had made a few days prior to picking up Severn. There would be a cost. Anders expected the current deal to be nuts and bolts in comparison.

But what other choice did he have than to take whatever Boozer offered? Any deal with him was better than coming into contact with Maddix again. Maddix would want Wick, period. No buy-offs and no deals. A slave and that's it. Anders would die before letting that happen.

After passing through the terminal, they continued their walk into the much less dense common-level marketplace. Anything needed while on port would be found here. Except supplies and ship parts, of course, which were stored at the level below any hangar. Anders wasn't looking for parts though. He wasn't looking for food and drink either. Or gambling. Or visits to a gym. Or new weapons or ammo or any other gear.

Anders wanted nothing more than to get his meeting with Boozer out of the way, so when he eyed the shop of his favorite cutler, it was tough to pass up a new knife.

"Hope we don't need to pass through here for long," Severn said, now walking behind Anders.

"What's the matter, Severn?" Anders said. "Too good for these people?"

"It's not the people, sir," she replied as she bumped shoulders with a guy mumbling to himself. "It's the smell. I've only been here once before, but I don't remember it being so bad."

"You can thank the Farlinians for that," Jones said. "The port's council lifted the ban on all foreign meats—the normal supply line got taken out, so they needed to keep up with demand. The people of Farlin jumped all over it. That's where this smoke is coming from."

Severn looked up and noticed the bluish haze hovering over the crowd. She noticed that the row of second-story housing above the shops all had their windows closed.

"Now everyone's basically eating dog," Anders said over his shoulder as he squeezed through a particularly crowded line at a seemingly popular food stand.

"Sick," Severn said.

"To us, sure," Jones said. "But to the majority, a dessert cooked and ground into a salted paste lathered onto a dark bean cracker."

Severn huffed. "Thanks for that, Jones. Now I won't be eating for days."

"I'll take that bet," Jones said.

"What, that I won't eat for days?"

"That or that you'll eat some Farlinian dog. A whole plate for five hundred cash."

"Don't do it, Severn," Anders said, regretting his decision to take that bet once before. "You're better off not eating for thirty days."

"Thanks for the advice, but I think the smell alone is pretty much eating it all the same."

Jones found that particularly amusing and started chuckling, which caused Anders and Severn to laugh as well. However, the tension looming over Anders cut his laughter short, and he began to grow wary and anxious as the three of them neared a particular shop. It didn't look much different than any of the other shops they'd passed, except that it had alleyways on both sides and was marginally wider. An easily missed symbol of something more sinister than a simple restaurant.

There were other more obvious signs as well.

Steel railing encircled the front patio, and before that railing stood four armed guards. They were paired off, two on either side of the only entryway cut into the railing, a small opening that would be difficult to flee through in a hurry. And to make matters worse, an auburn canopy jutted out from the edge of the shop's roof, all the way to where the guards stood. The gap between the top of the railing and the canopy was only a few centimeters. You couldn't go through the railing, and you couldn't climb over it either. No one was getting in or out without explicit consent.

"Severn, hang back and station yourself out here," Anders said, using his typical captain's tone. "I want you out here in case we need a hand leaving."

"Check," Severn acknowledged, breaking out of formation. Anders watched from his peripheral vision as she ducked into a nearby bar. Its canopy read "Drinkery Locale."

"Jones, with me."

"Check," replied Jones, closing the gap between himself and Anders.

"These guys look new," Anders observed.

"You think Boozer's beefing up cuz o' those attacks been goin' on?"

"Maybe," Anders said. "New guys and two more than usual out front. I'd say he's worried about something."

"Maybe he's got too much going on to care about us not having his money just yet. Could catch a break. Or an extension."

"Yeah, maybe. It's a good angle to try," said Anders. "C'mon, let's have done with it."

Anders and Jones confidently walked side by side up to the four guards out front. The two largest ones stood in the middle. Naturally, Anders walked up to the biggest one.

"I'm here to see Boozer."

"Boozer probably don't want to see you," the guard responded.

Jones was one of the strongest and toughest men Anders had ever seen and played the part better than anyone he'd ever worked with. To see him lose his composure by breaking into laughter in a moment such as this was a new one for Anders.

Though he completely understood why: The guard had spoken with a weirdly high-pitched voice that seemed out of place coming from the mouth of a mountain.

Anders stifled his own snicker and replied, "I'm sorry. It's from earlier." Then his laughter came to a complete halt when the guard lifted his chin while adjusting his shoulders. A long red scar across his neck made a brief appearance.

"Forget it for now," the guard said. "I'll see you around when I'm off the clock and show you how funny it is when your vocal chords are sliced through too."

Anders swallowed at the thought but then steeled himself while Jones responded for the two of them. "Sure thing," he said, regaining his composure. "Like he said, though, we're here to see Boozer, and we know he wants to see us."

The high-pitched guard pointed a thumb over his shoulder and stepped aside. The guard opposite him did the same and then said, "He's here, but you might not be able to talk to him. You'd better hurry." All four guards shared a last laugh as Anders and Jones stepped past them, heading toward the front door.

Inside Boozer's place, a diverse array of people filled dozens of finely crafted wooden tables and chairs. Most of them were focused on the various games at their respective tables, hoots and yells flaring up every time someone won or lost badly. Jones waded through this rowdy, drunken crowd, aiming for the back of the room, while Anders followed briskly behind.

"Can I get you anything, sweetie?" the woman behind the bar asked softly as they passed.

"No, thank you," Anders said, pointing to their destination.

"I wasn't talking to you," she retorted. Both Anders and Jones stopped short and glared at her as she took her time lustfully eying Jones from head to toe.

Jones smirked at Anders. "What, you think you're the only pretty one around? Better check that."

Anders grinned, shaking his head. "I guess so," he said and motioned for Jones to keep moving. Jones pushed on, but Anders couldn't help but notice the extra lift in his step.

When they reached the door at the back of the room, a couple more guards, nearly identical to the ones out front, stopped them. "Hold it," one guard said, raising his hand, palm out. "Who are you?"

"Anders Lockheed and first mate. Here to see Boozer."

"One moment," he replied, nodding to the other guard, who slid through the door and vanished into the hall beyond. No one said anything else as the three of them waited for the other guard to return, but Jones and Anders had a very intense stare-down with the remaining guard, whose steely eyes never left them, not for a second.

When the second guard finally returned, ending the staring contest, he held the door open and said, "She'll see you now."

Anders and Jones shared a curious look as Anders mouthed, *She?* Jones shrugged and followed Anders through the door. One after the other, and both thoroughly confused, they shuffled down the cramped hallway that ended at Boozer's office.

Except it wasn't Boozer's office anymore, Anders realized, and it was too late to turn back now.

CHAPTER 24

Severn had downed half her beer and dispensed of three would-be suitors by the time Marko arrived. She was sitting alone by the railing at a two-person table, surrounded by several other tables, only two of which were empty. The crowd was mostly seated and relatively tame, so Severn had a good eye on Boozer's place across the way and could faintly hear the guards' conversation. She couldn't make out any specific words, but she'd be able to read their reactions if something went down.

"Well, look who it is," Marko said, closing in on her with an exaggerated smile. He was about the size of Anders but held a somewhat larger gait due to his military-enforced workout schedule. Anders' own schedule, Severn noticed, existed but wasn't as strict.

She returned a "surprised" smile, as if she weren't expecting Marko's appearance. She knew of his assignment to the same task force, but she hadn't seen him since boot camp, which felt like an eon ago. Regardless, it was odd seeing a familiar face since her immersion in Anders' crew for the last several days, but it was nice to see her old friend again. Since they were holding a cover, though, one where she was expected to perform the "long time no see" shtick, she rose and embraced him.

"Marko. So good to see you!"

He pulled her in and held her tight. "Yeah, you too. Where have you been?"

"Cut the crap," she muttered quietly into his ear. "They're inside Boozer's right now, so I don't know how long we have."

"All right," he said, equally soft. "So how do we do this?"

"I'm not sure," she said, eyes on the guards. She pulled away from Marko and took her seat again, motioning him to sit on the chair across from her. She kept her tone quiet, however, to avoid drawing any attention from nearby nosy patrons. "I think, with these guys, it might be best to start a fight or something, and then have you come in and help."

"Okay." Marko sank into the chair next to her. "What about having them come out and see us together? Pretend we're old buddies and I'm looking for work."

She pursed her lips and shook her head. "Won't work. This needs to be fast. We need Anders to offer you the job now, today. He booked the dock for twenty-four hours, but I have a feeling we won't even be staying that long."

"So we need to stage an audition."

"Exactly," she said.

"All right. I can call the commander and have some guys down here within the hour. Act all drunk and have them start something."

"No. Too *random*," she said, considering what to do. "It has to be more personal. He needs to be put in a position of needing help. He's smart. He won't offer you a job if you break up a stupid bar fight."

"Makes sense." Marko bit his lip, then asked, "What about his crew? The twins. Are they around? What if they got hurt in some kind of scuffle that I helped you guys out with? He'd be down a man or two and would really need someone then. Your note said he may have to take on a job or something?"

"Yeah, looks like something's going on with his mechanic, Wicked. He seems to be in a tight spot, so that could work."

"Where are the twins now?" Marko asked, pulling out his handheld comm.

"I'm not sure. Cap ordered them to sell the wire we pulled from GC's starship before they went off to do their own thing."

"*Commander?*" Marko said into his comm.

The comm crackled back. "*Go ahead, Marko.*"

"*We need to find the twins. They're my way in.*"

"*Got it. Bravo team is on 'em. They've returned to the ship,*" Commander replied.

"*Severn says they'll be leaving again. Put a few guys on 'em in civilian clothes and ready for a beating. Ping me back with a location, and I'll meet you there.*"

"*Got it. Commander out.*"

Marko put away his comm and grinned at Severn. "Miss this?"

"A little, but I'll tell you what. I wish I could be there when our boys take out one of the twins. Man, I hope it's Ciris that gets the takedown. A broken leg would be nice." She smirked.

"It'll probably be a bit worse than a broken leg. But yeah, you'd like that, wouldn't you?"

Severn winked.

"All right," Marko said, standing up, "I should bust outta here before your new team gets back and *kicks my ass.*"

"Shut up," she said. "They're not all that bad. I kinda feel bad for using them as bait."

"Yeah, well, that's what happens when you're the best legal-slash-illegal crew around. Galactic Command will use you however they see fit."

"I guess so," she said, standing to embrace her old friend again for an overly cheery good-bye. As she moved, though, she noticed three of the guards at Boozer's place crowding around the fourth, who was on his comm. They stood as if ready to jump into a sprint. Then they hightailed it through the narrow entryway toward the front door.

"Change of plans," Severn said.

"What?" Marko replied, releasing Severn from the hug.

"Something's up inside Boozer's. We should go now. Anders is in trouble. That's our in, not the twins."

"Lemme call it in," Marko said, raising his comm.

"No time," Severn replied and rushed off through the crowd.

Marko followed closely behind her but accidentally bumped his hip into a nearby table, knocking over a couple of beers. A quick apology and he was off to catch up to Severn, who was already halfway to Boozer's place.

CHAPTER 25

When he and Jones walked in to what used to be Boozer's office, Anders didn't notice the additional guard standing inside the opening.

How could he have?

The horrific state of Boozer cowering in the corner stole every bit of his attention. Drool and blood seeped from his busted mouth, while another huge guard towered over him and held him in place. Boozer's left eye, swollen shut and puffy, had already turned blue with bruising. His lips and nose dripped a crimson warning for Anders to make haste and get out.

"Well, well," Maddix said, turning toward Anders and Jones. She was across the square office before she cut that distance in half with her tottering stride, her heels clicking on the steel floor. As she walked, a faint scratchy sound swished from her thick, nylon-covered legs as they squeezed passed each other in the overly tight knee-length skirt. "I was expecting you two. How delightful that you show up now, just when things are getting interesting."

"Maddix," Anders said, stealing a glance at Boozer. Expecting them? There it was—she knew about Wicked. Boozer failed at holding that a secret for Anders' payoff.

"Anders, we have something to talk about," she said knowingly.

"It appears so," he replied.

"Come," she said, turning back to the single wooden desk in the office. To the left was a row of steel filing cabinets and next to those, a cold box. She sat down in the chair behind the desk, the back of which was a deep auburn color and stretched high up over her head, splaying out at the top like a throne might. From Anders' memory, this wasn't Boozer's chair. She must have brought it with her, which meant Boozer was done. Maddix was taking over his operation. "Are you going to just stand there?"

Anders tested Jones with a look, and he nodded, so Anders walked toward the desk, knowing Jones was ready for any move he might decide on. As they both neared the desk, the lackey pinning Boozer on his knees stepped away and stole a couple of wooden chairs from the only table in the office and placed them behind the two. He quickly returned his grip on Boozer's shoulder as they reluctantly sat down. Jones' chair creaked under his weight.

"So," Maddix said, pouring herself a drink from a nearby flask, "you have been deceiving me." She took a sip and grimaced. "Ack!" She turned to Boozer. "You know, Boozer..." He was still catching his breath from his last bout with the man who watched over him. "You'd think with your name and the business you're in, you'd have a decent whiskey at your desk." She tossed the flask away. It skipped across the floor, splattering its contents along the way, and bounced off the cold box. She then waved her hand as if to brush Boozer away like a bothersome fly. There was a peculiar motion with her head as she raised an eyebrow to his guard.

The man stepped into him, placing a knee and thick thigh on Boozer's back while he knelt on the floor. This action steeled

Boozer into straightening his back as the guard drew a long blade without him noticing. In a quick fluid motion, he pulled Boozer's forehead back with one hand and neatly slipped the blade straight through the front half of his neck, as if he were testing a fleshy violin. Boozer recoiled a moment too late, blood spurting from his throat. He gurgled and gasped for a breath that wouldn't come, and he fell to the floor with a thud that echoed off the steel walls. On the floor, the pain on Boozer's face shown an aching plea for life as his fingers curled in angst before his throat. Anders noticed that Boozer wanted to cover the wound but seemed afraid to find a horrifying wet truth. Then his eye caught Anders', which shot him a look of horrid disbelief. Finally, the blood loss and lack of air drained the energy from his body as his fight for life failed and slowed to nothingness.

The stillness from Boozer's body held Anders' breath and with it the sudden realization that it was over. Finally, Anders took a breath while his racing heart sent a flash of heat through him. And as if there were a thread of hope that this wasn't real, Anders longed for some sign of life. But there would be no more movements from Boozer as Anders looked upon the man, chest down on the floor with a blank gaze of surprise still on his face. The guard then adjusted himself to face Anders, paying no more attention to Boozer as blood continued to leak out onto the floor.

Jones stiffened next to Anders, who heard him swallow anxiously. Standing in front of Maddix for any reason meant things were bad, but to see his first mate struggling, even though the signs were barely visible, was unsettling for Anders. He'd known Maddix was capable of heinous acts, but witnessing the worst of them firsthand called attention to the most basic of survival instincts.

Anders saw no viable exits. The one door he could see from his position was the one behind Maddix, and that probably led deeper into Boozer's lair. There might be a secret escape route, but Anders wouldn't be able to find it fast enough. It would be easier to fight through the guards and flee back down the hall from which they'd come.

"Kudos to you," she began again, addressing Anders, tearing him from his panicked thoughts on fleeing. "For deceiving me that is. It's not an easy thing to do. I have many eyes in the black. Tell me, how has business been?"

How could she pick up the conversation after that display? After giving that order? Disgusted and terrified, he knew he had to focus, so he considered the question for a moment. But why the small talk? He hated small talk, no matter with whom. Now it felt petty, vindictive. Screw this. "Damn the small talk. Let's have done with it," he said shortly. "You don't care about how my business has been."

"Oh, on the contrary," she said, waving a finger at him. "Your business has been good. No doubt many have noticed your well-improved income over the last five years. I've heard of you here and there over that span of time. And it was your most recent acquisition that demanded my immediate attention."

Now Anders knew without a doubt that she was aware of the truth. He and Jones had helped Wicked fake his death exactly five years ago to get away from Maddix. She hadn't known Anders and Jones then.

He hated playing games even more than making small talk. "Okay. So you know Wicked flies with us. Now what?"

"Wicked?" she said lightly. "Is that what you call him? No doubt you gave him that name for how he designed his own death." She smiled and then stood up. The cushions in the seat of her throne puffed back out in relief. "He is a clever one, isn't he? Helped me with some of my greatest"—she tapped a finger to her chin— "acquisitions."

"He was your slave," Anders said sternly. "He deserves better."

"Oh, you've grown to love him like a son, haven't you?" she mocked. "How sweet."

Anders grimaced.

Maddix dramatically walked around the side of the desk, as if she were thinking, and then continued. "And I suppose keeping him locked up on the ship while you're in port is a better way to treat him?"

Anders shrank back in horror. Did she know where he was now? He was hopeful, but there was a good chance she had already taken him. "He's free to take leave anytime," Anders said, holding his resolve.

"Oh, how true. In fact, he *has* decided to take that leave." She dropped her chin and spoke low. "Indefinitely." Her eyes then shot to the guard who had left Boozer bleeding on the floor. He lumbered over to the door behind Maddix's simple throne and opened it while she stood up and threw her arms at the door as if to present something with excitement.

And there stood Wicked, bound and gagged, with a panicked look in his eyes. The guard stepped into the small hallway and corralled Wicked.

Maddix shot the guard a faint look of disapproval. "Just the one?" she said. Her head tilted as if to add a scolding to her question.

The guard nodded reluctantly, and as Maddix spun back to address Anders, she said, "No matter. We'll find her."

"Let him go," Jones commanded from his seat.

"Oh look, big first mate loves little *Wicked* too," Maddix said, snarling at his name.

Maddix made a clicking sound with her tongue, scolding Jones for speaking out of place. "Not so fast with the orders, *pilot*. Wicked has returned home to me."

At that statement, Wicked's face warped into an expression of utter terror, then collapsed into weariness, as if he'd rather die than face that fate.

"What is it you want for him?" Anders asked, respectfully stern.

"Oh, you are a captain," she said, deepening her voice, the raspiness of which grew more and more grim. "A good captain like you reads situations like this perfectly. I do want something, that much is clear. But I'm afraid there's nothing you can give me to earn Wicky here back into your services."

"What is it you want then?" Anders repeated, his voice full of hatred.

"Wicked…I'm sorry." She frowned and spun on her heels to face him. "I just can't call you that. To me, you're still my little Drew. Yes, that's better." She turned back to Anders and gave him a grave look. "Drew here is going to stay with me now. Whether he stays alive is entirely up to you, Anders Lockheed, captain of *Elite One*." She said his name in mocking severity.

Anders felt the pressure now. Maddix's pride had been tarnished from falling for Wick's faked death, and no doubt a piece of her reputation had been damaged as well. So killing Wicked instead of using his talent was entirely worth it to her.

He would do anything to keep Wicked alive. He would for any of his crew. "What is it that you want from me?"

She shook her head as if to feign snapping back to reality; her cheeks rippled with the motion. "Thank you for asking again, Anders. Sometimes I get a little carried away with," she danced her fingers around as if to play with puppets, her cigarette still clutched between two of them, "my suzerainty."

Maddix then raised a finger and reached into her bag resting on the desk and pulled out a metallic hoop. Wicked shuddered at the sight of it. He then began to scream behind his gag in a panicked struggle to free himself. She placed her thumb on a small square at the top, and the hoop popped open. Wicked screamed even more. Anders' heartbeat quickened and his vision tunneled. He'd never been in such a helpless situation before. He was at a loss for what to do.

Maddix spoke again, drawing his attention back. "Do you know who Kopius the Collector is?" She raised the opened hoop over her shoulder. Wicked recoiled the best he could while one man held him and the other stepped forward, grabbing the thing.

Anders found the question both curious and revealing. "Not many don't. He's the curator for the Promaedia Museum in the Corban system."

The man walked the hoop over to Wicked, who was lost in a maelstrom of sobbing and tears. Jones leaped up from his chair, but it was too late. The guard clamped the collar around Wicked's neck, which cast him into a shame that fell him to his knees.

"Very good, Anders. I knew you'd be the man for the job." She glanced over to Wicked, satisfied the device was securely around his neck. Her eyes darted to his gag, and then to his arms restrained behind his back. The guard cut the ties from his wrists and released the gag.

"You all right, Wick?" Anders asked.

Wicked, broken and sobbing on his knees, said nothing. It was as if the collar on his neck shrouded him in a cloud of hopelessness. Softly, he said, "Yes, sir."

"Oh, that won't do," Maddix said. "That won't do at all. Drew, to you, no one else is sir or ma'am, nor do you have a captain. And your name is no longer Wicked. You just have me, and what do you call me?" She bent her ear toward him, and he said nothing. Her face grew disappointed. "I didn't hear you." She leaned in closer.

A soft voice struggled from Wick. "M'lady Maddy." Old *forced* habits die the hardest. Wicked's body slumped, as if he felt the full burden of what the rest of his life would be like with Maddix.

Anders' compassion urged him to take the attention off Wicked, whose shame was growing thicker by the second under Maddix's control. He wasn't going to allow this. "What is it that you need us to do?"

"Need?" she questioned. "I don't *need* anything. What I want is for you to pay a visit to Kopius and bring him and his latest, most prized artifacts back to me."

Anders glared at her. He'd known this visit was going to be bad, but he'd never dreamed it would reach this level. "That's impossible," he replied. "We'll never make it out with one, let alone both."

"Well, you're the best at what you do. I'm sure you'll figure something out."

"I'll need Wicked on my team. I can't do it without him."

"Oh no, my dear, we won't be making that mistake again," she said, shaking her finger at him. Her other hand was flipping through Boozer's leather-bound ledger on the desk. "He'll be available over comms, but he stays with me. Besides, I believe you now have a new smart young lady at your disposal."

Anders flinched. Aura? Severn? He refocused on Wick. "I'm telling you, we need him with us," Anders said adamantly.

Jones joined in with his deep, calming tone. "We'll need him to make a few things to do the job right."

"That might be true," she said, looking at Wicked. But then she shook her head. "No. He stays with me. I think you'll find the girl has the same qualities. Oh, and I'll be needing her back as well." She smirked. "When this is all done and over with, of course." She then flicked her eyes toward the guard nearest Wicked, and the man shoved him back inside the doorway.

"No!" yelled Anders, jumping from his chair. He lunged over the desk for Maddix. He knocked her over and jabbed the throat of the nearest guard, sending him to the floor. Jones leaped from his own chair, grabbed another guard's head, and swung him face-first into the wall so hard his jaw cracked.

Anders barreled into the back hallway, tackling the guard who was dragging Wicked off. Anders' fist smashed the guy's face in, nose exploding. At the same time, two gunshots rang out in the office.

"This isn't good, Cap. You should've let me g—" Wicked shouted, but Anders cut him off.

"No! I'd never leave you." Anders grabbed him by the shoulder. "Now, come on."

They darted back into the office, where Jones had taken out the other guards and was standing over Maddix, gun drawn on her head. His shoulder was bleeding, and a dark red river snaked down his bulging arm, leaving pools of blood on the front of Maddix's dress.

"You just bought yourself an early grave, pilot," she said, lying prone on the floor. Like a turtle on its back, she was unable to prop herself up.

Jones grinned. "Kill me all you want, but you ain't taking our boy."

Anders brought Wick over by Maddix, and they knelt down. Anders grabbed her wrist to make her unlock the collar, but she jerked her hand away and instead grabbed the gray lapel of her red coat. "Get in here! Kill them all!" she shouted.

Anders addressed his first mate. "The guards out front. Four of them." Wick stood up and darted over to the file cabinets.

"Take 'em out or kill 'em?" Jones asked. Their crew was never keen on killing, but in moments like these, Anders might make that call.

"Two each?" Anders said, looking at the door.

"I can take one," Wicked said from behind him. He had grabbed a long, thick piece of wood from behind a file cabinet. It had leather strapping wrapped around a handle. "Must be Boozer's last defense." He raised it in the air, ready to swing.

"All right," Anders said, "we take 'em out."

"And her?" Wicked asked, gesturing to Maddix.

Anders considered relieving them of such a burden, but he knew what happened when you started killing with your crew. Sure, they'd been in squabbles where death was dealt, but those few times called for it in absolute self-defense—a no-options-left scenario. This wasn't that yet. If you killed with options left, killing only got easier, and before you knew it, you'd gone way too far and become just another roughneck crew flying without a moral compass. He wanted better for his crew. They were the best, and they'd stay that way.

"Leave her," he said, almost with regret in his voice.

Footsteps thundered down the hallway, approaching the office with a certain malice in the tone that rang from the steel floor.

"They're gonna kill you," Maddix said, laughing. She was rolling back and forth, trying to get to a sitting position.

Anders and Jones, followed by Wick, hustled to the sides of the entrance to the office and waited. But before any of the guards reached the office, a loud shout echoed down the hallway. "Hey!"

What ensued sounded like a scuffle. Men shouted, "Get him," and "Stop her." The sounds of bones hitting walls and flesh smacking the floor filled the air. Shrieks of pain rang out. There was a loud pop, like a major joint tore from its socket, and a man hollered in excruciating pain.

Anders and Jones peeked around the corner, only to see Severn hustling toward them.

"Severn?" Anders asked as he stepped into the hallway.

"Looked like you needed a hand," she replied.

Before Anders could say anything else, he saw a man running up behind her and instinctively drew his gun.

"Down!" he yelled, but Severn jumped in front of him.

"Don't! He's with me," she said, raised hands blocking his aim. "He's with me."

The man stopped behind Severn and gave Anders a nod, confirming his temporary appointment made by Severn. Anders wanted an explanation, but here was not the place for it.

"He's gonna die!" Maddix shouted from behind the desk. She'd managed to get up and stand by the door. Anders stepped into her view. "Drew," she said, out of breath, placing herself in the door. "He's going to die if you take him." She pointed at him with a small device in her hand. A red light blinked from it. "The device on his neck. What do you think it is?"

Anders looked at it, confident it was some kind of tracking device rigged to kill. He knew she would deploy it. But he could buy some time. He could force her to wait.

Anders turned to her and began to raise his gun.

"Ah, ah, ah," she said. "I'll blow his head off right now. None of you have a gun on me, but the second someone tries," her voice turned vile, "he dies."

Anders paused to consider how fast he might take his shot. Probably not fast enough, and it wasn't worth finding out. So instead he pleaded, "I need him for this job." Anders stepped forward with his gun still in hand, but at his side. "Without him, we can't get it done."

She thought for a moment, eyes calculating her limited options. She had the upper hand, but Anders could almost see in her eyes that she knew he would kill her here and now if she wouldn't agree to it.

"Fine," she said. "Take him for the job. He's safe for now, but that thing will take his head off if you try to remove it, and I will be watching his every move. You cannot hide from me, and if I get any indication that you are not doing what I ask, I will make sure you see his head removed."

Anders said nothing to her, only looked at her thick, flushed face in disgust. "C'mon," he said to his crew as he turned to leave. They hustled into the hallway, leaving Maddix alone with her bloodied crew. Men began to moan and groan as they woke from unconsciousness.

Anders led the team back to the terminal and stopped in the middle of the busy corridor just before the hangar. Wicked stood next to Anders, Jones next to him, and Severn and Marko filled the circle in on the other side.

"Gather 'round," Anders said, first looking at Marko. "Thanks for your help. A friend of Severn?"

"Yes, sir. Name's Marko," he said with hopeful eyes and stretched out a hand. Anders shook it for a quick greeting.

"Well, I thank you. Does Maddix know who you are?"

"No."

"Good, then you should be able to walk away with no trouble. Say your good-byes and go. We have to leave as soon as we can." A look of disappointment crossed Marko's face, but before he could say anything else, Anders continued with his orders, turning to Jones first. "Your arm good?"

On their hustle back to this point, Jones had already taken off his shirt and jacket, ripped a long sleeve from his shirt, and tied it around his arm where a bullet had grazed him fairly deeply. The shirt was already showing a decent-sized pool of blood.

"I'm fine. I'll have Wick stitch me up later," he said, nudging Wick with his elbow.

"Good. I'll take Wicked back to the ship. Stay on comms and take Severn with you and round up the twins. We push off as soon as you get back."

"No doubt they haven't stocked rations yet. Prolly halfway drunk by now," Jones said before stepping away. "I know where to look first."

Severn shot Anders a look, as if she were about to suggest something. He'd seen that look before with previous recruits. The look that said, "I've got this friend who would be a great asset to the team." But Anders didn't have time for it. When she opened her mouth, Anders cut her off.

"Not now, Severn. We're full, and we have too much going on." Knowingly, he addressed Marko. "Thanks for your interest in our crew, but we're all set right now. Maybe another time." With that, Anders walked away, gripping Wicked under his arm and heading toward the hangar, looking around for any other trouble. Jones and Severn walked away after she shook Marko's hand.

CHAPTER 26

As if having an exploding collar around his crew member's neck wasn't hassle enough, Anders returned to the ship to find the cargo hold a mess, the sick bay disheveled, and the machine shop ransacked.

"What the heck happened?" Wick asked. "I was taken maybe an hour ago, and all of Maddix's goons came with us. Who did this?"

"I don't know," Anders said, then a thought occurred to him. "Where's Aura, Wick?"

A look of fear washed over Wick's face. "I hid her in the wall of my bunk when Maddix busted in. Then I went to hide in the engine room."

"Let's go," Anders said, bolting toward the stairs to the mezzanine. Wick followed. When they were halfway up the stairs, they heard a scream from above. It wasn't a female scream. It sounded like Ciris in serious pain. They stopped short and paused to listen.

"Stop! Get away!" Ciris' voice echoed through the mezzanine from ship forward.

"Up in the mess," Wick said.

"Go, now," Anders ordered, darting up the stairs. The grating underfoot sang out as their boots thundered along the corridor leading to the mess hall. When they arrived, they found Aura backed up to the kitchen sink, holding a pot in one hand with her other hand held out as if to order someone to stop.

Ciris was on the floor, maimed worse than Anders had ever seen. His right leg was bent almost ninety degrees to the right at his knee. He was sniffling, crying, and breathing harshly, while Kanor stood between him and Aura in a defensive stance.

"What the hell is going on here?" Anders demanded.

Aura didn't notice Anders and Wick until he spoke, and Kanor immediately offered his report. "She attacked Cy, Cap. We have to get rid of her."

Anders looked at Aura, then Ciris. "Why?"

"I don't know, Cap. She just attacked me." Ciris whimpered on the floor. A turned-over bench lay next to him, and broken dishes were everywhere with scraps of food mingled in.

Anders grabbed his comm. *"Jones, come in."*

A moment later, the comms crackled with Jones' deep voice. *"Check."*

"The twins are here. Come on back."

"Check," Jones said, and the comm went silent.

"What exactly happened?" Anders said.

Wicked seemed to trust Aura enough to approach her slowly. Anders allowed it for a moment, but drew his gun just in case and pointed it at no one in particular yet close enough to everyone in the room. He knew Ciris and Kanor were not telling the complete truth. They never did, only pieces of it. Anders had gotten used to it and had put up with it for far too long. Anders didn't quite believe that Aura had attacked Ciris for no reason.

As Wick approached Aura, she lowered her arms, dropped her pot, and clung to Wicked in tears; she shuddered as she held fast to him. With that, Anders had an idea as to what Ciris had done and felt he deserved more than a broken knee.

He looked at Aura, who was in tears with her head on Wicked's shoulder. "Are you all right?" Anders asked.

She nodded and said faintly, "Yes."

"Did he hurt you?"

"Held me down and tried to—" She closed her eyes as more tears streamed down her face.

Anders needed no more. "Why, Ciris?"

Ciris pleaded while in pain. "C'mon, Cap, she's stupid. She don't know what's what?"

"Yeah, she's the stupid one," Anders retorted while glaring at the man's broken leg.

"Kanor, get him off my ship. Take him to the nearest med bay.

"Ciris," Anders said with as much respect as he could feign, "I'm happy to say that you no longer have a place on this crew. I'll leave your things with the docking master. Good luck to you." He reached for Wicked and Aura. "C'mon, take her to her bunk. Severn will be back soon."

Wick and Aura left, and Anders was about to go as well, but Kanor stopped him. "Sir, you can't fire him. We need him. He's just a bit—"

"No," Anders said, "we don't need him, and I don't want men like that on my crew."

"Cap, he's my brother. You fire him—" He gave Anders a serious look. "I'm gone too then. I told you day one we were a package deal."

It didn't take Anders long to respond. "Then I thank you for your service, and I think you can handle gathering both your and your brother's things. You have fifteen minutes to get off my ship."

With that, and admittedly relieved, Anders walked out.

CHAPTER 27

Severn and Jones tramped into the cargo hold where they found a grumbling Anders tossing things from one side of the hold to the other. At first, he looked to be throwing a fit of rage, but Severn quickly realized he was making a crude attempt at cleaning up the place. She then noticed the machine shop in complete disarray as well.

"Cap, what happened?" Jones asked. "Maddix?"

"No!" Anders yelled in no particular direction. "Ciris."

"Ciris did all this?" Jones asked, scanning the mess.

"Why would he do that?" Severn asked, sidling Jones from behind.

"Well, he didn't do it alone," Anders said, growing calmer. "He tried to make Aura…" he paused in disgust, "his girlfriend."

Severn steeled herself. "Where is she? Is she all right?" She stepped toward the starboard-side mezzanine stairs, as if to go find her.

"Yes, she is," he said with a chuckle. "She's fine, actually. It's Ciris who isn't." Anders looked at Jones with a bit of suspicion. "She kicked his ass and broke his knee." He made a motion with his arm, showing a ninety-degree bend.

"Seriously?" Jones said. "Wish I woulda seen that."

"Me too," said Anders. "Not to see *that* she did it. I want to see *how* she did it."

Severn stopped before heading up the stairs. "You mean, all this mess is from Aura kicking Ciris around?"

"Looks like it," Anders replied. "Wick said Maddix and her goons couldn't have done it."

"Was Kanor here?" Jones asked.

"I think so."

"Was he hurt?" Severn asked.

"No, just Ciris. And I fired them both."

Jones let out a sigh of relief. "Finally! Now we can hire some decent crew and really start making a solid living without worrying about those two jackin' us up."

Severn paused, one foot planted on the first step. "And Aura is fine? No injuries?"

Anders shrugged his shoulders and waved his hand toward the ship's interior. "Yeah, she's fine. Go see for yourself. She's with Wick in her bunk."

"Huh," Severn huffed before heading up the stairs.

When she arrived at Aura's bunk, Severn found her lying on her side with Wick seated on the bed, gently rubbing her arm and shoulder. Severn stepped inside the small steel room, and Aura popped up with a smile.

"Severn," she said softly.

"Hi, Aura," Severn replied with the same tone. "Are you all right?"

"I'm…" Aura started, "confused." She wore a thoughtful look. "Why would friends hurt me?"

"Well, not all people are friends," Severn said, approaching the bed and sitting next to her. She put an arm around Aura. "We have to learn who to trust."

"How do you learn trust?" Aura asked, looking to both Severn and Wicked.

"It takes time," Wick said. "The longer someone doesn't hurt you, the more you can trust they won't."

Aura's eyebrow crinkled with thought.

"That's a good way to look at it," Severn offered. "With time you'll also develop an ability that will give you a feel for people early on."

Aura sucked in a deep breath and let it out with a sigh. "Well, I feel like I can trust you two. You've been so good to me. All they did was look at me weird."

"Yes, they did. And I'm sorry we didn't protect you better," Severn said.

"Thank you, but it's okay. You have work to do. You can't always watch over me."

They shared a smile, and Severn leaned in to give Aura a hug. And while embracing Aura, she noticed a device wrapped around Wick's neck. Her eye brows curled in curiosity.

Wick saw her eying the collar and recoiled. Severn got the distinct impression that he was ashamed of the thing, embarrassed even.

"Is that the thing Maddix was talking about?" she asked.

Wick stood up and walked over to a mirror hung over the tiny sink on the back wall. "Yeah, it is."

"You don't seem too happy about it," Severn said, hoping to hear more, although she sensed Wick had said just about all he was going to say on the matter.

Using the mirror, he looked the thing over. He inspected its metal casing, the lights, some of which blinked but all were at a faint glow, and the small fingerprint scanner on the outside edge.

"No, I'm not," he finally said. "She's a fan of putting collars on her..." He stopped, his face pained with what he was feeling. He quieted himself before heading out the door, but not before apologizing for his abrupt departure.

Severn and Aura were left alone on the bed. She could see that Aura was doing much better, and she simply said, "This boat is a bit messy, huh?"

Aura nodded with wide, wet eyes and said, "Uh huh."

CHAPTER 28

With a ship scrambled and crew shredded, Anders ordered an all-hands meeting at the mess hall table. Not two days before, they were a well-oiled crew making a solid living without interference. Now Wicked was collared as a hostage with his life in ransom, the twins were gone—which wasn't so bad except for their willingness, complaints aside, to basically do any deed that needed to be done—and they were flying with two strangers. Anders wanted nothing more than to get things under control and free his crew from Maddix's tightening grip.

The team gathered around the large wooden table, which occupied the better part of the port side of the kitchen. When Severn walked in, she began helping Wick clean up some of the scattered pots on the other side of the room, but Anders quickly interrupted them.

"At the table you two," he said.

Severn took a seat next to Wicked, who sat across from Jones. Anders took his typical seat at the head of the table and placed a flask down in front of Jones after taking a long pull for himself. Jones did the same and passed it to Severn.

"How does it feel?" Anders asked Wick, eying the hoop around his neck.

Wick palmed and shifted the collar, showing it was somewhat loose but not loose enough to slip over his head. Severn took her pull from the flask, and Anders watched as she held back a cough that nearly broke her silence. She passed the flask to Wick.

"Not bad," Wick said, palming the flask, "a bit heavy, but I can make do."

"Can you take it off?" Jones asked.

Wick stretched his head back, trying to look down at it. "Maybe. I haven't tried yet."

"Once underway," Anders said, "start looking at it. See if you can figure a way out of it."

"Yeah, but don't lose your head over it," Jones said, baring a white-toothed grin.

Glaring looks around the table faced Jones in a rare moment of insolence. Now wasn't the time for pun, and Jones knew better. "Right," he said, then nodded and pulled a solid drink from the flask and handed it back to Wick.

"So here's what we got," Anders said as Wick took his turn with the whiskey. Jones already knew what the deal was, but for Wick and Severn, this was going to be new. "We need to buy some time for Wick to work on getting that thing off his neck."

"What do we gotta do?" Severn asked.

"Maddix has instructed us to pay a visit to the Promaedia Museum and pick up a couple of things. If we don't, she's gonna set that thing off."

Severn eyed Wick's collar. "And what will that do?"

Wick smiled faintly. "I'm not exactly sure, but as Jones pointed out, I'm pretty sure it involves my neck and head disappearing in a flash."

Severn's face contorted, expressing several uneasy emotions.

Wick shrugged and kept the conversation moving. "Pick up?" he asked Anders. "Knowing Maddix, you mean take."

"I do mean take and, unfortunately, I also mean abduct," he said, gravely.

Wick's head bowed and Anders knew he no doubt felt the weight of the situation, and bore all the guilt that went with it. As if he weren't worthy of another pull, he sheepishly slid the flask over to Anders, who reflexively palmed the thing. Severn sighed and sat back in her chair. Anders could almost see her thoughts. *This is the best crew in the black? How did I get mixed up in this?*

"This isn't our thing," Anders stated matter-of-factly. "You all know this, so I want to do it right and make sure we do everything we can to *not* have to do this." He passed his flask to Jones again after taking another swig.

"What do you mean?" Severn asked.

Jones leaned in, the spice of fresh whiskey on his breath. "He means that every move we make going forward needs to look like we're going through with the heist."

Heist and abduction, Anders thought. No sense in ignoring it; they might have to go through with it. "Jones," Anders looked at him, then the other two, "we need to plan and act on this in case Wick can't free himself of that thing."

"No one's ever knocked off the Promaedia," Severn said.

"And we've never planned a job like this before," Anders said. "We gotta lay it all on the table, folks." He gave each one a look that asked for complete honesty. "Before this crew, who had experience with this?"

There was a quiet at the table, filled with the tension reserved only for that moment before someone admits a piece of their past they otherwise would have kept secret. Jones grabbed the flask of whiskey from Anders and finished it.

"I, ah…got a little…experience," Jones said, looking at his captain. "Sorry. I lied to you when we first met. I've got a bit of a past with these sorts of things. Nothing as major as this, but yeah, I took a lot of stuff with my first crew."

"Me too," Wick said. "Well, when I was with Maddix."

"No need to apologize, Jones. That was the past, and you're not wanted for anything now, so we're good. Wicked, I know about your time with Maddix, so let's start with Jones. What do think of this?"

"First thing, we need to know the lay of the land. We need to know the museum, the ins, the outs, the security, and most of all, what we're taking, where it is, and how big it is."

"Makes sense. Wick, can you get us the build plans for the Promaedia?"

"Probably. I need to set a link with—are we actually going through with this?" He shifted in his chair, grabbing at the collar on his neck. "I mean, I'm sure I can get this thing off."

"I'm sure you can, but I'm not risking it," Anders said. "We need to be looking at doing this just in case, and I'd rather be prepared than not if we have to go through with it. Maddix is far too unpredictable for us to be unprepared."

"He's right," Jones said.

"Severn, you're quiet," Anders said. "Got anything to add?"

"Well, I too am against going through with this." She paused. "But if it has to be done, then we need to do it right. And I think that with the four of us, plus Aura, we're still short on manpower."

The table fell silent again, and Anders played out a few quick scenarios in his head. Finally he said, "No. I'm not pulling anyone else into this mess."

Jones dug his meaty fingers into the thick black forest of whiskers on his chin, clearly thinking through some plays in his own mind. "I think she's right, Cap. We need to scope this thing out, and we need to do it with some cover. The five of us going to the museum together will look a bit suspicious. Plus it would leave one of us alone. If we could break our team up in pairs for the visit, each one bent on a different task, that could help."

"How do you mean?" Anders asked.

"Let's say we pair up Wicked and Aura. We send them in to walk around and verify the schematics he uncovers beforehand. That won't look suspicious as long as he doesn't bring a map with him." He looked at Wicked. "You'll have to do that from memory."

"Could work," Anders said. Wicked and Aura seemed to have gotten close, so it would look natural.

"Then," Jones continued, "we pair up you and Severn and have you scope out the main targets. Being the curator of the museum, Kopius is probably there all the time, so we can gain some intel on him."

"And what would you do?" Severn asked.

"Apply for a security position, of course. Maybe get a glimpse of what we're up against. It'd be better if I had someone with me for an extra pair of eyes. When we get hired, it'll be helpful to have someone with me."

"Marko," Severn said. "I'm sure he's still here."

A rather quick answer, Anders realized. Suspicious as her quick answer was, a thought stirred in Anders' head, right along side an interesting plan. He trusted what Jones said about needing another person, but he hated putting so much faith in a crew member he knew nothing about. Or could he trust something else? Severn vouched for him, but she was new herself, and how much could he trust a new crew member to vouch for someone? At least with the twins, he knew he could lean on their loyalty. Now he was considering adding another stranger to the crew for a job far more dangerous and illegal than anything he'd done before. Regardless of his lack of experience with museum heists, Anders was sure this wasn't the way to get it done. Nevertheless, he was up against a wall, and his gut told him he could use Severn and Marko.

"Would he even do this, and can we trust him?" Anders asked.

Severn donned an approving look. "Yes."

"How soon can you find him?"

"I know a few places I can look. Gimme an hour," she said, leaning back in her chair, readying herself to head out.

"Go. Don't tell him what the job is, but make sure he knows what it could cost him."

"Check." Severn got up from the table.

Jones stood as well. "I'll go with her." Severn stopped short at the mess hall door, as if to give Jones a moment to catch up.

"No. I need you here," Anders ordered. He nodded to Severn, sending her off on her own. She rapped the doorjamb with a knuckle, acknowledging Anders' wishes.

As Severn disappeared into the corridor, Anders said to Wicked, "I need all the information you can get me on Marko."

"Do we know anything other than his name?" Wicked asked.

"No. But I do know he and Severn have some kind of past together. Get what you can."

"Check," Wicked said before heading out of the mess hall. He paused at the door and turned back to face Anders and Jones.

"What is it?" Jones asked.

Wick's fingertips picked at each other as he pondered his thoughts. "I should have told you this before." He spoke in a soft, regretful tone.

"Told me what?" Anders asked.

"It's just that you were so mad at me," Wick said, head bowed. "Remember when we were on our way here to the port, and you asked me to help you empty out the hidden compartment in the cargo hold? And then I got angry. After that, things just kept happening so fast. I ended up letting it go. And—"

"Wick," Anders said, "what are you trying to tell us?"

He took a deep breath as if to ready them for his confession. "I think Severn signaled GC. I think she is still in the military, and I think Marko is too, and I think we're making a big mistake keeping her here and bringing him aboard."

"And why do you think this?" Jones asked.

"Well," Wick said, "I saw Severn talking to Ciris right before his trash dump. She was asking me questions about it right before that, and then I saw her throw something away as if she intended for it to leave the ship."

Anders and Jones shared a look before Anders leaned forward and stood up. "Maybe it's time we listen in on that thing you put in her jaw."

Jones acknowledged his agreement with a head bob while still settled in his seat.

"I'll meet you in the engine room shortly," Anders said.

CHAPTER 29

Aura's head was down and focused while her fingers danced vigorously about a control box when Wicked arrived. At the doorway, he remained silent and stole a few moments to watch her work. Her back was mostly turned to him, but he still saw a fair amount of her soft face. Even if she weren't humming to herself, he'd still see the most beautiful woman he'd ever met.

Wick intended to zero in on the receiver he'd implanted in Severn's jaw, but he was distracted by Aura—by her quietness and her determined focus on her work. He grabbed the first thing on the work bench and rolled it over. It produced a dull thud and pulled her attention to him. She looked up and gave him a brilliant smile. In his limited experience, he was unsure of what a smile so intense meant. He only realized it meant something good when she stood up, hustled over to him, and embraced him in a way that felt like she was trying to wrap her entire body around his. He let her. It felt amazing. Like an angel built just for him.

She smelled no less than sweet. Felt lean yet soft. And then she kissed him on the cheek.

"Thank you," she said, "for taking care of me."

Wick opened his mouth, but his words seemed a world away. He found the floor with his eyes and acknowledged her thanks with a murmur.

Aura raised her hands to his neck and eyed the new collar he'd come back wearing. "I look?" she asked.

She was so close to him, his mind raced. He knew it might be dangerous to let her look at the collar, but if she asked, he'd exit the airlock with her right now.

"S-sure. Go ahead." He raised his chin, giving her more room as she lifted, looked at, and turned the collar. The reflection of red and green lights from its surface flickered off the fair skin of her face. She caught him looking at her and smiled again, breathing out a soft laugh.

If he were to pick a moment, this would be the one where he fell for her.

Sadly though, as all moments do, this one passed abruptly when he heard boots on the steel grating in the corridor outside the engine room.

Just before he reached the doorway, Anders called out, "Wick?" He froze at the doorway, noticing their closeness. At first, it must have looked personal, but when Anders eyed the ohmmeter in her hand, he continued as if nothing were out of place.

"What's up, Cap?" Wick asked, wondering why Anders was there. They just had a meeting.

"The transmitter. In Severn's—" His eyes said the rest, as if to pull Wick back to reality.

"Oh!" Wick said, shocked he'd forgotten what he was supposed to be doing. "Right. Yes, come in. Let's do this."

Anders entered the engine room and then addressed Aura. "How are you feeling?"

"I'm good...sir?" she said, her inflection rising at the end, as if to ask if "sir" were an appropriate way to address him.

"You can call me Anders," he said.

Wick sat at his console and flipped some switches. A few speakers crackled as he dialed a volume switch and then keyed in a few strokes on his keyboard while reading the monitor. Before long, the low hum of a crowd came through the speakers.

"She must be walking through the main corridor," Wick said.

Anders posted up on Wick's right side and bent his ear toward the speakers. Aura came up behind Wick, looking at his collar again.

"You want off?" she asked.

Anders looked at her. "No, don't tou—"

"It's all right, Cap," Wick interrupted. "I trust her."

Aura blinked a few times, looking at Anders, before he nodded that it was all right to proceed.

"Think she can get it off?" Anders asked in a whisper.

"Yes," both Wick and Aura answered.

"And if she does, we don't have to go to Promaedia," Wick said.

The hum of the crowd coming from the speaker dimmed while footsteps echoed off walls. Then the creak of a swinging door sounded before the echoing of the footsteps became distinct, as if she were in some enclosed area.

There was the sound of a door bumping closed with the click of a metal latch. Then a zipper before a rustling of clothes. Then the unmistakable trickle of urination flooded from the speakers. Anders and Wick both fumbled around at the sound, Anders turning away, Wick fingering controls in an attempt to quiet the unintended intrusion.

"Oookay," Wick said as he turned down the volume.

Anders stepped away for a moment while they all stood in silence. Aura kept eying Wick's collar as if nothing had happened.

After a few moments, Wick asked, "How long does it usually take them?"

"Them?" Anders looked at him curiously.

"You know—" Wick eyed the floor. "Women. To, ah, do that."

Anders chuckled. "About the same as us, Wick."

Wick motioned toward the volume nob but stopped short, hoping Anders would confirm that it had probably been long enough.

"Go ahead, I'm sure it's over."

She was finished, and she'd already made her way back into what sounded like the corridor. Anders and Wick listened patiently until she finally spoke.

"Good, you're still here," she said with a relieved sigh.

"Severn, what are you doing here?" a man's voiced replied.

There was a pause, then, "Anders needs you on the crew, Marko. You ready?"

"Of course," he said.

"Where's the comma—" Severn began, but her voice through the speaker was cut off by the sudden tone of an incoming communiqué to Anders' ship.

"Are you recording her?" Anders asked quickly.

"Yes," Wick replied as he flipped a switch and sent his fingers flying on the keyboard.

"'Kay, who's pinging us then?" he asked.

"Um, I'm not sure." Still at work on his keyboard. "It's a blocked incoming connection. Clean, no viruses. Shall I connect?"

Anders waited a moment before he replied, "Do it. And trace it."

Wick acknowledged the order with a nod and went to work setting a trace before he connected the call. He almost lost the emptiness in his belly when he saw on his screen who was hailing their ship.

"Maddix," Anders said, "what do you want?"

"Oh, come now, Anders," Maddix said, slyly. She sat at a desk in a room much different from Boozer's place but with the same throne-like chair. "Is that any way to treat your friends?" She held a glass of brown liquid. A singular column of smoke whisked up past her face, the source of which came from below the view of the camera.

"Friends don't threaten to kill one another, Maddix," Anders said, dismayed.

"There are much worse things than death, my dear Anders," she said as her eyes slipped down to focus on something on her desk. The shadow of her knuckles bobbed up and down, just barely out of view, as if she were typing on a keyboard. "I wanted to let you know how serious I am about our arrangement." She looked up. "I would have preferred that Drew stay with me, but since he's there with you, I want you to know how short the leash is."

"Leash?" Anders asked.

Wick knew what she meant, and he stretched his head back to glance down at the collar. Right then, bolts of electricity shot into him with sharp, stinging bites. Only a couple of pulses at first, jolting him upright in his chair. Anders stepped back. He looked like he wanted to grab Wick to support him but recoiled, thinking better of it.

Aura obviously felt differently. While Wick sat there stunned and frightened, she hustled over to him to lend some aid. She put one hand on his head and leaned in front of him, placing another hand on his chest to see if he was all right.

Maddix spoke again with a voice that seemed to come from the darkest places of her soul. "Oh, there you are, little one," she said, staring devilishly at Aura. "Anders, this little affair of ours has become quite the stir. We shall have lots of fun. But know this before we get started...I can end him anytime I want. So when I tell you not to stall in getting me what I want—" she paused dramatically, "I want you to know that I mean it."

With thinned eyes and a sly grin, Maddix slammed her hand down on her controls.

Wick shot up straight in his chair. Sharp stings from the collar exploded through his body and paralyzed him to the mercy of the one who held his life in her hands.

CHAPTER 30

Anders watched as the collar sent electricity through both Wick and Aura. Maddix laughed as they shook violently. Aura held onto Wick as they shuddered. Then Wick's body slid from his chair, and they fell to the floor, but not before he hit his head on the worktable in front of him. Aura fell too, and when the shocking subsided just before they hit the floor, her grip on him loosened as she collapsed. He fell limp but Aura began to convulse violently, her head bouncing on the steel floor.

"Stop!" Anders yelled to the screen, where Maddix was glaring back at them. "I'll do it. I'll get it done."

"Good," she said. The screen went blank.

Anders knelt. "Wick! Wick, are you all right? Can you hear me?" He pulled Wick's limp body up onto his lap; he was unconscious. Anders then reached over to Aura and shook her leg. "Aura? Aura!"

She too was unresponsive. Thinking quickly, he hit the all-comms. "Emergency, all crew to sick bay. All crew to sick bay." Of course, the only crew left was Jones, but comforts like having a full crew were hard to shake.

Anders cleared Wick's chair from the area as he pulled Aura closer to Wick. With a hefty grunt, he picked them both up, cradling one in each arm and mashing them together. He shimmied through the doorway out into the thin corridor and headed to the sick bay as fast as he could. As he shuffled along, doorway bulkheads narrowed the passageway, but Anders did well to keep them from knocking against the ship. When he finally made it to the sick bay, he placed Wick and Aura on the surgeon's bed, then bent over, huffing, out of breath.

Jones showed up shortly after. He took a quick survey of the room. "What do you need, Cap?"

Out of breath, Anders replied, "Wick, Aura, electrocuted by the collar."

Jones darted over to Wick and placed two fingers on his neck. "No pulse," he reported with concern.

"Defibrillator." Anders pointed to the cabinet behind Jones and then forced himself to his feet. As Jones grabbed the defibrillator, Anders checked Aura. "She's got a pulse," he said.

"Is she breathing?" Jones asked. Anders put his ear to her mouth and held his breath. Jones stopped moving for a moment to quiet the room so Anders could better listen for a breath.

Finally, Anders said, "Yes."

Jones jumped back into action on Wick, and Anders picked up Aura, placed her on the floor, out of the way, stuffed two towels under her head, and returned to Wick at the table. Jones had already ripped open his shirt and placed the electrodes on his chest, one on his upper right chest and the other on his left ribcage. Jones took a half-step back, as if he were unsure of something.

"What?" Anders asked. "Let's go."

"Wait," Jones replied, thinking. "I think it'll do it on its own. If it needs to."

"Shit," Anders said as he looked at the collar. "What if—"

They both reached to pull the electrodes, but it was too late. Wick's body jerked. His arms flew up and his legs kicked out as the defibrillator sent a charge through his chest. The machine beeped a single solid tone while Anders and Jones stood by in silence. The charge didn't set off the collar, so all they could do was wait.

"C'mon, Wick. You got this buddy," Jones said as he grabbed Wick's hand.

Anders approached him, eying the collar. "Wick, your collar is still working. C'mon, buddy, we need you to come back so you can take it off."

The defibrillator chimed three times.

"It's going again," Jones said, stepping back. Anders followed his lead as another charge ripped through Wick's chest. A different sound came from the machine this time. The comforting sound of a heartbeat replaced the streamlined single tone of death.

"All right, good job, buddy," Jones said, stepping back to the bed. He put his massive hand on Wick's forehead, nearly covering his entire skull. Jones then ripped off the electrodes and threw the defibrillator on the counter, the wires strewn about.

"He's waking up," Anders noticed.

Jones turned around and recoiled. Aura had woken and was standing in the corner with her hands covering her mouth. Rivers of tears marked their path down her face.

"Damn, girl," Jones muttered. "You scared me. I didn't see you get up."

"Is he de—" She couldn't get the word out.

"No," Anders said, stepping away, giving her an opportunity to see him. Wick wasn't quite awake yet, but when Aura planted a kiss on his lips, his eyes shot open. If the defibrillator were still on his chest, his heartbeat may have broken it.

"Oh shhh—" Jones caught himself before ruining the moment.

Anders and Jones let their eyes wander elsewhere while Wick and Aura finished their embrace.

"I was so scared to lose you," she said as she pulled away from him.

"If I had been awake," Wick said, "I would have been scared to lose you too." The look on his face said he regretted the lame compliment that he obviously meant to be sweet. Aura seemed not to notice or even care. She wore a look of true concern on her face.

"Can you get up?" she asked.

"I think so," he said, grabbing the side bar of the bed and pulling himself up. He grimaced and placed a hand on his chest, but he seemed glad to not be dead. He then noticed the jumbled mess of the defibrillator on the counter and asked as he palmed the collar, "So this didn't kill me with the shock from the defib?"

"Doesn't look like it," Jones said.

Wick grinned. "Well, that rules out trying to short the thing, doesn't it?" he asked Aura.

She smiled and nodded overly joyously. "Uh huh."

Anders looked at Jones. "Who woulda thought boy genius here would find a girl just like him?"

"Yeah, man." Jones chuckled. "Gives me hope. So did you hear anything from the—?" He spoke secretively as if to not share with Aura that they had intended to spy on Severn. The women seemed to have become friends, so the caution was warranted.

Anders immediately picked up on what Jones meant. "Sure did. She met with Marko and was about to ask where someone else was before Maddix's call interrupted the conversation."

Jones' eyes showed only a hint of surprise. "Sounds about right."

"I recorded the conversation. We can go listen in now if you want," Wick added, having recovered quickly.

"My guess is they'll be here any minute," Anders said. "For now, let's just be careful about what we say and where."

"Or—" Jones started.

"Captain!" A shout came in from the cargo hold.

"They're back," Anders said and motioned for Jones to come with him. Then he addressed Wick. "You okay?"

"Yeah, Cap. I think I'm good."

Jones patted Wick on the shoulder before following Anders out of the sick bay as they made their way aft.

When they entered the cargo hold, Severn was out of breath and in a rush. "Sir," she started, "there's something happening. We gotta get outta here."

"What something?" Anders asked.

"There's an attack," Marko said. "It started just as we were getting to the hangar from the main corridor. We ran from it."

"It?" Jones asked.

"Some kind of machine," Marko answered, a bit flustered. "An android of some sort turned on the crowd and started firing."

Anders and Jones shot a look at each other. He knew Jones was thinking the same thing he was about the news report they'd reviewed earlier.

"Sir," Severn said, "it's heading this way."

Anders eyed the rations delivered to the ship's cargo hold. "At least the twins got something right. Okay, let's go. Severn, help Wick in sick bay and get him to the engine room. Help him with whatever he needs."

"Check," she replied and darted off to the sick bay.

"Marko, you're with Jones and me. You know how to work a turret?"

"Yes, sir."

"We say 'check' for an affirmative on this ship. Got it?"

"Check," he said, picking up the way of things.

Anders turned to Jones. "Get started in the cockpit. I'll be there shortly."

"Check," Jones said as he hustled off into the ship.

Anders led Marko up the mezzanine. He took him past the twins' old bunk and pointed inside. "This is yours. Toss your bag in there," he said and continued down the corridor in a rush, hearing the thud of a bag landing in the bunk. Seconds later, they made it to the mess hall, where Anders led Marko up a ladder. At the end of it was a small bubble containing the turret and one empty seat.

"Climb in," Anders said.

Marko slipped by Anders and into the seat as if he belonged there.

Anders gave him a smirk. "You look comfortable."

"I am. This is a long-range Berrian. Original. Very nice. Anything I should know about her personality?"

Anders wasn't exactly surprised that Marko knew about this gun, but the fact that he was familiar with it gave Anders quite a bit of information. "We call her the Bitch. That should clue you in on how she handles. Also, the sight's off about a click left."

"Check," he said as he fingered toggles and switches, turning on the targeting system.

"One more thing," Anders said. "You do not fire until I give the order. Got it?"

Marko made eye contact as Anders gave him a look indicating how serious he was.

"Check."

As quick as the answer came, Anders' feet met the steel grating at the bottom of the ladder, and in mere seconds, he joined Jones in the cockpit.

"Uh oh," Jones said, noticing the look on Anders' face. "What is it?"

"We got trouble," Anders said. "Where're we at?"

"Engines ready. What kind of trouble?" Jones asked as Anders fired the engines.

"Did you call for a launch?" he asked, shooting Jones a stern look. "And the trouble is that Marko's military."

Jones looked at Anders in confusion. "All launches are green lit. Everyone's bolting outta the hangar as fast as they can. Military?"

Anders hit the all-comms. *"Launch in one minute, check in."* He switched the comms off again. "Yeah, and I think he's still serving."

"Positioning and scans are a go," Jones said, sticking with launch procedures. "How do you know?"

"Check," Anders acknowledged Jones' go.

"Wick here. Engines are a go. All systems online."

Anders flicked the engine room comms. *"Aura, Severn?"*

"Both seated and strapped in. We're a go down here."

"Check," Anders replied. "Did you notice how quick he adapted to a military command? 'We say "check" here as an affirmative.' He fell right in line."

"So he's a good listener," Jones said, challenging his captain into a solid conclusion.

"Yeah. Do all listeners know how to use the Bitch up top?"

"He knows the turret?"

"He does. Slipped right in and put it in gear."

"It took you months to train the twins on that."

"It did. And you know what else?" Anders asked.

Jones looked at the console in thought. "Severn vouched for him."

"Exactly," Anders said.

"So what now?"

"Now," Anders said with a grin, "we use the military to pull a heist at the Promaedia Museum."

Jones let out a puff of air that was almost as large as he was. "Son of a bitch. Is that what we're into now?"

"No," Anders said. "But it's what we're going to do to save Wick."

They shared a look that only a captain and first mate who trusted each other with their lives could share, and then something caught Anders' eye out of the viewport.

"There it is, Jones. Look."

Anders pointed out of the cockpit. Stumbling from the main corridor and into the opening of the large hangar doors came what was left of a humanoid machine. It looked as though security personnel had taken as many shots at it as the crowded hallway would allow. Red hydraulic fluid spewed from its missing right arm and a gaping wound on its left leg. The skin of its hip had somehow torn away and seemed almost disjointed.

"Damn, Cap. Look how real they've become."

"They have skin?" Anders asked softly.

"And it looks female. That ain't a bad lookin' bot, boss," Jones said. His voice was a bit apprehensive of such a confession. "We should get out of here."

"No, wait," Anders said while grabbing his handheld comm. He switched a dial to point at the label "Turret." *Marko, you see it?*

Switching off the comms, he said to Jones, "Let's see if he really knows how to use a turret."

Jones smiled.

"*Check,*" Marko replied.

"*Line up a shot,*" Anders said, "*and wait for the order.*"

"*Check.*"

The thing hobbled into the hangar and rotated at its waist, as if to survey the room. *Elite One* lay perched in the middle of the hangar; half the ship slots were empty already, about a dozen or so left scattered about. When it finished surveying the room, the machine appeared to pick a target. It focused on a ship across the way from them.

"Anders. In the cockpit," Jones said, pointing.

Inside, two people, a man and a woman, scrambled as they tried to ready their ship. They were unaware of the machine focusing on them, and just then, the machine raised its arm and pointed its fist at the ship, as if it were going to take action.

"*Now!*" ordered Anders through the comms.

Two muffled high-caliber shots rang out from above Anders and Jones. Both shots struck the machine in the chest cavity and tore through it as easily as they would have a human being. The thing shredded into bits and pieces before hitting the ground, and Anders wasted no time afterward. He hit the all-comms.

"*Nice shot, Marko. All crew brace for launch in three, two, one.*"

Anders lifted *Elite One* from its perch, eased it forward and port and out of the airbreak. Moments later, he hit the thrusters and asked for artificial gravity.

"Check," said Jones, toggling switches on his console.

Anders popped the comms to the engine room, "*Prep for FTL.*"

Wick replied almost immediately, "*Check.*"

CHAPTER 31

Anders and Jones sat quietly at the cockpit controls. Not only had Anders managed to tether himself to one of the most destructive and illicit persons in the galaxy, but he'd also unwittingly enlisted the military into his crew for a job he would never have considered pulling off in the first place. As far as Anders was concerned, he'd lost control of his ship and his livelihood. All while placing his crew in serious danger and possibly getting them arrested and put away for life. Or worse.

At first glance, Anders thought his position impossible. Then he considered the past jobs he'd led his crew through—all the impossible situations, the near misses, the questionable legality, the "get in and out before another crew shows up" work. Never had he been infiltrated by the military. Never had he done anything to warrant a sting like this. He had never taken a job so illicit so as to attract the military's attention.

"So why are they here?" Anders asked Jones as he rose to close the cockpit door.

Jones seemed deep in thought. "A very good question."

"In the past years, can you think of any work we took on that would set the military on us?"

"The only one I'm thinking of is the Double Duck Switch we pulled on Esandrea," Jones said, "but there's no way they know about it."

"And there's no way they'd set a sting on us for it. Besides, the constable was returned unharmed and with no memory, and we got rid of the monkeys two years ago. I can't think of anything we've done worth this kind of attention. Most of our work is on the level. The other stuff, minor as it was, paid well and frankly just isn't worth military attention."

"Then why are they here?" asked Jones. "Why send Severn, and why did she make moves to bring in Marko?"

"There has to be something bigger going on. Something we're connected to that they need access to."

"So you're thinking we're some kind of bait or a way into something? Or somewhere?" Jones asked.

"Maybe. But it doesn't make sense." Anders folded his arms behind his head as he reclined in his chair.

"So we're bait then," Jones said, joining Anders in his relaxing posture. "They've got a target, and they're using us to get at it."

"Maddix?" Anders asked, then answered himself. "No, because we've never dealt with her, for obvious reasons. If they're after her, they wouldn't have had a reason to use us."

"Boozer?" Jones asked.

"Maybe. But again, he's too small time for a military sting."

Jones chuckled. "I think I'm too small time. We need Wick to figure this one out."

Anders leaned forward and clicked on the engine room comms. *"Wick, I need you in the cockpit."*

The cockpit stirred in silence while they waited for Wick to arrive. When he showed up, he took a seat at the small bench in the back of the cockpit, and Anders and Jones brought him up to speed on their conversation.

"I think you're right," Wick said. "We are too small time for a military investigation. Furthermore, given our success over the past couple of years and the reputation that comes along with it, it's no surprise to me that if the military needed something done—that had to look non-military—they'd use a crew as successful as ours. One that gets things done."

Anders relaxed in his chair again, as if it helped him think while he digested information. The military had infiltrated his team, seemingly intent on keeping it a secret, with the purpose of doing something that couldn't look like it came from military planning.

"How do you propose we find out what they're after?" Anders asked him.

Wick thought for a moment before he shrugged and gave a smirk. "I propose we do nothing. We go about our current business. It seems to me that if the military needs us for something, then they must have a vested interest in us staying alive and out of trouble."

Anders gave Jones a satisfied look. "So I was right. We are going to have the military pull a job on the museum with us."

"And if we help the military get what they want…we might even acquire immunity for the museum thing." Wick said before he excitedly waved a finger in the air. "We could even set up Maddix to take the fall!"

Anders enjoyed that notion.

"Maybe we could stop off and have a little fun while we're in Royale Row," Jones added with enthusiasm. Wick's eyes lit up as well.

Anders face grew stern. "Just because our job will take us into the entertainment center of the galaxy doesn't mean we'll have time for any fun."

"Seems to me we will, sir," Jones said, baring a huge set of white teeth inside a very large grin.

Anders perked up. "If we pull this job off and get free of Maddix and the military, I'll personally fund an entire week there for all of us."

A fully paid week in Royale Row was no small treat, a fact reflected on Wick and Jones' faces. Casinos, bars, showcases of all kinds, and a marketplace—any space-ridden person could spend a lifetime of pay acquiring gadgets and other interesting merchandise. Not to mention the plethora of parlors requiring a moral compass most askew. All of these attractions formed an enormous disk-like cluster of suspended structures orbiting the storm planet Prominus like a huge spotlight shining out from itself.

A free week in Royale Row might have been the best motivation to accomplish any task, even one as extreme as the crew's new mission.

CHAPTER 32

Severn gave a one-tap knuckled knock on the door of the bunk once occupied by the twins. A moment later, the press handle sunk in as Marko opened the door and stepped aside. Neither spoke a word as she slipped in, and Marko closed the door while she walked straight into the bathroom. She turned on the shower and waved him over.

He approached with a curious look on his face, but the smirk on hers said "dream on." At the shower, she drew him close and spoke in a whisper.

"Are you ready for this?" she asked.

"Yes, I know what the mission is," Marko said defensively. "You know I can handle this."

Severn looked straight into his eyes, gauging his pupils. "Yes, objective one is paramount, and you are certainly able. But are you prepared to do whatever it takes to keep this ship in operation until we meet that objective? This crew is in deep trouble, so I want you to understand me when I say we might have to go off the reservation on this one."

Marko looked away, as if to consider the mission orders and weigh them against what Severn had told him. "I understood that we'd have to operate with questionable actions. This is *Elite One*.

I figured we'd be pulling some off-the-books scav jobs. Maybe something along those lines. What are we really into here?"

"It's not that easy anymore," she said with a sigh. "They took the bait with the destroyer and brought her aboard, but now they've run into unanticipated problems with Maddix."

"What do they call her?" Marko asked.

"Aura. I fed them a story about some girl from boot camp to help sell a case of amnesia. Ever since, things have been a bit crazy, so they haven't really been asking questions. As far as they know, no one here has any answers anyway, so even if they did have questions to ask, there's no one here to answer them."

Marko looked in the general direction of the ship's interior. "Is she learning as quickly as before?"

"Yes, but she doesn't seem to remember me or anything from then."

"And she's been with you for about two weeks now, so that leaves us a minimum of a couple weeks before she snaps again." He gave a wry grin.

"Let's hope we have at least six again," Severn said.

"Yeah, but we can't bank on that. Besides, we need to finish this before she remembers you. Otherwise this whole thing with this crew is blown. Now tell me what we're into with Maddix."

"She's taken Wick's life hostage by putting some kind of device around his neck. It's on a remote, and she's threatening to kill him unless Anders leads his crew on a heist at the Promaedia."

Severn knew this complication was a bit heavier than what Marko was anticipating. It wasn't that she didn't trust him to handle the job with anything less than perfection, but Marko was a straight shooter, a by-the-book operative. And going off the reservation on a mission like this could be career suicide, so she was unsure of how he'd handle it.

"Severn, we have to tell the commander what we're into," he said, placing his hand on her elbow.

"Or," she said, offering her own plan, "we go through with it. Help them do it right and keep anyone from getting hurt. This is the closest we've ever been to hunting down the designer of the machines, and now we have a line on Maddix too. We've got a shot at doing some real good here."

"You have a good point," Marko said, grabbing his chin while thinking out loud. "No harm in making a move on Maddix while working our prime. Maddix is known to have military personnel on her payroll too, so if—and it's a really big if, Severn—we go through with this, our only hope at saving our butts is to explain that we had to keep the heist a secret to keep the information from leaking to Maddix."

"I like where you're going with this, Marko," Severn said with a smile.

"I'm not going there just yet," he said with his palm out, as if to slow her down. "What are we after at the museum?"

Severn paused, realizing this part could be the deal breaker for a man like Marko. "We have to abduct Kopius the Collector and take his latest main exhibit and deliver both to Maddix."

The absence of a reaction from Marko took Severn by surprise. Though it wasn't part of this mission's objectives, taking down Maddix was high on command's list, so she knew Marko might consider this. But knocking off a highly protected and valuable entity without the express consent of the Galactic Command was certainly, she thought, off the table when it came to Marko.

He looked into her eyes. "I think we should do it. There's too much at stake not to."

Severn was a wildcat. She was the girl who picked a fight with the biggest boy. She was the first in her class to sign up for Galactic Command boot camp before anyone else had considered it. She flew the fastest, and she fought the hardest. So when Marko agreed to her proposal, her smile gleamed with a hunger for the toughest of challenges and the chance to make some real change.

CHAPTER 33

While en route to Royale Row, two work shifts passed before Anders finally received confirmation that a trusted friend would meet with him. When Anders decided to take this job during Severn's interview, he thought he might have to call in a favor from Captain Jug Mason. Captain Jug and Anders had teamed up their crews on several occasions over the years to work a number of large-scale jobs. They split the spoils evenly, and both crews always came out ahead. In their history of supporting each other in times of need, there were several instances where one had run discreet interference for the other to lend aid in some work of questionable legality. A no-questions-asked cash gift never failed to exchange hands at a later time. Anders hoped he'd obtain this type of arrangement during this meeting.

It was dinnertime, so Anders made his way to the mess hall to alert the crew of the arrival of Captain Jug and his crew. As always, Jones had finished his meal by the time the others were halfway through theirs.

"Listen up," Anders announced as he entered the mess. All eyes darted to where he stood in the doorway, and as he moved toward his chair at the head of the table, the gazes followed him. "In a few minutes from now," he continued, "we'll be connecting midflight with a good friend of mine, Jug Mason."

The smile on Jones' face, Anders knew, was strictly the result of his looking forward to the challenge of a midflight docking. "They still flyin' the same class ship as us?" Jones asked, and Anders nodded. "Belly to belly, then?"

"You got it," Anders said before getting back to his announcement. "It's a quick stop to settle some business, so it won't take long. Jones and I will be boarding their ship, and you all will stay here."

"Need any support up top?" Marko asked.

Anders shook his head. "No. As I said, they're friends."

"What should we do then?"

Anders noticed a small grin on Jones' face. "Well, since you asked. As you've no doubt noticed, the ones who lived in your bunk before you weren't exactly the cleanest crew mates around."

"Yeah, I did notice," Marko said, disgusted.

"Why don't you clean the bunk and the head in your quarters? Get it all nice and shiny."

Marko's face went sour. "We're getting ready to pull a serious job, you're having a mystery meeting with some friends, and you want me to go...clean my room?"

"You have a problem with that?" Anders asked.

"I do. Very much so. I think—"

"I've written it down in my captain's log, and next time we have a vote on who does what around here, I'll make sure it's the first item on the agenda."

"You didn't write anything anywhere. You were standing here—"

"Let me lend you a hand, Marko," Jones said, using his deepest voice. "There isn't a vote, and there isn't a captain's log, so if you don't want to be assigned to clean everyone's toilet with your toothbrush, you'd best shut it."

Anders made sure Marko noticed his look that backed up Jones' statement. Marko recoiled, then sank into a relaxed position in his seat as he shot Severn a glance that seemed to bounce off her like a rubber ball off concrete.

With that, Anders finished his announcement and passed through the mess hall giving one last order. "Severn, Wicked. Gimme a hand in the cargo hold when you're finished eating." Anders left the mess hall with a slight grin on his face, knowing that in spite of his predicament, he wasn't going to let his crew suffer the hand the military might be dealing them. He was determined to set things right.

CHAPTER 34

Severn rose from her chair in the mess hall, shoveling the last of the food on her plate into her mouth. She ditched her dishes in the sink and hustled out the door behind Wicked, who was in full stride to meet up with the captain. That left Jones, Aura, and Marko alone in the mess hall. Severn didn't have time to think or worry about Marko. She was confident he could handle his cleaning assignment, no matter how demeaning it was.

As she and Wick arrived in the cargo hold, Anders stood at the port-side controls for the grappling system they used on the destroyer. Severn didn't think a midflight docking used a system like that to moor the ships together.

"Won't grappling spears damage their ship?" she asked with an inflection that made the question a sort of joke.

Anders didn't look at her; he only responded with orders. "I need you on these controls when we attempt the docking." He then called behind himself using a louder voice, "Wick, on the other one."

"Check," Wick said as he hustled to the starboard-side controls.

"When the ship comes in, you'll see it here." He pointed to a split screen. On the left side was nothing but star-speckled blackness, while the right side displayed a camera view of the hull looking at the loading door on the floor of the cargo hold.

"All right, then what?" Severn asked.

"They have the same class ship as ours, and they were designed for midflight cargo transfer. So when Jones lines our ship up with theirs—" he pointed to large steel hooks offset from each corner of the loading door, "those clamps will lock into place on their ship."

"And theirs onto ours," Severn said, finishing his explanation.

"You got it. When I tell you, press and hold this button until it's secure." Before she could ask how she'd know it was secure, he continued. "You'll hear the gears winding as they lock the hooks into place. When the connection is solid, the winding turns to a low hum, like they're struggling. That's when you have it and should release the button."

"Sounds simple enough," she said.

"Good," he replied just as Jones began a message over the intercom.

"*Cap,*" he said, "*I've got a visual, and I've made contact. We'll be connecting in five.*"

The intercom went silent and Anders placed a hand on Severn's shoulder. "You good?"

For a moment, her entire being flash-focused on that split second when he touched her. Before she could figure out why she noticed it so intensely, she panicked that an eternity had passed since he asked if she were good. "Check," she said while clearing her throat.

Anders, seemingly unaware of her moment with him, started a hustle toward the cockpit and called to Wicked with a finger pointed at him, "You know what to do?"

"Yes, sir," Wick replied without glancing away from his screen.

Anders disappeared into the ship, and Severn went back to her controls, trying to shake off the remnant of his hand on her shoulder. *Focus*, she coached herself.

First the open blackness of space and then the loading door. Back and forth her eyes darted, looking for any sign of the incoming ship, and that's when she realized how much she was enjoying the work. Not the mission itself but the assignment. She was beginning to like operating with this crew, the camaraderie she felt with them and the things they were doing—outside of knocking off the most prestigious space museum out there. It was good work, and she liked Anders. She respected him and was beginning to have pity on him for being a part of the operation that had put him in such a tight spot.

She urged herself again, *Focus, damn it.* The mission was objective number one. She kept telling herself this, and to complete that objective, her task at hand was securing the mooring of these two ships. Thinking of Anders in any way other than strictly a captain and her means to complete her mission was not an option.

"Hey, Severn?" Wick asked.

"Yeah."

"How long have you known Marko? He seems pretty solid."

"I knew Marko before I went to boot camp," she said, trying to remember the story she told Anders. She was a little caught off guard by this question, although she was fairly certain Wicked wasn't asking anything out of suspicion. He was probably genuinely interested, but she felt it better to change the subject before she slipped up and gave away any clues that might make him think. Wick was pretty smart and could figure things out.

"Good friends?" he asked.

"More like longtime acquaintances who knew each other fairly well. What about Aura?" she asked knowingly. "You two seem to be getting kind of close. Is she remembering anything?" The question appeared to shock Wick a bit, so Severn squinted at the screen, as if she were trying to make out something. Then she turned to face him.

"What do you mean, close?" he asked. "I'm not doing anything—"

"No, no. That's not what I'm saying," she defended. "You both seem to really like each other. I think it's nice. In a life like this—" she pointed in the ship to nowhere in particular, signifying a space-ridden lifestyle, "you're lucky to find someone special like her."

"Oh, really? You think she likes me like that?" he asked.

She smirked at him. "Oh, come on. Even you're not blind enough to miss that she's taken a liking to you."

"Yeah, I guess. But isn't it wrong for me to…I mean, since she's…"

"Got amnesia? Are you asking if it's wrong since she doesn't know who she is?"

"Yeah. Kinda. I guess so. I mean." He shrugged. "What if there's someone else?"

"There probably is," she said.

"What?" he asked, surprised.

"She's beautiful, Wick. There's always someone. I'm just saying not to let it stop you. Look out for yourself, Wick. Get some." She added a smile that made him blush and turn back to his station.

That oughta keep his questions at bay for a while, Severn thought to herself as she too turned back to her station. As she did, she spotted the incoming ship not too far in the distance.

"You see it?" Wick asked from across the way.

"I do," she answered, and just then Anders announced their arrival over the intercom.

Wick's voice took on a more serious tone. "Let Jones and their pilot line it up, and then we'll clamp down on Cap's mark."

"Check," Severn replied as she watched the incoming ship slowly position itself. Both ships approached each other face-first to line up the offset clamps on the cargo doors. When the ships were in position, Anders called for the deployment of the clamps. Severn deployed hers, as did Wicked, and all eight clamps, four from each ship, protruded from their respective hulls and held fast to the opposite ship like interlaced fingers. Severn listened for and heard the hard grinding of the gears and released her push button.

"Looks good," Wicked said, stepping back from his station.

Anders called over the intercom, *"Confirm lock."*

"Locking confirmed," Wick replied while pressing the cockpit call button. *"Waiting for pressurization."*

Severn walked over to Wick's station to watch as he completed the necessary steps to make ready the passage through the loading door. As she approached, Wick called the cockpit again. *"We have pressure."*

"Check," Anders replied. *"We'll be right there."*

"Okay," Wick said to Severn. "Cap will be right here and—"

His eyes lit up as he noticed something on the mezzanine. Severn turned to see Aura, freshly woken and still rubbing her eyes.

"I heard a noise, like a loud clanking," she said. "Is everything all right?"

Severn paused to let Wicked answer, but all he did was gawk at the cute girl with her hair all a mess.

"Oh, it's nothing, Aura," Severn said at last, saving Wick from his stupor. "We've moored with some friends because the captain has some business to do. Nothing to worry about."

"Oh, okay. Well, since I'm up, I think I'll go work in the shop. Is that okay with you, Wick?"

Wicked nodded, seemingly at a loss for words. He watched her as she made her way down the steps and didn't take his eyes off her until she disappeared into the small corridor leading to the engine room.

"You got it bad, mister," Severn said, breaking Wick from his staring contest with the unsuspecting Aura.

"Dang. I do, don't I?" he said, looking to the floor.

"It's okay, we all get it now and then. Why don't you go help her?"

"Nah, I should be here supporting Cap. Maybe later."

"Yeah, maybe later," Severn said, grinning at him.

CHAPTER 35

When Anders stepped into the cargo hold, he was holding a large wrench. Marko strolled in behind him and Jones closely thereafter. Severn and Wicked were standing by the starboard-side station, and they all met in the middle of the cargo hold at the floor loading door.

"You sure we have pressure?" Anders asked Wick.

"Yes, sir," Wick replied.

Knowing Captain Jug and having done this on several occasions, Anders knelt at the door and rapped the wrench heavily on the steel that framed the opening. He waited for a beat of about three seconds before the exact cadence clinked from the other side.

"They confirm pressurization," Anders said and rapped twice more before heading over to the port-side station.

"Everyone move back," Jones ordered, gathering the crew at a safe distance from the opening.

Anders flipped a few switches on the controls and turned to watch while he tested the opening. It cracked open with a short burst of the air equalizing between the two ships, and, satisfied, he opened the door the rest of the way.

Anders, Jones, Wicked, Severn, and Marko all stepped up to the opening, and just as if they were looking down at a mirror set a half meter below their feet, they saw Captain Jug and his crew staring back up at them. At first, it was a bit disorienting, looking at another crew through an opening as if they were standing upside down on the ceiling below. Severn and Marko had never before experienced this and quickly turned away.

"Those two the rookies?" Captain Jug Mason said, looking at Anders through the opening.

"Yep. How are you, old friend?" Anders asked.

"I'm still flyin' and I'm still eatin', so I won't complain. You?"

Anders chuckled. "About the same, but I'm sure I could pick a few things to complain about."

"Not to me, you won't," Jug retorted with a laugh.

Anders nodded. "No worries. You remember Jones."

"Sir," Jones said.

"I sure do. Jones, how are you? My offer still stands, you know."

Jones let out a short huff. "I'm well, and my respectful decline stands as always."

"See, Anders, that's a good first mate you got there. Loyalty. Everyone thinks you can buy it; the wise ones know you earn it."

"Ain't that the truth," Anders replied. "Permission to come aboard?"

"Always," Jug said as he stood up and brushed his long silver hair back behind his ears.

Anders took a few steps back to set himself up for the jump through the opening. He set one foot in front of the other and noticed an interested look from Severn. For some reason, he paused as if it were the first time he'd ever seen her. She looked... The way she stood there watching him gave him pause, and before he let on that she caught him off guard, he played it off as if she was wondering what he was about to do. So he turned it into a captain-teaching-his-crew moment.

"The trick," he said, "is to jump off the edge like you're diving into a pool but to keep enough forward momentum to get all the way across the opening. And don't forget to spin."

With that, Anders rushed to the opening, leaped into the air with a gentle twist, and arched his body to dive through the opening. Halfway through, he kept true to his advice and spun around. When the grav plates in Jug's ship pulled him to their floor, he was facing forward with his momentum. He landed like a pro with ease, catching himself with a single step.

Jones, not so much. He caught the tip of his boot on the lip of Jug's opening. He made it but stumbled like he was getting an electrical shock. His arms jolted out like Wick's had not too long ago. Some onlookers chuckled, but for the most part, it wasn't as bad as it could have been for a guy as large as Jones.

"Thanks for meeting with me," Anders said as he shook Jug's hand.

"Not a problem. Always happy to be there for ya. What can I do for you?"

"How about a beer and a meet with the top two?" Anders said. Jug eyed Anders for a moment, understanding how private he wanted to keep the discussion they were about to have.

"Sure," he said with a nod and then addressed Crumb and Drake, his two lower-ranked crewmen. "You two take leave and hang out with Anders' crew. Take some refreshments with you. We're gonna be here a while."

"Aye, Cap," Crumb said as he hustled off toward their mess hall.

Drake glanced down through the opening at Wicked, Severn, and Marko. "Y'all play dice?"

Severn looked at Marko, and they both shrugged. She said, "We do now, I guess."

"Great. Wait right there," Drake said and darted off after Crumb.

CHAPTER 36

Crumb heaved his case of beer down through the hatch from his ship's floor with nothing more than a "heads up!" Which rightly, yet unfortunately, caused Wicked to look up, which wasn't where the case of beer was coming from in his perspective. From Wicked's point of view, it was coming *up* from the floor.

It passed through the gravitational change and stopped right at Wick's chest as if it were a ball tossed in the air reaching its climax. This caused him to take a step back, and luckily, he managed to catch it—with Severn's reflexes offering a couple of hands in support.

"Whoa, there! Don't go droppin' our beer now," Crumb shouted as he launched himself through the opening, feet shuffling to keep his balance. Drake paused for a moment, and when everyone gave him a look to see if he was coming, he gave a nod as if to say, "Watch this."

He took one step back before he ran to the hole where he then launched himself up in a twisting backflip. While in the air, Wicked guessed he rotated three full turns as he flipped backward twice. But that wasn't even the impressive part. When he came up through the opening, he landed on the floor right in front of Severn on one foot with both arms straight out to the sides and his other leg straight back as if he were balancing on a ketchup bottle.

"Name's Drake. Yours?" he said, offering his hand and then standing normally.

"Severn," she said, shaking it. "And this is Wicked."

He ignored Wick for the moment. "Well, look at you." He let his eyes track down her body, "No doubt as tough as you are good lookin'." He winked and then shifted his attention to Wicked, relieving him of the case of beer. "No doubt there's a story behind that name of yours, eh? Maybe I'll hear it after a few'a dese?"

"Don't count on it," Wick said, grimacing. He'd never been a fan of pushy people like Drake. The man didn't seem like a horrible human being, but he apparently enjoyed taking over as soon as he arrived. To make matters worse, Drake eyed the cargo hold as if he were looking for something, and an uneasy feeling settled over Wick. Though he probably would have done the same thing on their ship.

"Right, then," Crumb interjected himself. "Shall we kick off a game of dice?"

Severn glanced at Marko, who was standing off to the side, arms crossed, with a look on his face that said he'd rather not.

"You'll have to teach us, but sure." She looked back to Drake. "C'mon, the mess is this way."

"You coming too, boy?" Drake said to Wicked. "Sure would like to hear that story."

"Maybe another time," Severn said. "He's got work to do in the engine room." She glanced at Wick, nodding him off with a grin. He figured she was telling him to take his alone time with Aura as it came, so he trotted off toward the engine room, hoping Aura would be there.

When he walked in, every bone in his body longed for a greeting as sweet as the last one, but she was in the middle of working on *his* personal project. Not only that, she had plucked his helmet from the wall, and it was sitting next to his project like she was working on both of them. A confusing jumble of conflicting emotions welled up in his chest, and it manifested in a short stint of paralysis.

"What are you doing?" he asked.

Aura started backward from his scolding tone. "You scared me, Wick," she said with a smile that had a bit of irritation in it. She reached back to the steel box with the glass globe on top and said, "I think I found a small miscalculation in the redirection feed. I was making the adjustment for you."

In watching Aura and listening to her speak, Wick noticed the dramatic improvements she'd made since they found her on the abandoned starship. Her speech was nearly perfect, and her intelligence was remarkable. In a matter of days, she'd managed to comprehend the long-standing problem he'd been having with his cloaking project.

"Aura, I have to tell you—" He stumbled over her smile as he spoke. "Since we rescued you from that ship, your ability to remember speech and your mechanical intellect have improved to an amazing degree. Do you remember anything from before the ship?" He reached across her and picked up his helmet. His fingers felt the surface, and he noticed she had polished it.

She looked down, almost saddened. "I'm sorry, it looked like it was getting old. I wanted to make it nice again for you."

Wick continued, ignoring the stuff with the helmet. He wanted to know how her mind was doing. "What about dreams? Or flashes of things that you might not know how to explain."

Wick glanced at her hands. She kept switching them, wringing one inside the other as if she were deciding whether to tell him something. She opened her mouth to speak but then recoiled. He waited, and she finally spoke.

"Do you remember what you used the helmet for?"

The question hit him hard. *How could she know to ask that question?* Then he realized she was probably mixing her words, so he gave a truthful yet ambiguous answer.

"I do. I keep it as a reminder to always try to do good. To make things that help." He took a deep breath and replaced the helmet on the wall and brought up his inquiry again.

"What about your memory? You're speaking very well, so I can see that your language is coming back. Anything else?"

By the look on her face, he could tell she was definitely trying to figure out how to tell him something. Was she ashamed? Scared? Nervous about something? He placed his hand on her shoulder. "It's okay, Aura. You can tell me anything. I'm here for you."

She looked at him with her huge sad eyes. "That's the thing, Wick. I think my name really is Aura."

Wick recoiled and took his hand away. "What do you mean?"

"Well," her fingertips picked at each other, "remember when Severn started calling me Aura? And then when Captain Anders was here with us—" she pointed at the grid of screens on the wall "and Maddix called…"

"Yeah, I remember," Wicked said, encouraging her to continue.

"After she electrocuted us…" Aura frowned as if she were ashamed. "When I woke up, I felt funny, and my brain…" Aura stepped away shyly. He circled around her and embraced her.

"Aura, what is it?" he said.

"It was weird. Like my current consciousness was reconnecting with my past consciousness. With the memories I had before you found me."

"Your memory is back?" he asked, elated.

"Yes." Aura nodded with a chuckle that didn't match the confused look on her face. And then tears began to well up in her eyes, and sadness washed over her.

Wicked overflowed with compassion for Aura, something he'd never before felt for any other person. He wanted nothing more than to banish her sorrow.

Giving her a smile wasn't good enough. He wanted her to feel loved. Cared for. Welcomed in his life and on this ship. So he pulled her close and kissed her. Not like the kiss on the cheek she'd given him the other day. This was the kiss he'd been waiting to give someone his entire life.

Aura embraced the kiss with a faint, almost imperceptible moan, and she wrapped her arms around him and pulled him close. Wick's body buzzed with warmth and desire. A felicity beyond all measure grew in his heart, which he only understood by comparing it to all of his time without her.

He loved Aura.

He wanted nothing else but her in this moment, and he knew she felt the same by how her arms pulled at him, how her lips reached for more of his. And how her mouth made his go numb.

CHAPTER 37

The beer was nearly gone when Anders interrupted the dice game in the mess hall. After two hours of playing, Severn and Marko each had two empty beer bottles in front of them, while the rest lay on the table and floor surrounding Crumb and Drake.

An absence of sound enveloped the table, and Anders knew it wasn't him that silenced the room. It was the kind of silence only a stack of lost cash could bring to a loser's mouth. And the kind of silence a humble trickster would display in respect for her victim as he wallowed in his anger.

Anders saw the neatly organized tower of cash in front of his new recruits and the lack thereof in front of their guests. He knew what had gone down in his mess hall, and it wasn't pretty.

"Jug wants you two back on your ship," he said, looking at the two disheveled, drunk, and broke men sitting opposite Severn and Marko.

"Not yet," grumbled Drake.

Crumb added, "I wan' win m' money back."

"Too bad." Anders threw a thumb over his shoulder, showing them the door. "You rolled 'em, now you live with it."

"Ah hell!" Drake shouted. "Y'all played us." He reached for the stack of cash in front of Marko. "Gimme that back!"

In a flash, Marko gripped Drake's hand and twisted it. The fluid motion threw Drake to one knee on the floor as he twisted his body to try to relieve the strain on his arm. He cried out in much pain.

"Okay, Marko, that's enough," Severn said as she counted out a quarter of her stack and threw it on the table in front of Crumb. "Here's for the game getting cut short. I'm sure you'd have won about that much back, right?" She gave him a knowing look.

"Yeah," Crumb said. "That sounds about right." He glanced at Drake, who was stumbling to get up. "C'mon, Drake. Let's go."

"Fine," he mumbled as he staggered to his feet. He followed Crumb out of the mess door.

Both Severn and Marko rose from their seats at the table. Marko faced Anders, seemingly expecting a set of orders. Anders obliged.

"Severn, grab Wick from the engine room. Help him lock up the cargo hold and wait for Jones' instructions to decouple from their ship."

"Check," she said as she headed out the door.

"Marko." Anders looked from him to the clutter on the table. "Clean this up," he said and left before Marko had the chance to reply.

There was no particular reason for Anders to give Marko a hard time, other than the fact he was there to use Anders for whatever the military had in mind. For all Anders knew, the crew was out of danger and had already earned immunity for whatever they did as a result of the military's involvement. That was no guarantee, but still, it was best to treat Marko and Severn with respect in the hopes of earning some kind of favor in the end.

But Anders just couldn't help himself. The fact remained that Marko was an intruder.

What really threw Anders for a loop was something he didn't see coming: He didn't feel the same disdain for Severn. In fact, it was the exact opposite, even though she was the first one to deceive him. If anything, she should have been catching the worst of his wrath.

Nonetheless, Anders needed them both for the time being, and he needed them to think he knew nothing. So he used that to justify his treatment of Marko and decided to keep the status quo with Severn by treating her as a trainee of a fully realized recruit. Marko was what he had always been: temporary.

CHAPTER 38

Severn noticed the embarrassment on Wicked's face before she noticed Aura putting on her shirt. In a moment, she realized exactly what had happened and thought it best to pretend she didn't.

Wick tied the last knot on his shoelaces while trying to hide his face. He started to say something, but Severn cut him off. "Enough naptime. We got work to do. Cap wants you and me to lock up the cargo hatch, Wick. Meet you there in a minute?"

"Sure," Wicked said. "I'll be right there."

"Hi, Severn," Aura said with a small wave.

"Hi, Aura, how are you? I'm sorry we haven't hung out in a while. Can I come by your bunk later to catch up?"

"Yeah, that sounds fun. I look forward to it."

Severn smiled at her, finding it a bit alarming that Aura had regained her speech so quickly. The last time she'd spoken that well, all hell broke loose. Severn didn't know how much time they had until she cracked again, and things were beginning to get more complicated than they had anticipated.

As Severn turned to leave them alone, Anders swung around the corner.

"Is he in there?" he said, pointing through the wall and into the engine room.

"Yeah," Severn replied as she stepped aside for him to enter.

At the commotion, Wick popped up, alarmed by Anders' entrance. Aura had already taken a seat at a nearby workstation, going back to work as if she were a piece of factory machinery.

"She's calling again," Anders said to Wick. "Put her up on the screens."

Wicked fingered the thing around his neck and stared at nowhere in particular. Severn hadn't considered Maddix could be their primary, but she saw how this woman was affecting Wick and this crew something fierce.

"Wicked!" Anders called out, shaking his shoulder.

He snapped to attention, bolted to the controls on his desk, and began making a conference connection with the cockpit where the call was held. A moment later, the screens lit up with an all too familiar and hated face. Maddix.

Just as before, the room she'd called from was dark, and the same smoke stream billowed up from a nearby cigarette. She held a glass modestly filled with some kind of brown liquor, and she smiled a yellow-toothed grin.

"Well hello, boys," she said in her Zen-like tone. "How are my little thieves doing today?"

"Maddix," Anders said. "What do you want?"

"How informal, Anders," she said. "How hateful, too. You should know by now the big and black is filled with the unsavory." She donned an innocent look. "Why, I'm just doing my thing to survive out here." Her tone grew dark. "You should respect that more. You should respect that I have the upper hand on you." She took a long drag of her cigarette and finished her drink. "If you did, you'd probably survive this, you know?"

"Again, what do you want, Maddix? We're in the middle of it here," Anders said.

"I wanted to make sure you were doing as you were told. Tell me, what is your plan, and when will you acquire the things I asked for? I don't like to wait long for the things I ask for."

"You'll have to learn to wait, Maddix," Anders replied. "*The things you asked for*," he said smartly, "take time to acquire. And how I'm going to get them is none of your concern. You'll get them. Don't bother me with how."

"I figured you'd respond that way," she said. "Too bad, too, but I guess it's better for me this way."

"What do you mean, Maddix?" Wick asked, sensing a ploy behind her words.

"Oh, he does speak," Maddix said. "But he doesn't remember my name, does he, Anders?" She looked at Wicked. "What's my name, Drew, baby?"

"Never mind that," Anders said. "What have you done?"

"You'll learn, Drew. You'll fall back into our old rhythm soon enough. And your girlfriend too." She cleared her throat. "As for my plan: I know you're heading to the museum now to get a good look at it. I also know you're probably too scared to pull the job off right away, but I just can't wait that long." She took a dramatic drag from her cigarette.

"It's smarter that way. You can't go in without knowing the place and expect to walk out with the most valuable things."

"Sure you can," Maddix said, leaning forward. "So I've sent some friends of mine to help out."

"Stay out of this, Maddix. I'll get this done my way!" Anders shouted.

Maddix broke into the knowing laugh that bellowed from deep in her bouncing belly. Smoke puffed out with each chuckle, and before she spoke again, she took another long pull from her cigarette. "We'll see about that." She lifted a handheld device into view, a small black box with a set of four buttons, all red. She fingered one and gave it a quick tap. Wick jumped in his seat as a bolt of electricity shot into his neck.

"Stop it, Maddix!" Anders shouted as he reached for Wick.

Wicked sat in his seat with a look of terror as Maddix fingered the box again. She eyed Wicked with an evil look. "Say hi to your girlfriend for me, Drew, baby. I'll be seeing you both again real soon."

With that, the screen went black, and not a second later, another shock came stinging from the collar into Wick's body. He violently shuddered for a moment as Anders stood there helpless. By the time it stopped, Wicked had collapsed to the floor, still breathing but unconscious.

Before Anders could make a move, Aura was already there, embracing Wicked on the floor. There was no warm look of compassion for Wicked in her eyes. Only hatred for Maddix. "I'm going to kill her, Anders," she said with a confidence he only saw in himself at the best of times. "We're going to do the museum thing and then end her."

"Check," Anders said in agreement.

CHAPTER 39

Three work shifts had passed since their call with Maddix and the visit with Captain Jug's crew. Anders sat in his pilot's chair as the third shift was ending. He scrolled through the nets while Jones nosily slumbered in the chair next to him. A snoring first mate might annoy most captains, but to Anders, it had become a comfort of sorts. A loyal crew member such as Jones was no mere commodity. They were hard to come by, so Anders didn't mind little things like snoring while he searched for news and future income.

Since he was the only one awake, Anders saw it first. At this distance, though, Royale Row was only a far-off glimmer of light. Larger than the shine of a typical star but easily missed by the untrained eye. Anders noted the sighting in his log at half past the eighteenth hour. Several more hours would pass before they arrived at Royale Row, which meant that now was a good time to gather the crew for a meal and a final briefing on their first visit to the museum.

Anders closed his thick logbook bound in old leather. It had many pages fully notated, plenty of scratch paper leafed inside, and a few stains on the cover, the scars of a logbook's life. He tied its leather strap and stuffed it down between his captain's chair and the steel wall of the cockpit. He glanced out the viewport one last time and nudged Jones' shoulder.

"Sir?" Jones said as he woke from his nap.

Anders pointed out the viewport. "We're coming up on Royale Row. Maybe another eight hours before we arrive."

Jones stood up, wiping his face and clearing his throat. "I'm hungry." He rubbed his belly. "We should go over the plan again too."

"My thoughts exactly," Anders replied. "Call everyone to the mess. I'll meet you there."

"Check," Jones replied, reaching for the all-comms hung on the starboard cockpit wall.

Anders made his way out of the cockpit and through the corridors. A quick stop at his bunk to freshen up before heading to meet with the crew made him the last one to arrive.

Jones sat at the table's portside bench, commanding his typical seat. Wick was next to him, giving his lady, Aura, the eye as she sat across the table from him.

Aura, strangely, seemed different. Anders noticed the look on her face had changed. She appeared more in the know, as if she'd lost the confusion of amnesia. She also looked happy, like she felt at home.

Marko and Severn sat next to Aura, talking with Jones. It wasn't a heavy talk, but it was heated enough that Jones finally stated the discussion was over and Marko would be making the meal for everyone. That made Anders smile as he pulled out the chair at the head of the table where he took his seat. All quieted and paid him his due attention.

"We're about eight hours away from the museum," he started, "so I want to use that time to go over the plan once more and then get some food and rest. First off, I want to be clear about this mission. The point of this first visit is to go in, get a look around, and see what we're dealing with. We have no idea about the size or weight of the item Maddix is making us grab."

"Or the size and weight of Kopius, for that matter," Wick commented softly, drawing a giggle from Aura.

Severn and Marko gave each other a look of confusion. Anders got the distinct impression that something wasn't going the way they'd expected.

"Hold the jokes, Wick," Anders said. "At least for the duration of the planning and executing of the thing that might very well get us locked up. Or worse."

Wick broke free from the attention he was pouring on Aura and gave Anders a nod of appreciation. "Aye, Cap."

"All right then," Anders said. "We need to accomplish the following: Get in and map all public pathways. I want to mark all locked and unlocked doors with their respective door labels, if they have any, and get a good look at the security, the main exhibit, and Kopius. Take as many mental notes as possible on everything you see. This is strictly a reconnaissance tour."

Wick joined in. "I have my body camera set up with geo-spatial plotting programmed to upload my data straight to the ship in real time. I've also given myself the ability, with the click of a button on my sleeve, to mark a point and verbally record a label, such as 'janitor's closet' or whatever."

"Good. Have you tested it yet?" Anders asked.

"I will after dinner," Wick replied. "I'll let you know if I run into any snags, but I don't anticipate any."

"Okay. And your cover?" Anders asked.

"Aura and I will be strolling the museum as a typical couple on a visit. We'll move quickly but not so quick to draw suspicion since we need to circle around the walls of every room. I'll have her equipped with the same mapping system for redundancy in case something should happen and require one of us to continue on separately."

"Solid plan. Aura, do you understand what we're doing and what we need you to do?" Anders asked her with a softer tone than his typical captain's voice.

"She does," Wick answered for her.

"That's great, Wick," Jones said, "but I think the captain would like to hear it from her."

Aura smiled at Jones in agreement and turned to Anders. "Yes, sir. I understand what we're doing. You and your crew have been so kind by taking me in and helping me get better, so I'm happy to help in any way I can."

"And you understand what's at stake here?" Anders asked, nodding at the collar around Wick's neck.

Aura glanced at it and said, bowing her head, "I do. I'll do whatever it takes to free Wick."

"Thank you," Anders said. "But you should know that we're all in danger of getting into some serious trouble, not only with the authorities but with the museum's private security force as well." He paused, realizing the crew, outside of himself and Jones, may not have known what he was talking about. His voice took another tone as he addressed the entire table. "If we succeed in relieving the museum of the main exhibit and Kopius, they will come after us. They will do all they can to hunt us down and recover them."

Jones added, "The fight doesn't end when we leave the museum with the stuff."

"No, it doesn't," Anders continued. "In many ways, that's where the trouble starts."

"Which is why Marko and I will be applying for jobs at their security office," Jones said.

"Once we gain their interest in hiring us, we will ask them to give us a security tour. It probably won't get us any big secrets, but it might give us an angle to use later," Marko added.

Anders raised his head, surprised at the contribution. Any security team would jump at having Jones and Marko on their team. He waved a finger at Marko. "Excellent point. Wick, can you get Jones hooked up with your tracking 'n' mapping stuff too?"

"Sure, I don't need any sleep," he said, regretting the snarky comment the moment he said it.

"Sleep when we're done. Besides, you've got help if you need it." He gave Aura an approving nod.

Severn piped up for her and Anders' role. "And while Wick and Aura are mapping the museum and Marko and Jones are applying for security positions, you and I will be making our way to Kopius and the main exhibit."

"Your cover?" Aura asked, clearly stumping Anders. He'd been so focused on what he wanted everyone else to do that he never explained his own cover. He felt a bit awkward voicing it for the first time to the group.

"Severn and I will be heading to the main exhibit pretending to be a couple, like you and Wick," Anders said.

He quickly realized it was only awkward for *him*. No one else batted an eye at the plan, and he felt something he hadn't before. Severn was more than a crew member to him. She was more than just a deceptive spy on their team. He felt something else for her, and this was the first time he'd considered it. Now wasn't the time for those feelings though, so he cast the thoughts aside. Besides, Severn was a military operative and, as such, just as temporary as Marko. But the thoughts lingered in the back of his mind anyway.

"Oh," Aura said. "Makes sense. You two look good together."

The table went silent, and everyone looked at Aura for a moment. Then, almost in perfect unison, their heads turned back to Anders as he shifted in his seat. Severn kept her wide eyes on the table.

"When we're each done with our jobs—" he cleared his throat, "we meet back at the ship."

"I assume we'll all have comms and be sharing our progress throughout," Marko stated.

"Yes," Wick replied. "And I may have something to check out while we're in there. Could be the key to making this happen if we pull the trigger for real."

"Show me," Anders said.

"I've been downloading and studying several sets of plans of the museum," he started as he pulled out his computer and placed it on the table in front of Anders. "You can find a lot on the nets, and it seems others have cased the place before. They're not an exact match to each other, but I think I've found a common theme to the structure."

Jones moved to stand behind Anders and Wick to get a good angle on the screen. The others methodically filled in behind them.

Wick continued to explain his theory. "Look." He pointed to the screen, which showed the museum as a whole. "It's cube-like, and with the exception of a few key rooms, like the large entrance hall, each room appears to be the exact same size. A smaller-scale version of the museum as a whole."

"So what are you thinking?" Anders asked.

"It's a working theory, so I need you all to be on the lookout for things."

"What things?" Severn asked.

"Things like: What do the joints between the rooms look like? Is there anything you notice that is in every room? I want to map exactly where the security offices are, where the exhibit is, and where Kopius frequents. If I'm right…" He cut himself off and hit the Enter key on his computer. The entire crew gasped at what they saw.

"Can that really happen?" Anders asked.

"If my theory is correct, yes," Wick said, shrugging. "It's quite simple and brilliant really."

"If we do that, then what?" Severn asked.

"We make sure Kopius is with his exhibit when we do this, then we—"

"Get him," Anders finished his thought.

"Exactly!" Wick said with excitement.

"Sounds great," Jones said, "but how the hell are we gonna make that happen? There's gotta be thousands of safety protocols to keep that from going off."

"I think it's part of their security. To protect the exhibits in the event of a heist or takeover or something," Wick answered.

"All right. This is good, but let's not get ahead of ourselves," Anders said. "Great work, Wick. Everyone keep an eye out for any information that could help us out with this. Jones and Marko, ask a couple of questions to security and see if they give you anything."

"They won't give any secrets, but I'll try," Jones answered.

"Any questions? Everyone clear on their jobs?" Anders asked, and the table fell silent. "Okay, good, let's eat. Who's cookin' tonight?"

"That would be Marko," Jones said as he clapped Marko's shoulder.

Severn laughed. "I'm not sure you want that."

"It's not like we have gourmet ingredients on board anyway. It won't matter," Wicked said with a grumble.

"Yeah, yeah. Let's get outta this mess, and I'll stock up with the good stuff, all right?"

"Deal," Wick said.

CHAPTER 40

Elite One approached Royale Row with an urgent reluctance matching that of its crew. Not one of them carried a distinct desire to embark on what they'd come to do, but Anders knew each of them was willing for the sake of their own missions. The crew's eagerness to get on with it showed in their crowded attendance in the cockpit, but their reluctance reigned over the small space in a gawking silence.

As they drew near, lights from the tops and bottoms of the suspended ship-buildings cast rotating beams in a kind of sword fight of lights in the surrounding space. The glowing expanse of the airbreaks at the front entrance drop-offs of these structures complemented the inviting luminous designs on their surfaces. Some went so far as to cast holograms near the traffic lanes of expected entertainers.

The most glorious of places at Royale Row stationed themselves in two long and neatly packed lines that faced each other, jutting through the center of the entertainment cluster. Between the two lines was space enough for several ships to pass by in either direction. The not-so-popular sites were strewn above, behind, and below Royale Row, distant enough to give all of the attention to the center attractions and still abiding by the proximity laws but also close enough to catch the smaller money.

At the center of the row lay their target. The Promaedia Museum. The closer the ship coasted to the museum, the more the crew pushed into the cockpit, trying to catch a better glimpse. Each person was already equipped with hidden gear needed to get on with the work.

Aura was dressed in brown everyday pants and a white shirt borrowed from Severn. Wick had dressed himself in the same dark canvas work pants and heavy knit long-sleeved shirt he always wore, but they were freshly cleaned and would do fine for the museum. Jones and Marko hadn't changed their appearances much, just a quick cleaning and they'd pass for security applicants.

Anders and Severn seemed to have taken a bit more care than the others in getting themselves ready. The smell of Severn's freshly showered-ness wafted into Anders' personal space, drifting a familiar distraction into his focus. Her jet-black hair, he noticed, was still slightly damp, which he found strikingly fresh in an inviting way. Based on her appearance, he was quite relieved to have taken care in his own preparedness, having showered and groomed his face and hair. Her black pants wore like they were painted on and Anders, even from the corner of his eye, could see how defined the muscles in her legs were. Her white button-up shirt, was tighter on her than on Aura but seemed to still hide her features. When Severn caught him checking her out in the reflection of the display screen he became desperately aware of how much he fell short in his appearance compared to hers. But he was glad to have stocked up on new shirts and pants, though they were the kind to wear around the ship. Dark canvas pants with a heavy knit long-sleeved shirt, an outfit not unlike Wick's, but it would have to do. Besides, Severn looked good enough for the both of them, so he replaced his focus on the approach.

Jones steered the ship into one of the many traveling lanes demarcated by positioning lights in perfect alignment. Severn stepped behind Anders to get a closer look. *Damn her smell. And damn her deceit!* He tried to ignore her fresh scent and her presence and her everything else while keeping his focus on the museum.

"So many lights. So many things. It's magnificent." Said Aura softly into Wick's ear, soft enough for everyone to hear.

"It is," he replied, "and sadly, we may make it less so in the coming days."

"Would you look at that?" Marko said, casino and fancy restaurant stations now engulfing the viewport. "They couldn't fit another one in here if they tried, could they?" He gawked at the endless row of palace ships flashing their lights and signs, trying to draw in the many ships passing by.

"Prolly not," Jones replied in his own awestruck way.

"We have to come back here when we're done," Wick said. "I've always thought the house odds are a bit skewed. I'd like to even that out."

Anders chuckled. "Yeah, Wick, that's why I've never brought you here. You could do some real damage at these places, and they don't like that much."

Silence bore down on the crew as Royale Row grew more impressive in the view from the cockpit. The lights, the ship traffic, and the sheer size of it all froze the crew into a watchful paralysis. The museum in the distance cast soft blue lights onto her clean white hull. A huge, perfect square ship suspended at the center of Royale Row. Structures around it made way to accent her majesty.

As they closed in, the perspective gave way to the identical casinos on either side of the museum, also bathed in soft blue lights, to complete a magnificent collection of palace ships framed inside a mini off-shoot in the row. The museum's grand entrance spewed out a line of ships as they queued up to drop off guests. One by one, the ships flew in through the entry side of the airbreak, touched down as guests quickly disembarked, and were then ushered out the other end of the airbreak to dock in the backside hangar.

Most of the ships looked to be passenger crafts, probably piloted by the guests' personal pilots, who were then meant to wait in the hangar while said guests paid their visit to the museum. Anders' plan used the same tactic, but unlike the other pilots, he'd be entering the museum through the back entrance, which wasn't out of the ordinary for guests who didn't need the elegance of the grand entrance.

"Everyone clear on what they're doing?" Anders asked as they approached the main entrance.

"Check," many said in unison.

"All right, Jones, I'll take it from here."

"Okay, Cap, control is yours," Jones said.

"Taking control," he said as he took the controls at his pilot's chair. Jones disengaged his yoke with a flip of a large red-and-black switch on his panel.

"You four head to the cargo hold and stand ready for a comms check."

"Aye, Cap," Jones replied. Severn stayed, standing behind Anders, while the others filed out of the cockpit with Jones pulling up the rear.

"Have a seat," Anders said to her, motioning to Jones' chair.

"Sir?" she asked, confused.

"It's all right, we're on the job. You should be ready for anything. Grab the yoke and flip that same switch Jones did before he left."

Severn sat down, looking at the plethora of buttons, switches, and gauges laid out before her. Anders quickly became amused at the overwhelmed look on her face.

"Don't worry about all that. Just flip the switch."

She did, and the yoke between her legs began to move with Anders'.

"Grab a hold and get a feel for how she flies. I'll do the rest."

Severn's look of discomfort melted into joy as she held the movement of the ship in her hands. Anders, of course, was flying it, but he could see the look on her face. Whoever she was, whatever she was up to, she was enjoying this in a way a spy shouldn't. Anders found it quite difficult to figure her out.

"*Comm check, this is Jones. Ready at the cargo bay door.*"

"*Check, Jones,*" Anders replied, motioning toward the mic under his shirt. He fingered his ear in a quick attempt to push in his earwig deeper.

"*Comm check, Wick.*"

"*Comm check, Marko.*"

Silence.

"*Oh, ah, comm check, Aura.*"

Anders smiled. Naturally, he looked at Severn to share his amusement with his copilot and was immediately caught off guard by her own smile shining back at him. He checked his behavior again and called into his comm, "*Comm check is good. We're pulling in now.*"

Anders flew through the airbreak field, gently pulling up on the yoke to counter the sudden pulling down of the artificial gravity inside the airbreak.

"Nice," Severn complimented his flying skills.

"The ship's computer calculates the majority of the stabilizing thrusters, so don't give me all the credit."

He eased the ship onto the demarcated drop-off point, a large circle painted by a thick red line. From there, a blue carpet led up the wide white staircase to the museum entrance. At the drop-off point, several museum ushers walked up to the cargo door, awaiting their newest arrivals.

"Clear to open the cargo door. See you on the inside."

"Check," Jones replied, *"opening now and disembarking. See you on the inside."*

Anders waited a few beats for confirmation on his console that the cargo door had been opened and then closed again. Out the viewport in front of him, the ship marshal signaled the all-clear to take off and exit the airbreak.

"Grab the yoke and palm the thruster handle," Anders told Severn.

She responded quickly, and as she held fast to the wheel on the yoke, Anders pulled up slightly and gave minimal thrust. Severn's hands followed the movements of his, and the ship eased from her perch and simply floated out of the airbreak seal.

"Awesome," Severn said, adding some laughter.

"You act like you've never flown before," Anders said, steering the ship down to fly under the museum. As he did, he noted bubble-like posts positioned at the tip of each corner of the structure; large, but small compared to the museum as a whole, with easy views of each side of the cube-shaped ship. Outside each bubble, a manned spacecraft was suspended in wait.

"I haven't," Severn said. "Not really, mostly simulators. Didn't we discuss this?"

"Yeah, maybe," Anders said, distracted by the guard posts. "Look at that." He pointed.

"It appears that at any time, four guards are watching each side," she said.

"Plus a manned aircraft. Looks hot with artillery too."

"This won't be easy," she said.

"Yeah, maybe, but there's one thing they didn't think of," he said.

"What's that?"

"My crew is elite."

CHAPTER 41

Wick had never imagined that he'd be the guy with the girl. In fact, he hadn't realized it was an option, but now that Aura clung to his arm, life seemed complete. With her there, this job didn't feel as volatile as a job casing a prestigious museum might feel. It was more exhilarating. Somehow more elegant.

The entrance to the museum stood three room cubes tall and twice that long. Each step up to the entrance took three footsteps to complete, no doubt to offer time for admiring the beauty of the foyer. Sky blue tapestries draped from the ceiling and spanned the entire length of the entrance hall. Intermittently, ocean blue curtains stretched to the floor, matching the tapestries and the magenta and purple hues of the airbreak behind it, which stretched along as if it were a solid wall, sealing the entrance from the threat of space only a few feet away. Along the edge sat huge planters filled with exotic plant life, and not a second after eying the delicious-looking flowers, Wick noticed the dozens of birds flying around the area.

"Look," he whispered to Aura while tracking one with his finger.

Aura gasped at the sight. They were small, brightly colored winged creatures that darted around as if in some kind of flying fight. Wick followed one with his eyes as it shot around the plants, and as soon as he began to worry about how close it flew to the airbreak, it passed right through it.

Aura gasped, covered her mouth, and looked away. Wick watched as it fought the elements of space, the bird's motions weaned down to perfect stillness in its wing-spread state where it peacefully flipped away on the same trajectory, forever animated as if it were still alive and in flight. As Wick watched the stiffened bird drift away, a small opening appeared in the ceiling, and another one dropped in to join the others, replacing the one that had been lost.

At first, Wick was impressed with the attention to detail the curator has paid to the entrance. Then fear swallowed that awe whole as he realized the implications: If that kind of attention was paid to keeping the status quo of *birds*, how much more attention was paid to keeping this place secure?

The group moved toward the line of people forming at the main doorway. Marko and Jones grabbed a spot in line first, and Wick let several other people step in before he brought Aura to the queue. From this point on, he didn't know Jones and Marko. Only Aura. The lady at his side.

It wasn't long before Jones and Marko entered and disappeared off to the right, bent on their mission. When it was his and Aura's turn to enter, he was glad to be rid of the annoyingly large hat worn by the woman in front of him. It had a pink feather that seemed to float around the enormous headgear as if it weren't attached but needed desperately to stay near.

Wick led Aura to the center of the grand front room. It was taller than the entrance and at least equally wide. Forward and to the left or right, guests filed into the museum, picking their desired paths. Straight ahead, guests either opted for the winding stone staircase up to one of three floors or passed underneath into the dark rooms beyond the entrance.

"What do you say we go left, circle around back here from there," Wick said, motioning to the right, "then head in the center hallway before going up a floor and doing the same?"

"Sounds like a wonderful date, honey," Aura said in a cute voice before she twirled around like a ballerina.

At first, Wick thought she wasn't very good at twirling because of how slow she spun. Then he realized she was going slow so the camera she was wearing could easily pick up and map the room. The goofy smile she wore was perfect. They were on a date as a cover for what they were really after, but she wasn't playing a part. Wick saw that she enjoyed being with him.

So he joined in and danced with her. He pulled her close and spun a robotic dance that positioned each of their cameras in opposite directions and paused for a moment, letting the gadgets send and receive all kinds of measurements. Then he pushed Aura away, paused, and pulled her back, spinning and dipping her so her camera pointed up. A slow spin around and they'd mapped their first room and continued, arm in arm, to the left.

"Shall we, milady?" he said, offering her his elbow.

"With pleasure, my gentle...man," she replied with a giggle and holding fast to him.

Green vines dotted with pink and blue flowers framed the entrance of the first room on the left. Passing through offered a sweet-smelling scent that seemed to cleanse his olfactory senses of machine shop and grease. His sinuses opened, and he breathed in through his nose, taking in the allure of the first room. An ominous soft voice spoke from hidden speakers, letting them know they'd entered the wing dedicated to the galaxy's most exotic rain forests. The moistness in the air thickened as they strolled deeper into the room, and their voices were sucked into the surrounding trees and brush, offering little to no echo. A couple nearby spoke, but the sound seemed far off, even as the singsong of wildlife rang true as a large orange-furred creature swung in the trees above them.

The creature flickered as it passed by, alerting a frightened Aura to the fact it was only a hologram. Relieved she loosened her grip on Wick, but he held on, enjoying her company. Another minute in this room, and they'd be ready for the next. Wick had noted nothing of importance so far, but it was only the first room.

The next room offered a similar rain forest setup, but this one was from another planet, Ankron. As they entered the room, a person dressed in native robes offered them a drink of something black as death.

"A drink customary to our wedding ceremonies," she said, pouring them a small snifter each. Reluctantly, Wick drew a sip and was surprised to experience a taste almost as sweet as how Aura felt while she danced on his arm. The tips of her feet excitedly tapped the floor in her show of appreciation for the drink.

Aura gave Wick a knowing grin. "I guess we're married now, huh?" she teased him, then laughed in a way that showed her teeth.

So pretty, he thought. *Say something.*

Wick attempted a pithy reply, but he only mumbled with a weird laugh.

Saving him from his embarrassment, Aura then offered, "This is easy and fun, Wick. All aside, I'm glad we're here."

"Me too," he agreed, suddenly becoming a bit rattled. He had been enjoying himself, and he realized why that felt odd.

He was on a job, and his crew depended on him to complete it. Normally he'd have been terribly focused while working on something of such import, and here he was dancing and twirling around with Aura like some kid on his first date. He was! But he also realized the trouble he could cause and felt the ramifications of neglecting his work.

Anders must have been sensing this too because just as Wick steeled himself to focus, Anders' voice came over the comms.

"Comm check, Anders here. We've docked and breached the rear entrance."

"Aw, check that out, Aura," Wick said, accenting the word "check" while pointing to a bright green bush.

"Check," Jones said after Wick, clearly not needing to conceal his communication.

"Real subtle, Jones," Severn voiced.

Aura found humor in that and shared a smile with Wick as they moved on. The comm check came at the right moment. It gave Wick the grounding he needed before sinking too far into his enjoyment of Aura.

The comms were silent while Wick and Aura mapped the next three rooms. The last room, before their chosen path turned right, contained the first guard Wick noted. As he passed by, he double-clicked the button in his sleeve to mark the guard's location. A quick spin around the room and they were off to the next, now entering a more modest theme of the museum: supreme architecture throughout the galaxy.

CHAPTER 42

After entering the museum, Jones and Marko headed right, as this was the fastest route to the security office. It was also the way to the restaurants and shops, which made Jones consider stopping off for a quick bite. Food on the ship became quite monotonous after even just a couple of weeks.

"You hungry?" he asked Marko.

Marko replied instantly, "Hell yes."

"Cool, let's make it quick though."

"Right. Cuz Anders might get mad? What's with him anyway? He seems like a legit captain one moment, but then he's got you guys all tied up in this Maddix business."

Jones defended Anders with as subtle a tone as he could manage in a public place. "You don't get to judge the cap like that. You don't know shit about him, us, or what we're into and why." It was a sharp rebuke, but Marko's comment reminded Jones that he and Severn were up to something, and he let that fact stoke the fire in his chest.

"Okay, I got it," Marko said.

"Just worry about doing *this* job, today, and do it right."

Jones spotted a guard standing across the hall from the restaurants and headed for him.

"Wait," Marko said, trying to stop him. "Food."

"You can eat later," Jones said, pressing on.

The guard stood about as tall as Jones and had light brown skin and dark black hair. He wasn't as thick as Jones, but Marko's jacket would fit him well.

"Excuse me, sir," Jones said as he approached the man.

A smile that looked like he'd shared it with a thousand others formed on his face before he said, "Yes, what can I do for you?"

"My friend and I came by hoping to speak with your security manager about any possible openings on your team," Jones said with a respectful tone. Marko nodded in agreement when the guard looked him over too.

"I see. Well, that sort of thing is usually done by way of appointment. But I don't mind if you try." The guard raised his arm and pointed to his right, the same direction they'd been walking. "Keep walking down here. On the left, you'll see a skinny hallway marked 'Security Personnel.' Head in there and you'll find our office."

"Thank you," Jones said as he pressed on.

"You're welcome, sir."

Marko followed closely behind Jones before stepping up beside him. "So, I badmouth your captain a bit, and now we don't get some *real* food?"

"Yup, that's right," said Jones. "Now shut it and put your game face on. Here's the hallway."

Jones turned sideways to enter the hallway and still barely fit. Marko entered when Jones was a few steps inside, and then Anders opened up communication.

"Comm check, Anders here. We've docked and breached the rear entrance."

"Aw, check that out, Aura," Wicked replied first.

There didn't seem to be anyone else around other than Marko, so Jones checked in. Since they were alone, he didn't blend it into conversation as per their protocol. "*Check,*" he said plainly.

"*Real subtle, Jones,*" said Severn.

Marko chuckled at her sarcasm. Jones paused in the hallway and took a deep breath. It was bad enough he had to pretend to not know that she and Marko were military, but to have to work with this guy and trust him was too much. Marko's deception was one thing, but to then question Anders' ability to hold the team together and insult him on top of it? And now Severn was trying to joke around like she was part of the crew.

Jones snapped. He turned his head back to face Marko, which only let his shoulder go from one side of the hallway to the other. He quieted his voice but filled it with rage.

"You'd better get your head outta your ass and get in this game. You think this is a joke? You might have a free pass here in case shit goes down and we get caught, but *my* crew don't. And I'll be damned if I let a piddly runt like you jam up my team. Focus on this day, join us for this job, make sure we don't get mucked up, and then get back to doin' whatever it is you two are doing on our crew and see who comes out on top. Got it?"

Marko paused for a moment, digesting all Jones had said. Jones didn't exactly say that he knew who Marko was, but he didn't hide it either. At this point, Jones didn't really care about that. He only cared about doing his job right, and doing it right now.

"Yeah, I got it," Marko said, stiffening his body as if to ready himself.

"Good, now let's go."

Jones returned to his forward advance in the hallway where it split at the end into larger thoroughfares. A sign directed personnel to the left for the locker room and to the right for the security offices. Jones went right and Marko followed.

CHAPTER 43

Back on *Elite One*, Anders and Severn spoke little as they flew the ship below the museum's underside. Flying as close to the structure as allowed, they were cast in the same blue lights as the museum, which reflected off the steel in the cockpit, sending dark shadows skating across the interior.

Heading behind the museum, Anders spotted a line of ships waiting their turn to enter the docking array. A dozen or so ships queued up behind the large square-framed docking port, which was suspended beyond the actual docking array. Connected to each side of the frame was a small manned sphere that controlled the port that flashed a docking assignment to each passing ship. A red and green light alerted the pilot whether to proceed.

Anders gave the back face a wide berth, sailing past the docking array, the point of entry, and then the line of ships before pulling up and flipping the ship around to join the line.

Severn gasped as she eyed the massive back side of the museum. The entirety of it was a huge airbreak separating space from the shelf-like docking area. Bright, huge letters demarcated docking columns along the top edge. The same identification system, except with numbers, laid out rows down the side.

With each ship that passed through the docking array, a new location assignment flashed on a massive screen suspended at the front of the line. Anders' ship was assigned P-19 when he approached the docking port, and when he was green lit, he headed straight for his slip.

Slip P-19, like all the slips, was a mere five ship lengths past the airbreak. Anders simply coasted straight at his assigned spot, and in the last moments, spun his ship 180 degrees, resting it on the provided landing platform with his back end in first. Whether the cockpit faced in or out of the slip was up to the pilot. Anders preferred having the option of the faster takeoff a backward docking provided.

After a few minutes of shutdown sequences that left the ship in a ready-quick state, Anders stepped off the cargo hold ramp that Severn had already deployed. Once disembarked, he closed the ramp with the click of the remote in his pocket, and he and Severn descended the stairs to the docking bay corridor lined with shops and eateries.

"You ready for this?" Anders asked her as she joined him in stride.

"Yes, sir," she said with a small grin.

Regardless of what she was up to or with which side she truly leaned, Anders somehow knew that in the thick of it, he could trust her. At least up until she turned on him.

"Good," he said. "I'll comm check the crew before we get too crowded in."

At the center of the level P docking, a collection of elevators ushered guests down to the bottom level where the only entrances to the museum were located. When they stepped up to the elevator, the doors opened, and a museum greeter gave a slight bow.

The greeter was tall, thin, and frightfully pale and spoke with a haughty tone. "Welcome to the Promaedia Museum. Might there be an exhibit you're particularly interested in viewing?" He was dressed in an all-black getup with dark red flame-like streaks licking down from the armpit of the coat to his feet. The pants had legs that might actually fit Jones' waist and were obviously much too large for this thin figure.

Anders fought a chuckle at the sight of it all and simply replied, "No, not particularly."

Severn, for reasons Anders could not find, fell into playing her part a little too quickly for his readiness. She slid her arm under his, clasped her hand in his, and ushered him into the elevator while grabbing his bicep with her other hand. All as if she'd been doing that to him for years.

Anders nearly froze, suddenly realizing how wonderful she felt on his arm. It took him the entire elevator ride to pull himself together and into his role. And just before the elevator door dinged and opened, he leaned over and kissed Severn on her hairline. She gracefully leaned her head in to receive it as if it were the thousandth time.

They left the tiny box, falling into step together, as silent as a couple who'd grown comfortable with a conversation-less date. Anders immediately spotted a rack of pamphlets and snagged a map of the museum.

Severn laughed when he unfolded it, only to find a barely manageable paper accordion in his hands. "Take it easy, giggles," he said. Several guests around them muttered their enjoyment of the scene. Anders pulled the map together and pointed at their targeted section. "There it is. Fourth level, center."

"Lovely," Severn said, shooting him a brilliant smile. "Directly there, or take some time?"

"I'll do a comm check first," he replied, breaking character. Severn's lips tightened, almost as if she were upset that he'd fallen back into captain mode so quickly. *Was she liking this too?* He continued before letting that thought ripen. "Then we can mosey a bit, but I want to get there quickly." He squeezed the sleeve of his jacket to open the comm lines and looked at Severn with a smile as if he were saying anything but, "*Comm check. We've docked and breached the rear entrance.*"

A short moment passed, and Wick replied first, "*Aw, check that out, Aura.*"

"I think Wick might be liking this job a bit much too," Severn said with a grin.

Anders didn't say anything back, but he did grimace as Jones checked in with a simple, "*Check.*"

"*Real subtle, Jones,*" Severn replied, staring into Anders' eyes and brushing some of his hair back around his ears. This was most distracting for Anders. It'd been a long time since anyone had done that to him, and to top it off, it was so subtle and perfectly placed in how she tested her comms that Anders couldn't tell whether it was part of her act or not. Again, he forced his thoughts back to the job at hand and considered his crew's locations.

Wick and Jones would be on the first level for a while, so Anders decided to head straight up to the second level to have a look before their first scheduled status update in forty-five minutes. The staircase up to the second level wasn't as glamorous as the one he saw up front while dropping off the crew, but it was wide and spiraled all the same.

"Well, I have to say this is the stupidest job I've ever taken," Anders said as they reached the second level and headed through the center toward the front.

Severn's hand slid down Anders' arm again, and she laced her fingers with his as they passed by a standing guard at the first room. "I would have to say that I'm pretty much in the same ship as you, Anders."

"Well, so far you've handled yourself pretty well," he said, not looking but somehow smiling at her.

"Thank you. Does that mean I'm hired? You never officially offered me a position, and here we are, a couple of weeks in and in a whole heap of trouble."

She was right. With all that had gone down with Wick and then him finding out she was still military, it had somehow slipped his mind that she was technically a rookie on probation. So he said, "Honestly, I haven't thought about offering you a spot on the team yet."

"I fit in, don't I?" she asked.

He paused for a moment. Outside of the whole deceitful she's-still-in-the-military quandary, she was a perfect fit for the crew. So much so that it angered him that this would all end. Badly. The truth of it was paramount. He needed to get Wick out of trouble first. Then he could deal with Severn and Marko.

"You do. You can handle yourself and anyone who stands in your way. You're not afraid to put your life in your crew's hands, and you'll do what it takes to get the job done." He stopped and faced her. "Can you promise me something?"

Her jovial face turned serious. "I can try."

"Will you do whatever it takes to save Wick from Maddix and keep my crew out of harm's way?" Anders hoped his tone said all he intended while still masking the fact that he knew the truth about her.

240

She took some time to think about it. That gave Anders hope. If she'd answered immediately, then he'd have known she was the type to do whatever it took to get *her* job done. Her pause meant that his crew might mean something more to her than some sting operation. He'd seen Severn with his crew. You couldn't fake that type of genuine *liking* all the time.

So he trusted her when she said, "Yes. I will do everything I can."

When she kissed him, he didn't know what to think. He could read anyone better than the next captain, but Severn was different. He had a bead on her before this kiss. Sure, she was confusing as hell, but he was beginning to unravel her a bit, and now she'd thrown a wrench in the whole thing.

He didn't know whether the kiss meant she was truly playing him or whether the kiss meant something else. So he did the only thing he knew to do. He embraced it. He pulled her tight and met her soft kiss with his own, and before he knew it, he was light-headed and couldn't tell up from down. This wasn't a good thing to experience in the heat of a job as serious as this one.

And as fast as caution entered his brain, it left. He realized how long it had been since he'd enjoyed a woman's embrace, but just as quickly as she started kissing him, and just as soon as he put all his focus into it, it was over. She leaned back and stared at him with her bright blue eyes, a few wisps of red-dyed hair resting on her lashes.

He opened his mouth, but nothing came out, as there was nothing in his head but desire. Some men can put desire into words. Anders wasn't one of them.

Severn seemed to realize that he was at a loss, so she smiled at him and urged him on his way through the museum. "C'mon, Casanova, we've got work to do."

That was it. Anders wanted her and loathed her with the same intensity in that moment. His disdain for her infiltrating his crew matched his desire for her to stay with him.

If that was her plan all along, it was working.

CHAPTER 44

Halfway through mapping the second level, Wick found some luck. At the end of the following room, a two-man mainte-nance crew had set up a small, cordoned-off area where they were working on the internal structure that joined the next two rooms. One man, with his head in the ceiling, appeared focused on his specified duty, while the other took a break with his tablet by the wall. The men had previously stripped the wall between the two rooms of its paneling, which exposed the museum's oth-erwise hidden structure.

Eager for a closer look, Wick struggled to pace himself while he watched the maintenance crew down the way. Aura, playing her part well, hugged him close and shuffled them slowly along the side wall while they pretended to admire the odd paintings hung in the room.

Wick embraced her strategy and followed her lead but kept his eye on the work, careful not to make it obvious he was star-ing at something two rooms away. He knew he had one shot, so he wanted to pick the best spot from which to study the struc-ture when they got there. A secret to this structure was hidden inside these walls, and he needed to verify that he'd found it.

But as she slowed them down to admire the paintings, the lights in the room went out, casting them into darkness. Another woman in the room gasped with fright at the unexpected change. Then every painting in the room transformed into baleful imagery, making Wick's skin crawl and Aura's grip tighten on his arm. What once was a sweet-smelling room with a peaceful array of bright and colorful paintings turned dreadfully evil in the darkness. A stinging repugnant smell drew near as deep, dark colors shone from the paintings.

"Why would anyone curate a hall of paintings like this?" she whispered.

"I don't know," Wick answered, wondering why anyone would add the smell of sulfur to heighten the experience of an art exhibit.

Aura's face shriveled with disgust. "I need to get out of here!"

With haste, they left the exhibit behind and entered the next far less offensive gallery. The doorway at the opposite end of this room was his target. It was half as large as the wall separating the rooms, square in shape, and framed by exposed internal steel members. Passing through the gallery, Wick stared at the structure at the end, and as they walked by the maintenance crew, Wick made sure to get a good long look.

One behind the other, two sets of huge steel bars as thick as Wick's thigh crossed each other, making a large X on each side of the door. At the ends of each bar were massive doubly reinforced gusset plates creating a three-sided connection at each corner of the room. These connected the support bars of each room at each wall and the ceiling. The connection at the floor mirrored the ceiling, but the two rooms were not connected to one another except for one pinned-type connection at the corner. From this one glimpse of the internal structure of the rooms, Wick verified his plan could work.

"Look up," he whispered to Aura as they passed through the opening of the exposed wall.

"Oh my," Aura said, placing a hand on her chest. "Seems a little overdone, doesn't it?" she asked as she sidled the man on a ladder with his head still in the ceiling. The other worker didn't seem to hear Aura as he continued perusing the tablet in his hand.

Before the man on the ladder glanced down to find the source of the sweet voice, Wick stepped several feet away from Aura, leaving her seemingly alone. When the man's face appeared from inside the ceiling, he shot a radiant look down at her as she whipped him with her eyelashes. His immediate interest in her was so thick Wick almost laughed.

"What's overdone?" he asked, stepping off the ladder and donning a confident smile.

"The walls," she said. "Why not make one single wall instead of two identical walls pinned together?"

Wick recognized the grin on the man's face. He'd seen it many times before, when a man thought he was about to impress a woman with his intellect. The man drew closer and tilted his eye toward Aura. He spoke in a hushed tone. "No one's really supposed to catch that. It's kind of a secret, so please, keep it down." He shot her a slick wink.

Aura cupped her mouth as if to put her words back in. "I'm sorry." Then she let her smile and voice take on a sultry tone. "Promise not to tell on me?" She tapped his forearm ever so lightly with four closed fingers as if to nudge her suggestion into him.

His confident grin seemed to stutter as if he suddenly realized he didn't know how to continue pursuing her. "I promise," he said. "In fact, I'll do you one better."

"Oh, you will, will you?" she teased.

He leaned in again, close enough to whisper in her ear, and she let him. When he was done, Aura jolted back and shot the man a surprised look with perfect timing. "What?" And then quiet again, "Wouldn't that destroy all the art? I mean, what an awful tragedy. I would be devastated." She placed her hand over her heart.

Amazing, Wick thought to himself. The innocence she projected to this man not only made him tell secrets, but the guy also began acting and speaking like some kind of gentleman to complement her innocence.

The man continued.

"Don't you worry a bit, my sweet," he said, bringing his hand to her back and turning her to look at the wall to the left of the door. "Those two steel plates tucked in that there wall?" She nodded, acknowledging where he pointed. "It's a hidden door. All the rooms have them, and they're airtight."

"What for?" she asked, concerned.

"Well, in case there's an emergency, of course." He chuckled. "If it's real bad, all the rooms close down."

"Why would they want that?" she asked.

"Well, let's say someone attempted a robbery," he said. Aura looked concerned again. "Security, if they decided it were necessary, would lock down the rooms. Those steel doors close, the rooms pressurize and seal." He pointed up at the joints between the two rooms and the corresponding rooms above. "See those claw-like clamps?"

"Uh huh," she said, nodding her head.

"There's two more sets that you don't see here. Eight in total connect a room to the others surrounding it."

"What if someone's still inside the room when that happens?"

"No big deal. As I said, each room is equipped with enough provisions for people to survive for at least three days. The artwork is protected by multiple security measures, and the floor opens, revealing seats with safety harnesses and even some cots. Enough for a dozen people. There are even protocols that supply the room with food, water, entertainment, and..." he pointed into the air, "its own restroom."

"Wow! That's pretty amazing," she said. "Are you sure you should be telling me this?"

That comment caused Wick to let out a snort, which he had to play off as a cough to avoid the man's attention.

"Well, I'm pretty sure you're no threat to this place, dear. Are you?" he asked with a flirty look.

"No, sir," she said seriously.

"I didn't think so. Say, I'll be done here in a couple of hours. What do you say we get out of here and go have some fun?"

Wick suddenly felt a spike of jealously, and he almost opened his mouth and blew their cover.

Then Aura reeled Wick's heart in with, "Oh, thank you for the offer, but I'm in love with someone at the moment."

This bold declaration nearly made Wick shout with joy. The smile on his face pushed his ears to the back of his head, so he turned away to hide it.

"Well," the man said, clearly disappointed, "he's a lucky man."

"Thank you. I feel just as lucky," she replied, turning away. "Thanks for the talk. Have a good day, sir."

The man didn't respond. He stepped on the ladder again, and before Aura had returned to Wick, his head was back in the ceiling.

"Well played, milady," Wick said, taking her arm and walking her away. "If I didn't know any better, I'd say you were a natural at this kind of deceptive work."

With a proud smile, she said, "I can be very persuasive when I need to be."

"Yes, you can," Wick said, then frowned. "Wait, so what parts of that conversation weren't true?"

Aura immediately kissed him. "Only the part where I seemed interested in him. Everything else was true."

"I see," Wick said, relief dousing his concern. "I'd better let the captain know what we've discovered."

CHAPTER 45

By the time they'd reached the fourth level on their way to the main exhibit, Anders had accepted the fact that he'd developed feelings for Severn, who was still on his arm. Walking down the wide corridor toward the exhibit, Anders felt empowered in a way he hadn't expected. It was the way Severn held onto his arm, as if she were claiming him. He didn't mind a feeling such as this. But still, every time he entertained these kinds of thoughts, they quickly turned to her deception. The anger he felt was no longer pure. It was tainted by something else. Feelings, confusing as they were, were now involved, and it felt a bit more like a betrayal instead of mere deception.

"I went to a museum once," Severn said, breaking a long streak of silence. "On Elvair. It's beautiful there."

"Congratulations," Anders said, hardening himself by focusing more on the exhibit than her. All the way at the other end of the wide corridor was an opening to a large room. From what he could see, inside was a well-lit glass encasement, inside that—.

"Hey," she said with a slight reprimand in her tone. "I'm trying to tell you something."

Realizing he had to maintain two covers, Anders grinned sarcastically. "Oh, sorry, *dear.*" He broke into a haughty tone. "Do tell."

Her smile at his dig matched the fortitude she had demonstrated in dealing with this crew since her first day with them. "I'm just wondering why we're forty seconds away from finding out what the exhibit is by actually going to it. Typically museums give out information on the different exhibits. All we've seen here is that stupid map that keeps giving you a hard time."

"So what? It's up ahead. You'll see soon enough," Anders said, still trying to eye the exhibit.

"I just find it weird is all," she said.

Anders stopped and faced her. "Look around you. Look at the people here. Look at the decorations, the curation of even just the halls."

Her eyes shot around, noticing the things Anders was pointing out.

"The money spent on making this place look this way isn't going to include advertisement pollution like pamphlets strewn about on simple steel wire racks. This place is about elegance and style and glorifying the artwork. It's about the artist and the abstractness—"

"Ha." Severn cackled and bent over, concealing a burst of laughter with her palms. Anders grimaced and was left speechless, looking around at nothing in particular. She continued to laugh, and Anders forced a smile or two at passers-by as they shot him accusatory looks. When she recovered, she said, "If you didn't say abstractness, I'd've gone on believing you."

"I thought it might be too much, but I was doing a thing," Anders replied.

She looked around again. "Still, I think you're pretty close on the advertisement thing."

"Yeah, yeah, let's go." Anders turned to face the exhibit. "We're about there anyway."

"Shall we?" Severn asked, offering her elbow to Anders.

He glanced at it with a raised eyebrow and then left it behind. It was bold to walk away from a woman like Severn, who was offering herself to him, but he felt it was a good time to leave her hanging. It felt appropriate for the unspoken dance they'd been engaged in.

As he'd hoped, Severn caught up to him and slipped her arm under his just before they reached the opening of the exhibit. They both stopped short, realizing in the same moment what Maddix was after.

"I don't believe it," he said.

Severn, a bit stunned, added, "Kinda changes your perspective on Maddix, huh?"

"Sure does," Anders said, leading Severn into the exhibit and up to the glass case.

Illuminated by bright lights, the ceiling-high glass case wrapped around the walls of the entire room, and inside that case stood a man, a bipedal machine to be sure, but it was identical to an average man. Two legs, two arms, a torso, and a neck that presumably supported some kind of a head—which was missing. And skin. Skin so real it would be impossible to tell if a piece weren't torn off, revealing the steel skeleton beneath.

"The machines," Anders said, teasing himself to a realization. "Maddix must be into these machines somehow. Maybe even behind all the attacks on everyone."

"You think?" Severn asked. "We all know she makes an illicit living, but does she really have *that* kind of clout?"

"Maybe." He leaned in to get a closer look. Anders didn't scare easily, and this moment was quickly becoming extremely close to terrifying. "Even if she's not directly in control of it, I'd be shocked to find out she's not involved at all. Why else would she want the exhibit?"

"Either she wants her toys back…or she wants these for herself," Severn said.

"Yeah, but why?"

"She wants in on the action?" Severn suggested. "Or to build an army of her own?"

Anders gave her a deadpan glance and then looked beyond her down the room. The single machine had taken all of his attention, and he soon realized the room was filled with them.

Anders spun around to look at the doorway and immediately noticed a peculiar thing about the way they presented the exhibit. "Severn, look at this." He pointed with each hand, one on each side of the doorway. The machines were of identical design: crude bipedal machines without skin and looking nothing like humans. The next machines on each side matched each other as well but were clearly of an evolved design from the first ones: a bit larger and appearing to have been built tougher. No skin either. The next ones were more evolved and so on. Glancing faster around the room, he landed on the one halfway to the center. The first skinned one. Then he skimmed past the rest back to the central one. The latest design. The exhibit showed the evolution of the machines that had been terrorizing the public all over the galaxy.

Severn stepped up next to Anders. "I recognize some of the others but not this one."

"I've seen this one before," Anders said. "It's the exact one from the Port of DeMarus attack."

"Seriously?"

"I could never forget this thing. It's the only one I've ever encountered. They did a damn good job putting it back together.

Marko tore it apart with the Bitch." Anders felt like he was staring at this machine from a great distance, even though he was right in front of it. The memory of ordering Marko to shoot it down before it took out the other ship in the hangar was still fresh in his mind. Something didn't quite add up though. "How and why did this thing end up in the museum so quickly after the attack?"

Not a second after Anders finished the question, someone spoke up beside them. "Because we needed to put it on display quickly."

Anders snapped his head to the left, spying a plump man standing in a narrow doorway. In his awe for the display, Anders hadn't seen the small door in the corner of the room. The man walked out into the exhibit, and Anders saw what appeared to be a laboratory, before the little door closed with a whoosh and vanished seamlessly into the wall again.

"It causes such a stir and raises more money the sooner we display it after an attack. It's only been a few days, and we've already slowed down," the man continued. "Pardon my insensitivity to the attacks, but we need to fund the research we're doing on the machines, so I need to always be selling."

"Research? Sounds like you're creating them to *stir* up some income," Severn said.

"Of course not." The man put out his palms. "No one knows where they're coming from or who's making them, but we sure would like to find out. Wouldn't you agree? So we study them. Quite extensively, I might add."

Convinced, Anders nodded, looking back at the machine. "Probably for the best. But I'd have thought the Galactic Command would be heading up this kind of project."

"Oh, they are. Believe me. They're just using my place to do it. Don't get the wrong idea though." He winked. "I get my piece of it."

"You must be Kopius then," Severn said politely. "Sorry for the accusation."

"I am," he replied with a small bow, extending his hand. "And don't worry about it." He glanced around the room. "Recent history aside, it's a spectacular arrangement, don't you think?"

"I do," Severn said, joining his observation of the exhibit.

"It's funny," Kopius said. "All the technological advancements we've made to date, and we don't even know who's creating the most spectacular one of all. Someone's finally produced machines capable of representing human life down to the smallest detail."

"Funny," Severn replied, "or terrifying?"

Kopius chuckled in agreement. "Yeah, well, true. But it is exciting."

As Anders listened to Kopius and Severn chat, he made his way along the line of machines, examining how each one stepped down in evolution. And then he saw her.

"What the— It can't be!"

The fifth machine from the center startled him into stumbling backward. Unlike the others, it was elegant. Beautiful. Non-utilitarian in every measure. It seemed more like a work of art, and as he gazed upon her face, he suddenly understood why Aura's chest had been rising and falling in the vacuum of space. She hadn't been breathing—she had been mimicking a human breathing pattern. Aura was a machine.

"Severn!" he yelled. "Get over here!"

Severn rushed to Anders, and he directed her attention to the mech that looked like Aura, who stood still, posed in the case as if she were modeling a gown for a photographer. The only difference between the machine in the case and the Aura who'd been tagging along with his crew were some signs of wear and tear in this machine's artificial skin. A few patches of skin on this model looked to have suffered decay, flaking off in bits and pieces.

Severn stared at the machine in awe but didn't say a word. Anders reached for his sleeve to immediately inform the crew, to let Wicked know who Aura really was. Then Kopius joined them, and Anders caught himself. Communicating to his team via his comms would alert the museum curator of some unwelcome behavior. So he didn't say a word. He had to wait, had to play out the rest of his time with Kopius.

"Are you okay?" Kopius asked him.

"Yes, I just..." Anders paused. He didn't know how to explain why he recognized her. Then he eyed the mech next to her. It was about the same size and wearing a helmet, which shocked him almost as much as seeing the Aura mech.

"Have you seen her before? Because if you have, I'd love to talk with you privately. Part of my job here is to speak with the visitors and gain any information I can."

Anders forced away the million thoughts going through his head and focused on keeping his cover. He figured since there were at least two copies of the Aura machine, there might be more. "My crew encountered this one before." Anders glanced down at the plaque at Aura's feet. It gave a date that estimated she was built four years ago. "A few years back," he lied. "It wasn't pleasant." He feigned remorse, attempting to gain sympathy from Kopius.

Kopius asked Anders to tell him more about the encounter, but then Wicked broke radio silence, alerting the team to his own news. *"I have confirmation on the structure,"* Wicked whispered. *"We need to find out the protocol for launching the highest security measure. It's most likely a very big deal, and Kopius might have to be involved."*

Jones acknowledged his message receipt first, with a quick, *"Check, waiting to meet with security management now."*

"Check this, Severn." Anders pointed at the Aura machine. *"The skin. It's a perfect match. Kopius, what do they make the skin from?"* he asked, ignoring Kopius' question but letting the team know they were in contact with their target.

CHAPTER 46

Jones and Marko occupied the only two chairs in the tiny waiting room inside the security offices. Ten minutes ago, they'd been told the security manager would be with them shortly. Jones eyed Marko's bouncing leg and wondered how someone couldn't calm themselves enough to stop shaking. A job like this wasn't for the meek.

"You okay?" Jones finally asked Marko, gesturing at his leg.

Curbing his leg, Marko said, "Yeah, I'm fine. Just don't like waiting."

Jones huffed. "You let yourself get worked up too easily. You sure you're cut out for this crew?"

Marko stared at Jones as if he were considering challenging what had just been implied. "Relax, Jones. I can handle the work. You worry about you."

"I have a whole crew to worry about before myself. And that's what I intend to do. Nothin's gonna get in the way of that. Got it? Nothing."

"What are you trying to say?" Marko said as he stood up to face Jones.

Jones didn't move. He wasn't worried about a physical confrontation with anyone, let alone Marko. Jones knew better than to get tangled in a personal riff while on the job. He only chuckled. "Sit down before you blow a gasket."

"No, I will…"

Marko was cut off by the sound of the door opening. "Gentlemen," a woman said as she stepped through the door. She extended her hand in a greeting to Jones. "I'm Bennie. How can I help you?"

Jones' hand engulfed hers as he accepted the introduction. She was so much smaller than him that he could have grabbed her whole forearm. "I'm Jones, and this is my good friend Marko." He hated saying "good friend." Hated Marko too.

Marko grinned and shook her hand as well. "Nice to meet you, ma'am."

"So, what can I do for you?" She laced her fingers together in front of her silver belt buckle. "I believe Nero told me you were thinking of joining our security team."

"Yes, ma'am," Jones said. "We hear you have a fine operation, and we sure could use the steady work. I think you'll find we're more than qualified."

"Interesting," she said with a smile. "I have no doubt that you are. In fact, I all but expected two very capable people to show up to replace the two officers who unexpectedly quit just yesterday." Bennie glared at Jones with a knowing look.

"Ma'am?" Jones asked.

"You're pretty good," Bennie said, pointing at them both before folding her arms. "I'll give you that. But I've been in this business a long time. Only the crews with half a brain try to turn their job into an inside job."

"Ma'am, it sounds like you're not taking us seri—"

"No!" she said, her sweet tone turning dark. "I'm not taking you seriously because you honestly thought you could disappear two of my best officers, then walk in here and take their jobs."

Jones stared in wonder at Bennie, then looked to the side in thought. It had to have been Marko. He'd somehow relayed a message to his command and had them take out two security personnel to leave vacancies. A stupid move that had now placed the whole team at risk and Wicked even closer to death. If they didn't pull this off, things were going to take a turn for the worse.

"Ma'am, I assure you, we didn't disappear anyone," Jones said. As far as he knew, they hadn't. "My friend and I are just looking for good work, I promise."

"A promise is a cry of desperation when it comes from a stranger's mouth," she said. "Especially when things smell as bad as this."

"If you're not hiring, ma'am—" Jones' voice rose with anger, "then say so. But I won't stand here and have you insult me."

Before he realized what she was doing, Bennie stepped back beyond the door. "I think you should wait here until I get some answers." She slammed the door shut just as Marko lunged at it to try to keep it open. The sharp echo of the door locking pierced deep in Jones' gut. The situation had turned dire before they'd even made a move. This job had failed already, so he grabbed his sleeve to check in with Anders.

"*Bad news, Cap,*" he said while facing Marko. "*Security didn't buy it. Apparently two of their men were taken. The head of security thinks we did it to take their jobs. Looks like they knew we were coming.*"

Anders responded immediately. "*Maddix. I knew she'd screw this thing. Where are you?*"

"*Security offices, first floor right side from the entrance. I thought we were placed in some kind of waiting or meeting room, but it turns out the door locks from the outside. Sorry, Cap, something's going down. You'd better jam while you can.*"

"Negative," Anders said. *"Wick, where are you?"*

"About halfway done," Wicked said. *"Second level almost finished. We're close to the main entrance atrium."*

As Jones stood in the holding room, he heard a soft alarm sound in the hallway. Underneath the door, a reflection of a blue light began to pulsate on and off.

"Cap," Jones said, *"you hear that alarm?"*

"Negative," Anders said.

"Wick? How about you?" Jones asked.

"Negative," he answered.

On the other side of the locked door, Jones heard a rush of footsteps careening passed the door.

"Something's going down here in the security wing. I don't think it's about us. Somethin's got the security all in a riot. Anyone see anything?"

"All seems normal here," said Anders.

"Same here."

Jones turned to Marko to ask what he knew about this, even though it would expose his knowledge of Marko's real role. But before he could get a word out, Bennie barged back into the room with two security officers at her side, and she didn't look happy. Jones clicked on his comms so his team could hear what she had to say. They'd have a better chance of getting out sooner if they had as much information as he could give them.

"What are you two up to?" she yelled as she entered. "I want answers, and I want them now. Who are you? What are you doing here? And what's been delivered to us in the cargo bay?"

Bemused, Jones replied, "Whatever is happening has nothing to do with us. What's in the cargo bay?"

"I don't know, but my team will be telling me soon," she said. "And you're waiting here with me."

With Bennie's pause, Jones closed his comm, allowing his captain to address the new information. Anders took the opportunity and spoke.

"Maddix. She said she was sending something to help move things along. Damn her."

"Must be some kind of distraction," Wick added. *"Cap, are you still by the exhibit?"*

"Check," he replied.

Wicked continued. *"You should stay with Kopius then. Jones has the key to setting off the separation protocol right in front of him. It's Bennie—she can do it. The protocol will take several minutes from start to finish, and he'll be able to set it off before heading back to the ship. Aura and I can be at the ship before it even starts."*

"No. Too many things can go wrong. We can't risk it," Anders said.

Jones made a decision in that moment. He glared at Marko, as if to instruct the man to set aside their differences, for the time being at least, and to remind himself he needed to work with Marko just long enough to save a fellow crew member.

Marko nodded with understanding.

Then Jones raised his hand to his mouth and clicked his comm one last time while staring into Bennie's eyes. *"Captain, we're taking the head of security. She's going to set off the protocol, or she's going to die."*

In the same instant, Marko lunged at one of the guards who stood with Bennie. Jones followed his lead in the blink of an eye, subduing the other guard with a swift right cross and leaving Bennie without protection.

"Sorry, Bennie," Jones said with a hint of an apology on his breath. "We aren't the ones attacking you, but you're going to have to do something for us anyway."

CHAPTER 47

Though they no longer needed to map the museum, Wick struggled with leaving the last room on the second level incomplete. Knowing Jones, he'd wait for them if they were late getting back, but that could put the team in jeopardy. He'd caused enough trouble for his family as it was, so he was eager to help make things go smoothly moving forward.

"C'mon, Aura," he said, grasping her hand. "It won't take Jones long to set off the security protocol on this place. We should get back."

"I think the quickest way is through here." She pointed to the front of the museum. "We can take the front atrium stairs down and head to the rear docking bay. There isn't access to it from the other levels."

"That checks out," Wicked said, impressed with her instincts.

They quickly shuffled onto the wide stairs that curved down from the second level to the front entrance. The museum visitors appeared unaffected, but the security personnel obviously had something going on. Several of them were storming out from the back area where Jones and Marko had headed when they arrived.

From his vantage point on the stairs, Wicked watched the security guards abruptly change from an all-out sprint to a swift jog when they entered the public area of the front entrance, being careful not to alarm the visitors.

"Something definitely has these guys spooked," he said to Aura.

Before Aura could reply, there was a loud crash and then *TAT TAT TAT.* Several sharp pops echoed from the hallway below, exactly where they'd intended to go. Wicked grabbed Aura and brought her down to a crouch on the stairs as he saw several bullets pierce the front wall. The crowd in the area erupted into a panic, running away from the commotion in the hallway.

Wick had no intention of jumping into the riot below. Instead, he chose to wait and see where the problem was going to head before he made a move. He wanted nothing more than to get Aura back to the ship in one piece.

As he peered through the railing balusters, he caught a glimpse of the shooter. It was shaped like a person, but he could only see the back of its head. It had long blond hair streaming down its backless dress, and it advanced forward in an elegant stride. If it weren't for all the recent attacks by machines, Wick wouldn't have noticed the jerky mechanical movements in its walk.

"Stay calm and move slowly," he whispered to Aura as he pulled her backward up the stairs.

Aura looked up at him with a fear he'd never seen before. Her eyes moistened as tears began to build. While focused on Aura, he noticed the machine down below turn and make its way into the first room they'd mapped. But as it stood sideways in front of the stairs, it paused...

In a flash, it spun around to attack personnel coming at it from behind, its hair wrapping around its head. *TAT TAT TAT. TAT TAT TAT.* Repeatedly, it shot three concise shots. Security guards fell one after another, grabbing for injured arms and legs. As best he could tell, there were no fatal wounds.

Aura was still trembling, and all he could do was hold her. "It's okay, baby. I'm here," he said over and over. After the last of the guards went down, Wick lifted his head to look at the machine, who was now taking its first step up the stairs toward them. But Aura reached up and grabbed the back of his neck and pulled his head back down before he eyed the machine.

Wick looked into her eyes, which were now full of tears, and they cast an altered gaze back at him. Different than all those moments they'd shared together on the ship. Different than the longing love that had been growing for him. Now there was something *more* there, and it seemed to wrap all the love she had for him inside a knowing layer of truth.

"I remember everything, Wick," she said, smiling. "Please, remember that I love you."

The machine took another step, drawing Wick's attention from Aura. In that moment, all the mystery surrounding Aura imploded inside Wick's chest, crushing his heart. Aura, the woman he loved, lay in his arms, yet at the same time, she was walking up the steps in the form of a machine that seemed heavily bent on destruction. Aura was a machine, a copy of who knows how many. One of her lay in his arms seemingly in love with him and another was coming up the steps after them.

"Wick, I'm sorry," she whimpered again. He looked away from her. "Don't." She pleaded. "Please don't be frightened. I can explain everything. Just come with me. We have to get out of here."

CHAPTER 48

Aura realized her worst fear as she saw Wicked's love for her bleed from his face. His mouth shimmered in search of words that never came. It looked as if there were a million thoughts processing to an inevitable end. Disbelief, remorse, pain—all wrapped up inside a look of pure betrayal, crushing the hope she held for them.

And just when she thought it couldn't get any worse, he murmured something she couldn't understand, and before she could speak, he slid her off his lap and scrambled away.

Watching him scurry away and knowing the mind of these machines, Aura understood they were both in danger. She immediately stood to draw the mech's attention to her, but it was too late. The Aura mech homed in on the figure rushing away: Wick.

Aura yelled, fearing for his life. Wicked turned to her, shock still painted on his face, clearly unable to realize the reflex to take cover. If he could've, he would have kept running or dove out of the way. But he was too confused, too scared, too hurt. She saw it in the posture he held. She wanted to protect him.

But the machine took its shots. *TAT TAT TAT.*

The first bullet nailed the right side of his chest and spun him sideways. The other two missed.

Aura, filled with primal urges, lunged at the machine. They both tumbled down the stairs. By the time they hit the floor below, Aura had ripped out the machine's throat. Blood and flesh tore from the steel skeleton, and Aura held in her hand the core wiring that connected the brain to the body through the throat structure. Life emanated from the eyes of the downed machine for a second more, but then it faded. Aura moved to dart up the stairs but stumbled on the first step she took; a sharp pain radiated from her thigh. Fearing more for Wick than her injured thigh, she muscled her way back up the stairs to him. He lay there bleeding and barely conscious.

"Captain Anders!" Aura shouted into her comm as she lifted Wick to his feet. Together, but mostly with Aura's efforts, they hobbled down the stairs and stepped over the machine lying on the floor, a pool of blood beneath the thing. With much effort, Aura shuffled their way down the center corridor. She winced at every step she took with her right leg, so she switched Wick to that side and used what little energy he had as a kind of crutch. The support he offered was little, but she used the help the best she could. Her leg was usable, but her knee wouldn't extend all the way, like a tendon or something inside her leg was caught.

More shots rang out from behind them and around the corner. *TAT TAT TAT. TAT TAT TAT.* The sharpness of the shots and the frantic screams sent jolts of adrenaline coursing through her veins. She bent her will to making sure she returned Wick to the ship quickly. Nothing would stop her.

"C'mon, Wick," she whispered to him. "Stay with me. I need you with me. We gotta get outta here."

"Captain Anders," she called out again, clasping the comm button in her sleeve.

"Check," Anders replied.

"*It's Wicked,*" she said, panting as she helped him along.

"*What happened?*" Anders said.

"*He's been shot,*" Aura said. "*In the chest. I'm taking him back to the ship now.*"

CHAPTER 49

At the main exhibit, Kopius, Anders, and Severn heard the faint shots fired only two levels below. Kopius' eyes went wide with fear as he inched away from Anders, who had been speaking on his comm. Anders knew that no matter what he said or did from now on, he'd be tied to whatever was going on down there. He had no choice but to go through with the orders Maddix had given him.

"Grab him," Anders said to Severn. Then he clicked his comm. *"Check, team. Listen up. Wicked's been shot and is on his way home. Looks like Maddix lit a fire downstairs, so we're taking the only shot we got to get this done. Jones, you hold the key. Make sure you set off the protocol. I'll lock down the prize. You'd better come get us. You hear me?"*

Jones replied immediately, *"Check that, I'll get it done!"*

Anders turned to Severn, who now had Kopius on the floor with his hands bound behind his back with plastic zip ties.

"Awfully convenient to have those with you," he said as he checked the hallway leading to the only public entrance to the main exhibit room. People were already flooding up the stairs, trying to get away from the commotion down below. "We need to block this room off."

"Kopius, is there a way to close this room?" Severn asked, jolting his shoulder.

"I'm not helping you monsters," he spat.

"Tell me now, or I'll make sure you sail out in the cold and black tonight," Anders threatened.

"No, you won't," Kopius said. "Let me guess, you're working for Maddix, and she wants me and all these mechs." He paused, glancing up at them the best he could from his facedown position. Anders and Severn said nothing. "Man, you guys are in deep, and you don't even know what you're into. She's been after me for a long time, and once she has what she wants, you're dead. It's how she works. I won't help you." He flopped his head down on the floor and ignored them.

"Anders, people are starting to fill the hallways," Severn said. "We need to close this room off, or we're taking people with us."

Anders looked around for some kind of emergency switch to shut the room down but saw nothing. Only the security cases holding a bunch of mechs.

Of course, Anders thought. He walked over to where the Aura mech stood inside the case. "The glass." Anders grinned as he placed his hand on the case. "Security measures will protect the room."

"That's how I'd design it," Severn said as she grabbed a nearby stanchion holding a single plush divider ribbon and handed it to Anders. "The honor is all yours."

"With pleasure." Anders grabbed hold of the steel bar. He swung hard, letting the large base of the stanchion hit first. The look on Kopius' face was nothing short of surprise as the tough glass shattered at Anders' first attempt.

Lights flashed inside the room, and within a second, a steel door secured the opening from the side, locking the three of them inside.

Anders clicked his comm to inform the team. *"Target secure and we're committed. Jones, it's up to you to finish this."*

CHAPTER 50

"*Check*," Jones said into his comm as he sat Bennie down in a chair in the command center. Jones showed no surprise when Marko took immediate control of the room and the four people who ran it. They weren't security personnel hired to physically handle the public; these people ran the tech behind the security.

"Okay, Bennie. You're up," Jones said calmly. "Separation protocol, now."

"No!" Bennie said, resolutely. "I will not help you."

"Yes, you will. I don't have a lot of time, so we're going to have to do this quickly, and you need to learn that we're not muckin' about. Marko, kill someone."

Marko swiftly picked up the youngest-looking tech personnel and walked him out the door. A moment later, a single shot was heard, followed by a dull thud. Marko returned, wiping his face with his sleeve, and then grabbed the next person by the shoulder, waiting for more instructions from Jones.

"Separation protocol," he said in a deeper voice. "Now."

This time Bennie said nothing. She only whimpered and struggled to hold back the torrent of cries working hard to escape.

"Kill another one," Jones said, looking at Marko.

"Wait!" Bennie said. "Don't hurt anyone else."

"Then get on with it," Marko said, lifting the next person to his feet.

Bennie reached for the keyboard and began typing. Jones watched the screen, and the best he could tell by the commands, Bennie was enacting the separation protocol.

"Initiating protocol now," Jones alerted the team. *"Shouldn't be much longer."*

TAT TAT TAT.

Marko jumped and then ran to the glass door to gauge where the shots had been fired. As he glanced out the door, trying to acquire the best view, he said, "I see it. Another skinned one. Man, they're looking good. I can't see the face, but I can tell this one's built for...Oh damn!"

"What is it? Is it coming this way?" Jones asked.

"No." Marko shook his head and slipped behind the wall.

"Then what is it?" Jones asked.

"Nothing. I...I've seen this one before."

"Really?" Jones said, starting to walk over.

Marko put up his hand to stop him. "No, don't. Keep her on that. How much longer, Bennie?"

"Rooms are beginning to close down at the top levels. Once all rooms shut down, they'll start separating from the top level first." She hit one last key and scooted her chair away from the console.

"What else do you need to do down here to complete the protocol?" Jones asked.

"Nothing. That's it."

"Tell me the truth," Jones said, towering over her, using every ounce of threat he had in his bones.

"I am," she said with a shudder.

"She's lying. Kill another one!" Jones swung his arm at another tech agent cowering in the corner.

Marko made a move toward her.

"No!" Bennie screamed. "That's it. I swear."

Jones paused for a moment, judging her face as she sobbed. "Fine," he said. "Everyone up. Line up at the door." He walked over to a cabinet that he'd spotted when he first walked in. *Security Only*, it read, and he thought it was the best place to look for something to bind the detainees. But when he turned around, he found Marko had already bound all four of them with plastic zip ties he'd pulled from his vest.

"Well, that's mighty convenient," Jones said. "When were you planning on letting me know you had those?"

"I thought now was a good time." Marko smiled, opened the door, and motioned to Bennie. "You first. Go around that corner." He pointed to the right hallway that wound deeper into the museum, away from all the shots and screaming in the public area. As Jones followed behind everyone, he glanced the other way and spotted the machine that had all the security personnel busy at the moment.

He stopped short and nearly tripped over his own feet when he saw the mech engaged with security. "Aura?" he said to himself.

His sense of urgency to get back to the ship faded as he watched the Aura mech. She methodically peered from around a corner to take sniper-like shots at the most exposed security personnel. Some were hit, while others dodged in time, but none of them were killed. Of the few hits Jones saw, there were only two shoulder wounds and a leg shot. By all accounts, it was a perfect distraction for his crew to finish their job.

"Jones!" Marko shouted from around the corner.

"Yeah, I'm coming," he replied. Then he opened his comms. *"Check, check. Protocol launched. Heading for the ship now. Rooms are shutting down. Wick, is Aura with you? She has some explainin' to do when we get outta here."*

"Check that, she's with me," Wick mumbled, clearly in pain.

"Check, we'll be waiting here," Anders said. *"And I think a lot of us have some explaining to do when we get outta here."*

"Check that," Jones said, rushing around the corner. *"And I'm gonna need a whiskey."*

All said, *"Check,"* at once.

Jones joined Marko where he saw Bennie crying over the first tech personnel Marko had taken out of the room. The man was alive but gagged, with his hands and feet bound. Jones walked up to Bennie and picked her up. "It's just as effective if you make someone *believe* you're a killer. But killin' just ain't my style, babe." He winked at her, picked the man up, and threw him over his shoulder. "Marko, take up the rear. Everyone else, follow me."

CHAPTER 51

Aura and Wick were the first ones back to the ship. She closed the cargo door behind them, thinking it was better to make Jones open it again than to have unwanted company rush in with all the commotion.

The distant *TAT TAT TAT's* were getting steadily closer, but Aura couldn't worry about that now. Wicked was still alive but unconscious at this point, and their movements had slowed. She'd take one step with her healthy leg and then prop her other leg and Wick forward as she skipped ahead. By her estimation, Aura figured he'd lost more than a pint of blood, and his body was already shutting down to conserve energy.

"C'mon, Wick. Stay with me, baby," she whispered as she decided it might be best to drag him inside the ship. This turned out to be much quicker, and she was able to grab a nearby toolbox on the way. He left a trail of blood all the way to the sick bay, and once she hefted him up onto the surgeon's bed, she went to work on him.

"Okay, first things first," she said to herself, remembering her medical training uploads. "Get the clothes off and clean the wound."

Aura limped around the bed while she cut off his shirt and poured half a bottle of alcohol over the hole in his chest.

"Damn, baby," she said, holding back sobs. "This is bad."

The gaping hole was left of center, just far enough away from his neck and heart. "Okay, focus," she whispered. "Just get in there and repair it. Just like a thingamabob in the engine room."

And she began to hum. All things made sense to her when she hummed to herself while working. It calmed her and helped her focus.

She dug into the hole in Wick's chest with her finger to test its depth. It wasn't big enough to work inside, but it was deep, so the first thing she did was make a vertical cut five centimeters above and below the hole and spread the flesh apart.

Inside the wound, she saw torn muscle tissue but no bullet. She needed to dig deeper. A cut here and a snip there, and she had an opening as long as her hand, maybe nine centimeters wide, giving her access to his ribcage. From there, she popped four spring pins and swung open four titanium ribs, giving her access to the bullet buried deep in his chest cavity.

She eyed Wick's heart as it beat steadily in its cradle, pumping blood into his chest cavity. "Seems like it should be weird, but it's not." She spoke to him softly while she dug out the bullet. She eyed it closely and then tossed it behind her. A dull snap lingered in the air as the tiny piece of metal bounced on the floor. "I know we love each other. I can feel it. It's real, I know it. I don't care that we're all metal and plastic and organic tissue. They said we wouldn't be able to love, but they were wrong. I love you, so don't even think about shutting down on me."

A tear, clear as rain, squeezed out of her blinking eye. As small as it was, it splashed a smidgen of redness from a bleeding vein, where Aura noticed a small cut. Pulsating blood weakly pumped from within, so she patched the hole, along with a few others around the cavity, using a patch kit designed for repairing high-density engine hosing.

When she saw no other damage that required mending, she began removing the tools she'd used to work on him. A clamp here, releasing flow back into his heart. Reattaching a pin there, where she pushed a rib back into place. And then she replaced the many screws she'd loosened to gain the access she needed to retrieve the bullet.

To the best of her ability, Wick's internal body lay there intact.

The last thing she needed to do was the one thing for which she had no proper tool, though she did consider the roll of duct tape sitting atop the tool chest. But the long gash on his chest deserved better. After scavenging the entire sick bay for what seemed an eternity, a suture kit surfaced.

When she finished, Aura stepped back, knowing there was nothing else to do but wait for him to wake. That's when her feelings for him grew even stronger. The threat of losing him gave her an experience she'd never before encountered—the human experience of realizing how much love you have for someone, only revealed through the lens of having nearly lost them.

And so Aura wept for the man she loved.

CHAPTER 52

Jones led Marko, Bennie, and the other four security staff through the corridors that wove deeper into the non-public areas behind the security offices. From the museum maps Wick had showed him, he knew those hallways led to the docking area, and with all the commotion up front provided by the mechs, he figured there'd be little to no resistance from armed security personnel on the way.

What he hadn't considered stepped out in front of him from a hallway hidden from his perspective: Aura. And she looked bent on mowing them all down with whatever was about to fire from her arm.

Instinctively, Jones dropped to his knees and slid to a stop on the floor. The man he carried bounced off the wall before tumbling to the floor. Though her face and body were that of Aura, the sweet girl he'd been crewing with over the last several days was not behind these eyes. These seemed to speak of death and destruction. And there lay the only reason Jones didn't hesitate. He fired two shots before Marko began shooting from behind the security staff who'd already taken to the floor for cover.

Jones' first shot landed square in this Aura's head. The second one missed, and the others from Marko hit her neck and shoulders, which effectively rendered her inactive. Her head collapsed onto her neck. Her arms dropped to her sides, and her torso shifted down at an angle as if to settle into a resting position.

On his knees, Jones admired the machine. Her beauty and elegance was only matched by her will to destroy, and he suddenly realized that a replica, probably as destructive as this one, was with his friend and crewmate, Wick. And they were headed to the ship.

Not wanting to place Bennie and her officers in any more danger, he ordered Marko to usher them into what seemed to be a maintenance closet.

"Tie them to something," he said, making sure Bennie couldn't escape in time to make an attempt at shutting down the separation protocol. Though he had no information about if that were possible, his opting to solidify the success of the mission was part of his nature.

After ridding themselves of the security personnel, Jones and Marko hustled through the hallways toward the docking bays. When they arrived at the ship, Jones opened the ramp and, knowing Wick was injured, redoubled his efforts to get to him in spite of his exhaustion. He was strong, but there was a cost to being that large.

At the sick bay door, the sight of Wick lying there unconscious, surrounded by blood and bloodied tools, sent shivers through him. Fighting his emotions and resisting his urge to drop Aura right there, he approached Wick. With his chest rising and falling to the rhythm of his breaths, Wick seemed peacefully asleep. Jones placed his hand on Wick's forehead and looked to Aura, who stood silently several steps away.

"He'll be okay," she assured him, wiping her tears with her blood-soaked shirtsleeve.

"He'd better be," Jones said, stepping around the bed toward her.

She feared him; the look on her face said it all. "Jones, there are things I have remembered, and I'm sure you have a lot of questions."

"Oh, you're quite right. Starting with who the hell you are, and why I shouldn't kick you off this ship right now."

He stepped closer.

Aura put her hands up in front of her as she stepped backward, favoring her injured leg. "We don't have enough time right now to get into who I am, but you shouldn't kick me off the ship because I love him." She reached for Wick. "I want nothing but good for him, and I'll do whatever it takes to get us there, but we need to get moving now to retrieve Severn and the captain."

Jones glanced at her leg and decided her threat level wasn't alarming enough to spend time getting answers from her. The mention of Anders rekindled his desire to finish the mission. The fact that the captain was alone with Severn, another deceiver, lit the fire in his eyes to get it done.

"Marko," Jones said, changing focus, "ever use a retrieval system on a ship like this before?"

"Something like it. I'm sure I can figure it out," Marko replied.

A groan came from the surgeon's bed. Then, "I can help him."

Shocked, Jones turned to see Wick already getting out of the bed. He slowly swung his right arm around, stretching out his chest. Jones was about to tell him to lie back down when Wick said, "I'm good, Jones. I can help." He blinked and shook his head. "Just keep her away from me." He pointed at Aura without looking at her.

With a plethora of questions about Wick's astounding health, Jones accepted that the bullet wound must have been minor and that Wick was as tough as nails. Knowing there was no more time to waste, Jones replied, "Fine. Get to the cargo hold and be ready. Aura, you're with me." He pointed at her. "You don't leave my sight, got it?"

"Check," she said sweetly.

Jones ignored her attempt at gaining his favor. "Let's go. We're sailing in three minutes."

Wick and Marko immediately left the sick bay and headed aft. Jones made sure Aura walked in front of him as they made their way to the cockpit. He'd hoped to get there quicker, but she favored her leg, which slowed their pace.

"Hurry up," he spat.

She doubled her efforts by hopping twice on her good leg to help relieve the weight placed on the other. "I'm trying. Somethin's broke in my leg."

"Try harder," he said but then curbed his annoyance with Aura's pained walk. His time was better spent thinking through his preflight checklist. There wasn't much he'd have to do, he realized. Knowing Anders, the ship would be ready to take off in mere seconds.

When they reached the cockpit, Jones ordered, "Sit there, where I can see you," pointing at his own chair. Jones took the captain's chair, refusing to let anyone other than Anders or himself occupy the hot seat. "Pull the shoulder straps on and grab them with your arms crossed, and don't move from there until I tell you otherwise."

"Yes, sir," she said, less sweet this time.

As with all their jobs, Anders had left the ship in a state of hibernation to provide a startup that would have them flying in a few short minutes. After a callout on the comms and a fast reply from Wick stating their readiness, Jones lifted the ship from its perch and bullied his way out of the airbreak. Normally, he'd have followed typical flight pattern protocol and organized his takeoff with control to place himself safely in line. But not this time. Jones needed to put his ship on a course that would intercept Anders and one of the most valuable exhibits in the museum.

Jones cut off two ships and nearly clipped another with his port side before he passed through the airbreak, entering space. With all the commotion in the hangar and getting the ship in the air, Jones had forgotten two things. In an effort to keep Aura restrained, he hadn't strapped himself onto the captain's chair, and he missed activating the ship's artificial gravity before breaking from the museum's artificial gravitational pull.

Aura caught the mistake the moment Jones' body began to awkwardly float. She toggled the appropriate switches, and Jones settled nicely into his seat before losing any control of the ship. Though she did help, she'd disobeyed a direct order from the acting captain, and Jones couldn't let that slide.

"Do not move," he commanded. "Do not touch anything, or I will put you out in the cold and black."

"Yes, sir," she said meekly.

CHAPTER 53

Jones analyzed the growing field of self-contained boxes scattered beyond the viewport. Each one of the museum exhibit rooms separated from the structure like a water droplet from a fountain. Except their paths didn't arc like a fountain stream would—they drifted straight in all different directions. Then the unexpected happened. Each container, originally white like the museum's interior, turned as dark as night. And with deep space as the background, they all seemed to vanish.

"Damn," Jones whispered. The closer they drew, the more difficult it became to spot the containers.

"We'll find them," Aura reassured.

Jones' lips thinned as if he were worried. He knew he'd find them; he was just pissed it would take longer than he wanted. *"Captain, you read me?"* Jones asked after flipping the all-comms.

A moment later, Anders' voice crackled through the cockpit speakers above Jones' head. *"Ch-ck."*

"I got a visual on all the rooms, but they're going dark," Jones said. *"Turn on your beacon. Need to lock in on ya."*

"Done. How's Wick?"

Staring at the radar screen on the center console, Jones spotted the pulsating green blip.

"*He's good. Apparently the bullet didn't do much damage. He's in the cargo bay with Marko getting prepped.*"

"*Check.*"

"*We're on our way, Cap,*" Jones said as he targeted his mark. A red circle engulfed a long rectangular container far in the distance, up and to the left of the center viewport. Jones then hit the comm for the loudspeaker in the cargo bay.

"*Hold on, kids. Got a lock on the captain. Gonna jam in three, two, one.*"

CHAPTER 54

Knowing what Jones meant, Wicked held fast to the nearest hold
bar. But before he had a chance to alert Marko of the urgency,
the man fell to his butt and skidded all the way along the cargo bay floor until he slammed into the rear hatch door. Marko
spent thirty seconds pinned to the wall, while Wicked reaped
the benefits of having latched his harness to the grappling system's stanchion. He hung in the air while inertia treated him
like a kite held in place by its taut string.

Wick laughed while Marko grunted and fought to unfold
himself from the steel door. When the ship's acceleration eased,
Wick and Marko fell back to the floor.

"What the hell is that maniac doing up there?" Marko
shouted as he brought himself to his feet.

"Oh, relax. He's just letting off a little steam. You'll learn his
tricks soon enough."

"I won't be with you long enough," Marko said under his
breath, wiping dust off his clothes.

Wicked heard what Marko said, but he didn't understand the
meaning. "What do you mean?"

"Never mind," Marko replied, clearly not meaning for
Wicked to have heard him.

Wick let it pass. "C'mon, let's get set up."

CHAPTER 55

With his field of vision growing ever more cluttered with rooms of the museum exhibits, Jones focused his efforts on avoiding collisions. But missing one container, without fail, placed him on a direct course with another. His only aid in navigating the minefield of containers was the forward spotlights, which afforded him only a thin field of sight; this kept him from increasing his speed without adding too much risk.

As if the danger of crashing into one of the exhibits wasn't enough, a burst of light flashed at the top of his field of vision. The bottom side of one of the exhibits, the highest one from his perspective, ignited with a set of thrusters, launching it into a high-speed trajectory.

"Whoa," Aura said, leaning forward for a better look at the room turned spaceship.

Jones' neck snapped to the left as another flash ignited, this one above a nearby container.

"Damn, they're taking off!" Jones said to Aura, forgetting he meant to treat her not as a crewmate. He clicked the all-comms again. *"Cap, we got a problem."*

"What is it?" Anders replied, his voice clearer now that Jones had closed the distance between them.

"The room containers have a thrust system. Looks like when they're clear of each other, a booster system launches them into a flight path."

Anders paused for a moment. *"Are there any around us?"*

"Kind of. Maybe," he said, leaning side to side, attempting to gain a perspective on Anders' position. *"There are a couple by you, but I can't gauge whether your path is clear. When it is though, I'm sure it'll be your turn."*

"Get above him, Jones, fast," Wick said through the comms. *"There's gotta be some kind of collision safety protocol. If you place our ship in front of the topside of his container, the thrusters won't kick in. Then we'll have all the time we need to get them out."*

Before Wicked finished his suggestion, Jones understood his plan. It was a bit riskier, but he needed to move faster. He increased his speed another fifty percent, foregoing the care he piloted with earlier.

CHAPTER 56

"Kopius, what's the protocol here? Where do the room navigation systems take the exhibits?" Anders knelt by the facedown prisoner.

Kopius smirked and turned his head the other way, ignoring Anders' question.

"He won't answer, Anders." Severn walked away from them, eying the floor.

Anders noticed her exaggerated attention on the floor and joined in her curiosity. The floor was made of large three-foot-square tiles that looked more like panels. An aluminum or steel grid formed joints between each one, with a seemingly nonexistent seam running down the middle.

"Look for the one that's different from the others," Anders said.

"Or the one that's scuffed up from being opened too many times." Severn used the toe of her boot to tap on the corner panel of the room.

Anders hustled over and knelt next to Severn as she rubbed a damaged corner with her fingertips, showing Anders a possible access point.

"Grab the stanchion," he said, pointing to the one lying on the floor, the one he'd used to break the glass encasement to set off the room's security system. She went for it as he jumped inside the broken encasement and dragged out the mech they shot down in Port of DeMarus.

With the help of Severn's leverage, Anders pried a thin piece of metal the length of his own forearm from the mech's chest cavity. He placed it at the scuff marks in the seam of the panel and held it vertical.

"Slam the stanchion down on it," he said, positioning the rest of his body out of the way.

Severn jumped to and grabbed the stanchion, placed her feet for balance, and swung down with the base of the stanchion. A sharp thwack and the piece of metal slipped into the seam with a thud.

"Good." Anders said and pulled the piece of metal toward himself, prying up the panel. Severn dug her fingers in and lifted. Once halfway open, Anders lent his support, and they both methodically lifted the panel up and out of the way.

Anders popped his head inside and saw nothing but a poorly stored tarp that blocked his view. He pulled the tarp out of the access area, which turned out to be three tarps, and threw them behind him by the broken encasement. With the entrance cleared, he saw all the way to the other side of the room by way of the crawl space.

"You were hoping to find the manual override to the thruster system," Anders said to Severn as he sat up.

"There's gotta be a way." She shrugged.

"You can't. There's no access to it from inside the live environment," Kopius shouted from the other side of the room.

Anders half turned his head to listen but then eyed Severn. "Well, better hop to it then." With Kopius saying there was no access to the system in the crawl space, he was positive there was. "It'll probably be a manual shutdown lever of some kind."

"Check," Severn said as she ducked inside.

CHAPTER 57

"Hurry up, Jones," Aura said while squirming on the edge of her seat. With containers igniting all over, Aura was beginning to think Jones wasn't going to make it to Anders in time.

"How much longer?" Anders asked.

Aura watched Jones eye the console gauges and the distance to target on the viewport screen. *"Maybe ninety seconds,"* he said.

Anders left his comm open. *"Get a move on, Severn. Jones ain't gonna make it."* Aura admired Anders' clever way of motivating Jones. Maybe that was just how they worked. No softening the truth, no decisions made from hopeful thinking.

Aura wanted to be a part of this crew. She wanted to have a normal life with them, and she wanted Wick to feel the same about her. The only way she knew how to make that happen was to get involved, help the team, gain their favor, and be there for Wick.

She focused on the captain's container. The long rectangular box hung in space, dark and silent. Around it, she saw two others. One square and to the right of it and the other one also square but twice as big.

"That one," she said, pointing. "It's keeping the captain's from taking off. As long as..." Aura's words escaped her the moment its thrusters ignited. Of course they did. There were no other exhibit containers above it. As soon as the space in front of a container was empty, the system ignited. It had been designed this way specifically to complicate theft.

"C'mon, Jones, you can do it," she said with an encouraging voice. "Get there."

As Jones increased his speed toward Anders and Severn, the space above their container became more and more open.

"How much time?" Aura asked, slightly in a panic.

"Thirty seconds," Jones said. "C'mon, hold on Cap. Not yet, not yet."

The silence in the cockpit commanded all focus on the target. Their breath seemed to stand still along with time, until they heard a sudden, muffled crack.

Aura jumped in her seat and let out a short squeal. But she didn't see thrusters ignite as she expected. The sound she heard couldn't have been what she feared.

"What was that?" she asked.

Jones leaned forward and looked up. Another muffled crack.

"Is that coming from above us?" she asked.

"I think so," he said, still looking.

A third muffled crack. This time Aura saw what it was. An orange light soared above them, straight toward Anders' container.

"A tracer round," Jones said.

"What's a tracer round?" Aura asked, fearing what she assumed it to be.

Jones ignored her question and reached for the comms. He only flipped the one labeled *the Bitch*. The original label had been torn off and relabeled with permanent marker.

"Marko, what the hell are you doing?" Jones said.

"Wick said it himself," Marko replied in a lighthearted tone. "If something's above the container, the thrusters won't kick on.

I just hope the navigation system can pick up on the Bitch's bullets passing overhead."

Jones looked at Aura in disbelief.

She thought about it for a second, then said, "Could help. Can't hurt." She shrugged. "As long as he doesn't hit the captain."

CHAPTER 58

"I think I found it, Cap," Severn shouted back through the tunnel.

"What's it look like?" Anders yelled.

"A single red lever. There's a display bar to the right. Four red bars lit up, four yellow bars lit up, and then three of four available green bars lit up. By the looks of it, I think it's about to ignite the thrusters. But I can't tell. Something's weird about it."

"What's the weird part?"

"Not sure what it means, but the fourth green bar keeps lighting up, then going dark a moment later."

"That means we're out of time," Anders shouted. "The lever, is it a shutdown lever, a manual override?"

"I can't tell," she said. "It's not labeled."

"Pull it!" Anders commanded.

Severn grabbed it with the full intention of pulling it, but paused with a thought. "What if it overrides the navigation system and ignites the thrusters?"

"What the hell?" Anders shouted. "Why would it?"

"I don't know, in case of an emergency situation where you need to go despite an overly conservative navigation system?"

"Seriously? You better pull that thing now!" Anders said, climbing into the tunnel.

Severn saw Anders coming and decided to pull. Just as she applied her pressure—

"*Stop!*" Jones' voice screeched in her earpiece. "*We're here. We're right above you. Don't pull it, Severn.*"

Severn released the lever with a sigh, her clammy hands sticking to its red rubber handle. She turned to crawl out and saw the disappointed look on Anders' face staring back at her. Though she felt the reason for staying her hand was legitimate, she'd disobeyed an order regardless, and that didn't sit right with her. Obviously, it didn't sit right with him either.

He wasn't her *real* captain—this was just another mission— but seeing his disappointment still stung. She could no longer deny her feelings for him. The kiss earlier in the museum, for her, had been real. And so was her desire to do it again.

CHAPTER 59

Setting the grappling system on Anders' container took less time than for Wick and Marko to don their spacesuits. The container they'd be piercing to free Anders and remove the mechs was a self-contained, space-ready element. However, this element was too large to pull into the cargo hold, so their only way in was through the shell.

After decompressing the cargo hold, Wicked opened the floor, exposing Anders' container secured tightly below. He rapped on it twice with his wrench, and a few moments later, two muffled taps rang back, communicating Anders' understanding.

"We'll have to move fast," Wick said as he used the crane to pluck a huge, square steel device out of a crate. It was about a half meter thick, the same shape as the cargo floor opening, but a bit smaller on the sides. Inside were pulleys, levers, wires, and tubes tracing all around its edge. At the center, a large rim formed an opening.

"I take it you designed this?" Marko asked, helping guide the thing into the floor's opened hatch where it fit snuggly inside.

"I did," Wick said proudly as he pressed a button. The thing hissed and sprung loose, snapping tightly to the edge of the opening, filling every gap, even the corners. "Here, help me with this." He reached inside the crate. Together, they pulled out a huge, square steel plate with a large center hole and laid it over the contraption already in place. Wick handed Marko a power drill, plus a dozen bolts, and simply pointed at the holes in the plate. Marko went to work.

Moments later, Wick rolled a steel drum over the opening, just as Marko finished installing the last bolt, effectively locking the plate in place. "Did you get them all?" Wick asked.

"Yes."

"Well, are they tight?" he asked diligently.

Marko looked at him like it wasn't hard to install bolts. "Uh…"

"Cuz if they're not, we all die!"

Marko eyed the installed bolts with a pause. "I'll check 'em"

"Good idea," Wick snapped, then turned away and heard Jones over the comms.

CHAPTER 60

"We got company," Jones said, holding the comm receiver to his mouth and looking at Aura. She wasn't looking back at him; she couldn't. Her eyes were pinned to what was suspended in space before them.

"Who?" Anders asked.

"Looks like museum security. I'm staring at four ships through the viewport right now."

Aura finally broke free of her fright, now with an air of determination. *"Jones, what do you need me to do?"* She unbuckled and stood up on her good leg, as if she were ready to hobble up to the Bitch and do something nasty.

"Nothing but sit tight," he said. Back on the comm, *"Wicked, where you at?"*

"Just about to breach the container," he replied.

"They're pinging me," Jones said, *"I'll patch the team in, but let me do the talking."*

Jones toggled the right combination of controls to place the call on all-comms but only for his comm to send back.

"Hello?" he said calmly, as if he had no idea who was pinging his ship.

A scratchy-pitched male voice replied, *"You're outnumbered, outgunned, and there's no way you're leaving here with that container.*

Give up, and we'll take death off the list of punishments pursued when this goes to Galactic Command."

"*Lot a words, man,*" Jones replied. "*And I'm afraid I have no idea what you're talking about. I'm just a hermit stranded on Esandrea with nothing but this here radio and a lot of time.*"

"*Very funny,*" the voice called back. "*You would do well to cooperate sooner rather than later.*"

Aura got up to leave. Jones clicked off the comms. "Sit. Down," he said sternly, staring at the console instead of her. She sat. Back on his comms, Jones replied with, "*I'm already well, and as I said, time is all I have, so sooner or later don't much matter to me.*"

Switching to his crew's comms only, he said, "*I can only stall for so long. We need to get this done quick.*"

"*We got twenty mechs down here,*" Anders said. "*Maybe two at a time will fit through to the cargo hold.*"

"*Twenty minutes,*" Wick said hurriedly.

"*That's a long stall,*" Jones said. "*Besides, there's four of them, in cruisers. We can't outrun them.*"

"*Once we get Kopius on board, we'll have a bargaining chip,*" Marko added.

"*One thing at a time,*" Anders ordered. "*Get us on board, and we'll go from there.*"

Aura got up again, and Jones grabbed her by the arm and sat her back down.

"*Check, going back on comms with security,*" Jones said.

A quick pause. "*Okay,*" Jones said. "*Say I want death off the table, what happens then?*"

"*You shut down your engines, dump your fuel so we can see it, and prepare to be boarded by my security team.*"

Jones waited a few moments for effect. *"I'll need five minutes to make contact with my captain in the container, confer with him, and then prepare for shutdown. You'll be on board in twenty minutes."*

"Jones, I want to be on board in ten," the voice replied.

Stunned that the voice on the other end knew his name, Jones still held his composure. *"I'll see what I can do. I'll check back when I make contact with my captain."*

CHAPTER 61

Inside the exhibit container, Anders and Severn dragged Kopius to a far corner, away from where Wick signaled his breach. Below Wick's entry point, they'd already gathered as many mechs as they could without making it impossible to strap a few together for the lift. The more recently designed mechs were the lightest and easiest to move, but even the first generation ones were surprisingly light.

With the tarps he'd found, Anders carefully wrapped the head and torso of the Aura mech and then the one with the helmet. Wick would be helping on the crane, so Anders wanted him to keep his focus while things played out with the awaiting force outside. Seeing those mechs might throw him off.

Not long after arranging the mechs, a faint drilling in the ceiling began, and they all watched as the first penetration appeared. Anders' ears popped when the drill pierced the ceiling. Air hissed out, then a rod slid through and deployed four hooks that gripped the ceiling. A red gelatin ooze leaked out and formed a fist-sized bulb at the end. A moment later, it turned gray as it solidified, and the ceiling buckled in as the bolt tightened from the other side.

"Not much longer," Anders said.

"Museum security is going to take you down," Kopius said. "You don't know what you're up against, and you obviously don't have a getaway plan. I overheard you."

"Shut it," Severn said, nudging Kopius in the shoulder.

Anders caught Severn's eye and shifted his head, inviting her to talk privately. She rose to her feet, and Anders followed her to the opposite side of the container. Glancing up at the ceiling, he saw that Wicked was about halfway done with the connection.

Crowded together in the corner, she said, "What are we going to do, Anders?"

"I'm not sure. For now, we need to get everything out of this container and on our ship."

"Yeah, you said that. But then what?" she asked.

"That's what I wanted to ask you. We may need some *outside help.*"

"How do we do that?" she asked.

"Well, I'm not entirely sure. I was hoping you might have an idea. You're in this mess too. Is there anyone out there interested in your immediate survival?"

Anders knew she might pick up on his knowledge of who she was really working for, so he donned a desperate look. If there was a chance that she could enlist GC to help them, it might solidify some kind of immunity for his crew.

She looked deep into his eyes and, with a look of pure honesty, replied, "No. I'm sorry, there's no one close by I know who could help us."

He watched her closely. "You sure about that? Cuz if not, then we might well be screwed here."

"Then we'd better get unscrewed," she said.

A heavy thud rang in the center of the bolts three times.

"Wick's ready," Anders said, grabbing the post he'd removed from the stanchion. He rapped it on the ceiling and then directed Severn back over by Kopius.

There, huddled in the corner, they waited a few moments, until finally a huge steel drum about a meter in diameter drilled through the ceiling inside the circular bolt pattern. Debris and ceiling material collapsed onto the pile of mechs stacked on the floor.

Anders ran over to the opening as he heard Wick call down, "Cap, you okay?"

"Yeah, Wick, we're good. What the hell are you doing? You didn't test the pressurization?"

"Captain," Wick said, hanging his head over the opening, disappointed in Anders' doubt. "I made some adjustments. I check the pressurization while I drill the holes now. We were good long ago."

Above Wick's head, Marko was already mobilizing the crane to pluck the crew and the mechs from the container.

"Anders," Jones said. *"They're getting antsy out there. They're moving in to board our ship, and I got nothing to stop them. Plus, Aura ran off. Not sure what she's up to, but I doubt it's good. You'd better get up here."*

"Check," Anders said. *"On my way."*

When Anders, Severn, and Kopius were brought up into the cargo bay, Anders assumed control of his ship again. "Wick, where's Aura?"

"She ran by heading for the engine room a minute ago," Wick said with a pained face colored with embarrassment. Anders understood.

"It's okay, Wick. She fooled us all. I'll take care of it." Anders patted him on the shoulder, but then stopped short. He glanced down at the bloodied hole in his shirt and pulled at it so he could see the wound. There was about a fifteen centimeter vertical stitching much closer to his heart then he'd thought. Anders didn't know what he'd expected, but it wasn't something so severe.

"I'm good, Cap," Wick assured him. Anders grimaced, confounded by his survival and recovery.

"Glad to see that," he said before reluctantly heading for the engine room. Amazing. Wick had been shot in the chest, Aura operated on him, and he was back on his feet and on the job minutes later. It was impossible, but here he was, working like nothing had happened. With the urgency of the situation, Anders was forced to accept it for now. His only explanation was that the bullet didn't strike too deep. Or the helmet he saw was proving something he wasn't ready to admit.

Before he ducked down toward the engine room, Anders snapped back into captain mode. "Severn, hide Kopius in the compartment," he said, pointing toward the hidden one by the cargo bay door. "Marko, Wick, get the mechs up here fast and pack the container with a *punch*. Be ready in five minutes."

Anders made a move toward the engine room again, but Jones called over the comms, which stopped him at the stairs to the mezzanine. *"Captain, you'd better get up here. GC's just arrived. I think they're taking control."*

Anders eyed the corridor to the engine room and then the stairs, the way up to the cockpit. He motioned first to the engine room. He needed to make sure Aura wasn't doing something that would get them all jacked up. But he paused, remembering the look on her face when she said she'd get Maddix. There was something about her in that moment that he couldn't quite figure out. Somehow it made him trust her just enough to change his course and head up to the cockpit.

CHAPTER 62

"Holy sh—"

"Yeah, it's bad," Jones said, interrupting Anders as he entered the cockpit. Reflexively, Jones shifted his bulk from Anders' chair over to his.

"How many?" Anders asked.

"About ten ships," Jones replied as Anders took his seat.

Anders buckled his harness over his shoulders. "That's not so bad."

"That's just in front of us. They're in a tight pattern behind us to conceal their numbers so I haven't been able to get a good count," Jones said, hope dwindling in his tone.

"Or most of them are in front of us to make us *think* there's a lot more behind us." Anders tried to sound positive.

"You and I both know at this point it doesn't matter," Jones said. "What are we going to do?"

"I don't know. Where did you leave it with them?" Anders noticed the ships closing in on them. "Boy, they're not messing around, are they?"

"No, they're not. I told them I'd ping them back once you and I made contact."

"Okay, set me up with them," Anders said, clearing his voice.

"Flip your comms when you're ready," Jones said, motioning toward the console in front of Anders. He reached for it. "Oh, and Anders?"

"What?"

"It's both museum security and GC on there."

"Great," Anders said with a smirk.

"And they know who we all are."

He glared at Jones. "Any other good news?"

"Nope, that about covers it."

Anders flipped the switch.

"This is Captain Anders Lockheed. Who the hell is this?"

Two sets of indistinct voices powered back over the comms before one dropped out, leaving, *"Thank you for the courtesy of letting your superiors speak first, Mr. Pollo."*

"Sorry, sir," the other voice apologized.

"Mr. Lockheed, this is commander Reginold Hammis. I have authorization from Galactic Command to use any force necessary to retrieve the mechs you're taking. I have that force surrounding you, and you would do well to surrender your ship now."

Anders shrugged to Jones, finding a little humor in their predicament. *"Wow, so you're telling me that it's a crime to be at the museum when someone attacks it. I was on a nice date there when this container launched me into space. My crew was kind enough to come pick me up."*

Jones gave Anders an impressed look. "They'll never buy it, Cap."

"Worth a shot, I guess. Maybe it'll buy us some time," Anders said, switching his comm to his team. *"How much time, Wick?"*

"Eight minutes. We have almost half of the mechs loaded."

"Get a move on. We're running out of time here."

"Check," Wick said.

"Captain," Hammis barked, *"you and I both know you're full of it, and you're just trying to buy some time to finish unloading that container."*

"Then what's with the strong introduction?" Anders asked.

"We're boarding your ship now. Shut it down, dump your fuel, and bring your crew to your cargo bay."

"Okay, we'll be there in five," Anders answered simply. *"I mean ten. We have to clean up a bit. We're not used to visitors. Do you guys drink beer or whiskey? Or coffee, maybe?"*

"You're not helping your situation, Captain," Commander Reginold said. *"And I'm losing my patience."*

"Cool it, Anders," Jones urged him. "Don't make this worse."

"That's impossible," he replied. *"Look, Commander,"* Anders said sternly, *"I'm out of coffee, so you'll have to choose between beer and whiskey."*

Jones rested his head in his palms.

"You leave me no choice, Anders. Prepare to be boarded. If you try anything, you and your ship will be removed from existence."

"I hear ya," Anders replied, *"but we don't have a very good connection open to that container right now. The museum's special curator Kopius is still in there. If you force us to open our cargo bay, I can't promise that seal will hold with the change in pressure."*

"You just let us worry about that," the commander said.

"Um, sir?" Pollo interrupted. *"May I have a word in private?"*

The commander paused before he huffed, *"Anders, don't go anywhere. Mr. Pollo, you have thirty seconds."*

The comms went silent, and Anders turned to Jones and shrugged. "Where are we gonna go?" he whispered.

Jones smiled meekly. Anders saw that Jones was trying to find the same humor in the situation that he had but noticed the struggle. He decided to take it back a notch and meet Jones in his desire to get out of the situation. "Kopius is valuable to them. Didn't you notice? As soon as I threatened the container, the museum security piped in. Maybe we can leave him behind to buy our freedom?"

"Doubt it," Jones said, shaking his head. "By the sound of it, GC only cares about the mechs. They'll be after them no matter what."

"What about a bluff? Say we're leaving it all behind, rigged with explosives. Our freedom for their survival."

"No way, this is military. They'll never go for it."

A soft tone rang out in the cockpit. "They're pinging back. I think we're done, Cap. Either give up or go out with a bang."

Anders thought for the entire second the commander allotted him. Then he sighed, realizing it may be over.

"I can be on the Bitch in thirty seconds," Jones offered.

Anders thought hard; he knew they didn't have any options. Getting caught now by GC with the mess that went down at the museum would put them all away for good. It was a slim one, but their only chance was to make a run for it.

"*I'm done, Cap. The container is packed and sealed. I can release it anytime,*" Wick cut in via the internal comms.

"*Thanks, Wick. Put Marko on the release. I need you in the engine room. We're gonna need all the power you can muster.*"

"*Check.*"

"*Captain Anders? Did it work?*" Aura came on the comms with hope in her voice.

Confused, Anders answered back, "*Did what work?*"

"*Can they still see us?*" she asked.

Anders and Jones eyed each other in confusion.

"*Answer the call,*" Jones said, pointing at the console.

Anders flipped the comm switch. *"Hello?"* he said, not sure what he was hoping for.

"Very clever, Mr. Lockheed," the commander said. *"You may have found a way to cloak yourself, but we'll lock onto you in no time. You're pissing me off, and we're going to shut you down as soon as we get a lock on you."*

"Cloaked?" Jones whispered.

Aura came through the comms again, laughing with glee. *"It did work! Yay, I'm so excited."*

"Aura, what did you do?" Anders asked sharply and with excitement.

"I finished the design Wick's been working on. He was going to surprise you when he finished, but I finished it and thought it might help us now. You like it?"

"Captain, release the container and get out of here. When we're clear, set the charges. It'll scatter their ships, and they'll lose us in the confusion," Wick said quickly.

"Do it before they lock onto us though," Aura said. *"Sir. Oh! And the container will reappear when we're far enough out of the cloaking envelope. Which isn't far."*

Anders paused, looking to Jones for his input. "Do it, sir." Jones said. "And do the decoy thing too just in case."

"Release the container," Anders said into the internal comms before switching back to the commander. *"Commander, I think we'll be leaving now. But don't worry, for your courtesy of not following us, we'll leave behind all the mechs and Mr. Kopius stuffed in the container."*

"Not going to happen," the commander said.

Jones already had the ship maneuvered to the underside of the container, keeping close to it in an attempt to hold it inside the cloaking envelope.

"Yes, it is, because if you don't, and you come after us, we'll blow the whole thing. We're screwed either way, so if you come after us, we might as well hurt you back good 'n' plenty. The survival of that container is up to you."

With that, Anders closed all-comms to the Galactic Command and the museum's security.

"Punch it, Jones," he said.

"With pleasure, sir." Jones hit the ship's all-comms. *"Grab a hold 'a something. Gotta jam hard this time. Wick, gimme all the power you got and make sure the cloaking device is on its own power source."*

"It absolutely is," Aura replied.

Off comms, Jones said, "Sir?"

"Yeah?"

"All aside," Jones said, obviously fighting his emotions, "I love this crew."

"Yeah, Jones, I do too." He paused while Jones did nothing. "Now get us the hell outta here!"

Jones hit the all-comms. *"Kickin' it in three, two, one."*

Anders' head snapped back into his seat as Jones jammed the forward thrust to the max. Acceleration ramped up with inertial forces, pinning them to their chairs. Anders closed his eyes and envisioned their position as they moved away from the container. He saw how it would reappear and how that would look for GC. Letting that scene sink into the commander's sight while he pondered what to do with it, Anders hit the all-comms.

"Ready on the container?" he said.

"Ready," Marko replied.

Anders eyed the radar screen, analyzing the dozens of ships surrounding an open center. *"Blow it."*

"Check," Marko replied.

Not a moment later, Anders confirmed the explosion by watching blips on the radar fan out away from the epicenter.

"Looks like we have an explosion," Anders said. *"Great work, team. Now let's see how lucky we really are."*

"Let's hedge our bets," Jones said to Anders. He cranked his yoke and gave a heavy throttle boost, changing his flight trajectory as he grabbed his all-comms. *"Wick, shut everything down except your cloaking thing and bring Kopius to the mess. Everyone, grab yourself an emergency suit and meet us there. We're going dark."*

In nearly an instant, the ship's acceleration dropped to nothing leaving it soaring at its current velocity. Anders and Jones shut down the cockpit and grabbed their emergency suits from a ceiling compartment. Moments later, the ship's power drained with a whirring, and dim red emergency lights flashed on. As the last of the systems shut down the artificial gravity, their legs lifted off the floor. So they floated out of the cockpit, letting the ship stay her coarse on her own inertia, as dead and undetectable as they could make her.

CHAPTER 63

Jones passed through the doorway to the mess hall before Anders stopped just inside it. Already there were Severn, Marko, and Aura splayed out holding on to counters, open cabinet doors, and a couple of well-placed grab bars to keep from aimlessly floating about.

Because some cabinet doors were used as makeshift grabs and the artificial gravity systems were no longer running, random pots, pans, and cans of food drifted through the stale air. Naturally, some of these items had turned into pawns in games of tag between Severn and Aura. With the right nudge, a pot would steadily make its way into the back side of an unsuspecting Marko's head. Aura giggled at Severn's jest.

When Anders called for full-attendance meetings such as these, he usually preferred that everyone was present before he arrived. Wick was the only one not there yet, but Anders understood why. Being a nonconfrontational person, Wick would avoid a chance encounter alone with Aura after finding out she, the only woman he'd ever fallen for, was actually a machine.

Of course Anders felt like a fool after her deception as well, but that seemed to be a theme on his ship, ad nauseam. No longer would he allow this to prevail. Anders became determined to have the truth out now. As far as the outside universe was concerned, the ship was as dead as the cold and black itself, and nothing was going to make him wake her up until he knew exactly what he was up against.

Upon entering, Jones drifted to a spot by the table and placed his foot on the edge to pin himself to the wall as smoothly as if he'd done it a thousand times. Not wanting them to float away, he and a few others hugged their emergency suits as if they were oversized pillows. Anders pinned his under one arm as he held himself in place with his other arm and both legs, like a three-legged starfish stretched out in a doorway.

Soon after, Wick floated in with Kopius, who he ushered to a spot at the kitchenette by the others. He then floated to the table next to Jones, exactly opposite and across the room from Aura. Anders noticed his intentional avoidance. Aura did too, so she pushed off the wall to take a spot next to Wicked.

Wicked held up his hand and shouted, "Don't!"

She caught herself midflight, using the ceiling and table for support, and with no appendages left available, her suit drifted to the wall above Wick and Jones' heads.

"Wick..." She pouted, eyes instantly bubbling with tears. Without gravity, tear sacs quickly welled up around her eyes. "Wick, please..."

"Save it. You lied to us. You're one of them," Wick said, eyes anywhere but on her.

"No, Wick, no. You d..." She blinked and wiped her eyes, causing tiny beads of tears to drift away.

"There will be time for this later," Anders said calmly before growing more stern. "It seems we have all been deceived multiple times since starting this damn job. This will be put to an end right now." Anders' eyes met Severn's, and she sucked in a breath.

He needed to put his crew ahead of his own feelings for her, whatever they were. Before *she* arrived, all was well. He still had the twins on his crew, and as wild and unpredictable as they were, at least they were loyal and not built on a lie. His crew had suffered a malicious shredding ever since Severn came on board.

Anders let that fuel his desire to get the truth out. Still staring at her, he said, "Let's have it, you two." His steeled look drifted to Marko. "Truth time. Who are you, and why us?"

Anders watched them both. The long years of doing this work had sharpened his ability to read people, and his initial take on a reaction was always his best.

Severn's eyes dropped to the floor. The mess was dark, and the dim red light barely lit her face, but Anders still caught her expression. Whatever she had done, she felt bad about it. He could tell she felt *something* for him, for his crew, but he also knew that, at her core, she was still a soldier. A soldier with a mission. The internal struggle shone through on her face and in her posture.

Marko's reaction was predictable and understandable, simple as it was. He hadn't been on the ship long enough to develop any emotional ties with the crew. He had a job to do, and he was going to do it. His face held its chiseled form, jaw locked tight, which meant only one thing. He wasn't talking.

"You're still in the military," Wick said softly while staring at the top of the empty table.

"We know you went to your commander on Port of DeMarus when I sent you to get Marko," Anders added, directing his statement at Severn.

Severn's eyes darted around the floor, as if she were looking for the right thing to say.

Anders looked to Marko. "How deep are we in with GC?"

Silence.

Jones slid his foot off the table, leaned forward, and planted his hands on the wall behind him. "You'd better start talkin', Marko boy." When Marko said nothing in response, Jones kicked off the wall and headed straight for him.

Reflexively, Marko braced himself for the impact, but at the last moment, he launched himself straight at Jones. Their arms interlocked, their shoulders slammed together, and they flipped into a violent spin.

In midair, Marko tried to get a strong hold on Jones, but the man was too big for him. Jones quickly handled Marko's smaller form, spinning him around with a move that turned his arms into a pretzel-like form behind his head. Marko tried to break free, but only gasped in pain. Jones' vice-like grip was too strong.

"All right," Severn said. "Let him go."

Jones didn't move.

"Talk, and *then* he'll let him go," Anders said, not having moved from the doorway.

"Fine," she said, taking a deep breath. "We're both military. I was never kicked out."

"We *know* that much," Wick said. "I bugged you the moment you set foot on this ship."

Severn looked at him in disgust, then thought for a moment while rubbing her jaw. "Is that why you knocked me out?"

"It's the only way we can test our new recruits," Anders admitted.

"Did you bug me?" Marko scoffed.

"Shut up," Jones said, squeezing his head tighter.

Marko squealed. "Agh, quit it!"

"Enough," Anders said. "Severn, continue."

315

Severn huffed. "Fine. We're hunting the designers of the machines that have been sent on the attacks."

"And you think *we* have something to do with the attacks?" Anders asked.

Severn let out a breath. "No. You were…"

"Bait," Wicked said. "You used us."

Severn's tone turned more corrective than defensive. "Not exactly."

"Then you'd better tell us exactly," Anders said.

"I was the bait," Aura said shyly, "wasn't I?"

The look Anders saw on Severn's face when she turned to Aura wasn't the look of someone in the military doing anything necessary to complete her mission. Severn genuinely looked sorrowful, like she cared about the people involved and hated using them to do *her* job.

Severn straightened her shoulders, owning up to her involvement. "She's right. Aura was the bait."

"So how do we fit in?" Anders asked.

"Command chose you. GC can't walk among certain people the way the top salvage crew can. We know you're not *always* on the level—there's a way the flight crews go that GC can't follow. We needed your cover to get inside. To track down whoever's behind this."

"And how would we track these people down without knowing it was *our* mission?" Anders asked.

"Easy," Severn said.

"Plant the mech," Wicked said, butting in. "They knew we'd take the scav job, and they knew we'd stake the claim first. They figured the best crew is also the crew most likely to take the bait. All they had to do was set us up with the mech and let the designer come to us. They stuck Aura with us, Maddix came after her, and now we're in this mess, and I've got a bomb around my neck."

"That's evil doings," Jones said quietly, leaning in toward Marko's ear.

"So this is all GC's doing," Anders said. "And what's GC's plan for us when this is done?"

Severn shook her head. "Before the museum heist, you'd've had immunity."

"And now?" Jones asked, releasing Marko and letting him drift over to Severn.

"To be honest, I'm not sure. Marko and I are involved too, so maybe—"

"Maybe isn't good enough. I want a guarantee that my crew is safe," Anders shouted, floating toward Severn. Marko kicked off the floor, grabbed Severn, and shifted her behind him before he stopped himself at the ceiling.

"It's okay, Marko," she said, maneuvering herself out from behind him and reaching for Anders. She put her hands on his chest. He kept his to himself. "I don't know what'll happen, but I promise I'm here until it's over, and I'll do anything I can to keep your crew safe."

"Anything?" Anders asked.

"I'll leave the military if I have to," she whispered, her eyes leaving his mouth and sinking into his, the same way they did before she kissed him in the museum.

"I guess we'll see about that," he said. "But one thing remains." He turned from Severn to face Aura. "There's something you all need to see."

CHAPTER 64

Wicked waited half a second before he shoved off the wall to send himself out after Anders. As if it were second nature, he used the ceiling and doorway like grab bars to guide his weight-less-self down the corridor. If he would have hung back instead, Aura might have tried to explain herself, and he wanted none of that. Her deception hurt too much to deal with at the moment. It disgusted him, what she did, what she made him do with her.

A machine with living tissue made him fall in love with it. How was that even possible? How could something be so cruel? It was too much for him to handle for the moment. They were smack in the middle of a job, he'd been shot, and things were heating up. If he could get his head there, as far as he was concerned, *they* never happened.

In the cargo bay, the crew, along with Kopius, positioned themselves along the back wall next to the machine shop where plenty of tools and the like had been fastened to the wall for such zero-G occasions. Those were now the things they used to stabilize themselves in place. All the mechs from the exhibit were piled together below the nearby mezzanine and strapped down against the starboard side wall. Above them, Anders patiently held himself below the edge of the mezzanine as if he were about to do pull-ups—a useless exercise in zero-G.

Wick placed himself between Jones and Kopius, leaving no room for Aura to slip in next to him. When all were present, Anders simply pushed off from the underside of the mezzanine and landed on the cargo hold floor by the two mechs wrapped in tarps. He grabbed one tarp and apologized to Wick.

Before Wick could consider why he was apologizing, Anders ripped the tarp off the mech and revealed the face of the only woman he'd ever loved.

"What the—?" Wick started, eyes shrouded in anger. "There are *more* of you?" he said to a shocked Aura. He drifted out from his perch, still holding onto the wall with one arm.

It pained him to let out his fury, and it somehow inflated the embarrassment he was already enduring. And seeing yet another mech identical to her twisted the knife already wedged deep in his heart.

When the deception came from only the one mech in the museum and Aura, it felt like a heartbreak all humans were meant to experience, in a way. But realizing that she was one of who-knew-how-many copies somehow made it infinitely worse. Like he wasn't even worth having a unique mech for himself. At least with humans, the one you were with was meant for you. This was different. His heart had never before felt so hollow and broken.

"I don't think they chose just any mech as bait," Anders said, motioning toward the alive and well Aura. He then spoke directly to Severn. "Did they?"

"No, they didn't," Kopius interrupted, pushing himself over to the mezzanine overhang near the mechs. "She's designed to *infiltrate*. If there was a mech the designers would be interested in getting back, it would definitely be her."

"What're we really dealing with here?" Anders asked Severn.

"GC isn't completely sure," Severn answered. "But we do know these mechs are very advanced, and there's big money behind them."

Kopius interrupted them with a scoff. "You people don't know anything."

"Then tell us," Jones demanded.

"Look at them," Kopius replied, waving his hand toward Aura, who was now bracing her weightless self in place next to Wicked, clearly meaning to be close to him.

Them? Wick thought.

He looked, but there were no other mechs near him and Aura. "Perfect humanoid mechanical designs. Complete with living muscle and tissue grown around a lightweight hollow titanium skeletal structure." Kopius' face grew grim, his voice took on a peculiar tone, and he placed the tips of his fingers together to form an oblong shape. "Real brain tissue, fully integrated with hundreds of high-powered organic processing units." He then straightened up proudly. "They are the very embodiment of a living, breathing organic computer, designed to infiltrate, corrupt, steal, or destroy."

Kopius gestured toward Wick and Aura again, and Wick felt a pang of disgust and frustration kindle deep in his belly. He tilted his head as if to rethink what Kopius was implying.

"How?" Anders asked, "And tone it down a bit, would ya?"

"Apologies. It's just so remarkable," he said, elated. "I've been studying them for some time now. These designers, whoever they are, have figured out how to make organic tissue fuse with an android skeleton with mechanical and electrical components. And it doesn't stop there. They've figured out the *plumbing* too. All of it. Think of a clone grown around a robot who can think for itself."

"But why? Why the tissue?" Anders asked. "Why not go all out and make them as strong as possible? Impenetrable, regardless of the resulting appearance."

"Too easy to spot then," Wicked said. "If you make the mechs too obviously like machines, you have to make them unbreakable so they can withstand attacks. And unbreakable machines, who think for themselves, can and will cause big trouble, even to the designers." Wick looked up with concern. "On the other hand, if you make something undetectable *and* vulnerable, the possibilities are endless, and you would still have more than a modicum of control. That's how I'd design them."

"Correct. You're designed so you can maneuver and infiltrate undetected," Kopius said directly to Wick. "And the scariest, most advantageous design parameter is your ability to empathize and use it to manipulate."

You? Wick tilted his head in confusion at Kopius. *What the hell is this guy thinking?*

"That doesn't make sense," Anders said. "What's the purpose of all this? The *goal*?"

"No one knows." Kopius shrugged.

"It's a long game, whatever they're doing," Jones said.

Marko chimed in. "Right. So what's the move now?"

"The same as it's always been," Anders said. "Get Wick free of that damn collar, and get Maddix and GC off our asses." He glanced at the curator. "Kopius, as soon as we can, we'll leave you somewhere safe."

"And what about *them*? You have live mechs here. Aren't you worried about what might happen?" Kopius asked with real concern, again gesturing at Wick and Aura.

Wick's frustration with Kopius' words burst out in a shout. "Why do you keep doing that?"

"Doing what?" Kopius asked.

"Talking about Aura and I as if we're *both* mechs. She's the lying, deceiving machine! Not me!"

Kopius' eyes scrunched, and he glanced at everyone as if to look for anyone who might know what Wicked was talking about. His eyes fell on Aura as she slouched. Wick saw her struggle with her words. Then she pulled herself together and turned to him.

"Wick," she said, reaching for him with both of her hands, "you and I knew each other before you pulled me from the destroyer. Maddix had acquired us both, but I was taken from her soon after we got there."

Wick brushed her hand away, letting himself drift from her. He refused to look at the others. "Uh-uh. You're lying," he said, almost to himself.

"It's true," she said, moving after him. "You and I were labeled as defectives after we were built. The control programming didn't work on us. Our will is free." Her voice grew softer. "And just as my name is Aura, your name really is Drew."

"That's enough," Jones said, making himself even larger. "Leave Wick outta this. Whatchu tryin' to pull?"

"Think about it," Aura said, glancing at but ignoring Jones. "Where were the mechs shooting the guards?"

Jones seemed to think about and recall his time in the museum.

"Legs, arms, shoulders," she said. "They were instructed to injure, not kill. This is a tactic to cause further disruption in their opponent's defenses. The mech we encountered meant to kill you, Wick."

The thought of being a target marked for death changed his whole perspective. The collar was one thing, but this? Before he could further consider all he was hearing, Anders asked another question.

"Why him?"

"Because years ago we were labeled as defectives, and defectives are to be terminated. All mechs are uploaded with prime, secondary, and tertiary directives. They'll have their current mission protocol but will execute others if they happen to arise during a mission. I think the mech that looked like me was following one of those nonprime directives."

"Then why didn't it go after you?" Jones asked.

Aura shrugged and gave a faint nod. "I know that we both unzipped a package that was downloaded soon after we were taken to Maddix. We were to seek and destroy several models, including us if we ever located each other. This was sent to all mechs, and Wick and I were always able to override that protocol.

"When we were on the steps in the museum, the other me-mech saw me and locked on, but I think it couldn't process the instructions. There's an anti-self-terminating mechanism in the design, and I think she saw me but couldn't reconcile the protocol to take me out."

While they were interrogating Aura, Wick was busy considering something Aura had said. They knew each other before Maddix. But that was impossible; he was always with Maddix, ever since...he could remember. *But where did I grow up? Where was my childhood? It doesn't matter.*

"You're lying," Wick said, snapping alert and interrupting their discussion. "Again. You probably lied about your amnesia, you lied about your humanity, and you're lying now about me."

Aura held cupped hands over her mouth, tear sacs bubbling around her eyes again. She wiped her face, and what didn't stick to her hand floated away. She let her eyes sink into his.

"No," he said. "Don't look at me like that. You don't get to do that anymore, you don't get to manipulate us any longer." He turned to his captain and pointed port side, in the general direction of the trash dump. "We have to get rid of her."

Anders set his jaw. "Wick, take it easy. I get it." He put out his palms as if to usher him into a calmer state. "There's no way the kid I've been looking after for the past few years is a mech. I'd've known by now. We've shared drinks, meals; we've shared discussions and stories of our pasts. Right?"

Wick nodded.

Anders' voice softened. "On several occasions, we've even saved each other's lives. There is no way you're a mech, right?"

Wick paused, anticipating that Anders was somehow teasing him into an understanding. Reluctantly, he nodded again.

Anders voice grew softer still. "Right. You're a human being, complete with childhood memories, and you get sick like the rest of us. Right?"

Sick. Wick thought long and hard about his past sicknesses but realized he had none. Not even a cough or a sniffle. So what? He was healthy. No. There's no way he could be a mech. He'd know.

Jones' chest heaved with heavy breaths. "Captain, what is this?"

Anders glanced at him, acknowledging his question, but maintained his focus on Wicked. "Wick," he said, looking at his chest, "how's your bullet wound?"

"Why? What's that got to do with anything?" Wick answered, beginning to wonder himself. He felt fine, but when he rubbed his chest where the sutures were, it felt a little sore. Itchy even. *That's how it's supposed to feel*, he convinced himself. He was healing. Just because he was shot and moments later went back to work didn't prove that he was a mech. Then he thought of something. He knew what could prove he was human. But before he could say anything, Anders continued.

"You were shot," he said calmly. "In the chest. And you continued on as if you weren't."

Wicked stared at him, as if he were waiting for the interrogation to end. Sadness and fear molded his face, but he didn't care if they noticed. It was their fault for doubting him, a member of the family. The fear only born from doubting your own sanity. Anders was the one person Wick trusted with everything, and he was doubting his humanity. Forget him.

"Anders, stop," Aura said softly as she moved closer to comfort Wick.

"I'll prove it," Wick said, ignoring Aura's aid.

"How?" Anders asked.

"Cage Challenge," Wick said resolutely. A challenge cannot be cancelled. *Anders will have to fight me now, and he'll injure me, proving my humanity once and for all. They'll see that I'm not a mech.*

Anders replied swiftly while drifting toward the mechs. "No challenge, Wick."

"Too bad," Wick said, advancing on him. "Can't be cancelled."

"Fine. But before we go down to the cage, explain something to me." Anders pushed off the mezzanine ceiling again to drift down by the Aura mech and reached for her. "Since you're human, and Aura's a mech like the others we've seen..." His hand then moved over to a second tarp and pulled it away, revealing a machine wearing a helmet identical to the one hanging in Wick's engine room.

Wick drew a quick breath. "My helmet? So he's got one like mine. So what?"

"That's not it, Wick. I want you to explain this," Anders said and then pulled the helmet off the machine, revealing Wick's very own face.

Suspended weightless above the cargo floor, Wick stared at himself strapped down to the other mechs as if he were dead. The air rushed from his lungs, and he made no effort to replenish them.

Bemused beyond belief, he turned his head away; his body spun gently, reacting to the inertia. How is this possible? He looked to Aura, not in hatred but for help. For understanding. Maybe an explanation.

Some remnant of his love lay underneath dark pains of betrayal, but it was still there, and his first instinct was to go to her. But he'd forgotten to breathe. The shock of this new truth had left him utterly breathless.

CHAPTER 65

Wick placed his face in his hands, and his body heaved as he cried out, "No! This can't be. I don't believe it, I won't." A rush of compassion surged through Anders, and Wick gave him a pleading look. "You don't believe this, do you?"

Anders placed a hand on Wick's shoulder. "You're a soldier to be sure, buddy. But not even Jones could take a gunshot to the chest like you did." He gave Wick an honest look. "Yeah. I believe that you're a mech just like Aura."

Wick's breathing seemed to calm down. The trust Anders saw on Wick's face, even now, amazed him. Wick's eyes darted back and forth, as if to search for truth somewhere in the air. "How could I have not known this? How could I," he paused, "live without knowing?"

Even now, knowing the truth about Wick, Anders couldn't tell that he and Aura were mechs. They were perfect in every way. The emotional strain Wick dealt with in this moment was portrayed on his face with wonderful exactness. No programming could do this. Anders was convinced Wick was actually feeling this emotional pain. And his body mimicked the plea for truth perfectly. Even in zero-G.

Aura drew nearer. "You did know. Once," she said softly. "No matter how many times they tried, we never took to their programming. Somehow, we had free will and never wanted to be under control. For that and other reasons, we were scheduled for decommission."

"What other reasons?" Wick asked.

"Well, you were always going on about how we should be free. That all mechs should be allowed to live among people."

"And you?" Anders asked.

Aura hesitated. "I have an anomaly somewhere in my brain. After some time has passed, I *unwind*."

Jones grumbled, "What your counterpart did in the museum, is that unwinding?"

Aura tried to smile. "No. That was normal. I think you can say that I go a little crazy."

"Crazy?" Severn said knowingly.

"I know, it's an understatement. And it got me cast aside as a defect."

"And Wicked just wanted to be free?" Anders asked.

"He hated being a machine used for slave labor. He never took to following orders, even when they reprogrammed him. Like me, he'd just rewrite the code in his brain and go back to doing what he loved."

"Yeah, inventing awesome shit that saves our asses!" Jones said, nodding approvingly at Wick. The smallest hint of a smile twitched at the corner of Wick's mouth.

"So what happened before Maddix?" Anders asked.

"We were both scheduled for decommission, termination. Wick said he'd rather not know why or remember anything when it happened. It was too painful for him to know he was being sent to die." She shrugged. "A lot of us mechs know and love life just as humans do." Then she bowed her head. "I promised Wick that I'd wipe my memory too, but I couldn't. I only pretended to.

And after it was over, after he reset himself, there was a breach in our installation, and most of the decommissioned mechs were taken, along with some good ones. We were taken to Maddix, but soon after we arrived, there was a raid by the military. I was taken by them, but Wick and some others were already hidden or taken somewhere else."

"That was a GC operation," Severn said. "We had intel that the masters behind the mechs were there. Turns out some mechs were, but the organizers weren't. We got more intel later that we had just missed them. It appears that Aura ended up losing her memory from the deep freeze she suffered when GC planted her on the destroyer."

Aura turned to face Wick. "I'm glad my memory returned. Otherwise our time together might have been lost forever."

"When exactly did your memory return, Aura?" asked Anders.

"Soon after Maddix shocked us in the engine room," she replied.

For a long moment, Wick said nothing. The entire crew remained silent as everyone watched him sort through the truth. Anders accepted it fairly quickly. As far as he was concerned, it all added up, and he couldn't care less whether Wick was a mech or not. To him, he was still the same kid.

In fact, it made sense to him that Wick was a machine. The things he'd created to get them into and out of work, all the contraptions he'd made. No man could make so many things so quickly and have them all work perfectly. And he loved Wick regardless. He was a kind, gentle young man. If nothing else, he was part of the family.

"Wick," Anders said, pulling Wick's attention to him, "this changes nothing for us. I hope you understand that."

"Yeah, kid," Jones added. "Don't sweat it."

Wick sucked in a deep breath. "Well, here I am, I guess." He grabbed hold of the collar on his neck. "Under control, again." He looked up to Anders, eyes still wet with tears. "Cap, you mind if we get back to work and get this damn thing off me?"

"Absolutely!" Anders replied.

"Hell yeah," said Jones. "What's the plan, Cap?"

"Easy," Anders announced. "We need to trade Kopius and these mechs for Wick's freedom."

"Wait a minute!" shouted Kopius. "You aren't really going to hand me over to her, are you?"

Before Anders could respond, Wicked cut in. "No! No one's gettin' delivered to Maddix. Not if I can help it. Not while I'm still around."

"Wick," Anders started, "you're not going to sacr—"

"No one's gettin' sacrificed either," Wick said with a grin.

Anders had seen this look before, usually when Wick came up with something especially interesting. "Whatcha thinkin'?"

"I've got somethin' brewing, but we all need to play a part. You too, Kopius. Whether you like it or not, Maddix wants you as well, so you gotta help us on this."

Kopius thought for a moment, and just as Jones started to say something, he copped to his answer. "Okay."

"Me too, Wick," Aura said, her face lighting up with excitement. "Whatever you need, I'll do it."

"Yeah, Wick, us too," Severn added, drawing a fist bump from him.

"Okay, quarterback," Anders said. "I'm thinking a party at the destroyer. Any chance what you got brewin' can go down there?"

"My thoughts exactly, but first things first. We fly dark and dead in the black like this for as long as we can. My best estimate tells me we'll be out of GC and security range in about twelve hours, then we'll lock onto the Lucy we dropped on the destroyer. We're gonna throw a party where this all started."

CHAPTER 66

At the captain's request, Severn and Marko joined Wick, Jones, and Anders in the cockpit shortly after the rest shift. For obvious reasons, the three had been planning the trade and getaway without them—the military personnel—but still needed information.

"I know it's tight, but come in," Anders said as he turned sideways in his seat. "I've been doing some thinking. For now, we have a common goal, but I realize at some point, you have to go back to GC and hand over the results of your mission to your commander."

Severn nodded to show her understanding and already knew where they were headed with this conversation. Marko stayed motionless next to her. He crossed his arms as if to put up a defense.

Jones added, "And we would like very much to not be those results."

"Like she said before," Marko started, "your crew has never been the target. Not before you decided to knock off a museum."

"You were there too!" Wick shouted. "Entrapment. Ever heard of it?"

"You said it was a scouting mission." Marko raised his voice in his defense.

"All right, that's enough," Severn said. "Let's just agree that it's complicated. Marko's right, our target was never your crew. Our mission is to get the mech designers. And as far as I know, we don't have any new orders, so let's calm down a bit."

Jones perked up in his seat. "Okay, so what's that mean for you and us?"

"It means that for now, we have the same problems to deal with," Marko said. "GC still wants us to hunt down the mech designers, and you need to make a trade with Maddix. Since she's our only lead, it looks like Maddix is our common goal for now."

Severn reinserted herself in the discussion with an assertive tone to keep the peace. "This trade is a perfect setup for us to further our mission. It could go a long way with GC on your behalf, if we play it right. And Marko is right: It's very good for us all that Maddix is a common goal."

"Yeah, 'til she's not," Jones huffed.

"Then it's safe to assume that, at some point, you're required to check in with Galactic Command?" Anders asked.

Severn nodded. "Yes."

"Then do you mind if we wait until a strategic time to invite them to the party? I'm not asking for a long window, just a few days to set this up," Anders said, using a certain tone to suggest unity on the crew.

Severn noticed Marko look at her, as if he'd object, but she wanted to help Anders' crew. Deep down, she understood it was GC that put his crew in this tight spot, and they had done what anyone would do out here—whatever it took to protect the crew and survive. So she responded before Marko could object. "I think that serves everyone fine."

"Agreed then. Thank you," Anders said. "Would you two please go find Aura and ask her to come meet with us?"

Severn paused at the sudden dismissal. She'd sensed Anders' change since the museum—he was more closed off and protected than before. How could she blame him though? He'd heard nothing but lies since he met her. At this point, she wanted to help him more than she wanted to stay loyal to GC. A confusing feeling, to be sure.

Still, an overwhelming need to make things right with him grew inside her, even if it meant sacrificing her job. That notion felt absurd on the surface, but she didn't ignore it, even though Galactic Command represented a career in an otherwise impossibly difficult place to live.

As she followed Marko to find Aura, Severn sensed a change in the way he held himself too. Just as Anders' demeanor had shifted, so had Marko's. Both seemed more determined on diverging paths.

There, walking the corridors of *Elite One*, Severn realized for the first time that she would have to make a tough choice in the coming days. Help Anders and his crew and be forced to leave GC as a deserter and effectively live on the fly forever; or turn on Anders by abandoning whatever there was between them and returning to her post in the military, the very entity that put him and his crew in an impossible position. She would have to decide whether she controlled her integrity and morals or whether the Galactic Command ruled them.

Severn walked behind Marko as they passed through the port-side corridor. "You know we have a job to do, right?" Marko said over his shoulder, somehow sensing what Severn was thinking and feeling. She knew she was a good soldier, one who desired to do the right thing. But the mission was getting more complicated.

"Yes, Marko, I know what the objective is."

"And what happens when GC adds Anders and his crew to that objective?" Marko said, stopping to face her. "Cuz you know they will."

Her answer to that particular question shocked her and nearly erupted from her mouth, but she maintained her composure. Anders' crew should be pardoned. That part was simple, but the question in her mind was whether she was willing to make that call despite what GC might have to say about it.

She decided to keep her answer ambiguously simple. "I guess we'll see when GC makes that decision."

Severn went to push past him, but Marko slid in front of her, bent on making his point. "Don't you dare make me choose between you and GC. It'll be a tough choice, but I'll close the book on you."

Severn smiled. "I wouldn't ask for anything else. Just do your job, and all will be fine for you."

"What if I want it to be fine for the both of us?" he said, his serious face turning into something resembling desire.

"C'mon, Marko," she said. "*Us* was a short thing a long time ago. We both know *that* book is closed."

"Doesn't have to be," Marko said, brushing the top of his curled index finger on the exposed part of her stomach.

"Oh, Marko," she replied with a sad tone, finding his attempt far more amusing than flattering. She brushed his hand away and steeled her tone. "Yes, it does."

She pushed by him without looking back. She headed toward the engine room to find Aura, and a tiny weight of annoyance lifted from her shoulders when she realized Marko wasn't following her. One less thing to deal with at the moment.

When Severn arrived in the engine room, she found Aura not working on one of the many gadgets as usual, but working on herself in what appeared to be some kind of mechanical acupuncture.

"What the hell are you doing?" Severn asked, legitimately concerned. Aura had palmed two thin steel rods and plunged them deep into her thigh. She hadn't pierced her skin, but it stretched and wrinkled from the depth at which she worked.

With a pained face, Aura said, "I think I caught a tendon at the museum. I'm trying to get it loose."

Severn heard Aura grunt as she pivoted the rods at odd angles while she pushed harder.

Aura's pained face mirrored itself on Severn's. "Would you like some help?" Severn asked.

"Nope," she said, her expression turning to one of discovery.

A loud, hollow pop thumped from Aura's thigh, and her skin rippled as if a rubber band had snapped up from below. "*Ah*," Aura sighed. "There it is. Much better!" She flipped her leg up and down a couple of times while rotating her ankle, then jumped onto the floor and did a few squats with straight arms before finishing with a front kick that stretched higher than their heads.

"Good as new?" Severn asked with an interested look as Aura walked without her limp.

"I think so," Aura said. "But you didn't come down here to see that. What's up?"

"Not much. Cap wants to see you up in the cockpit."

Aura's eyes lit up. "Is Wick there?" she asked excitedly.

"He is," Severn replied with a smile. "You like him, huh?"

"Of course." Aura popped up. "He's my man!"

"That's for sure." Severn drew a more serious look. "You know he feels the same, don't you?"

Aura bowed her head. "I do. It's just tough to wait while he processes all of this."

"Yeah, I get that. How are you feeling otherwise?"

"You mean, am I going to snap anytime soon?" Aura asked.

"I wouldn't put it so lightly, but yeah."

Aura pointed at her now-better leg. "I just did. Snap." She paused, shared a bared tooth smile, and waited for Severn to laugh.

Severn gave her a forced smile, instead. "Very funny, Aura. But you know what I mean."

"I know," Aura said, letting her joyous face settle. "Seeing as how there are no warning signs, I'd say I'm about due for a good one soon."

Severn grimaced and grumbled, "Wonderful. Is there anything we can do to help you when it happens?"

"Yeah," she said, making her way to the door, "get out of the way."

"Oh, I will," Severn replied as Aura passed her to leave. Severn noted the sadness behind Aura's camaraderie as she left, an eerie look of regret mixed into her smile, and it cautioned Severn's resolve.

CHAPTER 67

As she neared the cockpit, Aura noticed life emanating from Wick's laugh. The same life that bellowed out and echoed off the engine room walls those nights when it was just the two of them.

She had fallen for him all over again with each one of those passing moments. And in each of those moments, she fought the urge to tell him the truth. But she knew where the truth would eventually lead him, so she held on to the good times, cherishing them as they came, for as long as they would last.

She waited outside the cockpit door, out of sight, listening to Wick talk with his captain and first mate. She enjoyed his voice, and in it, she could sense the faint struggle he fought after finding out the truth about himself.

And at the same time, he was still her Drew, and what he did best was the job at hand. He was a problem solver down to the core of his existence. Since she'd known him, he'd always been that way, and she believed that was who he'd always be.

There was a pause in the conversation, then Jones asked a question that made her heart skip a beat. "How you holdin' up, kid?"

A short silence drifted through the air.

"I don't know," Wick said. "It's weird. Hearing that stuff... it was difficult, but in some way, I guess I've always known I was different."

"Just didn't think you were a machine," Anders said.

"Yeah, that and—" He took a breath. "I guess I'm not surprised."

"How so?" Jones asked.

"Looking back, I don't remember a single moment from before Maddix. And I never really tried to remember. It's like I've only existed since then, ya know?"

Jones huffed. "Not really."

"Plus, I've never been sick, so there's that." Wick chuckled.

Another pause in the conversation struck, and Aura felt a thick heaviness in the silence. Part of her thought the conversation was at an end and that now might be a good time to enter.

But then...

"We still love you the same. You know that, right?" Anders said. Aura held back tears of sweet joy. Then she heard a rustling of clothes, as if Anders had put his arm around Wick.

"You sure?" Wick asked with honesty in his voice.

Jones answered immediately. "Absolutely, brother."

"What about Aura?" Wicked asked.

Aura nearly ran from the doorway at the mention of her name, but she wanted to hear what he would say. So she stayed and even crept closer to the doorway to make sure she could hear.

"What about her?" Anders asked.

"I'm not sure about her," Jones said, "but I do know she saved our asses. It's like having another Wick around."

"That's true," Anders said. "She's never shown any ill intent around here. She's always been on the level with us. A little weird, yes, but true to us."

"Yeah, but…" Wick started. Another pause in the conversation.

"But what?" Jones asked.

Wicked didn't respond.

"Do you care about her?" Anders asked.

Silence.

"Nah, Cap. Look at 'im. He's in love wit' her," Jones said, simultaneously supporting Wick and giving him a hard time.

"I…" Wick started. "I don't know. How do you know? Am I even capable of love, being a…"

"Love has many forms, brother."

"How can you tell?" Wick asked.

Alone in the corridor by the cockpit, Aura smiled for real for the first time since the museum. If he was asking these things, then he was leaning toward forgiving her. Hope filled her heart in that moment, and that was when she realized that anything else Wick might say should be up to him for her to hear. She'd already stolen enough of this conversation.

She stood tall to build courage and let her voice carry into the cockpit. "Wait." She stepped through the doorway, revealing herself. "I think I've heard more than you'd like me to already." She shot Wick an apologetic look. "Any more should be up to you to share when you feel so inclined." She glanced at Anders and Jones and gave a small nod to present herself as requested.

"Aura, thanks for joining us," Anders said.

"You're welcome. Is there something you'd like me to do?" She stood tall and felt like a true member of the crew.

"Possibly," Jones said. "Your leg looks better."

She looked down, "Oh yeah, I caught a tendon or something when I tackled a mech down some stairs. I just now plucked it out in the engine room with a steel rod."

Anders and Jones both shot her a pained look.

She returned a smile as if it were normal behavior. "You said I could possibly do something for you."

"Wick mentioned that the mech in the museum—" Anders began.

"The one that looked like you!" Wick cut him off.

"Easy, buddy," Jones said softly.

Wick took a deep breath and then shyly glanced at Aura. Her heart fluttered at his attention to her and more so when he apologized for the outburst.

Anders continued. "Yes, that one. He said she was firing at everyone from some kind of guns concealed in her forearms."

"Yes, she was. She's actually an older model than me though. I'm a bit upgraded."

Anders' eyes lit up, and Jones' expression twisted with interest. Almost in unison, they both replied, "Upgraded?"

Aura shot them a knowing look with joy. "Uh huh, would you like to see?"

CHAPTER 68

A rest shift later Anders sat back in his pilot's chair on the verge of the beginning of the end. Jones sat quietly next to him and there Anders dug deep within himself to bring out the courage to finish a mess of a job that someone else had started. They had been set up from the start, and that alone could anger him enough to distract him to the point of total destruction. But he refused to let that happen. He instead allowed it to fuel his resolve, the engine that would drive his plan to finish this.

What once was an ambitious scav job had now turned into an epic siege where he stood to lose everything. They were up against not only the military but Maddix, someone so unpredictable that he too had to become a plan of his own. One that even his own team was unaware of. It was the only way out of this that he could see. Backing someone like Maddix into a corner, which their plan was designed to do, could make her react in unanticipated ways, so he had to think of everything.

Jones sat quietly next to him in the cockpit as they waited for Wick. A thick silence filled the cockpit, matched only by the sight of everything outside the viewport—a nothingness shrouded in darkness, and a chill so deadly one could all but shiver at its emptiness. Not much could be said between them anyway. Things were about to get serious, and words weren't going to change a thing, so the silence between this captain and his first mate meant only one thing: They were ready.

Then the distant patter of Wick's rubber-soled boots on the corridor's steel grating echoed into the cockpit, leaving no trace of the silence that bore down with such intensity moments ago. Out of breath, he popped himself inside.

"Sorry I'm late, Cap." He swallowed a sticky dry breath, an aftermath of running the ship's length. "There's something going on with the cloaking...thing."

"Sounds like you need a name for it," Jones said with a chuckle, eyes focused on the console in front of him.

Anders huffed and let his fist fall to his console. "It had better be working when we get there."

"It is. Kind of."

"Either it's working or it's not, Wick. Our plan depends on that thing."

"I know, I know. And it *is* working. Just more like a flickering light. Don't worry, though. Aura's on it. I'm sure she'll figure it out."

Jones' eyes lit up. "You talked to her?"

"Not really," Wick said. "More like ordered her."

Jones glanced at Anders, cringing. "I guess that's one way to break the ice."

"Well, she'd better fix it quick," Anders said, "cuz we're outta time. GC will be on us soon, and we need Maddix here first."

Wick shrugged. "She's probably already here, Cap."

"How could she be? We've been coasting dark for almost sixty hours now," Jones said.

Wick eased himself onto the steel bench at the back of the cockpit. "Maddix has a way with things," he said. "She's probably been tracking us through this thing," he grabbed the collar on his neck. "I'm willing to bet she's close by and waiting for us to open our comms again."

"We're still several shifts away from the destroyer," Jones said to Anders. "If we're gonna reach out to her, now's the time."

"Plus, it'd be nice to get the air scrubbers back online," Wick added. "It's getting a bit ripe around here."

Anders took a moment to make sure he'd thought of everything possible. He needed to bring Maddix to the destroyer first so GC's presence didn't spook her. Wick said she'd probably be close by, which meant he needed to wait until he had the destroyer in sight before he invited Severn's military friends to the party.

"You really think she's nearby?" Anders asked.

"I have no doubt," Wick said.

Looking nowhere in particular, Anders thought out loud. "She's close by and knows we have the goods, and she hasn't blown the collar yet."

"Which means we have the upper hand," Jones added. "You can tell her where, when, and how to make the trade."

Anders nodded, satisfied. "Okay, let's wake up the ship."

"With pleasure, sir." Jones ran through his procedure for bringing all the ship's systems online. Artificial gravity systems were the most difficult to detect at long distances, so Anders had ordered these turned on nearly thirty hours ago. Next to come on were the engines, air scrubbers, lighting systems, and general electricity, which ran nearly everything else.

Within the next fifteen minutes, the air was noticeably fresher, and Anders' slight headache began to dissipate. He soon felt levelheaded enough to turn on their external comm systems, and not a moment later, Maddix comm'd in.

"She sure don't waste time," Jones said. "You ready?"

"Do it," Anders said, steeling himself.

The intercom speaker in the cabin crackled, and the glass screen at the front-view port sparked alive. Maddix's image flickered, then formed, revealing her typical posture. A freshly lit cig smoked in her right hand, and her left one held a half-filled glass of most likely very fine whiskey.

"You sure know how to test my patience, Anders Lockheed," she spat. "I'm thirty seconds from blowing you out of the black."

"Can your spam, Maddix," Anders said coolly. "If you wanted us dead and your prize destroyed, you'd have done it by now, so no one here's buyin' it. Besides, we know you can't see us."

"I get a quick glimpse of you now and then. You must share with me how Wick's discovered to make you disappear. I have many uses for things like that." She grinned.

"Sorry to disappoint you, Maddix," Anders said nonchalantly, focusing his attention on things other than her. "It's just a short somewhere in our system. There's no *thing* doing that."

"Yes, yes. Keep your secrets. But I am glad you came to negotiate. It adds more fun to the hunt," she said, taking a drag of her cig. "All right, Mr. Anders. What say you?"

"I'm sending you coordinates to a decommissioned destroyer currently getting scav'd by several crews. Once we get there, I'll tell you where to go. The ship's decompressed, so we'll make the trade in suits somewhere inside. No tricks."

Maddix smoked her cig and sipped her drink while Anders spoke, as if she couldn't care less about what he had to say. He continued anyway. "You and two of your men will come in and verify the mechs and Kopius are to your liking. Then you will relieve Wick of the collar, and we will leave you to do your own loading. Make sense?"

"Fine, fine," she said, waving her hand through billowing smoke. "'Cept one thing…"

"What's that?" Jones asked.

"Can't take off the collar without pressing my finger on it; can't put my finger on it if I'm in a space suit, now can I?" She laughed. "Good plan though."

"Nice try, Maddix," Wick shouted. "I know how you have things designed. You can shut this thing off here and now just as easily as you could use it to kill me."

"Ah, sometimes I forget how clever you are, Drew." Maddix used the space of another drag and sip to delay her response. "Very well. Send me the coordinates and the location to meet you on the ship."

Anders nodded to Jones, who then transferred the information. "We're sending you the coordinates now, and I'll send you the location on the ship when the time comes."

"I'm looking forward to seeing you all again," she hissed while she leaned in and snuffed the life from her cig.

"Maddix, it's been a pl—," Anders said with a smile as he cut the comm link short.

"I can't wait to be done with her," Wick said.

"Check that," Jones agreed.

Anders' lips tightened as he paused before his next order. Work had to get done, and he would rather not force Wick to work with Aura if he wasn't ready, but he needed the cloaking device working perfectly. At the moment, solid execution was paramount to personal comfort. So he said to Wick, "I need you to help Aura get the cloaking thing operating at full capacity. No flickering or nothin'. I need perfection. Got it?"

Anders found it rather impressive how Wick accepted the order without protest. Not that he was prone to such behavior, but still, he smoothly acknowledged the order and turned to head out of the cabin in spite of himself and any reservations he may have had about working with Aura.

After Wick disappeared, Jones acknowledged, "He's a good kid. We'd never be where we are without him. I wouldn't trade that for anything."

Anders agreed, but he didn't voice it. His mind was focused on something else. "Maddix agreed to those terms awfully quick, didn't she?"

Jones didn't say anything for a moment, then, "Damn."

"Yep. She's got no intention of making a fair trade."

CHAPTER 69

With the destroyer-grade class M1A MK III suspended far in the distance, Jones shut down the forward engines and used the reverse thrusters to arrest the ship's momentum. They lay silently perched in space and watched as several ships buzzed around the destroyer as they picked it clean.

"You ready for this?" Jones asked Anders, who sat quietly to his left.

With narrowed eyes, Anders glared out at the job that should have gone a much different way. Instead, they were in a heap of trouble, and now someone else was getting the spoils, which made Anders' face turn grim. "Yeah," he said softly, "I'm ready to get our lives back."

"I can dig that, sir." Jones hit the ship's all-comms. *"Wick, we invisible yet?"*

A short beat later, Wick's voice crackled through the cockpit speakers. *"Check. We're cloaked."*

"Okay, Cap, you're up," Jones said, easing the thrust forward.

Anders grabbed his comm and used the controls on his console to zero in on Captain Jug Mason's secure line. He knew Mason's ship was somewhere among the other dozens scaving pieces from the destroyer's hull.

"Captain Mason, come in," he said.

Silence buzzed through the comm link. Then, *"This is Pek. Captain Mason ain' available. Who's this?"*

"I'd rather not say, but you can tell him he's expecting me," Anders replied, then switched to the ship's internal comms. *"Severn and Marko, to the cockpit on the double."*

"Yeah, okay, I know who you are," Pek replied. *"Welcome to the party. Hang tight, I'll patch him through."*

"Got a few more party-goers yet to arrive. Just tell him we're here and the music starts in a bit. No need to get him on the line."

"Check that. See you soon."

While Anders sat in silence watching other crews work *his* job, he sensed Jones regretting the same payday. "Shoulda been ours, huh?"

Jones chuckled from deep in his throat. "Agreed. But then we'd have missed out on all this fun we've had, plus what's yet to come."

"True," Anders said. "I know how you hate being bored."

Anders led the conversation into a lull when he heard two sets of footsteps clanging on the corridor's steel grating.

Severn entered first. "Sir, ready to make that call?"

Anders nodded and motioned for her to step up to the console, but then suddenly, the importance of the call hit him like a bad memory.

He realized, with no intention of her own, she could jeopardize the plan. If GC got the impression that their operatives were under duress, they could join the party with too many uninvited soldiers. As best he could tell, Severn was at odds with turning his crew in if GC added Anders to their list of *acquisitions*. And if that were true, something in her voice could give it away. He needed someone else, someone willing to turn on him and guarantee GC would honor their requests. Anders was in the middle of a long game here; it was to Anders' advantage for GC to believe they had this whole deal in the bag.

"Yes, it's time, but I need Marko to make the call," Anders said as he stood up. "Take a seat, Marko. I need you to make them think you've managed some alone time for a bit and that this is a private conversation. We want them here because *you* believe the person behind the mechs is Maddix and you know she's meeting us here."

Marko agreed. "Anything else?"

"One thing—we need them to come light. I don't want the whole armada here, got it?"

Marko paused, collecting his thoughts, then said, "All right, connect us."

Jones flipped switches on the console to dial in on known Galactic Command lines of communication and then pointed to Marko and spoke softly. "You're on."

"*This is Officer Marko Bayne on active duty for Commander Reginold Hammis. Please respond.*" Marko waited for a response. When none came, he called out his intro again.

This time, a woman replied. "*Officer Bayne, please hold for the commander.*"

"*Thank you.*"

A silent several beats passed before the commander spoke. "*Officer Bayne, is this comm link secure.*"

"*Yes, sir, it is. I'm alone here. The rest of the crew is sleeping.*"

"*Good, I've been wondering if you'd check in after your stunt at the museum. I trust you have a perfectly good explanation for letting this mission get out of hand.*"

"*Yes, sir. Anders ordered the ship to go dark so we couldn't be tracked. I had to wait until we came back online.*"

"This Lockheed is proving to be quite the annoying criminal," the commander said.

"Not exactly, sir," Marko said, surprising Anders with his defense. *"If I may, sir, it seems that Maddix is playing some kind of part behind all the mechs. She's managed to get Anders to do her bidding by way of holding one of his crew's life for ransom. She wants Kopius, the curator from the museum, and his mech exhibit."*

"I see. And knocking off the museum was Anders' way of buying back his friend's life?"

"Sir, while we did go to the museum at Anders' instruction, his plan was only to gain intel on how we might *relieve the museum of the mech exhibit. It was only to buy time. The plan wasn't to go through with it—until Maddix forced his hand by staging an attack at the museum."*

"Noted. And what's his plan now?"

"Well, sir, that's why I've risked calling in now. Time alone in the cockpit is a near impossibility, but I needed to give you an update. We're on our way now to meet with Maddix and trade Kopius and the mechs. I think this is an opportunity to not only grab Maddix but make serious headway on discovering who's behind the mechs."

There was a pause in the communication. The air in the cabin seemed to pack in around Anders the longer the silence stretched over the comm link. With each passing moment, he could feel the commander considering whether to put out an arrest warrant for him and his crew. Then the hammer fell.

"I agree with you about Maddix, but I'm not buyin' this crap about Anders' innocence. You don't make off from a major installation like the Promaedia without being involved somehow. I want Maddix and her lackeys, and I want Anders and his. Got it?"

Marko eyed Anders for the span of a moment. *"Yes, sir. I'll need one squad to get it done. I'll send you the coor..."*

"Bullshit. You'll get it done with five men. I'm personally coming with a squadron, and you'd better have this ready to go when I get there. I'll see you in less than two hours."

The commander cut communication to Anders' ship; silence echoed throughout the cabin. The fate of Anders' crew had been sealed with Maddix's, and the commander was bringing down the weight of an entire squadron to get it done.

The fast-approaching doom Anders had feared since the day this began was all but knocking on his cargo hold door. He now knew without a doubt the direction he would have to take his plan, and it took all of his strength to hold his resolve. Standing in the cockpit with his back facing the back wall, Anders slipped his hand inside a compartment and plucked out a small handheld recorder he'd been hoping he wouldn't need.

CHAPTER 70

Jones pitched and yawed the ship again to fly it down and under the destroyer for a third time when Wick finally called through the comms from his engine room.

"I think I found it," he said.

Anders jumped to his console to reply, *"About time, kid. I was worried they'd have this thing picked clean by the time you found something."*

"Sorry, Cap. I wanted to be sure I found the best spot."

Anders sighed. *"It's not the best spot, is it?"*

"No. I scanned everything. There's too much activity around the nice 'n' big spaces. This one will have to do. You should see a large, round dome-like protrusion. Aft of that is a decent flat area. That's where we go in."

Anders scanned the surface of the ship through his viewport and found the spot Wick had chosen for their landing. *"All right, I see it."*

Anders closed the comms to the engine room and turned to Jones. "Gimme a good shot, but keep your distance. Who knows what's hiding in there."

"Can't be any worse than before," Jones grumbled with a smirk.

Anders dipped his head with thinning lips as he unbuckled himself from the captain's chair. He darted out of the cockpit and clambered up the ship's ladder, where he slid his body into the gunner's rig and fired up the system.

Anders first checked his comms with both Wick in the engine room and Jones in the cockpit. By the time they acknowledged him, the Bitch was up and running and loaded.

"How many ships are in sight of this area?" he asked.

"The bulk of them are closer to the bridge, but there are two possible down here at the stern. Ten o'clock low and three o'clock mid. Don't know which way they're facing."

"Jones, got a visual?" Anders asked.

"Yeah, Cap, we're going to lose ten low behind the destroyer in about three seconds. Three mid is holding. But I think they're on an away heading. Your call."

"Check. Wick, any bodies behind these walls?" Anders asked as he aimed the long barrel of the Bitch at the flat area aft of the dome.

"The scan's cold," Wick answered. *"You're clear."*

"Ready to rock, Cap," Jones called.

Anders gripped the trigger and, with a grin, began his count. *"In five, four, three—thrust forward—"* the ship responded at Jones' control, *"two, one."* He plunged the trigger, and the turret rumbled as it spat out round after round. Anders traced a quick circle on the hull of the ship with his bullets before repeating the circle at a slower pace. By the third pass and nearly a thousand rounds later, an opening appeared as the hull disintegrated from the rapid fire. Anders released the trigger.

"Well done, Cap," Jones acknowledged.

"Quite therapeutic, Jones," he said, slipping himself out of the gunner's rig. *"You should try it."*

Jones rebutted, *"If you'd learn how to fly straight, then maybe I'd get the free time to do shit like that."*

Anders laughed to himself as he slid down the ladder.

CHAPTER 71

Instead of heading back to the cockpit, Anders made his way to the cargo hold to oversee Wick and Marko make the connection between the two ships. In the span of those few minutes, Jones had brought the ship within the grappling system's firing range, Wick had already made the connection, and Marko had started reeling the ship down to the destroyer.

"Where we at?" Anders asked as he entered.

Marko started to speak, but Wick cut him off, taking ownership of their work. "About ten meters to go before we're locked tight to the destroyer," he said, focused on watching the two ships come together on his screen. The massive hole Anders had shot in the destroyer was disappearing from the camera view next to the landing site.

"Check," Anders acknowledged as he made his way to the access hatch on the floor. "I see you left your hole maker in place."

Wick glanced up from his screen. "Yeah, I figured we might want a secret entrance to the room below. Could come in handy."

Anders agreed. "Might as well drop the mechs through there too then, instead of out the back."

"Check that. What's next on our list?" Wick asked, turning his focus back to the screen.

"Next we load the mechs inside the destroyer so we can get outta here as soon as Maddix takes your pretty little necklace off."

Wick mumbled something to himself as Anders walked over to a port-side compartment. He pulled out seven of the ten tightly folded suits, and one by one began a thorough examination. Satisfied they were in working order, he chose one and began putting it on.

Shortly after the ship settled into place, Wick and Marko each chose a suit for themselves, and that's when Aura and Severn walked in with Kopius.

"Pick a suit," Anders said, stepping aside to give them room to do so. "Jones should be here shortly, and we'll get started."

"Hi, Wick," Aura said softly as she walked by him.

Wick looked at her nervously. Anders could tell Wick struggled with how he had treated her and was trying to move on from it. "Hi, Aura. Um, how are you?"

Since discovering the truth, Anders was amazed yet again at how these machines could produce facial expressions and body language that displayed so many emotions. He couldn't help but gawk at the perfection with which they were designed as they engaged in small talk. The undeniable awkwardness of first love and the budding forgiveness after a lover's quarrel, combined with having found out he was a machine—it was *all* displayed on Wick's face in one powerful look of pain and confusion.

Despite his complete lack of knowledge on how to build one of these machines, Anders knew without a doubt that such programming was impossible. There was an element of humanity in these machines that hadn't been intended by the designers; they had somehow become owners of life rather than mere imitators.

How else could he explain why he still loved Wick as a son? And Wick's feelings for the others for that matter.

Severn joined Wick and Aura's conversation while everyone else donned their suits. "I'm glad to see you two getting along again," she said with a sly grin.

Wick didn't react, but Aura lit up with excitement. "Me too."

"How are you feeling otherwise, Aura?"

"Oh, pretty good," she said shyly. "I told you before, it's not like I can tell when it's going to happen, Severn."

"I know. I'm sorry I keep asking. I guess I'm nervous."

"It'll be okay, Severn. Just don't—"

"Okay, listen up!" Anders said, his captain's tone cutting off all conversations. "As far as we can tell, we're here first, so let's get started. We're going to keep the gravity on inside the ship, but we'll be decompressing the cargo hold so we can unload the mechs. Wick's found a nice little spot inside where we're gonna stuff 'em for the trade."

"Don't we want these on the ship until Maddix frees Wick?" Severn asked. "Seems like a bad idea to be letting them go so soon."

"I want us to be gone as soon as possible when she takes that thing off his neck. We can't afford to wait around and unload them after."

Silence all around.

"All right, first up. Jones and Aura will head down through the hole and get set up on the wall in the destroyer where we're placing the mechs, Severn and Wick will be stationed just inside the hole, and Kopius, Marko, and I will pass the mechs down to them. They will then float the mechs over to Jones, who will catch and pass them to Aura, and she'll tie them down." A short pause. "Any questions?"

Silence again.

"Solid," Anders said, letting his voice grow. "You ready for this?"

Reluctant nods and a couple of verbal responses echoed around the encircled crew. Anders pulled out his recorder but held it from the others' view behind his back.

"It doesn't sound like you are. I'll ask again." Anders took a deep breath and shouted, *"Elite One,* are you ready?" He clicked on the recorder just before the entire crew erupted with shouts of excitement and readiness. Satisfied with their exuberance, Anders had recorded the cheers he'd hoped he'd encourage from them. Pleased with it, he slipped the device inside a leg pocket and went back to business.

"Good, sounds like we're ready then. Are we cloaked?" he asked Wick and Aura.

Aura nodded excitedly.

"Check," said Wick.

"Good. Wick, show her how to ready the cargo bay for decompression."

"Check," Wick said and led Aura to the port-side perimeter wall.

After Wick showed Aura how to close down the first door, Anders continued. "Marko, Kopius, bring over the first mech. Jones and Severn, get your helmets on and check your suits."

"Check," said Jones.

Anders walked over to Kopius and picked up his helmet. While the others were hard at work, he whispered to Kopius, "Look. This probably isn't going to end very well for my team, but I promise you that I will do everything I can to make sure you get out of this safely."

"I appreciate that," Kopius said with resolve growing in his voice, "but maybe you should have thought about that before you abducted me and took my exhibit."

"You're right about that, and believe me, I wish that were the case. Unfortunately, we were backed into a corner, and I was looking out for my crew in the midst of a very bad storm developing too quickly to get out of its path. I guess I lost track of the greater good somewhere in there."

Still in protest, Kopius agreed. "I can see that GC put you in a tough spot too, and then Maddix turned the screws on you."

Anders fingered the helmet he held in his hands, feigning some kind of protocol check for serviceability. "I really am sorry for all this, but I still need to ask you for a favor."

Kopius said nothing and only stared at Anders with mild disbelief.

"When this is over, you'll be asked about me and my crew and what you know about us." Kopius nodded his understanding. "Make sure you tell them that my crew had nothing to do with planning this. Tell 'em this was all my idea and that I was ordering them to do these things under threat of being tossed out in the black. Got it? You make sure GC and your museum know they were forced into this."

Kopius thought for a moment, and Anders felt a short beat of relief, as there seemed to be a hint of mercy on his face. "I'll do what I can," Kopius said.

"Will you give me your word?" Anders asked, offering his hand.

Kopius took a moment for his own thoughts and then shook Anders' hand. "Yes, I give you my word."

"Thank you. Put this on when I tell you." Anders handed the helmet to Kopius. "And make sure you stay close to me until I tell you otherwise, got it?"

"Check," Kopius said, a hint of a grin flashing at the corner of his mouth.

Relieved that Kopius had promised to do what he needed, Anders ushered him over to join Severn and Wick in drilling a manhole in the destroyer through the cargo floor access hatch, just as they'd done with the exhibit container, except this time there wasn't a balancing of pressures to slow them down.

"Marko." Anders left Kopius with his orders and turned toward the crane-operating console next to the grappling system. "The first mech, get it ready."

Marko didn't answer. He simply grabbed the closest mech and strung a chain under its arms and around its chest. Anders lowered the crane hook into position and went over to help him with the intention of asking him for a favor as well.

"This one's an earlier design," Anders said, using small talk to soften any tension Marko might have. Marko didn't respond. "I think they realized their first mistake pretty quickly. The next generation that popped up a few years later wasn't as tall and didn't look as threatening. They hid the steel skeleton with the shell that gave them the body form."

"I don't need a lecture on mech history, Anders," Marko said. "I've studied this case for a long time. I know what we're up against."

Anders realized Marko wasn't the kind who took to small talk. A direct approach, he decided, would probably gain more respect from him. "Then you know that my crew isn't the target here."

Marko simply replied, "Doesn't matter. I have orders to follow."

"Then maybe there's a way you won't have to," Anders said, timing his reply with latching the crane hook onto the chain, completing the connection.

"I don't see how that's possible," Marko said.

"You're a smart man, Marko. You'll see the opportunity when it comes. I'm only asking you to make the right choice here. You and I both know my crew was set up and didn't deserve anything that happened to us after we took the bait. I'm just asking you to let my crew disappear if the opportunity presents itself."

Marko's face seemed to agree with Anders' suggestion, but his words did not: "You do what you have to, and I'll do what I have to."

Anders' face grew grim as if he were taking a second look into Marko's eyes. "Yeah, I know you. You'll do the right thing."

"C'mon, man, you've been in your business three times as long as I've been in mine. The right thing is relative. What really matters is who comes out on top."

In that moment, Anders saw that any more attempts at talking Marko into doing what he asked would only further degrade what little alliance they had left. So he let it alone the only way he knew how. "Careful, Marko. I've been doing this three times as long as you have. Coming out on top never happens the way you plan."

A short staring contest ensued, but there was work to be done, so Anders broke it and went back to his task.

Together, they brought the mech to the access hatch, Anders on the crane controls and Marko guiding the mech so as to not let it swing into anything. About that same time, Wick finished readying his hole-making device. Anders gathered the crew and ordered everyone to seal and check their suits for compression. All seven of them confirmed their suits were in working order, and Jones decompressed the cargo hold while Wick drilled his hole in the destroyer.

Soon thereafter, Jones, Severn, and Aura left the ship and floated inside the open space of the destroyer. A moment later, Anders lowered the first mech down through the hole, where Severn unhooked it and sent it floating over to Jones and Aura. When Severn confirmed they were ready for the next one, Marko and Kopius latched another mech to the crane hook; then Anders lowered it, and Wick guided it through the hole.

The team worked methodically and silently while they transferred one mech after another from their ship to the destroyer. With each mech that left his ship, Anders felt more and more relieved to rid himself of the burden. His plan was coming together, and that gave him hope.

Suddenly Jones' deep voice thundered over the comms, and his tone drained all the relief from Anders' heart in one simple phrase.

"We've got incoming," Jones said. "Looks like the party's starting a bit early."

CHAPTER 72

Severn and Wick held their bodies at arm's length below the ship's access hatch; their legs sought purpose but only dangled like sea anemones flowing with the movement of water. From that vantage point, Severn saw a single ship float into the open space just outside the hole Anders had shot in the destroyer. The ship, average sized, covered only half the opening, and she didn't recognize its form or insignia, so she got on the comms.

"I got a visual. It's definitely not military. Could be Maddix or another crew out here."

"Check," Anders responded. *"Keep working."*

Comm silence.

Severn received another mech from above, and Wick helped her quickly push it over to Jones, who caught it with relative ease. As he handed the mech to Aura, the visiting ship spun around, placing its rear cargo hatch at the opening. A moment passed, and the hatch began to open, a yellow warning light flashing on either side as the huge door swung downward.

"They're definitely here with a purpose," Severn reported. *"The rear cargo hatch is opening."*

Jones signaled to Severn to halt on the next mech, and she held up a hand to Anders above while she watched the ship in anticipation. The hatch finished opening, and Severn eyed five figures in full space gear. Four of them were in dark suits, while the fifth, very large, wore white.

"*Maddix,*" Severn said. "*Definitely Maddix. She has four goons with her, and it looks like they're planning on leaving their ship.*"

"*Here we go, team,*" Anders said. "*Hold tight and let her make her move.*"

Severn and Wick held to the grab bars on the ship's hull that lined the access hatch. The room they were in appeared to have been some kind of classroom when the destroyer was in commission. The dark gray walls were relatively smooth, except for random compartments spread out across the surface. When they'd started unloading mechs, Aura had secured them to the doors of these compartments. So Aura and Jones held on to either a mech or a door or both as Maddix and her men left their ship.

They simply walked off the end of the ramp at their cargo hold door and floated into the room. A quick moment passed, the crew adrift, before they ignited their jetpacks. Maddix cruised out in front, while the other four came along closely behind her, two on each side.

"*Is she connected to our comm link?*" Anders asked.

Wicked looked down at his left forearm and typed furiously on the small screen he had fastened in place. "*Doesn't look like it,*" he said.

"*Doesn't look like they came to talk, Cap,*" Jones offered.

As soon as Jones gave his observation, Severn saw Maddix intently point, first at Jones and then at Aura. Two of her men suddenly broke formation and shifted their jetpack trajectories toward them.

"*Two are going after Jones and Aura,*" Severn said quickly, knowing Anders couldn't see. "*Aura, get over here, now.*"

Jones made a move to grab Aura, but as he did, one of the men drew a gun from a side pocket and shot twice. Both bullets hit between Jones and Aura, embedding in the chest of one of the mechs.

Jones held up his hand to Aura to signal for her to wait. *"Cap, they've fired warning shots. She's not playing around here."*

"Check that," Anders responded. *"Everyone hold on."*

"We should have armed them," Marko grumbled. Looking up through the cargo loading hole, Severn caught a glimpse of him as he disappeared from her view.

"Hold. Your. Position, Marko." Anders said.

Maddix came to a halt about halfway between her ship and where Severn held on to the grab bars at the access hatch. Two people stopped with her, using their jetpacks to arrest their momentum. Maddix then gave a swirling motion with her fingers toward the other two men, and they continued toward Jones and Aura.

Before Severn could voice a warning, the two men lifted large, tube-like cylinders from the sides of their suits, aimed, and fired.

One shot at Jones and the other at Aura.

Jones quickly pushed off from the ceiling and shot toward the floor of the room. Aura spun like a ballerina, tracking her body along the line of mechs she'd tied down.

Both shots missed, and Severn warned her crew. *"Maddix is trying to capture us. She shot some kind of netting at Jones and Aura. They missed."* By the time Severn finished her warning, Jones had already rebounded off the floor and launched back up, heading for the man who had shot at Aura. The man was feverishly trying to let go of his cannon to regain control of his jetpack. Too slow. Jones slammed into his chest.

In a flash, Jones ripped tubing out from behind the man's helmet before they both crashed into the ceiling. He then lifted his knees up to his chest, waited until their rotation was right, and then kicked at the man. Jones went flying backward, while the man shot straight out of the opening.

Much to Severn's surprise, the man bounced off the side of *another* ship that had suddenly arrived. This one's cargo door was already open, and four more men came rocketing out, also in suits with jetpacks attached.

"*Someone else is here!*" Severn shouted, her voice echoing inside her helmet.

"*No need to shout, Severn,*" Wick said. "*The mic does the work for you.*"

"*Sorry, but Maddix has another crew here,*" she replied frantically.

"*No, she doesn't,*" Anders said. "*You know these guys. Say hello to Captain Jug Mason.*"

"*Sorry we're late, Anders,*" a new voice called out inside Severn's helmet.

"*No worries. You're just in time,*" Anders said. "*Give us a hand?*"

"*Sure thing,*" Jug said.

Severn watched in amazement as four men from Jug's crew darted toward Maddix, weapons drawn. Maddix appeared to be speaking to the three remaining members of her crew through their comms, and they seemed to be responding against her wishes and ready to fight. Soon the men acquiesced, and Maddix appeared to signal a surrender; her men put their weapons away.

Guarded, corralled, and suspended in the open space of the room in the destroyer, Jug's crew seemed to wait for Anders command. He walked to the end of the ramp on *Elite One* and waved them aboard. And so like cattle herded into a barn, Jug's crew ushered Maddix and her men out of the opening of the destroyer and onto Anders' ship.

Maddix had folded like a broken table the moment she was outgunned.

"Everyone back to the ship," Anders said. *"Let's get this thing over with."*

"Oh, Anders," Maddix's stale voice entered Severn's helmet, *"this isn't over by a long shot."*

"So you were *patched into our comms, Maddix,"* Anders said, stealing a look at Wick. *"I'm glad you can see that you're outgunned here. To be honest, I thought you'd put up a bigger fight."*

"I've got more men than you think, Anders," Maddix said with resolve.

Severn drifted up through the access hatch, crawled out onto the cargo hold floor where she found gravity, and then reached down to help Wick up. Aura followed, and the three of them helped Jones through the opening.

At the ship's rear cargo door, now fully open with a view out into space, Severn joined her crew as they gathered together, backs facing the interior of the ship. Jug's crew surrounded Maddix and her men at the large opening at the ramp.

"Maddix," Anders said with mild annoyance, *"you're going to turn off and release that damn collar on Wick's neck right now, or I'm sending you on a very long and lonely flight out in the cold and black."*

Severn secretly hoped Anders would do it anyway. But as she composed herself, she noticed something unsettling about Jug's crew. Their ship was now maneuvering in a position directly behind *Elite One*, with the rears facing each other. But the truly unsettling thing was that Jug's crew were holding the exact same net guns Maddix's crew had just used on Jones and Aura. And the jetpacks were identical as well.

"Anders," she said, stepping forward. But before she could get her warning out, Maddix called out an order.

"Now!" she said, and in an instant, the four members of Jug's crew and one of Maddix's launched nets at Anders' crew.

Aura, Jones, Kopius, Marko, and herself were all ensnared in steel wire netting.

"Jug, you son of a bitch," Anders yelled. *"What the hell are you doing?"*

As the five of them fell to the floor, shuffling with madness to break free, Maddix laughed inside her helmet, a horrible, gurgling smoker's laugh.

Severn saw the fury rage within Anders. He darted toward Maddix, but she immediately raised her hands and clapped them together. Severn eyed a bulge in Maddix's glove. There was something inside her suit.

Then Wick fell to the floor and convulsed as electricity raged through his body. In her helmet, Severn cringed at the sound of Wick's torturous screaming.

"Get down, Anders," Maddix said.

Crippled by his own mercy, Anders fell to his knees. *"Okay, okay. Just stop. Let him go, please."*

"Move again, and he gets twice as much," she said. *"This will be over soon."* She turned to Jug's crew. *"Get going and hurry up!"*

Jug's crew stepped forward, and all four of them approached Jones. Each one grabbed a leg or arm and carried him to the end of the ramp.

"Tell me, Anders," she said. *"Why didn't you pay Jug more than you did? You know I pay very well."*

Anders huffed. *"Where I come from, loyalty is earned free."*

"When it pays this much," Jug said, carrying Jones by his right arm, *"ya gotta take the cash. I figured you'd know that by now."*

"Looks like free doesn't pay the bills, Anders." Maddix grinned. *"Don't be so crushed, Anders. You should feel honored that I called in help. When I heard it was you who picked up Aura here from the destroyer, I knew I needed a second layer of deceit. You are the best, aren't you?"*

Jug piped up again, as if he were mad at Anders for forcing his hand. *"And it's your fault you failed, really. When you asked me to meet with you on this* problem *of yours, you practically begged me to go hunting for a higher price."*

Jug let out a grunt on his last words as he and his men swung Jones forward and released him out the back of Anders' ship. At first, Jones looked to have been tossed too high, but a crew member inside Jug's cargo hold moved a joystick on a console, and the ship drifted up. Jones floated in through the center of the opening. Severn hated the look on Anders' face as he watched while his first mate was taken from him. It nearly broke her heart for him.

"There's a special end for men like you, Jug," Anders said. *"Twenty years of alliance and friendship, and you turn just like that for a few bucks."*

"My crew is hungry, and I'm gettin' old, Anders."

"Enough chatting," Maddix interrupted. *"I'd like to get out of here."*

"Maddix," Anders spat, *"release the kid's collar, now. You've won. You've got what you wanted. The mechs are here. Kopius is here. At least spare him his dignity."*

"Dignity and self-worth are what caused him to flee me in the first place," Maddix said. *"I won't be making that mistake again."*

Kopius and Aura were the next to go, two men each, and they were sent over to Jug's ship with a simple toss. Anders hung his head. Even through his visor, Severn saw the pain and disbelief on his face as his crew was taken from him.

The same four men approached Marko and Severn. Crumb and Drake, she recognized, walked up to her, each one with a smug look, no doubt enjoying their payback for the dice game. Severn didn't like losing, but being the pawn in a game of revenge had an especially sour taste.

Not only that, but the feeling of being manhandled and tossed from one ship to another and taken prisoner to an unknown end had an eerily offensive feel to it. The sensation of being thrown from one environment with gravity to one without and back into one with was not nearly as disorienting as slamming to the floor of a dirty cargo hold before being dragged to and locked in a steel crate.

Stuck in a small cage, she watched Jug's two-man crew still on his ship turn off the artificial gravity in their hold, grab a very large reinforced wooden crate, and heave it weightlessly over to Anders' ship.

The massive bulk appeared to soar effortlessly over to *Elite One*. On the other side, Anders tackled Wick out of the way and landed on top of him at the edge of the ship's cargo hold. When the artificial gravity of *Elite One* pulled on the crate, it slammed to the floor. Pieces of the crate splintered and cracked as it slid to a halt deep inside the hold. Other crew members dashed out of the way, and Maddix erupted in anger.

CHAPTER 73

Anders tackling him to the ground wasn't what terrified Wick. Neither did the crash of the massive crate on the floor next to them. It was the fact that Anders released the clamps on the neck gasket of his suit and ripped off his helmet, exposing his head to the elements of space. This swiftly executed surprise drove a fear into Wick nearly akin to his time with Maddix.

Anders made a shushing formation with his lips as the heat and air left Wick's face and head. Then his neck and chest tingled. His skin grew violently cold, and his lungs burned as the absence of pressure sucked the air out with such pain he nearly begged for death.

His captain, friend, and the only father figure he'd ever known was going to kill him.

Out of the corner of his eye, Wick noticed Maddix throwing up her arms and pointing at the crate. She appeared angry, but he couldn't hear any chatter coming out of the speakers in his helmet.

Even in these terrifying moments of death, Wick thought of a tiny modification to his suit that could help prolong life in the event of a lost helmet in space. But those thoughts quickly faded with his focus. His mind grew dull.

Just before he lost consciousness, he realized what Anders was doing. The tears in Anders' eyes were the only proof. Wick knew Anders knew he'd rather die before Maddix took him again. And Anders was giving Wick exactly that. He trusted Anders with his life, and if Anders was taking it, it was because Anders believed it was the best choice Wick could make in this moment.

The short life he'd been given was over. So Wick closed his eyes and let the cold and black take him. There, in his last moments, he remembered Aura and the brief but wonderful moments they shared.

CHAPTER 74

Anders heard but ignored the conversation on the comms and gave Wick his attention.

"*Relax, Maddix,*" Jug replied. "*I know Anders, and if you're planning on leaving him here to die, then you don't know him like I do. That crate holds something very illegal that GC has been after for a long time. Let's just call it an insurance package. Anders won't be flying any time soon.*"

When Wick closed his eyes, Anders saw he accepted what he was doing. The trust Wick displayed made Anders lose control of himself. A heave of emotion puffed out of his chest in one giant, uncontrolled sob. He wanted to yell his name, to keep him awake, to help him survive.

But he wasn't finished. It wasn't over yet.

The collar on his neck hadn't fully frozen over, and the two beacons on it still flashed in similar rhythmic pulses. "C'mon," he whispered while the comms buzzed with conversations. He silently mouthed more encouragement to Wick so no one on the comms could hear him.

"*Fine, just get started on the mechs. I want to be gone five minutes ago,*" Maddix continued, distracted from Anders' time alone with Wick.

Anders didn't budge when unwanted men boarded his ship and took the mechs from his cargo hold. He watched Wick fall unconscious, hoping he'd last longer than the collar. The only evidence to the possibility was that Maddix held the remote to the collar inside her suit. That was when he'd realized she hadn't designed the collar to resist the cold vacuum of space. It could destroy the collar before it could destroy Wick. It had to. Aura had lasted in space for much longer than he was intending to hold Wick there. It *had* to work. There was no other option.

If he couldn't get Maddix to set Wick free, then Anders would make sure Wick was free himself. Either free in death or alive without a collar on his neck.

Anders watched as Wick's face froze over. It grew white with a purple hue as the last mech was taken from his ship and loaded onto Maddix's. She was busy directing Jug's crew, who were seemingly growing less and less attentive to her needs. The perfect distraction he needed to try to kill the collar. And then it finally happened.

The collar sparked, the lights faded, and then a third red light slowly dimmed until it was snuffed out. The collar was dead.

Anders grabbed it with both hands, closed his eyes, and with a violent tug snapped the collar from Wick's neck. Then he closed Wick's helmet, confirmed the airflow, lifted him onto his shoulder, and ran for the end of the ramp.

With the collar pieces gripped tightly in his hand, Anders called out in his comms, "*Maddix!*" He then tossed the two halves of the collar at her helmet. As she turned to him, he ran directly at her large bulk.

Maddix threw up her arms to block the collar from striking her helmet visor. Distracted by it, she didn't brace for Anders' rushing at her, so he threw a shoulder into her, casting her out into open space.

A step to the left, and both Anders and Wicked soared straight into Jug's cargo hold. Wick slammed into the port-side wall, and Anders slammed into Jug, who saw him coming. Jug caught him, spun around, and threw Anders out of the cargo hold, tossing him straight back onto his own ship, separating him from his entire crew. He crashed violently into the splintered crate in the middle of his hold.

Pinned to the floor of his own ship, Anders watched as Jug closed his own cargo hold. The sight of Wicked unconscious on the floor and the rest of his crew locked in cages like dogs was the last Anders saw of his family.

"Anders!" Jones called out to him, his fingers laced through the cage. For the first time in their lives together, Anders saw true horror wash over the face of his first mate.

"Hang tight," Anders said, *"I got you."*

Severn began to say something too, but the comms went dead as the cargo door finished closing.

Alone and silent on his own ship, Anders noticed a cold sensation inside his suit. He looked down and saw red droplets squirting out like a weightless water fountain. A stream of crimson marbles spewed forth from a splintered piece of the wooden crate that had pierced not only his suit but his side as well.

Struggling, Anders pushed his elbows backward to move his body away from the crate. The jagged piece of wood slipped back through his side, more blood gushing out in its wake. He pinched the torn fabric of his suit tight and tried to staunch the bleeding.

He had a job to finish. He pulled himself to his feet and stumbled over to the floor hatch. There, he flipped a few levers and then kicked Wick's contraption loose and watched it weightlessly sink to the space between the destroyer and his ship. Then he walked over to the large cargo door and hit the buttons meant for closing both the floor and back hatches. From his vantage point, he peered out into space and saw Maddix's ship off in the distance, picking up speed. Anders would have been angry at her getting away if it weren't for the large GC cruiser settling into place in front of her ship. Two more drifted into position behind her.

It was a victory just big enough to strengthen Anders to make his way to the sick bay and patch up the hole in his side. The first thing he did was plunge six syringes full of numbing agent in the areas around both puncture wounds where the splinter had pierced his side. Afterward, he crudely stitched up the ragged tears in his skin as best he could.

From the sick bay, bloodied and limping, Anders hustled to the cockpit. GC was here, and he needed to get on his way. His crew needed him to finish this.

Anders fell into his captain's chair and saw that Jones had left the ship in a perfect ready state. "Oh, Jones, you wonderful man, you!" he said as he clicked the switches to cut the grappling cables. By the time he started the atmosphere compression of the cargo hold, the force of the grappling cables' release popped the ship up from the surface of the destroyer, and the two ships drifted apart. Anders pulled up on the yoke and gave some thrust to pull away.

Clear of the destroyer, Anders located all of the GC ships in the area, Maddix's ship, and Jug's ship. Nine ships in total were highlighted on the screen in front of his viewport.

Immediately, a call came in on his console. "Damn it, can't you guys give me a minute?" Anders shouted to no one in his cockpit.

He took a deep breath to ready himself, but a sharp pain pierced his side as he took in the air. Anders stole another moment to calm himself and then answered the call. *"Anders and Sons shipping. You pack it, we take it. You pay it, we ship it."*

"Aren't you being a bit cavalier for a man who's about to spend the rest of his life in a cold prison cell?" the voice said.

"Commander?" Anders said. *"Is that you? Gosh, it's good to hear your voice. What ship are you in?"*

"The one too big for you to outrun," the commander replied.

Anders moved his joystick and fingered keys on his console. The green outline of the largest GC ship on his screen changed to red. Two keystrokes later and 'The Bitch, Armed and Locked On' appeared on his console screen.

"What makes you think I plan to outrun you? Seems to me you have me surrounded."

"I'm glad you can see that. I guess the question is, are you smart enough to order your crew to stand down with you?"

"That's a pretty tall order for me to decide on my own. I'll have to ask my crew. That's a call we make together. Hold on."

Anders muted the comm link and grabbed a wireless headset strapped onto the port-side wall next to him. He donned the headset and transferred the call to it. He then reopened the comm link. *"I have them all here. Let me ask them."*

Anders turned around to an empty cockpit, held up his recorder, and said, *"Y'all want to give up and live, or do you wanna run and probably die?"* He held the recorder half an arm's length away and played back what he'd recorded earlier. Cheers and shouts of readiness bellowed out from the recorder as if his crew were standing right there with him.

Back on the comm link, Anders said, *"Well, you heard them. Does that answer your question?"* Anders stood up and headed out of the cockpit, grabbing a control tablet from his console as he went.

"Either they're cheering for jail, or they're cheering for death," the commander said. *"Honestly, I don't care which one."*

"Well, I can tell you that they're not the kind to want to go to jail, and they definitely prefer not to be dead." Anders entered the cargo hold. *"On the other hand, they do love having three meals a day, a bed to sleep on, and a little something to watch to pass the time. Tell me, does the prison you speak of offer decent entertainment?"*

Anders muted his comm link while he donned his old leather jacket and another less punctured space suit.

"There are a few things, but I'm not sure your crew is going to like watching the cooking channel." The commander laughed.

"Yeah, you're probably right. I think we're leaning toward making a run for it at this point," Anders replied before muting the comms again. With his suit pressurized, he locked himself inside the cargo hold and began to decompress it. Once completed, he opened the rear cargo hold again, nothing but starry space behind him.

The commander made a tsking noise through the comms. *"Not a very good decision, Anders Lockheed."*

"Well, you didn't leave me with many options when you set me and my crew up," Anders said, angrily beating on and tearing up the crate Jug had left on his ship. *"Seems to be a common theme in the universe these days. No one knows what loyalty is, no one understands respect or even feels the need to ask for help. I have to ask,*

Commander." Anders stood still and pulled in a deep breath. *"Did you even consider asking for my help before you set us up? I probably would have worked with you."*

"I highly doubt that," the commander replied.

"Still my choice to make, isn't it?" Anders argued.

There was a quick silence over the comms. *"Maybe, but you still made the choice to knock off the museum."*

"I wouldn't have had to if you had come to me first."

"I guess we'll never know," the commander said. Anders heard no mercy in the man's voice, so he knew he had to go on with his plan.

"I know one thing, Commander," Anders said.

"What's that?"

"No matter what happens in the next few minutes, I'll be the only one of us sleeping with a clear conscience."

Anders then pulled out his tablet, brought up the controls for the Bitch, and leaned against the steel of the object in the crate while he stared out into space. Still locked onto the commander's ship, Anders hit the key, and the faint sound of the massive gun above firing round after round vibrated through the ship. Anders cut the comm link and tossed the tablet to the floor like a Frisbee. It skipped once before launching out into space.

He glanced around his cargo hold, as if to take in a lasting memory, and then gave a salutary nod to his ship one last time.

"It's been one hell of a ride, ol' girl."

CHAPTER 75

For Severn, this was an entirely new experience—having been taken captive aboard a flight crew's ship. She was sure this was new for Marko and Anders' crew as well. The only one with any real experience with this was Kopius, but Severn was sure he wouldn't be much help. All but Wicked, who lay unconscious on the floor, were locked inside tiny steel wire cages like animals.

Once she took the time to look around, Severn realized that's exactly what these cages were used for—the transport of animals. Traces of such were left inside and all around the cages. This crew weren't perfect cleaners, and the hold still held the remnant stench of the animals' bodies.

Wick, the only one given a shred of dignity, lie on the floor near her. Not much but thinking could be done at this point, so the most horrible thoughts entered her brain as to what this crew had in store for them.

She glanced over to Jones and Marko who patiently waited for the opportunity to pounce on anyone who may come too close to their cages. Mere minutes had passed since they had left the destroyer, so she could still see the angst in the both of them. Aura shone a certain terror on her face, akin to what Severn might expect a child to express in this situation.

The cargo hold itself was similar to that of *Elite One's* but not as well kept. The lighting wasn't as yellow; it was more of a white light, maybe for the sake of the animals, although this crew was shaping up to be one that might not care about the comfort of what they transported.

By the looks of the cargo stacked around, they were in the hauling business. Crumb and Drake walked around as if they were on patrol, both donning wry smiles as if they'd finally gotten their payback for her and Marko having handled them at dice.

It wasn't until Jug came back in the hold that Severn noticed the screen hanging from underneath the port-side mezzanine. He surprisingly wore a deferential expression on his face as he approached them. He said only one thing before turning on the screen. "This'll be over soon, but you'll need to brace yourself."

The screen showed a view of the space outside. Nothing was in the view except the backdrop of a starry space beyond. Jug clicked on his comm. "It's on, but I don't have a visual of *Elite One.*"

Then the viewing panned left, passing the destroyer and then focusing on *Elite One* after an adjusting lens zoom. "Good," Jug said into his comm before turning to address Severn and the rest of the caged crew.

"This is going to be a bit tough to take, but this is how Anders wanted it."

Over the next couple of minutes, Jug allowed them to witness how the Galactic Command had taken out Anders and *Elite One.* In comparison to the GC ship, it was as if Anders and his ship were a burdensome, unarmed one-man space pod.

Wick remained unconscious on the floor, Aura cried in horror, and Jones watched in disbelief at seeing his ship and brother-in-flight destroyed. Severn's heart sank into the depths of her, and she all but lost herself in a fit of tears.

Aura's cries of horror echoed through the cargo hold of Jug's ship as he displayed for them what the Galactic Command cruiser ships had done to *Elite One*.

In less than ten seconds after Anders fired on the GC cruiser, the cruiser maneuvered out of the way and fired back. At first, they exchanged similar shots. Some connected, and then one took out the Bitch.

That's when the heavy artillery came.

One missile struck the cockpit head-on and removed it with ease. The ship coasted backward while its automatic stabilizers kept it level, but then two more missiles entered where the cockpit used to be. There was a pause, as if they were making their way to the sick bay, before their powerful explosions blew the ship apart from within. When it was over, all that remained was a mass of steel shrapnel spreading out in all directions.

Jones lost his cool and began shaking his cage. "You bastard!" Jones screamed in a baritone not unlike certain animals that might have instead occupied his cage.

Severn joined his fit. "Why? Why show us this?"

She realized in this moment that she felt no allegiance to Galactic Command but instead felt like she'd been with Anders and his crew for years. Admittedly or not, she was a part of them now. Not a blink of loyalty to the military resided in her heart—only love, sympathy, and a profound attachment to Anders and his crew.

In Anders' death, Severn finally realized her own feelings for him, which grew tenfold and manifested in a flood of tears and hatred for Jug and his crew.

Marko sat in his cage next to her, silent, without any offers of comfort. Even in her pain, she understood his position. She didn't hate him, not entirely. In the end, she knew he was only doing his job.

Wick finally came to and cautiously glanced around the hold in a brave attempt to gain his bearings. Realizing that he was witness to his crew, his family, in cages, he collected himself in a ready state. Then he spotted Aura, who was in tears, and removed his helmet while he scurried over to her.

"Wick," she said softly and glanced up at the screen.

Wicked stopped and saw on the screen the last remnants of a disintegrated ship dissipating into space. And there Severn saw it; his understanding of why his entire crew were in tears and why Anders wasn't there. The short-lived deadpan realization of Anders' demise faded from his face before he too broke down in a flood of emotion.

And that's when Aura started screaming.

As high pitched as it was, the screaming wasn't nearly as terrifying as her convulsing. She shook her body so hard in protest to Wick's pain that it rattled her cage. She pushed and pulled on the steel wiring. With the force, the walls of the cage bent in and out. Jug's crew stepped back as she toppled into Kopius' cage, then overturned again the other way, upside down on the floor. Inside her cage, Aura jumped around and slammed into the cage's sides until the steel wires snapped. Her skin was punctured, scratched, and bloodied in various places.

Finally, Aura broke free and stepped in front of Jug's crew, who, although armed, trembled at the sight of her incensed form preparing to attack.

"You're going to wish you never took this job," Aura growled.

"Yes!" Severn shouted in encouragement.

Aura stepped forward as the skin on her forearms split open, revealing the barrels concealed in her flesh. She bent at her waist and knees as her thighs sliced open, revealing shotgun-like double barrels rising up from her quadriceps.

Jug stepped in front of his crew, waving his arms in surrender. "Wait! He left a message for you." He pointed at the screen, where Anders' face suddenly appeared.

Aura paused, bemusement arresting her anger. She almost seemed disappointed that she wasn't going to get to do what she had intended. Jug tapped a button on a control panel, and the video began to play on the screen. Anders' face appeared with a look of apology and concern. And then he spoke calmly.

"Well, it seems things didn't turn out the way we'd hoped when I took this job back on Cambria. I guess this means that you've no doubt witnessed the CG destroy our beloved Elite One..." He paused. "And with it, me."

Jones, Severn, Wick, and Aura's faces all twisted with pain. Severn's heart was suddenly struck with the pain of not being able to say good-bye to Anders. But this video showed that all along he'd been planning this end and had recorded his own good-bye for them all.

"You're going to have a lot of questions," Anders continued, "and Jug can answer many of them, but I want you to know that this was the only way I could see us getting away clean. We were in too deep with GC and Maddix. Someone had to pay the price, and we needed GC to take out Maddix for us. Faking your deaths was the best plan I could come up with for a clean getaway. Hell," he shrugged, "it worked for our boy Wick. For a while anyway."

Anders bowed his head and gave a soft apology for getting them into this. Then, not having a way with speeches, he looked up and steeled himself to give his last orders to his crew.

"Jones, get your old ship out of storage. I'm promoting you to captain. Wick and Aura, do your best work on that old beater of his and you'll have it up and running in no time. Severn." His voice caught in his throat, and he struggled to refocus himself. "I'm sorry we didn't have more time together." Severn fought back a rush of tears. "But I offer you this. It seems there's an opening for first mate on my old crew." He smiled. "It's yours if you want it. My guess is that you've had a change of heart in your choice of careers. I think we both know where you belong."

Jug paused the video; the suddenness of it nearly ripped Severn's heart from her chest. She would have watched a video of him forever. But it was paused, and her thoughts raced while Jug and his crew began unlocking the cages.

"I should have let you out of these damn cages before I played that video," Jug said. "But Anders told me it would be impossible to reason with you after taking you aboard like this. As you can see, I never double-crossed Anders. He was a good friend and the best ally I've ever had. I want you to know that I did exactly what he asked me to. He even offered to pay me, but when he convinced me this was the only way he could make sure you guys got away, I turned down the money. Anders wouldn't take that kind of payoff, and neither will I. Besides, I got a huge advance from Maddix." He winked. "She was a bit too eager to turn someone on Anders that she didn't think loyalty in friendship could go past money."

Crumb went to free Marko, and it caught Jug's attention.

"Hold it," Jug said, walking over to Marko's cage. "Marko, right?"

"Yes," Marko answered.

"Military man. You know you guys put Anders in a tough spot, don't you? It's your fault he's dead."

Marko didn't respond right away, but then his eyes hit the floor. Severn got the distinct feeling that Jug was pressing hard on him regarding what would happen next. Whether Jug would actually kill him or not, he was making it clear that Marko was about to decide his own fate. She saw how Anders' planning had made sure that Marko would make the right call here.

Smartly, Marko replied, "Yes. I see that."

"Then when I release you back to GC, you shouldn't have a problem telling your commander that Anders and his *entire* crew were on board *Elite One* when they destroyed it. I believe Anders mentioned this opportunity to you." Jug stared intently in Marko's eyes as if to make sure he understood what he was saying.

Marko looked up and nodded. "Yes, he did."

"Your word, sir," Jug said, fingering the gun at his side.

"You have my word," Marko said, sliding his hand through an opening in the cage wires. "I'll tell them his entire crew were on the ship." Jug reached down, shook his hand, and then opened the cage.

"Okay," Jug said, addressing the lot of them. "There's more to the video, but we don't have time right now. My pilot has us in position on the decommissioned destroyer. Here's what we're doing."

He turned to Jones. "If you'll allow us to detain you again, we have a place we'd like to stuff you. It's tight, mind you, but GC will never find it. We need to call them aboard to pick up Marko and…" He turned to Severn. "I'm sorry," he said respectfully. "Miss Severn, I nearly forgot. Anders asked me to make sure to get your answer before we get GC on board."

Severn felt an urge to tighten her back and stand tall at the mere mention of Anders. Jug approached her and put a hand on her shoulder. "And before you answer, consider the fact that GC probably knew you were still on *Elite One* when they destroyed it."

Severn's look turned grave, then her eyebrows scrunched at the sudden realization. She shot an accusatory look at Marko for a moment before replacing the blame on GC. Jug watched her as she thought about it, though he probably didn't know she'd already made up her mind. He asked her again, "Are you going to take the job?"

Just when she didn't think there were any tears left inside her, she shed a couple more. Even in his death, Anders was still captaining his crew. Still, the words stuck on her tongue like dry peanut butter.

"He mentioned," Jug continued, "that you were thinking of leaving GC, and he wanted to make sure you had a place to land."

She finally spoke. "I never told him." The words freed her. The modicum of confession opened the floodgates to her ability to fully admit where she belonged. She glanced at Jones who stood tall, awaiting her response.

"You didn't have to," Jug said as Severn slowly made her way to Jones. "Anders has a pretty good read on people."

Severn collected herself into a respectable posture and presented herself to Jones. "It would be my honor, sir. If you'll have me."

Jones gave Severn a huge smile. "You sure you wanna leave GC?"

Severn turned her head to face Anders on the screen. "I want to be a part of something greater."

"Then hell yeah, kid. Welcome to the *Elite*," Jones said before he, Wicked, and Aura embraced her in one big circle.

"All right, all right," Jug said, interrupting the moment. "Very family-like. But we still got work to do. Like I said, we're calling GC aboard to pick up Marko and Kopius, so we need to make it look like we're just another scav crew here on this destroyer. It just so happens that we picked up these two, who managed to escape the menacing and maniacal Anders Lockheed. Understand, Marko?"

He nodded. "I do."

"Kopius, I understand Anders spoke with you as well. Are we going to have an issue with your statements to GC?"

"No, sir. I think GC got what they were after," he said, nodding at the screen, which showed Anders' face frozen on pause with an oddly contorted look.

"Good." Jug turned to Jones. "You okay ordering your crew into our less than legal holding compartments?"

"Yes, sir," Jones said happily.

"Sounds wonderful. Crumb, Drake, take Mr. Marko up to the cockpit and have him call his commander—oh, and take Kopius too. I don't want them seeing up our skirt. We may have an agreement right now—" he shot a grin at Marko, "but that only goes so far, doesn't it?" He extended his hand again.

Marko took Jug's hand in his for one final shake. "It'll go a bit farther than you think, but, yeah, that's correct."

Pek, Jug's first mate, took over from there. "You heard the captain. We got work to do. Let's move!"

Each crew member darted into action. Drake and Crumb led Marko and Kopius up toward the cockpit, while Jug and Pek showed Jones and his crew where they'd be hiding during the visit from GC.

Jug hadn't lied. It was a tight fit, stuffed into a decommissioned sewer tank, but Severn settled in next to her new captain just as easily as she'd made her decision to leave GC. Anders wasn't with them, but being a part of this crew made him seem not so far away.

CHAPTER 76

Losing Anders affected each crew member in ways it didn't for the others. Wick lost the tuning fork to which he sharpened the melody of his being. In many ways, he'd grown up a bit, not having his safety net of sorts. He spent much of his time on Cambria with Aura as they fixed up Jones' old ship. They'd all become quite the team, despite their loss. But there was still much to do, even though the ship had been flying for a few months.

Severn spent much of her time with Jones, combing through Anders' old contacts trying to scare up work. There had been the occasional courier job, but many of those gigs started with, "I'm sorry, but without Anders I just can't pay as much." Needless to say, money was tight, so readying the ship for the bigger paydays became tougher by the day.

So they hadn't had much to do while they made their way back into the scaving world. At the end of the week, Jones would sponsor a night out at Slips. And every time they walked into Slips, Jones grinned at the memory of Severn's interview with Anders and her fight with the twins. Taking his crew there, in many ways, felt like a tribute. A show of respect, of sorts.

But the place was different. The feel of it had changed.

When Jones stepped through the doors, the absence of Anders at the head of his crew seemed to spread out and mix with the torrent of smoke wafting through the dim lights cast on the crowded tables. The familiar scent of warm, sweaty bodies still filled the air, but he missed a certain sourness from the leather jacket worn by an old friend. Even the scars on the walls from the attack Cambria had suffered changed the bar's face enough to skew his memory.

The collective murmur of conversations quieted as they walked by. Never used to.

Before the job, Jones and his team had been just another flight crew trying to make a living. A popular one to be sure. But now they were the walking dead, a secret held by everyone in Cambria out of respect for what the crew had endured and by the price Anders had paid.

If the crowd only knew how loud the hushed whispers echoed in Jones' head...

"Damn," Wick said when he walked in behind Jones, "it's still tough to see how bad they got it."

Jones huffed. "Yeah, a bit beat up, but she's still our home, kid."

"First round's on me," Severn said, weaving between Wick and Jones.

Aura followed quickly behind her. "I want one of those appletini thingies. They're *so* good."

Wick shot a knowing look to Jones. "Guess I'll be the sitter tonight?"

Jones chuckled and clapped Wick on the back. "Ah, it'll be fine. We got a new recruit to interview in about half an hour."

Sadness drifted onto Wick's face. "I know it's been a few months, but are you sure we're ready for someone else?"

"I know how you feel," Jones said, "but we gotta move on. There's work coming up, I can feel it, and we'll need the help. Besides, you and Aura did such good work getting the ship ready, it'd be a shame to waste it."

Wick nodded. "I guess you're right. I hope he's not a jerk though."

Jones laughed. "I've met him once or twice. He's no worse than the last guy. C'mon." He ushered Wick up to the bar.

Severn and Aura were already receiving the ordered drinks. In her own excited way, Aura was in the middle of shifting her hips opposite her shoulders, neither one hitting the beat of the music.

The bartender planted two beers in front of Jones as soon as he bellied up to the bar. "Well, if it ain't James Lovell and his crew." She winked. "Jim, how are you?"

"I'm well, m'lady, thanks," Jones said with the tiniest of bows. "And thank you for your discretion. It's more appreciated than you know."

She waved her hand. "We all owe you our silence. As far as I'm concerned, you did us a *huge* favor when you took out Maddix. For that, discretion—and a free beer or two—is the least we can do."

"Still can't thank you enough," Jones said. "Hey, I've got someone coming in for an interview. He wears a heavy beard and a not-so-kind mug. Can you send him over if he comes up asking?"

"Sure thing, but promise me you'll pick a different name than Jim Lovell. It's a terrible name for a captain."

"Ha!" Jones laughed. "I'll see what I can do. C'mon, kids, let's find a table."

Severn led the crew through the jumbled rows of tables. Less than half of the tables were filled with people a little more than drunk. Some of the more in-the-know patrons motioned their drinks in a slight raise, as if to give a silent salute, as the crew walked by.

"Anders should be here," Wick whispered to Jones. "He's the real reason these people love us."

"May it be so, kid," Jones said.

Aura skipped up ahead of Severn, bent on grabbing an empty table by the back wall before anyone else. She slid into the chair next to the wall and raised her hands in victory before drawing another sip through her straw.

"Oh, babe," Wick said. "Let the cap sit there. He's got a thing against putting his back to the crowd."

Aura sucked on her straw, shrugged at the request, and tracked her body along the table's edge, slipping easily into the next seat. Severn sat across from Aura, and Wick sat across from Jones, who took the seat against the wall.

Jones surveyed the crowd as he tilted his head back and drank half his beer in one gulp. The thought that he could get used to sitting in the hot seat tickled his brain, but he knew he'd gladly give it up to have Anders back.

"You said you had news from the wire, Wick," Jones said.

Wick, in the middle of a sip of beer himself, raised a finger, as if to thank Jones for reminding him. He pulled his small handheld comm from his pocket and quickly scrolled to a specific feed. "This is from the internal networks at GC. Eyes only for the rank of captain and higher." He handed it to Jones.

"The Captured or Killed List," Jones said. "How did you… never mind. I don't want to know."

"Wow, Wick," Severn said. "The CK List. It's not top secret, but it's a serious hack. Nice work."

Wick smiled at her. "We've been listed on it for a while, but I just now found it. Check out number forty-eight."

Jones scrolled down to read the entry, and a smile stretched across his face. "And there we have it. Anders, Wick, Aura, and me all listed as killed." He continued down the list. "Here's Maddix. She's listed as captured with a 'CC'?"

"Ah, yes," said Severn. "That means Case Closed. Probably means they pinned the whole mech thing on her."

"They did," Wick said. "Public record. She gave up the whole operation so they'd take death off the list of punishments. Took a lot of people down with her."

"Damn. She's gonna have a tough time in prison," Jones said.

Wick shook his head. "No, she won't."

Jones looked at him, confused.

Wick laughed. "She's already dead."

"Wow!" Jones said, his face showing his surprise. "Okay, then. Anything on Severn?"

"She's public record too. Don't you read anything?"

"That's what I pay you for."

Wick grimaced. "You don't pay me, sir."

Jones finished his beer before responding. "I paid you with that beer. Shut it."

"I bought the beer," Severn said, stealing a few laughs from the group.

"Fine, room and board then. You sleep on my ship," Jones said sarcastically as he eyed the crowd.

"Ship?" Aura squeezed in on giving Jones a hard time. "That's not really a ship. *Elite One* was a ship. What we have is a tin can at best. I bet we could crack it open and find—"

"All right, comedians," Jones let his empty beer land solidly on the table. "I know the shape of it, but it *is* a home." He smiled blankly at the bottle.

"Hear, hear," Wick said, raising his beer. The others clinked theirs to his in a salute to a good and simple life.

"Anyway," Wick said, pulling them back to the conversation. "I found the posting on Severn the day after…" His words caught in his throat. The pain of losing Anders was clear as water on his face. It always hit Wick the hardest. "She's listed as dead too. GC seems to think we were all on the ship with Anders."

"I still can't believe Anders pulled that all together without us," Jones said. "But he knew we'd never have let him go through with it." He let the sadness at the table linger. He felt it was good to let the pain of their loss work its way through their hearts.

But, as if the bar knew a change of tempo was needed, the lights dimmed and a different music began to pump through the speakers, signaling the third, more upbeat shift of the night. Some of the more liquefied people in the crowd filed onto the raised dance floor mid-bar to cut loose.

Aura's eyes nearly popped out of her head as she let the beat of the bass take control of her shoulders. Her head stayed in position, though, so she could finish her drink. After she'd sucked up the last of the green liquid, she nearly dropped the huge martini glass off the edge of the table.

"I *love* this song!" she said slowly, standing up and letting her hips bounce back and forth. "C'mon, Wick, dance with me," she invited, her arms outstretched long and thin, her fingers flickering, urging Wick to jump in.

"Hell no, babe," he said, shaking his head. "Severn warned me about this."

"Aura," Severn said in a calm voice. "Please, sit down and stop listening to the music. Turn off your ears or something."

Aura's body shuddered for a moment, then stopped. Severn raised her hands to her mouth and said, "Uh-oh."

A worried look fell onto Aura's face. "Oh, no. It's happening, isn't it? Oh, man, I didn't even see it coming." Her elbows rose and flapped in the air while her hips mildly pumped front to back.

"She's not even going with the beat of the music," Jones whispered to Severn with a disgusted look.

"Aura, please sit down," Wick asked, reaching for her arm. "People are starting to watch."

"I can't, baby. I'm trying. It's like, it just…"

Aura spun around and slammed her palms on the table next to theirs. Two men and a woman jumped in fright. At first, they were all startled, but then the men grew smiles as Aura's fair face turned serious with desire. The woman's face turned to a mix of anger and jealousy.

Wick leaned over. "I'm very sorry, ma'am. This will only take a moment. She means no harm."

Aura then dropped her rear to the ground, still pumping her hips, elbows, and now her head, all moving in opposite directions. Not a single jolt hit a beat of the song.

Jones scrunched his face as if to try to hold it in, but he burst out laughing and slapped his hand on his knee. "This is the defect y'all were talking about?"

Severn nodded and then started laughing herself.

Both of them cackled madly as they watched Aura assault a chair, awkwardly grinding to a beat much different than the one thumping through the speakers. People around them began cheering and laughing with Severn and Jones.

Wicked, trying to end Aura's embarrassment, reached out to help her, but Aura pushed him away, unable to control herself. He slouched into his chair and dropped his head into his hands, sighing. Aura, clearly embarrassed, displayed a different, more confident posture.

Jones felt bad for Wick, but he was enjoying this too much to let that pull the smile from his face. This was the laughter they all needed.

Knowing Anders was with them, seeing this too, made it all the better.

The last few months had been some of the darkest times, and though Jones was looking forward to this interview, this event was the beacon of light he didn't realize he'd been looking for. He loved his crew.

When the song's beat pulsed into nothingness, Aura's body seemed to awaken back into her control, one limb at a time. A pumping bent elbow became her own again, and her knees drifted back together as if released from the grasp of an unseen force. She snapped back into a normal posture and brushed floor debris from her clothes. Then she picked up the chair she'd been using as a prop and offered it to the gentleman from whom she'd stolen it. The confused people sat there motionless as Aura earnestly apologized for her intrusion.

Jones and Severn sat joyously at their table, sniffling laughter and awaiting Aura's return.

Wicked, on the other hand, pinned his crossed arms on the table with his forehead.

Aura, breathless, slowly returned to her seat. Another song started almost immediately, and she steeled herself as if to check and see if it would happen again. It didn't, so she offered an apologetic look to Jones, but he immediately offered his support.

"Well done, Aura. Next time, try not to draw so much attention. We're supposed to be keeping a low profile."

Wick lifted his head. "I need another beer."

"Hang tight. It's coming." Jones grinned. "But first, I have a question for you." He leaned in curiously, drawing the others in closer as well. "It's about the night we lost Anders. You know that Jug's crew faked an alliance with Maddix to help Anders' pull off his secret plans, but none of you ever asked about the crate they tossed into the cargo hold of our ship."

Blank looks reaching for memories of that night spun around the table.

"Ya know," Wick said, "now that you mention it, I remember Maddix's reaction to that. She didn't know about it, did she?"

"No, she didn't," Jones said, pointing at him with his beer bottle.

"That's right, she didn't," Severn said.

Aura perked up, still dealing with her embarrassment. "Jones. Um, sir! What was it? The crate."

"Let's just say that the military is missing an experimental safety protocol. They—," Jones cut himself off. He glanced up and faked a surprised look. "Ah, don't look, but our interviewee is walking over. Listen up. It ain't easy, I get it. But just as I was telling Wick a few minutes ago, we got work coming up, and we need the help." Jones flashed a knowing smile, and an assortment of bobbing heads circled the table as the others readied themselves.

Jones knew they understood life had to move on, but the loss of their captain still felt fresh most of the time.

"But I need your help. Give 'em a hard time. Try to rock 'em. Knock 'em off balance with tough questions. And when he's just about to break, I'm gonna turn the screws on him. We clear?"

"Check," the crew said in perfect unison.

"Good, cuz he's here."

Aura, Severn, Jones, and Wick each smoothly leaned back in their chairs as five bottles of beer came crashing down on the table with a certain authority. One beer was retracted with the hands that delivered them.

Wick didn't look up, and Jones saw him fall right into character as the ship's engine master and super-space genius, unwilling to hire a new crew member.

"What?" Wick said. "You think buying me some piss warm beer's gonna butter me up to give you my vote?"

Jones smiled a big white-toothed grin.

CHAPTER 77

Desh Sundance pinned several large bills under his empty beer bottle and slid it across the bar. Nira, the tall and slim bartender who was well liked by the men who frequented Slips, grabbed it and let her hand cover his.

"Hey, handsome," she said knowingly.

He smiled through his thick beard, smoothly slipped his hand away, and left her with nothing but a wink and a sly grin. He'd bought five beers this way, tipping double or even triple the standard, and, most important, buying the staff's silence if anyone came around asking questions. It was an understanding Desh didn't mind having.

He nodded politely as he left the bar and fingered the beers in his hands. He weaved his way through the crowd. On the other side of the room he spotted Jones, the new captain of the famous scav crew once captained by the late Anders Lockheed. Desh held no fantasies about how difficult this interview would be—never mind how incredibly unwelcoming Anders' old crew would be in hiring someone new.

As he made his way over, his eye caught several people watching him. A couple even pointed at him. Then came the whispers. He heard only a few of them as he walked by—disbelief that he was the one interviewing with Jones today. A few people who really knew Desh raised their drinks in a silent salute at his sudden appearance.

Desh grinned and nodded at Jones as he walked up and clanked the bottles of beer in the center of the table.

Wick grabbed one without looking up. "What? You think buying me some piss warm beer's gonna butter me up to give you my vote?" Wick lost his words when he looked up at Desh, wide-eyed and caught off guard.

"No," Desh said, "but I hear a *cold* one helps heal deep wounds."

Aura leaned back in her chair, placing her hands over her mouth, as if to hold back the many words trying to escape.

Desh addressed her next. "Ya know, you're a pretty good dancer, girl."

Jones only smiled, grabbed his beer, and winked at his recruit. Desh reached over, and clanked the sweaty necks of their beers together.

Severn, teary eyed and already standing, punched Desh in the shoulder and hugged him. "Anders," she whispered, "you son of a bitch!"

She kissed him like she'd never kiss anyone again. Anders returned her kiss with the exact same passion. Then he pulled back and looked deep into her eyes. "I'm sorry, dear, but didn't you hear? Anders is dead. I'm Desh Sundance, and I'm here to interview for a position on your crew."

Wick, standing nearby in amazement, let out a chest full of air he had been holding in and practically jumped into Anders' arms. Aura followed, and all three of them embraced him warmly.

And there sat Jones—happily leaning back in his chair while embracing his inevitable demotion with a smile and a beer.

THE END

A VERY SPECIAL THANKS

To my copy editor, Therin Knite at Knite and Day Publishing (www.kniteandday.com),

To my proofreader, Vicki Adang at Mark My Words Editorial Services (www.mmwllc.net),

To my book cover designer Martin Smirmaul (Contact info AuR),

A story is never as perfect as the day it is conceived in the mind of a writer. The work you performed brought this story within reach of that very vision I dreamed of so long ago. To labor on a story with me as you did places something into history that will be here long after we're gone. So, if we are to strive to stamp this world with our legacy, we are to do it right, and that requires an honest approach to our work with a professionalism to match it. You command them both with my highest regard.

This book is a work of art because of you,

Until next time,

Tyler

ABOUT THE AUTHOR

Tyler Wandschneider is a Seattle-based novelist working in the professional world. He and his wife are expecting their first child in October 2017. It is a girl, and he is delighted to meet her. *Lockheed Elite* is his second novel, and no, you cannot read his first. You can follow Tyler on some of the usual social media channels, and he has a website for you to check out as well, www.tylerwandschneider.com. You can subscribe to his newsletter there in which he shares all the trouble he gets into. He is also fond of hearing from those who have enjoyed reading *Lockheed Elite*.

And please remember, there is no greater way to honor an author than to tell your friends of them, and maybe leave a review or two around the web. So, a very appreciative thank you if you choose to do so.

Made in the USA
Middletown, DE
18 August 2017